SPELL OR HIGH WATER

By Scott Meyer

Magic 2.0 series

Off to Be the Wizard

Spell or High Water

SPELL OR HIGH WATER

SCOTT MEYER

47NORTH

Text copyright © 2014 Scott Meyer
All rights reserved.

Published by 47North, Seattle

www.apub.com

Amazon, the Amazon logo, and 47North are trademarks of Amazon.com, Inc., or its affiliates.

ISBN-13: 9781477823484
ISBN-10: 1477823484

Cover design by inkd
Illustrated by Eric Constantino

Library of Congress Control Number: 2014930081

Printed in the United States of America

SPELL OR HIGH WATER

The following is intended to be a fun, comedic sci-fi/fantasy novel. Any similarity between the events described and how reality actually works is purely coincidental.

1.

It was a normal evening at the inn called The Rotted Stump. Outside, the sun was setting and the town was getting quiet. Inside, candles were burning and the patrons were getting loud.

Martin materialized across the street. He marveled at how quickly people get used to things. Here he was, a grown man in a shiny silver robe and pointed hat, coalescing out of thin air, brandishing a staff with a bust of a masked Mexican wrestler at its peak, and nobody, not the medieval peasants nor he himself, found it odd.

A passerby said a polite hello as he stepped around Martin. Martin returned the greeting, and started across the street. Three months ago Martin was a twenty-three-year-old data entry drone in Seattle who poked around in corporate computer systems in his spare time. Two months ago, through a series of events that barely made sense to him, even though he'd lived through them, he found himself at this very inn, in the year 1150, trying to pass himself off as a wizard. About a month ago, with quite a bit of help, he'd passed his training as a wizard, and now Martin was about to meet his very first trainee.

It wasn't a huge surprise that the new trainee would turn up here at The Rotted Stump. When fleeing back in time, logic dictated that you use a geological landmark as a landing zone, and if you're going to England, you can't do much better than the Cliffs of Dover. The road nearest to the cliffs led to this town, Leadchurch, and the inn was the first public establishment you found if you followed the road. It was more surprising that Martin had been called to go meet the new arrival.

Martin was in his workshop when he got the call from Phillip. Word had come that a stranger had arrived claiming to have magical powers. Someone would have to look into it. Phillip was much closer, but part of his new job as chairman of the wizards' council was to delegate work to others, and in most cases *others* meant *Martin*. Besides, the new wizard was at the exact same inn where Phillip had found Martin, just two months ago. Phillip said he liked the symmetry of sending Martin as the welcoming committee.

Martin jumped at the chance. Almost since the day he started training, he had looked forward to training someone himself. Martin's training had been a humiliating series of mind games, confusing revelations, and immature practical jokes. He had found much of it profoundly unpleasant, and he wanted a trainee of his own. It would be his chance to take all of those miserable experiences and inflict them on someone else, instead of absorbing them himself.

Martin paused before he entered the inn. He remembered the night two months ago when he'd arrived, hungry and more than a little scared. He had introduced himself to the patrons, and proceeded to demonstrate his powers by transforming himself into a laughingstock. Eventually Phillip had challenged him to a duel and blasted him into the woods, where he'd hit his head on a tree and passed out. He smiled at the thought of having the upper hand for once as he entered the inn.

It was a warm, crowded room with exposed wooden beams. Candles and the sunset filtering through the windows were the only sources of light, which sounded more romantic than it looked. Indeed, not even romance itself would look romantic if it was being seen in The Rotted Stump.

Martin scanned the room. It was a busy night. Strong men were drinking strong drinks and using strong language. He was looking for a youngish man (like himself) who seemed out of place (like he did) and was most likely in deep trouble (which he had been). As he peered into the murk, he heard a deep, booming voice shout, "Martin the Magnificent!"

Martin tried not to cringe. One of his first acts upon arriving in Medieval England was to give himself that nickname, and as with all self-bestowed nicknames, it had been an awful mistake that now haunted him. Pete, the owner of The Rotted Stump, and whose absent right forearm gave the inn its name, got up from a raucous table in the corner and came to meet Martin, smiling broadly.

"Martin, good to see you, lad. Phillip couldn't make it?" Pete asked, patting Martin on the shoulder.

"Yeah, he's busy, so he sent me instead. Is there a problem, Pete?"

"No problem at all," Pete replied. "Just a new wizard in town, is all. He showed up dressed in strange clothes. I sent the boy to go fetch Phillip right away. I needn't have hurried though, he seems to be all right. He's already getting on much better than the last wizard that turned up."

Martin scowled. "I was the last wizard that turned up."

Pete's smile didn't even flicker. "Aye. He walked up to me, and asked if I was in charge. I said I was, and he asks what we have to drink. I point to the beer barrel. He looks at it and says, 'That'll do.' He's been back there drinking and talking ever since."

"Has he offended anyone?" Martin asked.

"No, he fits right in. I think Gert's sweet on him. Come 'ere, I'll introduce you."

As he crossed the room, Martin was able to pick the new wizard out of the group right away. It was his hair that set him apart. It was a fallacy that every man in medieval times had a flowing mane. There were a variety of hairstyles available to the stylish medieval male, but a perfectly trimmed, flat-top buzz cut was not one of them. Martin guessed that the new wizard was in his mid-fifties. Beneath his iron-gray military-grade haircut he had dark, severe eyebrows and a perfectly trimmed moustache. He was wearing a flimsy white dress shirt and a thin black necktie. Instead of a wizard's robe, he wore a tan trench coat. Martin kicked himself for having not thought of that himself. It seemed as if a dim bar was the new wizard's natural habitat, even if it was a dim bar in the Middle Ages.

Pete cleared his throat, and all conversation at the table stopped. The new wizard looked straight at Martin, making eye contact immediately. Gert sat next to the new wizard, towering over him like a slightly feminine oak tree. She had been smiling down at him, but when she looked at Martin, her smile turned effortlessly into a snarl. She liked Martin all right, but she already knew that she liked this new guy more, and she wanted Martin to know it as well.

Pete gestured toward the new wizard with his hand and said, "Martin, I'd like you to meet Roy. Roy, this is Martin."

Roy looked at Martin for a moment, then said, "Oh, yes, the apprentice. Your teacher couldn't make it?"

When Martin had arrived in this time, he had known next to nothing. He hadn't known that there were other wizards with the same kinds of powers that he had, that the other wizards were time travelers from the late twentieth and early twenty-first centuries, like he was, or that there was a training and orientation program in place for newly arrived wizards. Not knowing these things, he had made many mistakes. Clearly, the locals had already told this guy Roy all about the wizards and the training. They probably had told him about Martin's arrival, and from that Roy could have figured out that the other wizards were probably time travelers, like he was.

Phillip would have told Martin that there was a lesson in this about listening instead of talking, but Martin wouldn't have listened.

Martin smiled at Roy, and said, "Welcome to Leadchurch, Roy. You and I should talk."

Roy replied, "We will, as soon as I've finished my beer." He lifted the earthenware mug to his lips. Judging by how he handled it, the mug was over half full.

Martin leaned in slightly. "It's imperative that we speak, in private."

Roy said, "I figured you meant in private, or else you'd have just started talking. That's why it has to wait until I'm done with my beer. I doubt that Pete wants me to take his mug, do you, Pete?"

"No, Roy. My mug stays in my inn."

"See, Martin? So unless you want to put my beer in your hat, we have to stay until I've finished it."

Martin slowly, without breaking eye contact with Roy, removed his silver sequined wizard hat, muttered a few words under his breath, and pulled from the hat a mug identical to the ones Pete used for serving beer. He knew it was identical because he had made Pete's mugs in the same manner and given them to the innkeeper as a gift.

"There," Martin said, smiling. "This mug is mine, not Pete's, so we can take it wherever we like."

Roy said, "Good. Pete, please fill my young friend's mug with beer. It'll help him kill the time while I finish mine. Martin, you can take a seat, or, because that is your mug, you're free to take it and wait outside if you like."

Martin sat at the table in silence, barely touching his warm beer. Roy didn't talk much either. Instead, the patrons of The Rotted Stump seemed eager to tell Roy everything they knew about the wizards who lived in the area, and the events of the previous month. Martin's arrival. The duel in which Martin was defeated by Phillip. The mysterious deaths at Rickard's Bend. Martin's mood started to lighten as they described the battle at Camelot, and the duel between Martin, Merlin, and Phillip. He had to admit, he came off pretty well the way they told it. Going in alone. Facing a more powerful adversary to buy his friends time. Remaining brave in the face of what looked like certain death. Martin felt rather heroic until Roy summed up what he had heard.

"So, Junior bit off more than he could chew, and his trainer had to come bail him out."

There was a tense silence. Martin decided to play it cool. He was the more experienced wizard. He had the upper hand here.

"No, Roy," Martin said, shaking his head, "there's more to it than that."

Roy snorted. "What did they leave out? Did you cry?"

So much for feeling heroic, Martin thought.

Eventually, Roy finished his beer, and started to settle up with Pete, who refused to take any payment, calling the drink a welcoming gift. He charged Martin full price for his beer, pointing out that Martin had been in town a while. The two wizards walked out into the chilly night air. Martin had decided not to have a public confrontation with the inexplicably popular newcomer, but now away from Roy's fan club, and with a beer in him, Martin felt freer to talk.

"Look, Roy," he said, "when I got word you were here, I dropped everything and came out from London to meet you."

"Isn't it called Camelot now?" Roy asked.

"For the time being. We're gonna change that back. Anyway, I came all the way out here . . ."

"You teleported here. Don't forget, son, I found the same computer database you did. I know that our world is a simulation, and I know how to use the database to alter that simulation, or else I wouldn't be here in the first place. I know how to teleport. You probably do too, so don't pretend that the distance was some kind of big imposition."

Martin turned on Roy, poking him in the chest with his staff. "Look, Roy, I came here for your benefit. You can get into a ton of trouble around here if you don't let somebody show you the ropes. That's why I'm here, to show you the ropes. To help you stay out of trouble."

Roy brushed Martin's staff away from his chest with exaggerated care. "Okay, okay. Calm down, big guy. Don't get upset. I appreciate you coming to welcome me, but I'm a grown man. I don't need a kid to tell me what's what."

"See, that just shows how little you know. There've been guys like us here for over a decade, and others who went further back in time than we did. There's a whole system built on top of that 'database,' to do things you haven't even thought of, things like freezing the aging process. Just because a wizard looks a certain age, doesn't mean they are that age. I could be a hundred years old, for all you know."

Martin stormed off down the street. Roy followed, thinking.

Finally, Roy said, "That's a good point, Martin. I hadn't thought about that."

"There're a lot of things you haven't thought about, Roy. That's why I'm here."

They walked in silence for a moment. They rounded a corner and were in the town's central square. The lead-covered church that gave the town its name was across the square, but predictably, it didn't stand out particularly well at night. A few citizens milled about. One or two had torches, but most navigated by starlight. Roy and Martin continued walking across the square.

Roy said, "As you say, you could be older than me."

"Yes, I could."

"But, back in the bar . . ."

"*Inn*. You should get used to using the time-appropriate words. The Rotted Stump is an inn."

"Back at the inn, they said you only got here a couple of months ago."

"That's true."

"So, you only had your aging stopped then. You're twenty-five years old, right?"

"Twenty-three."

"Either way, you're a kid. This has been fun, but is there an adult available to train me?"

Martin stopped walking. Roy stopped after a step and turned around to smirk at him.

Martin switched his staff from his right hand to his left, looking thoughtfully at the small plaster bust of Santo, the King of the Luchadores, as he did so. He turned his attention back to Roy, and calmly said the words, "*Akiri grandan.*"

Martin glowed with eerie silver light that seemed to form a grid pattern on his skin. He divided along the grid lines into hundreds of small silver boxes, not dissimilar in shape to tiny coffins. The boxes blew apart, swirling around Roy, who was too stunned to move. The boxes multiplied and reformed into a new form which looked just like Martin, only three stories tall, and made of glowing silver boxes. As the giant form spun into shape, its empty right hand swept Roy up and lifted him to the giant's eye-level. Roy was held around the waist in the immense hand's uncomfortable grip. The other hand held a giant version of Martin's staff. Roy saw that the bust of Santo was also enlarged. Its eyes were glowing with the same sickly light.

A voice, clearly Martin's but louder and deeper, shouted, "Silence!" Then, Martin's normal, much quieter voice addressed Roy. "Look, the training isn't just to teach you what you can do. It also gives us a chance to learn what you're likely to do, and if we don't like what we learn, we will make sure that you don't do anything. That's not a threat. We won't hurt you, except in self-defense. We will strip you of your access to the file, that database of yours, and send you back where you came from in such a way that the authorities will be sure to find you. Do you want that, Roy? If so, just say the word. I'm your trainer. I can make that happen any time you like."

Roy squirmed, but the grip of the giant hand didn't loosen. They looked like a toddler playing with a Ken doll, only the doll didn't feel like playing, and the toddler wanted to practice his throw.

Martin pushed the head of the giant staff forward until it filled Roy's field of view.

"Do you want to go back, Roy?"

Roy gritted his teeth and said, "No."

Martin smiled, but didn't move the staff. Not yet. In a much quieter voice, he said, "Yeah, I bet you don't. Few of us come here because things are going well in our own time. Who's after you back there?"

Roy stared at the giant likeness of Martin's face until it was clear that he wouldn't be put down unless he answered.

"The CIA," Roy said, then after a breath, he sighed and added, "and the Department of Defense."

Giant-Martin's face cracked a huge smile. "Wow. I can't wait to hear that story." Martin pulled his staff away, but kept Roy suspended twenty-five feet above the ground.

"Here's the deal," Martin said, at a volume carefully calculated so that only he and Roy would hear it. "We wizards have to police ourselves, because there's nobody else who can police us. Part of how we do it is with the training. You can accept me as your trainer, and I'll show you how to fit in here in the past, how to use the powers we've created, and how to make new powers yourself. When I think you're ready, you'll face the trials, and once you pass them, you'll be on your own, free to do whatever you like, within reason. Don't accept the training and we'll assume you're up to no good, strip you of your powers, and send you back to your time. Perhaps we'll send you to the courtyard in the center of the Pentagon. Not a lot of tourists get to see that, do they? What do you say, Roy? Do you accept the training?"

Roy shrugged. "Yeah, kid, I'm sorry. I accept the training."

Martin said, "Good," as he placed Roy back on the ground. As soon as Roy's weight was back on his own feet, Giant-Martin silently exploded into thousands of silver boxes that flew outward, spun in space momentarily, then imploded back in on themselves, leaving normal-sized Martin in their place.

Roy smoothed out his trench coat and looked around sheepishly. "Geez, kid, you didn't have to get so sore about it. I was just messing with you."

"Well then you've just received your first lesson. 'Don't mess with me.' Did you learn it, or will you need a review?"

"No, no. I got it." Roy looked at the townsfolk in the square. There weren't many of them, but the few there were had stopped all activity and were watching the two wizards intently. "Did we have to do that in public?"

Martin said, "Yes. In fact, I put it off until we got here, 'cause I knew there'd be people and plenty of room. I wanted witnesses for two reasons. One: It's good to remind the locals what we can do every now and then. Two: It was important that everybody know that I'm more powerful than you."

"Important for the training?"

"Important to me, which as far as you're concerned, is the same thing." Martin reached out a hand to his trainee. "You'll be staying with me during your training. Take my hand. We'll teleport there."

Roy looked at Martin's hand as if he were holding a dead rat. "I'll just put my hand on your shoulder. That should work just as well."

Martin thrust his hand toward Roy. "Come on, don't be a baby. Take my hand."

Roy put his hand on Martin's shoulder and repeated, "I'll put my hand on your shoulder. That should work just as well."

Martin rolled his eyes, and said, "I can see this relationship is going to take some effort. *Transporto Magazino.*"

Martin and Roy disappeared.

2.

Jimmy walked at a brisk pace. He had a shocking amount of energy for a man in his sixties. That was one of the benefits of spending thirty years riding a bicycle. Another of the benefits was having plenty of time to think. Think and plan.

He wasn't riding a bicycle now, and if things went the way he expected, he'd never ride one again. It was just as well, since he'd sold his. The day before, Jimmy had watched Martin lead a low-speed chase to his parent's home, then evade the police by fleeing back in time to Medieval England (where he had caused Jimmy no small inconvenience). Once the police and two conspicuously out-of-place federal agents had left, Martin returned, a few hours later from his parents' perspective, several weeks later from their son's, the time traveler. After observing Martin leaving his parents' house by taxi, Jimmy had ridden straight to the homeless shelter he was using as a base of operations. The fluorescent lights flickered and the TV went wonky as he walked through the shelter's rec room. He had found over the years that as long as he walked through such areas quickly, his disruptive magnetic field would be chalked up to a temporary brownout. He could get away with this for a week or so before someone would notice that the brownouts always happened when he walked by.

For nearly thirty years, Jimmy had kept moving, both from room to room, and from place to place.

Jimmy retired to the private room he had sweet-talked the management into giving him. He went over his notes by flashlight. Batteries and incandescent light bulbs still worked for him. It was only integrated circuits that couldn't tolerate his presence, which included the ballasts in fluorescent lights.

He'd had a good night's sleep, then got up bright and early and sold his bicycle to a panhandler for thirty bucks. Jimmy took his newfound fortune to the nearest thrift store, where he purchased the nicest suit they had in his size, a white shirt that only had stains on the back, and a tie that didn't have any cartoon characters on it. He also grabbed an ancient Samsonite briefcase. He paid cash. He had to let them keep what little change he was owed because the cash register mysteriously stopped working. He changed into his new outfit in the fitting room and dumped the contents of his backpack into his briefcase. He donated the backpack and his old clothes to the Goodwill, suspecting that they'd more likely burn them than sell them, then set out to face the new day.

Jimmy had a plan, and that plan only called for him to look presentable for a few hours. After that, with any luck, he'd be under arrest.

Jimmy walked down the pleasant suburban Seattle street. He'd spent so long staking this street out the day before, he knew it as if he'd grown up there. He hadn't, of course. Martin had.

Jimmy stopped, checked his notes, made sure he had the right house, then strode up to Walter and Margarita Banks' door. He glanced at the button for the doorbell, then knocked. Three crisp, friendly sounding knocks. He heard faint sounds coming from inside the well-maintained split-level ranch house. After a moment the door opened a crack. A pleasant dark-haired woman close to his own age peered at him through the barely opened door. The chain lock was still engaged. Jimmy wasn't surprised. These people had been through a lot the day before, and were probably still pretty edgy.

The woman said, "I'm sorry it took so long. I barely heard your knock. We do have a doorbell."

Jimmy smiled. "I'm sorry. I didn't see it there."

Margarita said, "That's fine. So, what can I do for you?"

Jimmy's smile faded the exact amount he had predetermined would convey a sense that he regretted having to bring up the subject he needed to discuss.

"Mrs. Banks, my name is James Sadler, but I'd like it if you called me Jimmy. I know your son, Martin. I'd like to ask you a few questions, and I suspect you'd like to ask me a few of your own."

Margarita's smile froze, and all of the light drained from her eyes. She excused herself for a moment. Jimmy smiled kindly, and told her he understood. She closed the door and called out for her husband. Jimmy heard bits of the conversation on the other side. He couldn't make out words, but the tone came through loud and clear. Mrs. Banks was upset. Mr. Banks was angry. Mrs. Banks calmed down a bit. Mr. Banks did not. Mrs. Banks tried to soothe Mr. Banks. Mr. Banks responded. Quiet conversation followed. Jimmy took a half-step backward, to appear less threatening. The doorknob jiggled slightly, then there was a moment of quiet, just long enough for both Jimmy and Mr. Banks to take a deep breath.

The chain lock rattled, and the door opened wide. Mr. Banks stood, filling the doorframe. "I'm Walter Banks. What can I do for you, mister . . . Sadler, was it?"

Jimmy bowed slightly; just slightly enough that Mr. Banks wouldn't notice that he noticed it. "Yes, Sadler. James Sadler. Martin calls me Jimmy."

Walter Banks made a sucking noise as he thought. Finally he said, "I don't think Martin's ever mentioned you."

"No, Mr. Banks, I expect he hasn't. We haven't known each other for long. I'm very impressed with your son. He has a unique combination of intelligence and creativity. You should be proud."

"I am," Walter said, flatly. "You still haven't told me what you want, Mr. Sadler."

"Of course. Sorry. I'm a bit nervous," Jimmy lied. "I want two things. I have one question I want to ask you and Mrs. Banks, but before that, I want to answer as many of your questions as I can."

Walter stared at Jimmy for a long time, then asked, "So you're involved in Martin's . . ." Walter trailed off.

"Difficulties? Yes. At least, I was once. I know a great deal about it, and while I won't be able to answer all of your questions directly, I should be able to leave you better informed than you are now."

After another staring match that Jimmy was careful to lose at the exact right moment, Walter invited Jimmy in.

+=——=+

An hour later the Banks' front door opened and Jimmy walked out. Walter and Margarita followed him out the door and saw him off. Walter grasped Jimmy's hand with both of his and shook it vigorously. Margarita gave Jimmy a hug. Jimmy thanked them for their help, and for the sandwich, which he assured them was delicious. Goodbyes were said, and the couple stood for a moment and watched him walk away before finally going back inside.

Nice people, Jimmy thought. *Martin's lucky to have them.*

The conversation had gone well. There was an awkward moment early on when they offered to take his jacket and he refused, but that passed quickly. While he wasn't able to answer the questions they had asked, he had managed to answer the questions they should have asked, and he was gratified that he hadn't had to lie to them. *The easiest way to mislead people is to tell them the truth,* Jimmy thought.

"What did Martin do?"

"I can't tell you what he did, but I can tell you that he did not break any laws. What he did was so new, so unprecedented, there just aren't any laws on the books about it."

"Did he steal something, or hurt somebody?"

"Heavens, no! Listen, what those men yesterday are after your son for is nothing you'd recognize as a crime. Martin didn't take anything from anybody. He didn't claim to be anything he wasn't. He didn't do harm to any living thing, except maybe one tree, but it survived."

All, technically, true. Of course, he had both harmed and taken things from Jimmy, but that wasn't why the feds were after him.

"Please understand," Jimmy continued. "I wish I could say more, but all I can tell you is that your son discovered something the government didn't know about. He examined it to figure out if it really was what he thought it was, and in the process, he came to the attention of the authorities. Now I believe he's just trying to make sure that he doesn't cause himself any lasting legal problems."

That placated Martin's parents, but what really set the hook was when Jimmy made the observation that Martin had always been a little too smart for his own good. They figured he must know their son pretty well if he knew that.

After dancing around a few more questions, Jimmy asked them his one question, which they eagerly answered, then the next fifty minutes were spent eating sandwiches and listening to stories about Martin's childhood.

Jimmy reached the end of the street and turned left, taking an extra second to look at the tree that just the day before had been on the receiving end of Martin's car. It looked like it would be fine.

Jimmy reached into his pocket and pulled out the piece of paper on which he had written the answer to the one question he'd asked Martin's parents. There was a phone number, and the names Miller and Murphy.

When Jimmy asked for the contact information of the agents who had searched the Banks home just the day before, Margarita asked him why he wanted to help her son.

He thought, *I didn't say I did.* He told her, "Your son and I had a . . . falling out. It wasn't entirely fair. I . . . I just want to make things right between us. I owe Martin that."

All true statements, Jimmy thought, *and totally misleading. Oh well. She doesn't need to know that the falling out was over my attempt to kill him.*

3.

Martin and Roy materialized just outside the door of Martin's warehouse in London/Camelot. There were a few more people milling around, but it was after dark in the twelfth century, so a street in a large city like this looked pretty much the same as the street in the medium-sized town they'd just left.

Martin said, "So, this is Camelot. Not much to look at in the dark, I know. You'll see a lot more of it in the next few days."

Martin opened the door to his warehouse and motioned for the older man to come inside. They walked in to a large, open room, about one-third of the overall volume of the building. The walls were painted black. The wooden floor was also painted black, except for a blood-red pentagram inside a circle. At the points of the inverted star there were candles. They lit themselves as Roy entered the room, which startled him.

Martin shrugged as he closed the door. "Yeah, they do that whenever someone who isn't me comes in. If it bothers you, I can make them not notice you. It just takes a little programming."

The corners of the room were home to four ten-foot-tall stone statues of fearsome creatures undreamt of in this time's primitive mythology. Each creature stood atop a pedestal that also bore the creatures' names, which were all unfathomable to the ears of the locals. The far end of the chamber was not a wall, but a red velvet curtain. Roy pointed at it and said, "Looks like you stole it from a movie theater."

"I did. I worked there when I was in high school. The manager was an awful racist jackass. Now he's a racist jackass who has to explain to the owner how he let someone steal a huge velvet curtain."

As they walked across room, Roy asked who or what the monstrous statues were supposed to be. Martin pointed to each, listing their names.

"Optimus Prime, Boba Fett, Grimace, and the Stig."

Roy said, "Yeah, I can read. Are those names supposed to mean something to me?"

Martin had nearly reached the velvet curtain, but stopped and looked at his trainee, genuinely puzzled.

"None of them ring a bell? Not even Grimace?"

Roy shook his head.

"What year are you from?" Martin asked.

"1973."

"Wow," Martin said. "Seriously? Huh."

Martin took a moment to absorb this, then said, "Well, none of these guys existed yet in '73, except Grimace, and he probably looked pretty different. Did you ever eat at McDonald's?"

Roy said, "No."

Martin asked, "Why not?"

"Because I'm a grown man," Roy answered.

Martin shrugged and parted the curtain. He gestured toward the gap and said, "After you."

Roy walked through the curtain into Martin's living quarters, which took up the remaining two-thirds of the building. The walls were bare wood and plaster. The ceiling was a tangle of timber rafters. The floor was raw planks. The space between the walls, the floor, and the ceiling was filled mostly with furniture from IKEA. The layout was what designers in Martin's time called "open plan living." It was one space. The bedroom was distinct from the living area and the dining area, but they were delineated from one another not by walls or partitions, but by where and how the furniture was placed.

Now Roy looked confused. "You live in a barn?"

Martin smiled as he breezed past Roy. "Pretty much. I mean, the building is in town, so I think of it as a warehouse, but before I bought it, this building's main job was to keep hay dry before it was fed to horses, so yeah. I guess that pretty much makes it a barn."

Martin walked to his work table and watched Roy explore his living space. The furniture was loosely clustered together in a little over half of the room. The rest of the room was open and empty. Roy walked around the dining room table and chairs, then stopped and asked where the kitchen was.

"Don't have one. We don't really need to cook. Are you hungry?" Martin asked.

"No. Pete gave me some mutton. He said it was on the house."

Martin remembered that when he'd arrived, the only thing Pete had given him "on the house" was an assortment of threats and insults.

Roy moved on to the color-coordinated couch and easy chairs. They were modern, comfortable, and small enough to be easily maneuvered by one man. He slowly walked toward something he clearly didn't recognize. It was a large, flat slab of black glass and plastic, mounted vertically on a base that sat on top of a wooden cabinet. "What's that?' he asked.

"That's my TV," Martin said. He picked up a remote control and aimed it at the slab. It played a little jingle and displayed a spinning Samsung logo. Martin turned it off.

"There are no TV channels here, of course, but I use it to watch old movies from time to time."

Roy turned to Martin, and in a quiet voice asked, "What year are you from?"

Martin chuckled. "2012. Have a seat, Roy."

Roy sat heavily in one of the easy chairs. Martin looked at his closed laptop, thinking he'd give Roy a little more time to adjust before hitting him with that. He got up from his desk and sat on the couch opposite Roy.

"So," Martin asked, "what happened?"

"Huh?" Roy said, snapping out of his daze.

"What brings you to Medieval England, and how the heck did you manage to find the file in 1973?"

"Nobody else from the seventies is here?"

"No. Until you, the earliest year anyone had come here from was 1984, as far as I know."

Roy puffed up a bit. "So I found it first."

"Yes," Martin said, "but you got here last, so you can decide for yourself what that's worth."

Roy thought about that, then continued. "I was an engineer at Lockheed. It's a company that makes airplanes."

Martin said, "It's called Lockheed Martin in my time. Always kinda got my attention."

"I bet. Anyway, I worked in a division called the Skunk Works."

"Really?!"

"Yeah. We, uh, we mainly did top secret work for the government."

"I know!"

"High-speed, high-altitude stuff."

"I know!"

"Top-secret projects."

"I know!"

"Look, kid," Roy snapped. "Do you want me to tell you the story, or do you already know it?"

Martin put his hands up. "Sorry. Please, go on."

"Okay. So, back in '65 we got ourselves a computer. An IBM 360. We didn't know what the heck we were gonna do with it, but everyone figured those things were the future, so they ordered me to learn how to run the thing. I studied and experimented for a while. The company had a few more of them sitting around in other divisions. All of the magnetic tapes for the whole company were stored in one room. One day, I decide to see what other divisions are using the stupid thing for, so I just start loading up all the tapes in there, one by one. One of the tapes has a file on it that appears to be larger than the tape could hold. That got my attention."

"Understandably," Martin said. "How much could one of those tapes hold?"

"A hundred and seventy megabytes," Roy answered. "What's so funny?"

Martin said, "Nothing. Please, go on."

"Okay, so I load up the file, and I get a print of the first few thousand characters. It looks like a database."

"And eventually, you realized what you were looking at."

"Yes," Roy said, "proof that the world, and everyone and everything in it, is just a program controlled by a computer."

"And you had a file that could control the computer that controlled the world." Martin leaned forward and asked, "What did you do next?"

"I thought about giving myself a bunch of money, but I thought that was probably the fastest way to get caught."

Martin decided to never tell Roy how he had gotten caught.

Roy continued, "I decided to use the database to give myself an advantage at work. Make my prototypes stronger. Boost the output of my team's engine designs. I told everyone my secret was advanced computer modeling."

"Smart. Did it work?"

"For a while. There was one project I'd really put my heart into. The A-12. It was a spy plane. It needed to fly very high and very fast. Later they added a seat and called it the SR-71."

"You worked on the Blackbird?" Martin blurted, in spite of himself.

Roy smiled. "Is that what they call it?"

"Yeah, eventually, I guess. It went, like, Mach three, didn't it?"

"Officially. It could go a bit faster if it had to."

Martin leaned back heavily into his seat. "Wow. The SR-71. I had a poster of it in my bedroom. I always wondered how they managed to make something like that clear back in the sixties."

There was a long, awkward pause, as Martin's smile faded.

"And now you know," Roy said. "The damned Russians were just so much better with titanium then we were. I thought having good intelligence would prevent wars in the long run, so I found ways to make the plane work. Then I found ways to make it work better. I just got carried away."

"And that's how you got caught?" Martin asked.

Roy grimaced and said, "I moved to a different project, then they tried to build more SR-71s. It was top secret, and I wasn't on the team anymore, so I didn't know it was happening. They couldn't get the titanium parts to bond. Eventually they started asking questions."

"And you pictured yourself having a long talk with the CIA, so you decided to get lost."

"Bingo. I'd read a book that had just come out. *The Best Years to Live in Medieval England*, by some guy named Cox. It was a gift. Anyway, I snuck into the chart room and grabbed the coordinates for the Cliffs of Dover, made a side trip to the computer room, entered the coordinates, picked a date, and that's how I got here."

Martin considered this for a moment, then asked, "So where's your computer?"

Roy squinted. "I don't own a computer. I'm just a guy."

"What about the computer you used to get here?"

Roy kept squinting. "That's Lockheed's computer."

"Whatever," Martin said. "Where is it?"

"Where I left it, at the Skunk Works."

Martin had difficulty absorbing what he was hearing. "You didn't bring it with you? Roy? Oh man, it was a one-way trip for you!"

"Like I said, kid, I panicked."

"Without a computer here, how'd you plan to pass yourself off as a wizard?"

"I didn't," Roy said, chuckling. "I figured I'd use my engineering background to make a living. I walked into that bar, they took one look at me, and assumed I was a wizard."

"Yeah," Martin agreed, "I bet they did."

Martin spent the next hour laying out the situation for Roy in much the same way Phillip had done for him. He explained that there were communities of wizards all over Europe in this time, and in various other places, at other points in history. He told Roy that all of the wizards were guys like them, who had stumbled across the file in one of its many forms, gotten into trouble using it, and come back in time as a means of hiding.

They spent some time puzzling over the fact that while everyone else had found the file on some corporate mainframe, Roy had found it on a magnetic memory tape, but Martin eventually dismissed the topic as just one of the many things about the file, and the universe itself, that seemed counterintuitive.

Martin explained that women who found the file all ended up going to Atlantis, as life everywhere else wasn't particularly hospitable for women with magic powers. Martin was just explaining about chronological pollution, and how nothing they did to the past seemed to have any effect on the future, when Roy interrupted him by snoring.

Martin roused Roy just long enough to get him set up to sleep on the couch. As he tucked a sheet set into the cushions, Roy asked, "When do I get to meet the guy in charge?"

They guy in charge, Martin thought. *There's a thorny issue.* For a moment, Martin considered telling Roy about how the current chairman had only held that position for a short time, and how the chairman before had changed his name from Jimmy to Merlin, and then tried to reshape the entire country according to his whims, which included trying to kill all of the other wizards.

Nah, Martin thought, *that's a little too heavy to drop on him on the first night. I'll explain the whole thing later, when we talk about banishment.*

Martin answered, "I don't know when you'll meet the chairman. It'll happen at some point, but it's hard to say when. He's a busy guy."

4.

Some would think that Phillip enjoyed being the chairman of the wizards in spite of the busy schedule that came with the job. Phillip would tell you that he enjoyed being chairman *because* of the busy schedule. Many people found this hard to understand, but those people hadn't actually seen the schedule.

Phillip rolled out of bed at his official residence, the same hut he'd lived in for the last ten years. He stretched his back and regretted for the thousandth time that he hadn't gained the ability to freeze the aging process until he was in his forties, and predictably thick around the middle. He pulled some breakfast out of his hat and ate it in a bleary haze. When breakfast was done and he was mostly awake, Phillip grabbed his wizard staff, put on his pointy hat and light blue robe, and commuted to work. Some days he'd make a show of flying to his shop in public, but today he simply teleported there. He had a full agenda, and he wanted to get to it.

He appeared in front of his building, entered right away, and walked through the storefront that was just there for show. He went straight through the séance room, with its fake crystal ball. He climbed the staircase at the back of the building, and reached his goal, the second story, which was decorated with the finest furnishings and entertainment devices that 1984 had to offer.

He pushed a button on the massive Sony stereo, and the room quietly filled with the resonant sounds of The Alan Parsons Project. He walked to the chrome and white plastic bar and looked at his official schedule.

Item one: get up. Done!

Item two: eat breakfast. Done!

Item three: think up some busy work and delegate it to a wizard who'll make a lot of noise about it.

Phillip thought for a moment about the busy work, and about whom to make busy with it. His eyes drifted around the room, past his Commodore 64 computer, past the mint-condition Pontiac Fiero he kept inside as if it were a work of art. His gaze lingered on his original stand-up arcade GORF cabinet. He remembered how he had carefully dismantled it and transported it back in time one piece at a time. He saw the scratches around the cabinet's coin box, and remembered seeing Magnus, the younger of the two wizards who resided in Norway, trying to pry it open. That answered the question of *who*, but he still needed to think of a *what*.

After a few moments he called Magnus on what the wizards euphemistically called *the hand phone*. He raised his right hand in front of his face, as if imitating a Shakespearian actor reciting the "Alas, poor Yorick" speech. Phillip said, "*Komuniki kun Magnus two*." Almost instantly, Phillip's raised hand was filled with Magnus' place-holder icon, a flickering, semi-transparent image of the devil sticking out his tongue. The demon's left hand held the neck of a white, V-shaped guitar. The other hand was making a devil-horns gesture.

It's redundant for the devil to make devil horns, Phillip thought. *He could just point at his horns and send the same message.*

Finally, the image of the devil was replaced with a bleary-eyed Magnus. Clearly Phillip had woken him.

The image of Magnus' head said, "Hey, Phillip."

"Good morning, Magnus. How's Magnus?" Phillip replied. Magnus' best friend was also a wizard who lived in Norway, who was also named Magnus.

"He's Magnus," Magnus answered, "you know what I mean?"

"I think I do."

"What's up?"

Phillip said, "Official business, I'm afraid. As you know, I am now the chairman of the wizards."

"Well, yeah. I voted for you. It was only two months ago."

Phillip smiled. "Right. Well, I've decided that we need to take a census."

"A census," Magnus said, clearly thinking he'd misunderstood.

"Yes. We need to count and list every wizard in Europe," Phillip explained patiently.

Magnus squinted, and said, "But, Phil, you know every wizard in Europe."

"Well, that's the thing," Phillip said, "I think I do. We both think we do, but we can't be sure. For all we know, David, out in Russia, might know another wizard who he never mentioned because he assumed we already knew about him."

Magnus kept on squinting. "I guess that's true. Why are you calling me?"

Here we go, Phillip thought. "Magnus, I'd like for you to make a list of all the wizards in Europe that you know of."

Magnus nodded and said, "Okay, I can do that."

"Good," Phillip said. "Then I want you to call every wizard on that list, and ask them to make the same list."

Magnus' eyes widened. "You want me to call everyone?"

"Yeah," Phillip said, brightly. "It's not like I'm asking you to go see them in person."

"Yeah, I suppose not," Magnus agreed, grudgingly.

"Unless someone comes up with a wizard you've never heard of. Then I want you to go track them down and get their information."

"What kind of information?"

"You know. Who they are. Where they're from. Where they found the file. The basics."

"How soon do you need this, Phillip?"

"Oh, there's no particular rush. A couple of days, I guess."

Magnus sucked his teeth, then said, "That's fine if there are no new wizards. If I do have to hunt someone down I'll need more time. Can I have a week?"

Phillip looked disappointed, but said, "Of course, Magnus. If that's how long it takes."

They said their goodbyes and Phillip turned his attention back to the list.

Item three: think up some busywork and delegate it to a wizard who'll make a lot of noise about it. *Done for the week! On to item four.*

Item four: Do whatever you like for the rest of the day.

Phillip played some GORF, then settled in to his most comfortable chair to read his dog-eared copy of *Catch-22*.

He had been reading for about an hour when he heard the noise. It wasn't an inherently alarming noise. It sounded like someone at the foot of his staircase had rung a crystal bell.

The sound shook Phillip down to his bones, since he didn't own a crystal bell, and due to his magical security measures, it shouldn't have been possible for anyone to be at the foot of his stairs.

Phillip put down his book, grabbed his staff, and carefully crept to the head of the staircase. Carefully, he peered down into the distance below and was thoroughly confused by what he saw there.

5.

Martin didn't know what his next move would be, but he knew he'd have to make it in the next five seconds. He was flying as fast as he dared, at an altitude of seven feet above the forest floor, high enough to not get caught in the undergrowth, but low enough to avoid getting hung up in the canopy. He held his staff in front of him, tilted so as to be parallel to his body. The last thing he needed was his staff slamming into a tree trunk sending him falling in a heap to the ground. He couldn't slow down because one of his pursuers was flying right behind him. Martin was sure he was losing ground, since he had to find his way through the trees, while all his attacker had to do was follow him and fly through the Martin-shaped hole. Martin would have just flown straight up, punching through the canopy and emerging into the clear blue sky above, except that he knew there was a second pursuer lurking up there, waiting for Martin to emerge into the open, presenting a clear target.

Martin glanced upward and saw a black shape moving fast above the treetops. He lowered his gaze just in time to see and almost dodge a dead limb hanging limply from the live branches that supported its weight. He tried to swoop under it, but wasn't quite fast enough. It grazed painfully across his back, then fell to the forest floor. In an act of hopefulness Martin glanced behind him, and cursed when he saw the purple blur that was gaining on him zip right over the top of the fallen branch without having to alter course, or even decelerate.

He knew from memory that a river cut through the woods, and that he'd be reaching it soon. He would lose his cover and be a sitting duck for the bogey above the trees. If, on the other hand, he slowed enough to turn away from the river, the purple blur behind him would overtake him and knock him out of the air. To make matters worse, there was a third attacker out there somewhere who had been delayed at the start of the chase, but would certainly be back into the fray by now.

Martin only had himself to blame. He had gotten so caught up in the excitement of having a trainee that he'd forgotten that there were people who would attack him on sight.

+=+=+

The day had started on such a positive note. Martin awoke to find that Roy was already up. Martin produced breakfast for them, and while Roy was amusingly disturbed to eat food that had been pulled out of a wizard's hat, he was clearly equally disturbed that the breakfast consisted of a McDonald's bacon, egg, and cheese biscuit and a solid slab of hash browns.

Once breakfast was done, Martin set about getting Roy up to speed.

Martin showed Roy his top-of-the-line 2012 laptop, which, since Roy was from 1973, was as astonishing to him as any magic trick Martin had done. Martin explained that until recently the wizards from farther in the future had tried to keep later technology from the earlier wizards in the interest of not messing up the timeline more than they had to, but that recent events had shown that this put earlier wizards at an unfair disadvantage, and that the timeline didn't seem to care what they did.

Roy asked Martin to explain that last part, and Martin explained that most wizards went back to their original time on a regular basis, and that nobody had found a single change, no matter what the wizards did in the past. He briefly explained the two predominant theories: that they existed in a separate timeline created by whatever program used the file, or that at some point in the future something would happen to clean up the mess they were currently making. Martin trailed off when it became clear that Roy had lost interest in the philosophical discussion and just wanted to play with Martin's computer.

Maybe we'll get along after all, Martin thought.

Once Roy was done boggling over Martin's laptop, Martin explained about the shell program, the interface that Phillip and the former chairman, Jimmy, had developed to make it easy to utilize the file that brought them all here. He explained to Roy the powers that the shell could bestow upon anyone who knew that it existed and took the time to learn how to use it. He told Roy that he need not age. He'd never be too cold or too hot again. He could speak any language fluently. Most important, he explained that while he still needed food, water, and air, he was impervious to physical damage.

If Roy wore a robe and hat that met certain measurements exactly, the shell would recognize him as a wizard and he'd have the powers of flight and teleportation, and the ability to create food, money, and almost anything else out of thin air. Martin also promised Roy that when his training was complete, and he'd passed his trials, that Martin would set him up with a laptop, so that he could go back to his own time at will, if he wanted.

"That's if you accept the training. If you choose not to, I'll just assume you're up to no good and send you back home so the CIA can pick you up. So, Roy, do you accept the training?"

With a sales pitch like that, Roy didn't have to think long.

Martin spent a little time at the computer, getting Roy set up in the shell, then Martin announced that it was time to go. There had been some unpleasantness a while back, and now he and a few of his wizard friends were making a point of getting together once a week to compare notes and share new shell scripts they'd devised that could be used in an emergency. He brought Roy along so he could meet the guys and see what kind of things they'd been working on. Having worked in the defense industry, he might find it interesting.

Martin and Roy materialized in the middle of a large clearing about five miles away from Leadchurch. Martin's friend Gary had picked it because it was large, flat, and surrounded by thick woods on all sides. The wizards had all the room they needed to demonstrate and test new spells without having to worry about any locals sneaking up on them. Even if someone did sneak up on them from the forest, that person would have to move amazingly fast to reach the middle of the clearing before the wizards could react.

Martin, in his silver robe and hat, staff in hand, and Roy, wearing his trench coat, skinny tie, and sensible shoes, stood alone in the middle of the field. Martin spun around, then said, "Oh, no."

A gray shape emerged from the tree line, moving amazingly fast. Two more shapes, one purple, one black, were closing on their position from other directions.

Martin remembered Gary proposing a new plan to keep each other on their toes. He called it *the Kato Protocol*. It was a simple idea. The wizards would attack one another without any provocation or warning. It would ensure that they all stayed in fighting shape, it would force them to be aware of their surroundings, and, most important from Gary's point of view, it would be fun.

"Sounds good," Martin had said. "When do we start?"

"We'll see," had been Gary's reply.

The streaks of color were almost on top of them when Martin yelled, "Time out!"

The streaks stopped in midair, floating motionless in a rough triangle around Martin and Roy. Tyler's purple robes hung beneath him, flapping slightly in the breeze. The sun glinted off of the Rolls Royce hood ornament that topped his staff. Jeff landed, tucking his wand into the pocket of his gray flannel robe. Gary drifted around in front of Martin and Roy. His long, scraggly brown hair jutted out from around his jet-black hat. Beneath the hem of his black robe, his skinny legs and black canvas high-tops hung five feet above the turf. He pointed the head of his staff, adorned with KISS action figures, toward Roy, and said, "Hey Martin. Good to see you. Who's the new guy?"

"Gary, Tyler, Jeff, this is Roy, my trainee. He just arrived last night. He doesn't have any powers yet, and doesn't know what's going on, so it would be really unfair to attack him."

Despite his clear age difference, and uptight demeanor, the three younger wizards welcomed Roy in a genuinely friendly manner. Martin was relieved to note that despite Roy's age, cultural background, and year of origin, he didn't seem to miss a beat when introduced to Tyler, who was possibly the only black man in England at this time in history.

They all agreed that they couldn't attack him, since he couldn't really defend himself.

Jeff said, "I could explain to him what's going on, though."

"Good thinking," Tyler said, still floating in an aggressive posture. "That'll free Martin up to be attacked."

"And us, to attack him," Gary added.

Martin said, "Fair enough." He blurted out the magic word *flugi* and was off for the tree line like a shot. As he streaked away, a shiny silver ball of speed, he faintly heard Jeff talking to Roy. Martin thought Roy and Jeff would have much to talk about, both being engineers.

Martin made a mental note to work on some sort of fast-getaway sprint spell to help him really accelerate when he needed to fly away from trouble. Some sort of glowing projectiles flew past Martin, striking the ground in front of him. Martin chose to ignore them, figuring that, like bullets, they were only his problem if they hit him.

Martin made it to the tree line with Tyler in hot pursuit. Gary, who had been slower to react, chose to go over the trees and try to head Martin off at the pass, so to speak. Now the pass was in sight. Martin could see a dark shape hanging above the trees, clearly watching him, waiting for him to emerge from the woods. Unless he did something fast, Gary would almost certainly hit him with something. He didn't know what, but knowing Gary, it would be something unpleasant and probably immature.

Happily, Martin had been working on a few ideas. He had that big workspace in his warehouse; it'd be a crime not to use it.

Martin reached into his pocket and pulled out a small black beanbag. He aimed for a gap in the trees with empty space beyond, looked behind him at Tyler, who was closing fast, slowed a bit, then tossed the beanbag over his shoulder. It flew in a graceful arc, sailing over Tyler, missing him completely. Martin made a grasping gesture with his right hand and said, "Bamf."

Martin disappeared in a puff of black smoke, which violently dissipated when Tyler flew through it. In the same instant, Martin appeared directly behind Tyler, generating another puff of black smoke. It appeared as if he had materialized and miraculously caught the beanbag, but in truth, his right hand had materialized around the beanbag, and the rest of it with him.

Martin stopped all forward movement and watched as Tyler flailed, utterly confused by what had just happened. He sailed out of the woods, and instantly was struck by a pulse of energy from above. Gary had clearly mistaken Tyler for Martin.

For a moment Tyler spun in the air. Something clearly was wrong. Then, Martin saw that a small grayish object of some sort was stuck to the small of Tyler's back, right where he'd been hit. Purple smoke started shooting from the object with quite a bit of force, enough to push Tyler into an uncontrollable spin. The smoke was accompanied by a sound, similar to the sound of a whoopee cushion, but much louder and longer in duration. The purple smoke also had an odor. The odor was familiar, and not at all pleasant.

Tyler spun in the air like a foul-smelling pinwheel. The whoopee-cushion sound was drowned out momentarily by the sound of Tyler cursing at Gary. The thrust from the whoopee-rocket stabilized slightly, and sent Tyler corkscrewing helplessly into the sky, yelling and cursing as he went.

Martin dropped gently to the ground and crouched there in the thicket. He tucked his staff under his left arm and wound up so that he'd be ready to throw his beanbag.

Cautiously, Gary dropped below the tree line, looking for Martin. He hovered, staff in one hand, the other hand shading his eyes so he could see into the darkened forest. He expected to find Martin flying above the ground, but it didn't take long to spot Martin's shiny silver robe and hat in the dark brown and green of the woods. It also didn't take long to notice the black object flying very quickly towards him.

The beanbag struck Gary painlessly in the chest. A split second later, Martin was there, grasping Gary around the neck with one arm, pulling down with all of his weight. Gary toppled over forward. He found himself beneath Martin, who pushed off from him with both feet, driving him even faster into the ground. Gary hit the ground with great force while Martin drifted down gently to Earth.

Gary lay motionless for a moment in the scrub grass along the river bank, eyes closed, gathering his strength, hopefully luring Martin in closer. After a carefully timed interval, Gary sprung up into a three-point crouch, his staff held in front of him. His defiant laugh was made less dramatic by the fact that he misjudged Martin's location and had sprung up facing away from him. Gary felt something soft hit him in the back, heard Martin say, "Bamf," then felt Martin's full weight bear down on his back, buckling his arm and forcing him back into the dirt.

"You done?" Martin asked, standing on Gary's back as he lay prone in the dirt.

"Yeah, I guess," was Gary's muffled reply.

Martin stepped off of his friend and gave him a hand up. He didn't mention that Gary had two big dusty footprints on the back of his robe, and he hoped nobody else would tell him either.

They turned their attention to Tyler, who was still creating foul, purple curlicues in the sky. Gary muttered something under his breath, and the smoke and noise let out one last, powerful trumpet blast, then stopped. Tyler remained motionless, a dot in the sky, for a moment while he composed himself. When he was ready, he flew to Martin and Gary's position, landing in front of them, glaring at Gary the entire time.

After a thick, velvety silence, Tyler asked Gary, "When will this smell come out of my robe?"

Gary said, "As soon as you figure out how to make it come out. Sorry. "

"You will be," Tyler said. He then turned his attention to Martin. "So, what's up with the old guy?"

They were amazed to hear that Roy was from the year 1973, or as Gary put it, pre-*Star Wars*. Martin told them about how Roy had arrived the night before, copped an attitude, then settled down eventually. He hoped Roy wasn't giving Jeff a hard time. Jeff could be a little sensitive.

They took to the air to reconnect with Jeff and Roy. Martin was relieved to find them sitting in the grass, Jeff listening in rapt attention as Roy told him about what it was like to work at the Skunk Works.

Now that the pleasantries and the combat were over, they all formally demonstrated the new defensive power they'd brought to share. Gary described what he called his "gas jets," which he'd accidentally used on Tyler.

Tyler demonstrated his spell by deliberately using it on Gary. Tyler shot him in the back with one of the same glowing bolts Martin had seen whiz past him during their chase. As soon as it hit Gary, he was lifted into the air. Gary swung and lolled sickeningly in space. Clearly he had no ability to stabilize himself. He was also visibly vibrating as he hung in space, helpless.

"WHYYYYYYYY," Gary whined, in a goat-like, wavering tone.

Tyler walked toward the helpless wizard. He grabbed Gary's leg, stopping his motion.

Gary said, "Thaaanks."

Tyler said, "You're welcome," and gave him a good, hearty spin. "I'm sure this looks familiar to you all," Tyler said. "The spell lifts the victim three feet into the air, drops him, then places him right back there, three feet above the ground. It does this ten times a second. The result is that the target is helpless, and has no attitude control, although, in this case, the target had never been able to control his attitude in the first place."

Gary told Tyler to shut up. Tyler shoved Gary with all his might, sending him gliding away from the group, yelling plaintively the whole way.

Tyler continued. "Also, the vibration humiliates the target, and almost instantly gives them a splitting headache."

Roy asked, "Why would you think that would look familiar to us?"

"Oh," Tyler said, "sorry, Roy. I forgot you were so new. It's based on a spell Martin invented, and used in front of all us wizards once."

Roy turned to Martin. "You invented that? Kiddo, that's diabolical."

Martin shrugged and said, "Yeah, well, I hope never to have to use it again."

Jeff started to say that this was because Martin had created the spell for his own use, as a crude and utterly failed attempt at a flying spell, but Martin shot him a look that stopped him before he started.

In the distance, a weak, warbling voice said, "Tyyyyyylerrrrrr, pleeeeeease stopppp thiiiiiissss!"

Tyler yelled, "Stop it yourself. Any other spell will override it."

Gary said the magic word *flugi* and instantly drifted slowly into the sky, where he hung limply for a moment.

Jeff called out, "Hey, Gary, you okay?"

Gary held up one finger, as if asking for a moment to compose himself. He pointed the finger at Tyler and said, "*Ekskuzi vin.*" A ball of light streaked from his finger. He was far enough away that Tyler had time to react. He hiked up his wizard staff, and swung it like a baseball bat. The silver Rolls Royce hood ornament traced a glowing arc in the air. The staff connected with the glowing ball, which dissipated on impact. Tyler paused at the end of his follow-through, then craned his head to look at the end of his staff. There, just under the hood ornament, was another of Gary's *gas jets*.

After a half second of silence, the gas jet fired. Martin, Roy, and Jeff all ran as Tyler spun violently, trying to keep his grip on his staff. Soon, Tyler was invisible, at the center of a foul-smelling cloud of purple vapor. The wavering sound of the jet and the occasional glint of high-speed chrome were the only indications of the violent activity within the cloud. Finally, Tyler either let go or lost his grip. Either way, his staff soared off into the distance, whirling like a helicopter blade and leaving a purple contrail in its wake.

Tyler lay in the grass on his back. Gary approached and offered him a hand up. As he hoisted Tyler to his feet, he said, "We're even."

"For now," Tyler replied.

Roy shook his head and asked, "Are you boys sure these spells are meant for self-defense, or are they just designed to help you humiliate each other?"

Gary answered, "I think a really good spell ought to be able to do both."

At that moment, a subtle, warbling, repetitive chiming noise filled the air. The wizards all cocked their heads to the side. Jeff asked, "Okay, whose hand is that?"

Everyone but Roy looked at his right hand. Martin said, "Oh, it's me."

Martin lifted his hand in front of his face. A small, semi-transparent image of Phillip's head appeared in the palm of Martin's hand.

"Martin," Phillip said, "I need you to come to my shop right now."

"Why?" Martin asked. "What is it?"

"I don't know for sure, but I need you to help me figure it out."

Martin said, "I'll be right there."

Gary leaned in behind Martin's shoulder. "We'll all be right there."

Phillip rolled his eyes. "Is it too late to say that I want you to come alone?"

Martin said, "I'll come alone."

Gary said, "We'll all come alone."

6.

Moments later, Phillip's private sanctuary was crowded with wizards. Phillip liked to call it his *inner sanctum*. All the other wizards called it his rumpus room.

Martin asked what was going on. Phillip pointed to his wet bar. Sitting on the bar, there was a large salad bowl, the most beautiful salad bowl in the world. It was a perfect half sphere, made of the thinnest, clearest glass Martin had ever seen. The bowl was kept upright by three impossibly perfect clear glass dolphins that acted as legs.

"Where'd you get that?" Martin asked, approaching the salad bowl.

"The bottom of the stairs," Phillip said. "I was tending to some important chairman business and I heard a ringing noise. I went to investigate, I found that. There was no note, and before anybody asks, I checked, and the phrase 'So long, and thanks for all the fish' isn't engraved anywhere on it."

"So someone left it there and rang a bell to get your attention?" Jeff asked.

"No. You know nobody can get up in here without my permission. That's why Gary's waiting downstairs." Phillip looked at the floor and yelled, "Having fun down there, Gary?"

A muffled voice answered, "No."

Tyler asked, "So, what made the ringing noise?"

Phillip reached into the bowl and pulled out a glass disk, about the size of a coaster, but again, it was the most breath-takingly clear and beautiful glass coaster Martin had ever seen. Phillip held it a couple of inches above the bottom of the bowl, then let it go. When it struck the bottom, it created a loud, clear, yet somehow soft tone that filled the room.

Phillip said, "I figure whoever sent them put the bowl there first, then sent the disk, a few inches above it, to get my attention." He handed the disk to Martin. "Now, to get your attention, I'll ask you to take a look at this."

Martin held the disk up to the light. It weighed less than he expected, and was cold to the touch. As he turned it in the light Martin saw that it was etched with some sort of pictogram. It showed two figures in pointy hats standing, facing each other. Between them, they held a large half-circle, each supporting it with both hands. In the middle of the half-circle Martin could make out a circle that he was sure symbolized the glass disk in his hand. Beneath the two figures, there were words. It was hard to read such small, fine print etched so lightly on a transparent background, but Martin immediately recognized that the words were the names Phillip and Martin.

"So, Phillip, what do you think?" Martin asked.

Phillip said, "If they were trying to hurt me, they'd have just sent a bomb or something."

"Unless they wanted to hurt both of us," Martin said. "This bowl thing does put us in the same place at the same time, touching the same object."

"True," Phillip allowed, "but all the same, this doesn't feel threatening to me."

"Me either. Still, this could be dangerous."

"Agreed," Phillip said, before yelling, "Okay, Gary. You can come up now."

Gary, Tyler, Jeff, and Roy took shelter behind Phillip's beloved Pontiac. Even though it was from the eighties, it was the most advanced car Roy had ever seen. He was not impressed. "It looks like a doorstop."

"It's about as mechanically sophisticated as one, too," Jeff said, as they took up their positions, cowering behind the car.

Like any Fiero owner, Phillip had learned to ignore such comments. He and Martin stood in the middle of the room. Phillip held the bowl in one arm, the disk in the other.

Phillip asked, "You ready for this, Martin?"

Martin answered, "Not really, but we're going to do it, aren't we?"

Phillip said, "Yes. Yes we are." He placed the disk in the bowl, then held the bowl up so Martin could help support it. Soon, they were each holding the bowl with two hands, as the picture had demonstrated. For a moment nothing happened, then the rim of the bowl glowed a vibrant bluish-green. A pulse of light traveled the entire radius of the bowl, glowing brighter wherever Phillip and Martin were touching it. The pulse subsided, and the disk lying in the center of the bowl glowed and lifted into the air just above the bowl's rim. A shaft of blue-green light projected upward from the disk, grew more diffuse, then coalesced into the figure of a person who stood facing Phillip. It was a young female with short hair, large eyes, and an impish smile.

"Hello, Phillip," the hologram said.

"Hello, Gwen!" Phillip replied.

After a pause, Gwen said, "This is a recording. I can't actually hear you."

In spite of himself, Phillip said, "Oh, sorry."

After another pause, Gwen said, "Don't be embarrassed. I hope you're well."

Behind the Fiero, Roy whispered, "Who's that?"

Jeff said, "Gwen. Female wizard. She used to live here. She and Martin kinda had a thing."

Tyler added, "Martin had most of it. Then she took off for Atlantis."

The image of Gwen didn't show color, but her flared-sleeved, hooded cloak was all too familiar. Beneath it, she wore what appeared to be a lightweight dress and sandals. Gwen's posture stiffened, as if she were starting into a rehearsed speech, which it immediately became apparent she was.

"Phillip, as chairman of your colony of time travelers, you are invited to attend a summit to be held here, at the sunken city of Atlantis. You will meet with the leaders of all of the other known colonies. Together we will try to create a solid foundation upon which to build our mutual future. The topics of discussion will include chronological pollution, the ethical treatment of non-time travelers, and prevention of the abuse of our shared power. This invitation has been extended to you and a second representative." Holo-Gwen jerked a thumb over her shoulder, as if indicating something behind her.

"Specifically, it's been asked that you bring Martin." She looked back over her shoulder and smirked at Martin, then turned her attention back to Phillip.

"This is not a command. This is a request. You may choose to decline this invitation, but you won't. Regardless of whether you attend or not, you are welcome to keep this bowl as a token of Atlantis' goodwill. It is made of solid, molecularly pure diamond, the hardest material on earth. It is also dishwasher safe. You can give the disk to Martin. Maybe he can use it as a paperweight or something. When you're ready to depart, you and Martin are to recite the following phrase in unison: '*transporto unua Atlantis kunveno*,' at which point you will be transported here, to the sunken city of Atlantis, just in time for the beginning of the summit. You will be here for two weeks. It will be warm. Pack accordingly. Also, know that I've managed to get the shell program running here in addition to the system the Atlanteans already had in place, so all of your existing powers will work."

Martin leaned to the side to make eye contact with Phillip, who looked just as surprised as he was.

Holographic Gwen glanced back over her shoulder, to where she assumed Martin would be standing. She said, "That concludes the official message. I'm adding this last part because I know the two of you won't be satisfied if I don't."

Gwen turned so that both Martin and Phillip could see her in profile. She took a deep breath, put the hood up on her cloak. She looked from side to side in an exaggerated pantomime of fear, then said, "Help me, Obi Wan Kenobi; you're my only hope." With that, she bent at the waist, mimed putting a card into a slot, then disappeared.

The glowing disk went dark, wobbled for a second, then fell into the bowl, creating one last ringing noise. The three wizards and one trainee who had been hiding behind the car stood up.

"So, when do we leave?" Gary asked.

"You leave immediately," Phillip said, "and go home. Martin and I will probably leave for Atlantis in a couple of days. We need time to prepare and think things through."

Martin nodded. "Sounds good."

Gary agreed. "Yeah, that'll give you time to decide that you have to bring me along."

Tyler said, "Gary, give it up. You heard Gwen. They just want Martin and Phillip."

"But they've gotta take me with them."

Jeff asked, "Why is that?"

Gary was clearly amazed that he had to explain something so obvious.

"Because," Gary said, "I really wanna go." He turned to Phillip. "Please, Phil, please take me with you. I want to see *the ladies*. I like *the ladies*."

Phillip shook his head. "No way. You're not coming."

"Phillip, that's not fair," Gary whined. "Think of *the ladies*."

"I am," Phillip said. "Guys who act like you're acting are part of what they created Atlantis to get away from."

"And you're gonna let them get away with that?" Gary's voice grew louder. He was almost manic. "They'll have forgotten how to deal with suave guys like me. It'll be like shooting fish in a barrel, only instead of fish, it'll be *ladies*. And instead of shooting them, I'll be—"

"Yes, we know what you think you'll be doing," Phillip interrupted.

"And instead of *in a barrel*, it'll be—"

"Shut up," Phillip said. "You're not coming. That's final."

"Fine," Gary seethed, "I'll stay here. You two keep all *the ladies* for yourselves."

Roy had been making an effort to listen more than he talked, which doesn't come naturally when you seem to be older than everyone around you by at least twenty years. Now he couldn't contain himself. He had to figure something out. He turned to Gary and said, "Say, 'the ladies' again."

"*The ladies.*"

Roy shook his head and repeated. "The ladies."

Gary smiled, and repeated, "*The ladies.*"

"Why do you say it like that?"

"*Like what?*"

Roy said, "It's like you're talking in italics."

Gary arched an eyebrow. "*Italics?*"

7.

Two kinds of people spend time in police interrogation rooms: cops who have a suspect, and suspects the cops have. As such, interrogation rooms usually contain people who are happy to be there, sitting across a table from people who are unhappy to be there. Today was no exception.

Agent Miller sat down sullenly, took a moment to scowl at his partner, Agent Murphy, who glanced blearily back at him. Miller turned to the man across the table and growled, "Well, here we are."

"Yes," Jimmy said, smiling broadly. "Thanks for coming. I really appreciate it."

The two agents exchanged a look that was like stepping on a LEGO—quick and unpleasant. Agent Miller adjusted the frilly shade of the oversized decorative table lamp that had been scrounged from somewhere to provide light when the overhead fluorescents mysteriously conked out.

Agent Miller opened the manila file folder that was sitting on the table and started reading aloud. "James 'Jimmy' Sadler. Sixty-two years old. You graduated from Caltech with a solid C average, and got a job at Intel. You came under scrutiny in 1986 when irregularities were found in your personnel file; specifically, you were shown to have been given a promotion that nobody remembered giving you. Shortly after the investigation began you disappeared without a trace. You finally turned up yesterday, here, at the headquarters of the Seattle PD, where you ask to speak to us."

Jimmy beamed, and said, "Yes, I wanted—"

Agent Miller cut him off. "Shuddup, Jimmy. I wasn't done telling my story. I was gonna say, before you so rudely interrupted me, that the Seattle PD called our office. Our office then had to call us, because we weren't in our office. Would you like to know where we were, Jimmy?"

Jimmy said, "Yes," his smile fading slightly.

"We were at the airport. You see, we'd just gotten off of a plane. A plane from Seattle. So, instead of going home, like we wanted to, we had to hop right back on a plane."

Now, Jimmy did lose his smile, replacing it with a well-practiced look of regret. "Oh, I'm sorry. I hoped to get you before you went back home. I figured you'd be here a few days, investigating."

Agent Miller's eyes narrowed into slits. "Jimmy, do you know who we work for?"

Jimmy shrugged. "The American taxpayers?"

Miller scowled. "No. Well, yes, in a sense, but in a much more direct sense, we work for the U.S. Treasury Department. Do you know what the U.S. Treasury Department's job is, Jimmy?"

"To investigate—"

Agent Miller cut him off again. "To be tight with money. That's what the Treasury does. It obsessively tracks every penny of the taxpayers' money. Do you suppose they feel like spending a lot of money doing it?"

Jimmy nodded. "No, I suppose—"

"No, they don't, Jimmy!" Miller bellowed. "No, they don't. So, what do you think are the odds of them paying for hotel rooms for Murph and me to use while we stay here in Seattle, *investigating*, when they could just let the local authorities do it instead while they make Murph and me fly home stacked like cord wood in the coach section of the cheapest flight to L.A.?"

Miller stood and loomed over Jimmy. "We didn't have any time to do anything yesterday. We flew to L.A., checked our phone messages. Hung around the airport for two hours, then flew right back here. The only bright point was when we stopped off at that fish market they got here before we went to the airport."

"Oh," Jimmy said brightly, "the one where they throw those great big fish around?"

"Yeah, that's the one," Agent Miller said, wearily.

"How was it?" Jimmy asked.

"It was a fish market. You've been to a fish market, haven't you, Jimmy? It was exactly like that, only crowded, and with guys yelling and throwing around a big dead fish. Does that sound like fun, Jimmy? How they ever convinced people that that's a tourist attraction is beyond me. It's all a big sham. I'm pretty sure they kept throwing the same fish around no matter what anyone ordered." Miller sat down in his chair, breathing heavily. He exchanged a look with Agent Murphy, who shrugged. Finally, Agent Miller said, "There was a place that sold tiny little donuts. Those were really good."

After a carefully timed silence, Jimmy leaned forward in his seat and said, "Look, gentlemen, I apologize. If I'd realized you'd lose a day of productivity over this, I'd have contacted you faster. That said, you are here now, and we can help each other."

Agent Miller snorted. "Jimmy, I can see how we'd be in a position to help you, but how can you possibly help us?"

Jimmy said, "Yesterday, you tried to apprehend Martin Banks. He got away. I'm betting that in the process he did at least one thing that you cannot explain. Knowing him, probably more than one."

The agents made eye contact, then Miller said, "And you're saying that you have information about Mr. Banks' whereabouts."

"I can't tell you where Martin is now, but I can tell you where he went, and, more important, I can show you how he went there."

Agent Miller hid his excitement, which, to Jimmy, was a more obvious sign of excitement than excitement itself.

"Okay," Agent Miller said. "What do you want in return for this information? Immunity?"

Jimmy said. "I don't need immunity. I haven't been charged with anything, and anything I might have done happened thirty years ago. The statute of limitations has to be up by now, if I did anything illegal, which I did not. Even the thing I'm going to show you is not, strictly speaking, illegal."

Miller shook his head. "You say you're gonna show us what the Banks kid did, right? Well, he escaped from police custody after somehow depositing tens of thousands of dollars into his bank account that he didn't earn. How could he have done any of that legally?"

Jimmy hadn't known the particulars of how Martin came to the attention of the authorities. He was amused, but not surprised by what he heard. Jimmy explained, "It's not illegal because of how Martin got the money."

Miller leaned in closer and asked, "How's that?"

Jimmy leaned in and quieted his voice as well. "Through means that the lawmakers never thought was possible."

"And that is?" Agent Miller prodded.

"What I will show you." Jimmy prodded right back.

"So, what's in this for you?" Miller asked.

"The knowledge that I've done my civic duty." Jimmy answered. It was a transparent lie. Jimmy had designed it to be. Men like Agents Miller and Murphy were used to dealing with untrustworthy people. Sincerity would have only confused them. The only way to truly gain their trust was to confirm that he was what they expected: untrustworthy.

Jimmy let Miller stare him down for several seconds before making a show of squirming a bit, and admitting in a slightly higher-pitched voice, "And I'll need a few things. A place to stay. Some food. A computer."

Miller leaned back and laughed. "Old man, how are we supposed to sell our superiors on that?"

"Tell them you believe I have information that will help you explain what happened yesterday, and in numerous other unsolved embezzlement and bank fraud cases that have ended in mysterious disappearances over the last three decades."

Agent Miller considered this, then said, "Yeah, they might cough up a few bucks if I said that. The problem is, I don't think I will, because, like you said, I'd have to believe that you have the information you claim, and I haven't seen anything to convince me of that."

"Haven't you?" Jimmy asked. "Didn't you notice the big ugly lamp sitting on the table in front of you? Don't you think it's odd that the fluorescent lights have stopped working in only this room, or that they continued to not work after the janitor put in new bulbs? Did anybody mention that they had to keep me in an unused office because the electronic locks on the doors of the holding cell wouldn't work? Or that they couldn't take my mug shot because the digital camera died?" Jimmy paused for effect, then asked, "Say, have you checked your cell phone messages?"

Agent Murphy pulled his phone from his pocket, looked at it, pressed a button, then showed the phone to Agent Miller, who said, "Turn it on."

Agent Murphy said, "I can't."

Miller and Murphy excused themselves and left the room. Jimmy looked at his reflection in the large mirror that took up most of the interrogation room's far wall.

✦━━✦

On the other side of the one-way glass, Agent Murphy checked the video camera they had set to record just before having Jimmy brought into the interrogation room.

"I'll be darned. It's dead," Murphy said.

"You don't have to sound so excited about it," Agent Miller grumbled.

"Yeah, I kinda do," Murphy said. "This could be the break we've been waiting for. If he can explain how the Banks kid got all that money then disappeared into thin air twice, he might be able to help us figure out all the other stuff we can't explain."

Miller sighed. "Murph, just 'cause we can't explain why your camera isn't working—"

"Or Seattle PD's camera," Murphy interrupted.

Miller said, "Yeah—"

"Or their electronic locks."

"Okay—"

"Or my phone."

"Whatever, that—"

"Or the lights."

"Shuddup!" Miller barked, loud enough that Jimmy jumped in the next room. "Just 'cause we can't explain him doesn't mean he can explain all the other stuff we can't."

That was the real heart of Agent Miller and Agent Murphy's problem. There was far too much that they could not explain. When they had officially been made a two-man investigative task force, they had thought it was a promotion, until they came to fully understand their assignment.

Miller and Murphy were tasked with investigating obvious cases of embezzlement where there was no actual evidence of embezzlement. Any time anyone in the United States turned up with a large sum of cash and the local authorities couldn't figure out where it came from, Miller and Murphy would be brought in. It was like trying to catch murderers without ever finding a body.

They had spent the last several years receiving random calls (from detectives who always sounded delighted to get the case off of their hands), then dropping everything and flying (which cost the Department of the Treasury nothing, because the airlines could deduct the ticket cost from their taxes) coach (because airlines could give free fliers their worst seats and upgrade two paying customers) to wherever there was a lack of evidence for them to collect.

Miller and Murphy desperately wanted out of the task force, but leaving it would look terrible on their records and would compromise their chances of future promotion. What was worse, every passing day brought them closer to the inevitable moment when they would be removed from the task force involuntarily.

Whatever assignment they were given after a solid record of high-profile failure, they were sure it would not be pleasant.

Miller looked through the one-way glass at the man his partner thought might be the key to their salvation. Jimmy was sitting alone, smiling into the mirror.

"I don't trust him," Miller said.

"Neither do I," Murphy agreed. "But I don't think he's lying."

Miller nodded. "That's just because he hasn't really told us anything yet."

━━◆━━

After several minutes, Agents Miller and Murphy returned to the interrogation room.

"Okay," Miller said, "that's an impressive trick."

"I know it is," Jimmy replied. He gestured toward the mirror. "It's a shame the video camera you have back there didn't catch it."

"Shut up!" Agent Miller said. A thick silence descended while Jimmy waited for Agent Miller to say what Jimmy always knew he eventually would. "Okay," Miller said, "what will you need?"

Jimmy said, "Nothing fancy. A clean place to sleep, three meals a day, and we'll need a computer with high-speed Internet access."

Miller nodded. "I suppose you'll need the computer to be in your room."

"No," Jimmy said. "I won't be touching the computer. I don't want it anywhere near me, but we'll need it."

8.

For three days Martin and Phillip were quite busy. There were preparations to be made, and the fact that neither of them was sure what those preparations were did not make matters easier.

They thought that a first-of-its-kind leadership summit in Atlantis sounded like a big deal. They knew that they were representing their friends. They were absolutely sure that there would be many women. Martin could hardly think about anything beyond the fact that Gwen was certain to be there.

They each went back to their own original times for a serious makeover. Eddie, Jimmy's former right-hand man, turned out to be very helpful in this endeavor. They had all been loath to trust him, after Jimmy tried to kill everyone, but then again, he had tried to kill Eddie as well. Besides, in the two months since that incident, Phillip and Martin had gotten to know Eddie pretty well, and it turned out he was a really interesting guy, and obsessive about men's fashion. He showed them that by jumping to moments in time spaced several months apart, a wizard could get premium bespoke tailoring done instantly, from the wizard's point of view.

They each bought new black tuxedoes, which were timeless. They got new suits, which were carefully chosen to look digni-fied, and as such, were not terribly dated. They got casual wear and swimsuits (it was Atlantis, after all), which couldn't help being a bit dated, and haircuts, which virtually screamed *I'm from the year I'm from.*

Phillip decided that for the brief period he'd be gone, he would leave Tyler and Eddie to manage his chairmanly duties. It wasn't difficult. Essentially, he told Eddie to do what he always did and report periodically to Tyler. He told Tyler to be available to listen to Eddie's reports. On a certain level, Phillip liked the idea that he was leaving Medieval England in the hands of a black man and an Asian man.

Martin felt bad about not being able to complete Roy's training. He especially felt bad when Roy seemed happy about the situation, eagerly suggesting that Jeff take over as trainer.

Gary moped around for a day or so, angry that Phillip and Martin weren't letting him tag along, but then he and Martin hit on the idea of planning a grand entrance.

"Look," Martin said, "this is the first time representatives from all of the wizard communities have ever gotten together in one place. We want everyone to know that we've arrived."

Phillip said, "They'll know that because they'll see that we've arrived."

Martin shook his head. "No, Phil, you're looking at this all wrong. This isn't just a bunch of people showing up for a meeting."

"That's exactly what it is,' Phillip said.

"No, it's not." Martin said, before pausing, then adding, "Well, okay, it is, but it also isn't."

Phillip asked, "Did that sentence make sense to you when you planned it in your head, or do you just open your mouth and let the words fall out however they like?"

Martin took a moment to rephrase his thoughts. "It isn't just a bunch of people arriving for a meeting. It's also a group of important people greeting the world on behalf of their communities. It's like the opening ceremony of the Olympics."

Phillip said, "I was thinking it'd be more like a meeting of the UN."

Gary said, "Really, I was picturing the Tri-Wizard tournament from Harry Potter."

"Yeah, we know you were," Martin muttered. Then, to Phillip, he said, "Look, I've given this some thought, and I think we need to make a big entrance, okay? Will you just go with me on this?"

"Fine," Phillip said, just not wanting to argue about it. "Olympic opening ceremony. Whatever. Are you suggesting that we wear track suits and walk in a circle carrying a flag?"

Martin and Gary looked at each other. Martin said, "You know, that would be funny."

Gary said, "No, you need something impressive. Something that will grab people's attention."

Phillip suggested, "How about if we two grown men appear out of thin air, looking like responsible, rational adults?"

Gary said, "That's a start, but picture this: 'two full grown men,' as you say, crawl out of a fiery crack in the ground, spewing brimstone and damned souls."

"Is the crack in the ground spewing brimstone, or are we?"

Gary said, "We can try it each way and keep whichever looks better."

"I see what you're saying, guys," Phillip said, "but surely in a situation like this, less is more."

"Yes," Gary agreed, "and if less is more, then logically, more must be even more than that."

Eventually Phillip surrendered. He told Gary and Martin to do what they liked, but he begged them not to make it too ostentatious.

Gary's promise to make it just ostentatious enough did not make Phillip feel better.

Finally, the time came. Their suitcases were packed and in hand. Phillip's was a hard-sided chocolate brown Samsonite, Martin's was a black fabric rolling upright. Their hair was perfectly styled. Martin's was spiky and crisp, Phillip's was impeccably feathered and parted down the middle. They were ready to go.

The guys all gathered at Martin's warehouse to see them off.

"Okay, everyone," Phillip said. "We'll be back in exactly two weeks."

"Yeah, why is that, kid?" Roy asked. Being in his sixties, Roy delighted in calling Phillip *kid*. Being in his forties, Phillip delighted in finally having someone around who could plausibly call him *kid*. "Why come back in two weeks? You're time travelers. Why not just come back the second after you left?"

"For quick trips, we usually do," Phillip explained, "but sometimes, for longer trips, it's just less confusing this way. Besides, when you've lived in the past for a while, you begin to realize that you don't particularly need to see all of it."

Martin asked Gary, "Is our entrance ready?"

"Yup," Gary said, "I've got the macro set up so that it'll automatically trigger off of the same phrase that transports you there."

"Do I have to do anything special?" Phillip asked.

"No," Gary said, "we've designed the whole thing around the idea that you're gonna stand there like a stiff."

"Wise," said Phillip.

Tyler asked Martin, "What's your plan with Gwen?"

Martin said, "I'm gonna try to be cool."

It occurred to Phillip that the phrase *try to be cool* could mean *try to act like everything is all right,* which would be good, or it could mean *try to act like I'm a really cool guy,* which would be disastrously bad.

Goodbyes were exchanged. Instructions were imparted. Stern warnings were leveled at Gary. It was time to go. Martin and Phillip stood side by side, staffs in one hand, suitcases in the other, and in unison said, *"Transporto unua Atlantis kunveno."*

+>==<+

Many, many years before, and many, many miles away, two figures materialized. It was impossible to identify them further because they were cloaked in shadow, despite the bright sun that shone overhead.

For a moment the incongruously shady duo stood motionless, then they were bathed in brilliant light, making it easy to identify them as Martin and Phillip. Phillip winced in the blinding light, shielding his eyes. Martin leapt into the air, much higher and more gracefully than he'd ever be able to without magical assistance. He executed a perfect roundhouse kick, a feat that was all the more impressive for his still holding his staff in one hand and his full suitcase in the other. At the apex of his jump, he froze, motionless in mid-air. As he hung there, the vista behind him was filled with images of explosions, blood-thirsty orcs, and what appeared to be a white Pontiac Fiero jumping a ravine. Both Martin and the tableau held their position behind Phillip for a moment, giving the intended audience the impression that they were looking at the poster for an action-packed buddy movie about a kung-fu wizard frequent-flyer and his straight-laced, confused partner. From somewhere, an electric guitar solo played, then the images of cheesy B-movie awesomeness disappeared. Martin landed on the opposite side of Phillip from where he'd started. With a carefully practiced air of nonchalance, Martin lifted his gaze to receive the audience's reaction to their entrance.

Martin saw the bluest sky he'd ever seen, above the bluest ocean he'd ever seen. To his right, there was a lush, green forest of palm trees and scrub grass. Beneath his feet was sand the color and consistency of sugar. Directly in front of him, he saw Gwen, standing alone, barefoot on the beach. Her hair was still cut in a cute bob, but exposure to the sun had bleached it a lighter brown than he remembered. She was wearing a hooded cloak of the same design as the one she'd worn when she lived in England, but this one was made of a light fabric more appropriate for protecting the wearer from the sun than from wind and rain. Beneath the cloak she wore a light, knee-length sundress. Her sandals hung by their loops from her fingers, but her hands were still unencumbered enough to execute a perfect slow-clap.

Phillip cried, "Gwen!" He dropped his suitcase and rushed forward, seizing Gwen in a bear hug.

"Phillip," Gwen said. "It's so good to see you." As they hugged, Martin set down his suitcase and approached for his turn to say hello.

The hug finally ended, but rather than releasing Gwen, Phillip held her at arm's length and looked her up and down. "Gwen, you look great."

Martin silently agreed.

She thanked Phillip as he finally released his grip. Martin moved in for a hug of his own, but was stopped dead when Gwen offered him a handshake. With great effort, he shook her hand without any sign of disappointment.

"Gwen," Martin said, "it's great to see you."

"You too, Martin. Clearly you got the bowl okay."

"Oh yeah. Thanks for the *Star Wars* reference, by the way."

Gwen smiled. "Don't mention it."

Phillip, now done greeting Gwen, had turned his attention to their surroundings. "Gwen, this is beautiful! Where are we?"

"This is an island a few miles off the coast of Greece. It's the year 368 B.C., if you can believe it. Some of the other delegates were given transport coordinates directly into the city, but I wanted some time to say hello and explain a few things." She started walking down the beach. The two men walked with her.

Phillip said, "First things first. How are you Gwen? How do you like living in Atlantis?"

Gwen said, "Atlantis is amazing. You'll see soon enough. It's not perfect, but it's pretty close."

Martin said, "Really? Because, I gotta say, I was surprised to hear from you again so soon."

"What do you mean?" Gwen asked.

"Oh, just that when you left, I figured we'd hear from you again, but I expected it to take a lot longer. I thought you'd hold out longer than a month or two."

Martin looked at Gwen. She was looking back, but she was not smiling. Beyond her, Martin could see Phillip. His eyes were bulging and he was gritting his teeth.

"It's been a month or two for you, Martin," Gwen said. "I've been here over two years."

Martin stopped walking. Gwen and Phillip did not.

"Oh," Martin said. "That's closer to what I expected."

Gwen neither slowed down nor said a word. Phillip looked back at him and chuckled mirthlessly. After a moment, Martin ran to catch up.

"So," Phillip said, breaking the silence, "where are we going?"

"To Atlantis," Gwen answered. "It's a few miles away, but I've got a boat to take us."

"Why don't we just fly there?" Martin asked.

"Because we can't really talk while we're flying, and there are a few things you need to know."

As they rounded a bend, skirting the edge of the island, they saw a wooden dock extending off of the beach and into the water.

"Where shall we start?" Phillip asked.

"Let's start with the summit," Gwen said. "As the invitation said, representatives from each colony of time travelers have been brought here. We've brought two members from each group, the group's leader, and another, usually either the second in command, or the leader's best friend. It may please you to know that you're from one of the largest groups. Most colonies are quite a bit smaller."

Martin asked, "What are the biggest ones?"

"Well, there's you guys, because you represent all of Europe in one of the most obvious time frames. China and Baghdad are about the same size as yours, but the biggest is Atlantis."

"Really?" Martin said. "Atlantis is the biggest?"

"Think about it," Gwen said. "We have most of the women from most of the groups. Of course we'd be the biggest."

Martin held up his hands, signaling surrender. "No, I get it. You've got a point. I'd just hoped that other cultures were a little friendlier to women who do magic, so maybe they wouldn't feel the need to come here."

Gwen said, "Sadly, life is pretty nasty for women who do magic almost everywhere, and in almost any time. The only place where they get treated the same as the men is in the colony that's living as Gypsies in Paris in the 1480s, and that's just because the locals treat the male and the female Gypsies equally badly."

They walked quietly for a moment, contemplating human nature, until Gwen broke the silence. "So, we'll be deciding various issues that face our kind. How to prevent the abuse of our powers, what we will call ourselves, that sort of stuff."

"What's wrong with calling ourselves wizards?" Martin asked.

"We don't all pose as wizards. There are fakirs, philosophers, wise men, alchemists, medicine men, sorcerers, and a couple of magicians. You'll be meeting people like us from all over the world, and all over recorded history. For now we're using 'time travelers,' but that doesn't really cover it. In Atlantis, we call ourselves 'sorceresses.'"

"Because you're all women."

"And because it's fun. It kinda makes everything into a tongue twister. 'Send several sorceresses south.' See?"

Phillip said, "Great. Two weeks of planned disagreements with people who aren't used to dealing with equals. It'll be a miracle if we get anything accomplished."

"It won't be a problem," Gwen said. "Our leader, Brit, will be running the show. She's pretty good at this sort of thing."

"It's a shame your leader has to do that instead of acting as a delegate for Atlantis."

Gwen laughed. "Oh, she's also one of our delegates."

Wait," Phillip said. "Isn't anyone worried that she might somehow, I don't know, favor herself?"

Gwen said, "Believe me, it's not a problem. She seldom agrees with herself. Here's the boat." Gwen gestured toward the end of the dock, which seemed at a glance to have no boats moored to it. When Phillip and Martin actually looked, though, they could see another transparent bowl bobbing in the water. This one was much larger than the one Phillip had received. Even knowing it was there, it was more visible for the shadow it cast and the furrow in the water where it sat than for actually being visible itself. If Martin squinted, he could just make out a transparent floor and a shelf-like bench wrapping around the inside.

Gwen walked to the end of the dock, slipped on her sandals, and stepped over the rim, into the near-invisible boat. Martin and Phillip followed suit. When they were all seated Gwen said, "Take me home." The boat silently lifted a foot or so above the surface and started moving, fast enough to make real progress, but slowly enough that the wind was not unpleasant.

Phillip looked at the edge of the flying bowl-boat and asked, "Is this made of diamond too?"

Gwen smiled. "Yeah. It's laid down one molecule at a time by an automated algorithm. Makes incredibly strong structures, and if you think it through well enough you can make almost anything. Also, because they're so molecularly pure, you can manipulate, levitate, or teleport them at will with no danger of them breaking apart. It was one of the Brits' first great innovations."

Phillip puffed up a bit with nationalistic pride. "We Brits invented this? When?"

Gwen chuckled. "Not the British. The Brits. Two of our leaders are named Brit."

"Oh," Martin said, "like the Magnuses."

"No," Gwen said. "Nothing like the Magnuses. This is one of the things I wanted to warn you about." Gwen sighed heavily, thought for a moment, then plunged ahead. "See, there are three people in charge of Atlantis. They form a sort of voting council. There's the President, whom we all elect. At the moment it's a woman named Ida. Then there's Brit, our real leader. She founded Atlantis and is the smartest person I've ever met. She's there out of respect. She built the whole place herself. She's, well, she's just amazing. You'll see."

Martin said, "And the third, the other Brit. What's her deal?"

Gwen winced. "See, that's the hard part to explain. There is no other Brit. It's the same Brit. Brit is two people, or you could say she's one person twice. See, Brit went back in time, like a hundred years ago, and built Atlantis. She designed it, did all of the engineering, made it all work. Then she went out into the world and encouraged people to move to the city and populate it. They set up homes and businesses, gave her creation life, and made it a real city. She built the buildings, then she made it into the city it is today."

"She sounds great," Phillip said.

"She is," Gwen agreed. "The problem is that before she did all that, she came to the past for the first time, eleven years ago, and found Atlantis here, already up and running. Then she met herself and discovered that she had gone back in time and built Atlantis so that it would be ready for her when she arrived."

There was a long silence, which ended with Phillip yelling that this made no sense, and that the whole thing was preposterous, followed by Martin agreeing with Phillip, followed by Gwen agreeing with both of them, but assuring them that it was true, or at least it seemed to be.

"Brit has a theory about how it happened. When she explains it, it makes sense."

"Well, let's hear it." Martin said.

Gwen shook her head. "You'll have to ask her. It only makes sense when she explains it."

Phillip grimaced. "I don't like it," he said.

Gwen said, "I knew you wouldn't," putting a steadying hand on his shoulder. "You'll have plenty of time to ask Brit about all of this. For now, you just have to keep in mind that there are two Brits. We call them *Brit the Elder* and *Brit the Younger*, and they are the same person at two different ages."

Martin exhaled loudly. "That should be easy to keep straight."

Gwen added, "Oh, and I should mention that they're the same age. Physically. You'll see."

The men did not seem reassured.

Gwen pressed on. "The summit is Brit the Elder's idea. She saw early on that it would be easy for one of us to abuse our abilities. She wants to avoid that, but she needs everyone else to cooperate, and people don't like the idea of limiting their own power. Because she's the leader of the earliest known colony of time travelers, she has the luxury of time. She spoke to all of the girls who've come to Atlantis from all of the other colonies, pinpointed a moment a month or two after some time traveler tried to abuse his power, then invited leaders from that time to come here for a summit. That way, she knew they'd be in the right frame of mind to cooperate."

"And I'm sure Brit the Younger agreed," Phillip said, ruefully.

"No. Brit the Younger thought it was manipulative. They have a . . . difficult relationship."

"But they're the same person," Phillip cried.

Gwen shrugged.

"So that's why we were called now," Martin said. "Because Jimmy tried to kill us all two months ago."

"Which means she knows all about the Jimmy situation," Phillip said. "That's a bit embarrassing."

Gwen said, "Don't be embarrassed. I told Brit the Elder the whole story and she agreed that Jimmy had to go. She said that he was clearly dangerous, greedy, manipulative, and cruel."

Phillip said, "I'm glad we're in agreement."

Gwen shielded her eyes with her hand and peered into the distance. "She also said that he lacked vision, and thought too small."

"What's that supposed to mean?" Martin asked.

Gwen smiled. "Judge for yourself." Gwen gestured ahead. "Gentlemen, the sunken city of Atlantis." Martin and Phillip shielded their eyes, and in the distance, they saw it.

The ocean was calm and vast. There were no islands to interrupt the flatness of the horizon, but in the distance, there did appear to be a hazy collection of square-sailed ships. It was difficult to look at them. Something about how the light was shimmering made their eyes strain. It was also difficult to look at the ships because it was impossible to ignore what was above them. Hovering above the wavering, wobbling patch of sea there were what appeared to be a great many tall buildings, just hanging in space. Seagulls soared above the impossible skyline, and the small armada of ships bobbed below.

"Wow," Martin gasped.

"Yes," Gwen said. "The genius of picking Atlantis as a base of operations is that it's destined to disappear anyway, so Brit was free to build anything she wanted. Of course, that was before she knew that nothing we do seems to affect the future anyway, but still, it was clever of her."

Martin whistled, then said, "One person built that? No wonder it took her a hundred years."

"She spent the first week designing the city and writing the construction algorithm. She set that in motion, and the basic construction was done in a few days. The rest of the time was spent establishing a culture, encouraging immigration, and creating a system of government. That was the hard part."

Phillip said, "It took Jimmy years to build one castle, and he had an army of builders helping him. How on Earth could this Brit of yours build that in a few days?"

Gwen rapped on the side of the crystal-clear bowl that was whisking them toward the city. "The same way we built this boat, and the bowl we sent you. You know how you copy coins and food items? We do the same thing, with individual atoms, and instead of replicating the atoms in a hat, we place them precisely next to the last atom we copied, in a pattern pre-determined by and automatically carried out by computer code.

"Domes are the strongest shape, and the easiest one to program. She got the idea from a science fiction book she read. It had a lot of diamond domes in it, but she chose to make basins instead."

"That explains how she built the buildings," Martin allowed, "but how did she make them float in mid-air like that?"

Gwen said, "She didn't. They float, but not in the air." She leaned over close to Martin. She put a hand on his shoulder, and put her head next to his, looking off into the distance in the same direction as him. She pointed at a ship at the edge of the shimmering armada. "Look at that ship on the end, with the blue-striped sail. See anything odd about it?"

"Yes," Martin said, squinting into the distance. "It's sitting next to a ship with the exact same sail."

"No," Gwen said. "Look closer."

Martin squinted some more, then exclaimed, "It's sitting next to half a ship with the same sail." It was now clear to Martin what he was looking at, and it wasn't what he'd first thought. They weren't buildings: they were just the tops of buildings. The empty space beneath them wasn't empty at all: it was the reflection in a giant, curving, mirrored wall. The shimmering wasn't magic: it was distortion from the curvature of the mirror and a mirage from the heat it was reflecting. The gathering of ships beneath the city was a much smaller gathering of ships around the city, and their reflections. The city was not floating above the water, but rising up from it.

They were approaching the city quite quickly now. Clearly, the flying half-bubble that Gwen kept referring to as a boat was moving deceptively fast. With the city looming ever larger in front of them, Gwen turned to Martin and Phillip and said, "Look, guys. One last thing you should know. There are some things about Atlantis that I'm not entirely proud of."

"What do you mean?" Phillip asked.

"You have to understand," she said, "it's a society ruled entirely by women."

"We expect it to be different," Martin said.

"Yeah," Gwen sighed, "well, expect it to be different from what you expect."

The guys clearly did not understand what she meant.

"I'll put it this way," she continued, "have you ever been to a bar where a bachelor party was going on?"

Both men said yes.

Gwen asked, "Have you ever been to a bar where a bachelorette party was going on?"

Again, both men said yes.

Gwen asked, "Which one was more out of control?"

The craft started gaining altitude, flying above the ships, massed around the perimeter of Atlantis. Ancient Greek traders standing on their ships craned their necks and watched them fly overhead.

As they approached the rim of the wall, Martin said, "Gwen, if it's a walled island, why do you keep calling it 'The Sunken City of Atlantis?'"

Gwen said. "You're thinking *sunken* as in *sunken treasure*. You should be thinking *sunken*, as in *sunken living room*."

The craft crested the rim of the city and kept climbing. Looking at Atlantis from above, it was as if a gigantic hole had been dug into the ocean itself. The city was a perfect circle, and while there were tall buildings around its outer rim, the interior of the circle fell away sharply, forming yet another bowl shape, this one quite irregular, made up of windows, terraces, and rooftop gardens. All of the buildings were made of a smooth, gleaming white material, formed into flat surfaces joined with rounded edges.

Tracks divided the city like slices cut into a pie. Broad, flat lifts teeming with people slowly inched up and down the tracks. Terraced foot paths, crowded with pedestrians, radiated around the city at regular intervals, interspersed with large public plazas where people could meet and enjoy the view.

It was immediately clear to both Phillip and Martin that the outer wall of Atlantis was nothing more than another molecularly pure diamond bowl, only much larger than any they had seen before. Glancing at the edge of the city, the bowl looked to be at least three feet thick. What they had taken for a wall had actually been the upper rim of the bowl extending above the water line. Gwen confirmed this, and added that it had been partially silvered, for security, and because it just looked cooler that way.

In the center of the city, at the low point of the bowl, there was a large park. At the center of the park there was some manner of pointy civic monument. Large, impressive buildings festooned with domes and columns surrounded the park on all sides.

As their craft descended into the center of the city, it became clear that their destination was one of the buildings surrounding the central park. Martin could make out a low, flat building that appeared to be made up of various rectangles intersecting each other at right angles. It was as if they had taken the home of the wealthy villain from an action movie and covered it in reflective white paint. Large glass doors led to an immense balcony with two people standing at attention. Even from a great distance he could tell that they were on high alert. Martin asked Gwen where they were going.

"To Brit the Elder's personal quarters," Gwen answered.

"Makes sense," Martin said. "I'm sure she wants to personally greet all of the delegates."

After a silence, Gwen said, "Actually, no. She specifically said that she didn't want to meet any of the delegates until the formal reception tonight. Then, she pulled me aside and told me to bring you two straight to her."

Phillip didn't hear her, lost in his own thoughts. He looked down at the beautiful building and shook his head in disgust. "Typical. She builds the city and gives herself the nicest home, right in the center of the city."

Gwen said, "Brit the Elder's home looks different, but the inside is pretty much like everybody else's. The only real difference is the patio. She uses it for official meetings, that sort of thing. And yeah, the government buildings are pretty fancy, but they're sitting on the worst real estate in Atlantis. Think about it: everything's uphill. It's like living at the bottom of an open pit mine. The whole city looms over you all the time, on all sides. Brit says it gives the city's leaders the proper perspective."

"You like her, don't you?" Martin asked.

"Almost everybody does."

"Almost?"

Gwen sighed. "Yeah, well, Brit the Younger isn't her biggest fan. Like I said, it's complicated."

The craft gently touched down on Brit the Elder's patio, a space about twice the size of a basketball court. Instead of wood or stone, the deck was covered in soft grass. Rather than just being a uniform green, different species of grass had been employed, in various shades and lengths to give the effect of a tasteful inlaid design. Three sides of the terrace were edged by thin, decorative railings. The fourth was taken up by a perfect white wall. In the center of the wall there were large windows. There was so much light outside, and so little inside, that one could not see what was inside the building. The two people Martin had seen standing on the terrace as he approached were clearly guards, both male, both tall and slender, yet muscular. They had great definition. Martin could tell this because of their clothing, which consisted of a loose, light blue tunic, made of a semi-transparent mesh, and a sort of kilt, made of black fabric that managed to be clingy and rough at the same time. The kilt came down to just above the men's knees, exposing their powerful, hairless legs. They wore sandals with thick leather straps and chunky soles.

Martin asked Gwen, "Are we going to have to dress like that?"

Gwen smirked, and looked at Martin's full-length, silver-sequined robe and matching hat. "No, don't worry. If you're more comfortable you can continue to wear your robes."

"You made these robes," Martin reminded her.

"Yes, but you're the ones who choose to wear them," she replied.

The mirrored-glass windows parted smoothly, and two more tall, thin, muscular guards emerged, flanking a woman. She looked to be in her mid-twenties and was a bit on the short side. She was not overweight by any rational standard, but she was also certainly not skinny. She wore black-rimmed glasses and a light, gauzy dress. Her reddish-brown hair hung down to her shoulders. Though she looked young, she had the bearing of a mature woman, the kind of woman who wasn't too bothered about what you thought of her, because she knew what she thought of herself.

As the woman approached, Gwen said, "Brit the Elder, I'd like you to meet . . ."

Brit the Elder didn't seem to hear Gwen. She spread her arms wide and said "Phillip!" She walked directly to Phillip and looked at him, breathing in deeply. "Phillip," she repeated. "It is so good to see you. I just had to say hello to you before the reception, with all those other delegates around."

Phillip glanced at Gwen, who seemed thrown. He extended his right hand and said, "Thank you, . . . ma'am, uh, but I don't believe we've met."

Brit took Phillip's right hand in both of hers, and smiled. "Of course, you're right. We haven't met, but we will soon."

"Aren't we meeting right now?" Phillip asked.

"Yes, but not for the first time. That comes later." She smiled at Phillip for another moment, then she released his hand and pried her attention away from him. "Hello, Martin," she said, brightly. "How do you like Atlantis?"

Martin bowed slightly and said, "It's spectacular, but I gotta say, I'm really more impressed with how you built it. It simply never occurred to me to make a macro copy of molecules like that. It's brilliant."

Even though Martin wouldn't have thought it possible, her smile got even broader. "Yes, I thought you'd appreciate it more than most. That's why I told Gwen to invite you."

"Oh, uh, um," Martin stammered. "That was your doing?"

"Yes. She suggested that someone named Tyler might get more out of the visit, but from what she's told me about you, and from what I remembered, well, I knew you had to be the one to accompany Phillip."

She looked back at Phillip for another long moment, then she looked away, stood straight and tall, and said, "Gentlemen, it's wonderful to see you both. I'd love to chat, but we all have a reception to prepare for. Thank you, Gwen. I'll see you all tonight."

Brit the Elder turned and walked back toward the mirrored glass, followed by two of her four guards. The glass opened silently just as she arrived, then closed silently once the three of them were inside.

9.

Jimmy sat in his private jail cell, which, sadly, was the nicest home he'd had in thirty years. It was clean, the toilet worked, and he didn't have to pedal it. Of course, he couldn't leave, but he was sure that would change soon. Jimmy had expected to be taken into custody once he revealed himself to the authorities, but once he was officially working with them, he expected his treatment would improve.

Jimmy heard the agents coming long before he saw them. He heard the jangling of keys on the far side of the steel security door at the far end of the hall, which told him that someone was approaching.

Then, Jimmy heard the security door open and the sound of footsteps, which told him that the visitors were two men.

Then Jimmy heard the other prisoners greeting the visitors with a mixture of insults, threats, and insulting threats, which told Jimmy that the visitors were not the normal jail guards.

Finally, Jimmy heard one of the visitors silence the prisoners by shouting a torrent of the most viscerally horrifying threats Jimmy had ever heard, while the other man said nothing, which told him that the visitors were Agents Miller and Murphy.

Jimmy sat up on his bed and turned to face the iron bars. The electronic lock on his door and the doors of the two adjacent cells had mysteriously stopped working, so they were secured with several loops of thick chain and big, beefy padlocks that Jimmy could have picked quite quickly, if he'd had any wish to do so.

Agents Miller and Murphy arrived in front of Jimmy's cell. Jimmy waited patiently while Agent Miller finished a particularly long and intricate threat, shouted not at any specific prisoner, but at anybody who had the audacity to be listening at that moment. When he was finished, Jimmy said, "Good morning, gentlemen."

Agent Murphy's face split into a wide, goofy grin. "Why, good morning, Jimmy. I hope you slept well. We're awfully sorry about your accommodations. We're still working on getting you someplace a little more comfortable."

This was not unexpected. Miller and Murphy employed an exaggerated version of the old good cop/bad cop routine that Jimmy liked to call "violently unstable rage-aholic cop/friendly, talkative youth pastor cop." As soon as it became clear that Jimmy was not a perpetrator to be bullied, but an ally to be placated, Agent Murphy had taken over most communication.

Jimmy said, "I slept very well, thank you. I'd rather not be in a jail cell if I don't have to, but I know you're working on that. How was your evening? I trust the agency has found you some-place to stay."

Agent Miller remained silent and white knuckled, just staring at Jimmy and looking as if he were chewing on his own tongue. Agent Murphy chuckled lightly and said, "They've put us up at a charmingly rustic independent motel near the airport."

"Oh," Jimmy said, "that doesn't sound very convenient."

"Oh, the airport's not far from downtown. It's just a little over an hour commute each way, thanks to this amazing Seattle traffic.

The hotel's not much, but it's all we need. There's ten channels' worth of cable on the TV, and clean sheets on our twin beds, and a picturesque view of the gentlemen's club next door."

Jimmy thought he saw Agent Miller's left eye twitch.

Jimmy said, "I'm sure that's very entertaining."

Miller couldn't take anymore. "It might be," he said, "if we had a view of the inside, but all we can see is a parking lot full of desperate, lonely men, all of whom seem to look in our window. They seem to be fascinated by the sight of two middle-aged men lying in twin beds like Ernie and Bert, watching The Weather Channel because it's the most exciting thing on. It's like being an exhibit in an alien zoo, on the planet of the scabby pervs!"

Agent Murphy turned to look at his partner, and Agent Miller immediately stopped talking, clenching his jaw so hard that his teeth nearly cracked.

"Now, Miller, you know that the nice man at the front desk promised to get our blinds fixed so we could close them just as soon as he gets around to it." The agents turned their attention back to Jimmy, one viewing him with an air of friendly benevolence, the other with cold loathing.

Jimmy said, "Look, guys, I'm sorry. I wish we could go back to your home office in L.A., but you know I can't fly. You saw what being next to me did to your phone. Do you really want to ride in a plane with me?"

"We could drive it," Miller growled. "It can be done in eighteen hours if you're motivated."

Jimmy had no doubt that Agent Miller was motivated. "You'd have to get a car with no integrated circuitry, so that means an unrestored car from the fifties. Then you'd have to take roads where traffic would never get closer than thirty feet from us for more than say, five seconds at a time, so that would mean taking little roads through Eastern Washington, Idaho, and Nevada to get there."

"You seem to have given this a lot of thought," Agent Murphy said.

"That route is how I got to Seattle," Jimmy said.

"On your bicycle?"

"Yup."

The agents looked at each other, then looked at Jimmy. He was in his sixties, and very thin, but neither man doubted for an instant that he was telling the truth.

"If you must get me to L.A., the fastest way would be to get the Treasury Department to hire a boxcar on the longest freight train you can find going to California. It's faster than driving the long way, and it will keep me away from any electronics I might damage."

"How much would that cost?" Agent Murphy asked.

"Sadly, a lot more than your hotel room for a week."

Agent Miller grunted, "A week?" Jimmy thought he could hear tendons popping in the agents' hands.

Jimmy put his hands up, defensively. "Maybe less. Hopefully less."

Agent Miller muttered, "It'd better be less."

Jimmy smiled and said, "It will be! It will!"

"Good."

"Probably."

10.

After their meeting with Brit the Elder, Gwen explained that she had to prepare for the reception an hour later. She called out to one of the impossibly good-looking guards, who somehow managed to sashay over to her in a way that was still undeniably manly. He stopped less than a foot in front of Gwen, looked deeply into her eyes, and in a husky voice, said, "Yes, ma'am? What can I do for you?"

Gwen said, "Please escort my friends to their quarters and arrange for their transportation to the reception."

The guard glanced at Martin and Phillip, not like a man who was meeting new people, but rather like a man who was judging the weight of two heavy sacks of flour he'd been asked to carry. He looked back to Gwen's eyes and said, "If that is what you want, that is what I will do."

"Good. That's what I want."

"Is it?"

"It is."

"Is that all you want?"

"Yes."

"Really?"

Gwen frowned. "Yes, that is all I want, from you."

The guard smirked, but his eyes registered confusion. Martin made a note of it. Not hurt, confusion. The guard said, "Then it will be my pleasure to transport these," the guard paused long enough to glance down at Martin and Phillip again, "these *men* to their quarters." He leaned in closer to Gwen. "If you need anything else from me, anything at all, I trust you'll ask."

Gwen said, "That'll be all." She turned to Martin and Phillip, and her smile came back, but not as strongly as before. "Guys, it's just so good to see both of you."

Phillip asked, "Hey, Gwen, the reception—how formally should we dress?"

"What's the nicest thing you brought?"

"We both had custom-tailored tuxedos made."

Gwen laughed, but it was out of astonishment. "Wow. Class move. Well done. I'd say wear the tux, but use your robe for the top layer instead of the jacket. Just adjust the robe so it's open to the sternum, like a tuxedo jacket, or wear the robe open. Oh, and bring the hats and staffs. You won't need to do any magic, but it's good for show. See you then." With that, she turned and left via the same sliding glass door that Brit the Elder had used.

The four men on the terrace, Martin, Phillip, and the two guards, watched her leave with great fondness. As soon as the door slid shut behind her, the guards' demeanor changed completely. The guard tasked with showing the wizards to their rooms looked to the other guard and shook his head dismissively. The second guard chuckled mirthlessly and shrugged.

The guard assigned to Martin and Phillip looked down at them. He was a full head taller than Martin and had no noticeable body fat. He said, "Follow me. Keep up." With that he led the two wizards to a small staircase leading to the park below.

The grass was perfectly manicured. The trees were immaculately pruned. The flowers and shrubs were carefully arranged and lovingly maintained. They happened past a gardener, toiling in the sun. He was young and muscular. He wore a kilt and sandals, but no shirt. As he heard footsteps approaching, the gardener languidly turned to face whoever was approaching. He bowed his head slightly, pursed his lips, and raises his eyes to look through his long hair, which had artfully fallen into his eyes. He saw that the approaching footsteps belonged to a guard and two men and he immediately slouched. His expression soured. He made eye contact with the guard, who shrugged and shook his head.

Martin quickened his pace to walk next to the guard and said, "Hi!"

The guard said nothing.

"So," Martin asked, "what's your name?"

"Never mind," the guard replied.

"Oh, come on," Martin said. "You must have a name."

"I do, but it's not worth the trouble of telling you. What would you do with it? Use it to greet me if you see me again? What good would that do me? I'd have to explain to the other men who you are, *what* you are, and worse, how you came to know me well enough to use my name."

Martin said, "I was just trying to make conversation."

The guard considered this and sneered, "Is that what the males do where you come from? Make conversation? Do you squawk and titter like the womenfolk do?"

"Sometimes, I guess. It depends on what we're talking about."

The guard grimaced. "Well, that explains it."

"Explains what?" Phillip asked, still lagging behind.

"The one who brought you here. Gwen, she comes from the same place as you?"

"Yes."

"Well, if males like you are what she is used to, then it's no wonder she has yet to select a servant."

"A servant?" Martin prodded.

"The sorceresses who rule this city each choose a servant to tend to them. Some more than one. Brit the Elder has several."

"What all does the servant do?"

The guard squinted down at Martin. Phillip sped his pace slightly to be closer to the conversation. He wanted to know where this was going.

The guard repeated, "He tends to them."

Phillip asked, "And this is a sought-after position among the men?"

"Yes. Of course. Men from everywhere who consider themselves a likely candidate flock to Atlantis to be near the sorceresses in hopes of being chosen."

"Seriously? Your loftiest goal is to be a servant?"

"To a sorceress, yes. Their powers afford a servant every luxury you can imagine, and the prestige of being selected is second to none. In return for all this, a servant's only duty is to tend to the needs of his sorceress."

"Cooking, cleaning, that sort of thing?" Martin asked.

The guard snorted. "Never! There are menials for that."

Martin started to understand what Gwen had meant when she said that there were aspects of Atlantean society of which she was not proud.

As the trio walked, skirting the edge of the park, Martin and Phillip began to see that any job that involved being seen in public was being done by a tall, brooding man. The guards, the gardeners, the food vendors, the porters, they were all men, all beautiful, and all noticeably disappointed by the sight of Martin and Phillip. Also, most of them were shirtless—even, disturbingly, the food vendors.

At last they came to the elevator station. The guard called it the cable car, but it had no cable, and looked nothing like a car. It was simply an open platform bordered by a thin safety railing. An empty path that could be called a track led straight up the curved wall that defined the city, but there were no rails, cables, or cogs. At first, Martin thought the empty path had been painted an extremely dark green color, then he realized that it was clear, and that he was seeing into the ocean itself on the other side of the basin.

They waited a few moments while a few more men boarded the platform, standing as far away from the wizards and their chaperone as they could. Then, silently, the platform started working its way up the side of the city.

Martin looked down at the platform on which he stood. It was milky white and translucent, and it had a grid pattern cut into its surface. *For traction*, he supposed.

Martin stamped his foot, listening to and feeling the vibration. He muttered, "More diamond?"

"Maybe," Phillip said. "Or maybe a toughened glass, like Pyrex or something. I've seen a few different materials here, but they all seem to be crystalline."

"Makes sense. It would be easy to produce using her molecular construction method, and the structures she builds would be perfectly monolithic."

"Yes," Phillip said, seeing what Martin meant. "Then she could use the shell, or whatever her version of it is called, to move them around at will without any fear of them losing their structural integrity."

"It's . . . it's brilliant," Martin said.

"Yes, I have to admit, it is," Phillip said.

Martin and Phillip became aware that the guard was looking down at them, his face a mask of undisguised loathing. Martin changed the subject.

"So," Martin said, using his best nonchalant voice, "you say Gwen hasn't chosen a servant."

"Yes," the guard said, looking away. "That is what I said."

"And she's the only sorceress who hasn't?"

"Yes."

"I see. Have many of you tried to become Gwen's servant?"

"We have all tried to become her servant. We are all still trying to become her servant. She is the most sought-after woman in all of Atlantis."

Martin said, "Well, I can understand that. She is adorable."

The guard laughed. "If by adorable you mean that she is short and strange and that she talks in gibberish, like you two. She is sought after solely because she is the only sorceress who has not chosen a servant. That is all. Someday, she will choose a servant, and if that servant is me, it means that the most difficult work I'll ever need to do is pretending to enjoy her company."

They rode in uncomfortable silence for a moment as the platform followed the contour of Atlantis' massive bowl. Now that he was looking for it, the walls of the buildings were clearly some crystalline matter, colored a uniform milky white. Palm trees, footpaths, and small rooftop patches of soft grass broke up the jumble of buildings clinging to the wall's permanent incline.

For the first time, the guard spoke without being asked a direct question. "Gwen came from wherever you live. Tell me, was there a male there whom Gwen found attractive?"

Martin chose to ignore the question.

"Yes," Phillip said. "Yes, there was. Why do you ask?"

The guard looked around, then said, quietly, "If you were to tell me what this man that Gwen was attracted to was like, I might act more like him, and perhaps become her servant."

"I see," Phillip said, almost giggling with glee. "That's an interesting idea."

"Then will you help me?"

"Yes," Phillip said, "but before I can help you, you should at least tell me your name."

"I'm sorry," the guard said. He stood straight, and puffed out his chest as if he were about to say the most momentous thing Phillip had ever heard. "My name," the guard said in a deep, resonant voice, "is Ampyx."

Phillip said, "It's a pleasure to meet you, Ampyx. My name is Phillip." Martin kept looking at the city moving past and shook his head.

"So, Phillip," Ampyx asked, "what can you tell me about this man that Gwen found attractive?"

"I don't have to tell you anything. You've met him. It's my friend, Martin." Phillip put a hand on Martin's shoulder, and gestured toward him with the other hand like a game show spokesmodel displaying a new car. Ampyx looked at Martin with an undisguised mixture of horror and disgust. Martin glared at Phillip. Phillip beamed back at him.

Most of the balance of the trip to their quarters passed in silence. Ampyx watched Martin's every move. Martin tried not to show how profoundly uncomfortable Ampyx was making him. Phillip tried not to laugh out loud. The platform arrived at a station about two-thirds of the way up the side of the bowl. Ampyx led them off of the platform and down a broad, grassy footpath. They passed shops selling food, clothing, and hard goods, all of them small and tasteful, and all of them staffed by good-looking men. Ampyx asked Martin several questions, but Martin resisted answering, or even speaking to him. The only question that got any traction was when he asked Martin what he did. Martin tersely replied that he was a wizard and was met with a blank stare.

"You know, a wizard," Martin said. "I do magic."

Martin had expected that this would at least impress Ampyx. Martin was wrong.

"Why?" Ampyx asked.

"Why what? Why do I do magic?"

"Yes, why do you do magic?" Ampyx asked, as if it were the most obvious question in the world.

Martin looked at Phillip, who shrugged. Finally, Martin answered, "Why wouldn't I do magic? Wouldn't you do magic if you could?"

"Never," Ampyx said.

"Well, why not?"

Ampyx scrunched his face and said, "Magic . . . it is . . . woman's work."

Martin just stared at him. Phillip piped up, "You do understand that this entire city was built with magic."

"Yes," Ampyx said. "By a woman, and it's very impressive, in its way. I mean no disrespect to women. Someone has to do the magic, and they are very good at it, but it's not fit work for a real man."

"And what work is fit for a real man?" Phillip asked.

"Look around you, and see for yourself," Ampyx said. "Guarding things, tending to the flowers, selling clothing, serving food. Some of us cut hair."

"Manly work," Phillip said.

"Yes."

Now Martin had to make sure he was hearing things properly. "And what about building things, inventing, and running the government?"

Ampyx said, "The women seem to enjoy doing those things, and they're good at it, so we leave them to it while we tend to what's important."

Finally, they reached what Martin and Phillip instantly recognized as a hotel. Inside, the thin, handsome young man behind the counter told them they were expected. He checked with the manager, who was not a sorceress, but she was a woman, and got their room number. They boarded an elevator that had no noticeable workings, but which still transported them between floors. Ampyx took his leave of them, and they entered their room. They were so dumbstruck by what they found inside that they forgot for a moment to put their suitcases down.

The room was two stories tall, with a staircase and a loft forming the second floor. There was a bed and a bathroom and a kitchenette on the ground floor, and a second bed and bath on the second. The second-floor loft was slightly less deep than the first floor, giving the impression of a grand balcony. Both floors had an unobstructed view of the room's back wall, which was also the city's outer wall. Essentially, one entire wall of their room was a massive, curved window out into the ocean. The clarity of the ocean in this area and time meant that they could see light filtering down from the surface, itself an endless, undulating, silvery plane, extending off into infinity. Schools of fish swam past as they watched. Looking below them, they saw no bottom to the sea, just a hazy gradient shifting from light blue to dark blue, then to black.

"Wow," Martin said. "I did not expect that."

Phillip snapped himself out of his amazed stupor and said, "I didn't expect the guard's name to be Ampyx."

Martin rounded on Phillip and said, "Yeah, and I certainly didn't expect you to help him try to cozy up to Gwen."

"Oh, calm down," Phillip said. "Acting like you isn't going to help him get anywhere with Gwen. It doesn't seem to have helped you."

"Is that supposed to make me feel better?"

Phillip hoisted his suitcase onto the bed and started unpacking. "No, it's meant to be the truth. You need to get your mind off of Gwen. We have bigger problems."

Martin looked around them. "What problems? That this place is beautiful?"

"I know," Phillip said, "and I don't like it. Not one bit. I don't like this city, and I don't like that Brit the Elder. There's something wrong there."

"She certainly seemed to like you," Martin said.

"Like I said, wrong."

"Well, like Gwen said, she's the future version of herself, maybe . . ."

Phillip interrupted him. "No, Martin, she's not the future version of herself, she's one current version of herself, from the future, and I know what you were going to say. 'The two of you must have known each other in her past.' That is what you were going to say, right?"

"Yeah. So what? So the two of you met and hit it off in her past. That's nice."

"No," Phillip said, "it's not nice. It won't be nice, and if it is nice, that'll make it worse."

"You're not making any sense," Martin said.

"No, reality isn't making sense. I'm just describing it. By suggesting that we meet and get along, she essentially ordered me to meet her and get along. Now, when I do meet her, I'll be subconsciously primed to like her even if I don't, just because it's supposedly already happened."

Martin said, "Oh, okay. I get it. You're back on your 'free will' trip."

"I'm not back on it," Phillip said, "I'm still on it. I never wasn't on it. Make no mistake. For as long as you know me, for the rest of my life, I will insist that I have free will."

"But, if you're going to insist that you have free will no matter what," Martin said, "then that's not free will. Like I keep telling you, that's not a choice, that's a program. You might as well be an inanimate wooden sign that says 'I have free will' for all that proves."

Phillip looked at Martin for a moment, then, in an unnaturally calm voice, said, "It's true. You do always say that. And what do I always say in return?"

"That I should shut up."

"Indeed."

"And none of that does anything to prove that either of us has free will. In fact . . ."

"Martin?"

"Yes?"

"Shut up."

11.

Martin and Phillip arrived at the reception about a half hour before the official start time, and the place was already bustling. It was a large ballroom in one of the ridiculously impressive buildings at the center and bottom of the city. The ballroom was under a large dome that protruded from the roof of one of the buildings. Because all of the buildings in Atlantis were constructed from molecularly engineered crystalline materials, the walls were a milky, opaque white that faded to perfect transparency at their peaks. If one looked up, they were treated to a dizzying view of the city looming over them, and the dark blue Mediterranean twilight looming over the city. As the sky got darker, lights came on. Martin didn't know if the lights were fires, magical contrivances, or oil lamps, but they illuminated the buildings from the inside, like thousands of huge paper lanterns stacked all around him.

The outer perimeter of the room was populated at regular intervals by large white statues of various important women, depicted in the style of Greek goddesses, which worked well for Wonder Woman, but not so well for Margaret Thatcher.

Phillip and Martin spent several minutes soaking in the spectacle and scanning the room for a familiar face. There were many wizards, shamans, sorcerers, and other assorted magic folk, all of them men. There were many guards, servers, and hosts, also all male. They had given up seeing someone they already knew and were about to start actively mingling when they heard Gwen's voice. They turned, and saw her poking her head through a small door that was camouflaged by a particularly ornate molding. She motioned for them to come with her.

Philip and Martin went through the door and found themselves in a bustling room full of chefs, expediters, and important-looking behind-the-scenes management types, all female.

"Wow, you boys clean up nice," Gwen said.

The men thanked her. They had taken her advice and worn their tuxedos, only replacing the jackets with their wizard robes. Martin and Phillip returned the compliment, both feeling silly, because the fact that Gwen looked great that evening was self-evident. She wore a simple black, knee-length cocktail dress, which she had clearly designed herself. The dress had full-length sleeves that flared at the wrists to the standard, shell-specified width for a European wizard's robe. Where another dress might have been backless, or had a zipper, Gwen's featured a tapered hood, which pooled slightly around her shoulders and spilled down her back. She held a thin, graceful wooden wand in her hand.

Gwen looked at her own outfit and thanked the men. "I made it myself," she added. "I wanted to wear something that reflected where I had come from. Speaking of which, I have something for you." She reached into the hood of her dress, and pulled out two bowties, one sky blue, to match Phillip's robe, the other silver sequined, to match Martin's.

"I didn't have time to make cummerbunds, so you'll have to keep your robes pulled shut, but for a formal occasion like this, you probably should anyway."

The men quickly pulled off their black ties, replacing them with the new ties Gwen had made. When they were done, Gwen straightened Phillip's tie for him.

"Is mine straight?" Martin asked Gwen.

Gwen looked, and said, "Yeah, close enough. Well, guys, the Brits are going to get things started any minute. I've gotta run. See you out there."

Gwen scampered away, through the kitchen staff, around a corner and out of sight. Martin watched her go. Phillip watched Martin, smirking.

"Remember when you and Gwen first met?" Phillip asked.

"Yes, I remember. It was less than three months ago," Martin said.

"Remember how you would shamelessly try to get her attention?"

"Yeah."

"Then why don't you remember how well she responded to it?"

Phillip went back through the door, into the ballroom. Martin stood for a moment before following.

They spent a few minutes sampling hors d'oeuvres and making small talk with a wizard from China who had introduced himself to Phillip. His name was John, and he'd been educated at Cambridge. He knew of Phillip because he was still in contact with Eddie, who had originally time-traveled to ancient China before later moving to Medieval England and getting tangled in Jimmy's massive web of lies. The conversation seemed pleasant enough, but Martin couldn't concentrate on it, at first because of his preoccupation with Gwen, then because of the two men staring at him.

The men were standing by the wall at the far side of the room. They sneered and glared at Martin and Phillip as they spoke. They wore stiff black tuxedoes and white shirts with high, starched collars. They held top hats in their white-gloved hands. Martin smiled and waved. The men smiled back, and their white gloves added a hint of elegance when one of the men gave Martin the finger.

Martin considered walking over, asking them what their problem was, and offering to help them fix it, but then the lights dimmed and a hush fell over the room. A large, ornate door at the far end of the ballroom opened, and a long line of women emerged. There were around forty of them. They were all different from one another, yet they were all lovely. They represented every race and ethnicity, and their ages ranged from the late teens to a couple of women in their forties. Some were tiny, some were large, but all seemed healthy. Few were particularly thin, or noticeably not-thin.

Gwen would later explain that in their version of the shell program, which they called "the interface," they had found a way to set a sorceress's nutritional intake at an optimized constant, and as such, their weight tended to settle at a natural balance point.

The room was filled with men, and men cannot help themselves. As the Atlantean sorceresses filed into the room, the visitors from other times and places naturally noted how many of them they found attractive before losing count and succumbing to acute option paralysis.

Gwen was toward the back of the line, followed by a tall, slightly built young woman with black hair and a prominent nose. Behind her were two versions of Brit. The Brit at the end of the line stood straight and tall. She smiled brightly, and wore a spectacular evening gown and heels. She seemed completely at ease with herself and her surroundings. The Brit who was second to last slouched slightly, smiled weakly, and wore a blue cocktail dress and a matching pair of canvas high-tops.

The sorceresses lined up, dwarfed by several of the statues that adorned the hall. Together, they formed a dazzling backdrop for Brit the Elder, who walked forward from her place at the end of the line and addressed the room.

"Welcome, gentlemen, to Atlantis. We sorceresses summoned you here for this summit."

Martin and Gwen shared a smile at this.

"By now," Brit the Elder continued, "I'm sure most of you know why you've been invited. Each of your communities has suffered at the hands of one of our own kind who has abused his or her power. Some of you have been lucky, and your trouble has been slight. Others have had your entire community threatened."

Martin remembered Jimmy, his attempt to remodel all of England into a smaller, dumber version of Tolkien's Middle Earth, and kill all opposing wizards in the process. He wondered if any of these other people had a story that could top it.

Brit the Elder continued, "Starting tomorrow, in this very room, we will work together to prevent any such problems in the future. Tonight, our only task is to meet, talk, and get to know one another. We have, in this room, two representatives from each of our communities, which are spread out across the globe and throughout all of recorded human history. If you can't find an interesting conversation in this room, it's because you are boring."

A polite laugh followed, and faded to silence almost instantly when Brit the Elder waved it away. "Before I let you all start getting to know one another, I'd like to make a few introductions. Most of you know at least one of the women behind me, as all of them came here from one of your communities, and of course, it would be terribly time consuming to introduce them all by name now. Besides, who can remember that many names? Instead, I will take this opportunity to introduce my two fellow members of Atlantis' ruling council of three."

"I, of course, am Brit. I founded and built Atlantis." There was another round of applause, which she dismissed after a moment with another wave of her hand. Brit the Elder motioned vaguely to her right, causing a spotlight that seemed to emanate from empty space to wink into existence and focus on the tall, dark-haired woman who stood to Gwen's right. Brit the Elder said, "This is Ida. She is the duly elected president of Atlantis. She has served a little over three years of her four-year term." There was another round of polite applause as the president, Ida, stepped forward and bowed slightly to greet the crowd.

When the applause died down, Brit the Elder said, "And of course, this," pausing to make another, slightly more expansive hand gesture to her right, which caused the spotlight to shift to the second version of Brit, who started to smile and wave as Brit the Elder continued, "is a past version of me." Brit the Elder clasped her hands in front of her gown, causing the spotlight to cut off abruptly.

"So, that's it for the preliminaries," Brit the Elder said. "Please, have a good time tonight, and know that while we are here to do serious work, it'll be a lot more fun if we're all friends. Do make an effort to get to know each other, and be sure to fill out and wear your nametags." There was an awkward pause, followed by one of the women in the line stepping forward and whispering something to Brit the Elder, who turned and addressed Brit the Younger.

"Dear, didn't you see to the nametags?"

The other Brit replied, "You said you were going to do it."

"Yes, but I meant that you would. You are me, remember?"

"Well, how was I supposed to know that?"

"I knew it, so why wouldn't you?"

Brit the Younger gritted her teeth. "Well, I'm sorry I didn't read your mind."

Brit the Elder's smile grew strained. "It's your mind too, but that's okay," Brit the Elder said. "No need to beat yourself up."

Brit the Younger muttered, "Oh, I dunno."

Luckily, one of the first tricks every community of magic practitioners figured out was the ability to replicate small objects, so they very quickly had all of the adhesive nametags and felt-tip markers they could possibly need. Everybody wrote his or her name, time of origin, and time and place of residence. The next few hours were spent making small talk and eating small food.

Even with the nametags, Martin was overwhelmed by the sheer number of new names and faces to which he was subjected. Usually, in a situation like this, a few memorable people would emerge from the noise and get firmly cemented in his mind, but the problem was that everyone he met here was memorable. He met Chinese wizards, Hindu fakirs, Arabic sorcerers, and a Navajo medicine man. He met Aztecs, Incas, swamis, and gurus. One guy was wearing a loincloth and a hat made of a wolf's skull, which he insisted was his dress ensemble. Later, Martin worked up the nerve to ask him a few questions.

It turned out his name was Richard, and he was from Portland, Oregon, in the year 2003.

"Yeah, that's where you're from originally," Martin said. "But where do you live?"

Richard said, "Portland, in the year two thousand and three. I own a food truck."

And then there were the women. To Martin's chagrin, he still really only had eyes for Gwen, but those eyes were still able to see, and before them trotted a parade of smart, interesting women who knew about the file, knew how to use it, and understood Martin's situation better than anyone who didn't know those things possibly could. He tried to remember names, but it was impossible. Lisa, Rebecca, Mallory, Jennifer, Oui, Sabrina, Stacy, Allie, it all washed over him like he was a stone at the bottom of a river.

At one point, Martin found himself standing next to the woman who had been introduced as the president. She was deep in conversation with a particularly tall and muscular man in a net shirt and kilt who Martin suspected was her servant.

Martin had never met a president before. "Madam President," he said, in his smoothest voice, "it's a pleasure to meet you." He offered her his hand.

She tore her attention away from the muscular man, who was telling a story that was about, as near as Martin could tell, repeatedly punching someone in a novel manner. The president shook Martin's hand, and while reading his nametag said, "Welcome . . . Martin. Thanks for coming. Atlantis must be a big change from . . . Medieval England—oh!" The president brightened up immediately. "You're from Gwen's group. You're the ones who nearly got beaten to death by orcs."

"That's us," Martin said.

"What are orcs?" the tall man asked, now interested.

"They're these big creatures with bluish skin and horrible teeth," Martin explained.

"And you fought these creatures off?" the servant asked.

"Yes," Martin said. "Well, in a way. We created an army of demons to scare them off so we could make our escape."

"Ah," the servant said. "So, you had someone else fight for you while you fled. Impressive."

The president made an effort to hide her amusement. Her servant did not. After a moment of mirth at Martin's expense, the servant continued his story.

"So, it's a brawl, people fighting everywhere, but I want a challenge, so I decide I'm just going to hit guys on the top of the head, like this." The servant made an exaggerated swinging motion, wheeling his arms over his head and bringing his fists straight down in front of him. "I just wanted to see if I could knock guys out like that. Turns out I can."

The president seemed impressed. Martin moved on.

Elsewhere in the same room, Phillip was talking to a man whose nametag said "Goopta" about how their respective communities' versions of the shell program worked.

"The shell looks for certain details of our wizard robes and staffs to determine who should and shouldn't be allowed to cast spells," Phillip said with some difficulty, while eating a piece of fried shrimp.

"Clever," Goopta said. "We call ours *the gateway*. It identifies us based entirely on our fingernail length." Goopta held up his hands, showing Phillip his dark, curved nails, the shortest of which was at least five inches.

"Wow," Phillip said. "Impressive."

Phillip felt a tap on his shoulder. He turned to find himself facing both Brits. He smiled, but inside, he cringed. He considered Brit the Elder to be a walking refutation of everything he believed about free will, and as such, he found even looking at her unpleasant. This was made worse by the fact that on another level, he found looking at her quite enjoyable, which made him angry with himself.

It also didn't help that Brit the Elder again seemed delighted to see him. "Phillip," she said, positively beaming, "I have someone I'd very much like you to meet. Phillip, chairman of the wizards of Camelot, this is me, approximately 182 years ago, from my point of view."

Brit the Younger grudgingly made eye contact with Phillip while limply shaking his hand. Phillip said, "Good to meet you."

Brit the Elder's smile grew even brighter as she looked at Phillip and Brit the Younger, both of whom were radiating discomfort. "Yes, lovely. This brings back such memories. You two are going to get along famously, I just know it." She turned to Goopta, glancing deftly at his nametag. "Come, Mr. Goopta, let's give these two some time to get acquainted. I could introduce you to a servant who gives the best manicures."

Phillip and Brit the Younger watched as Brit the Elder led the bewildered man away into the crowd.

Phillip thought, *I could really begin to hate her.*

Brit the Younger said, "God, I hate her."

Martin worked his way through the crowd. He didn't want to admit to himself that he was looking for Gwen. He was so focused on scanning the distant corners of the room that he nearly ran directly into the two hostile men in top hats.

"Oh, hey," Martin said brightly. "I was hoping I'd bump into you two."

"Oh, were you?" said the top-hatted man on the left. He was stocky, tall, and angry-looking. His moustache was straight, waxed, and angry-looking. Martin suspected that this effect had to do with the angle at which the two halves of his moustache met under his nose. His nametag said "Gilbert," that he originally came from 2007, and that he currently resided in the year 1906.

"Yes," Martin said. "I noticed you eyeballing me and my friend earlier. I figured the civilized thing to do would be to come over, introduce myself—"

The second top-hatted man, taller, with a thoroughly oiled Van Dyke, a monocle, and a nametag that said "Sid," interrupted Martin, saying, "You're Martin Banks, also known as Martin the Magnificent, The Great Martini, and that git who hangs around with Phillip."

"Ah, we've met," Martin said. "I assume we meet in the future."

"Correct," said Gilbert.

"So," Martin said, determined to figure these two guys out, "you're magicians."

Sid said, "Yup."

"And you do magic."

"Yes, we are magicians. We do magic," Gilbert explained, slowly.

"Well, obviously," Martin said.

"You're the one who asked," Sid replied.

Martin said, "What I mean is, you two are like us. You can do real magic, as far as your audience is concerned."

"Yes," Sid agreed.

"But when you do magic, do you do magic? I mean, when you do your magic act, do you do fake magic tricks, or do you ... you know, do real magic?"

Sid pinched the bridge of his nose and shook his head.

Gilbert was aghast. "Are you suggesting that we would advertise ourselves as magicians, then get up on stage and do magic?"

"I was just asking," Martin said.

"We would never dream of such a thing," Gilbert sputtered.

"Why not?"

"It would be dishonest, that's why, or does that not matter to you?"

Martin said, "You're telling your audience that you're going to do magic. Why would it be dishonest to go ahead and do magic?"

Sid said, "Because, mate, the audience expects us to fool them. They don't think a magician can really do magic. They come to be entertained by a lie. We can't get up there and show them something that's not a lie. We'd have lured them in under false pretenses. Can't you understand that?"

Martin's mouth said that he could, but his face said that he couldn't.

"When people walk out of a magic show," Gilbert explained, "they say, 'I wonder how he did that?' They picture lots of mirrors and trap doors, strings that are too fine to see, that sort of thing. Imagine how unsatisfying it would be if they found out the answer was 'he did it with magic.' They'd be terribly disappointed."

"So you have magic powers, but your act is made up of normal magician's tricks."

"Yes. It's the only honest way to proceed."

"Do you invent the tricks yourselves?"

"No, we go to the future and copy them from modern magicians."

Martin said, "So you're thieves."

Sid smiled and said, "That's what you say later, when you find out what we're doing for the first time."

Martin said, "It's good to know I agree with me."

"Gwen had never..."

Gwen had never been much for parties. Her usual plan was to find the quietest part of the room, go there, and try not to make it any louder. She had spent most of the evening getting caught in, then escaping from, conversations with men she'd never met and knew nothing about. It would have been nice if she could have latched onto either Phillip or Martin and spent the evening teamed up with one of them, but Brit the Elder had specifically asked her to leave Phillip to his own devices for the evening, and Martin was acting strange, which, sadly for Martin, wasn't all that strange.

Along the wall, where Gwen could easily reach it, there was a door that led to a balcony. She might be able to get away from the crowd for a few minutes, but the whole point of this wing-ding was to meet new people. It would be bad form to spend the evening hiding from the very people she was supposed to meet. Instead of fleeing for the cool night air outside, Gwen stood there, alone in the crowd, looking and feeling tremendously uncomfortable.

Gwen didn't see the tall, muscular guard who slowly approached her, looking furtively around, checking to see if anybody was watching. She didn't see him close his eyes and take a deep breath, as if psyching himself up for something. She didn't hear him mutter encouragement to himself. The guard opened his eyes and took two steps to his left so as to enter Gwen's field of view.

Gwen saw the man approach, and at first she thought he was one of the typical city guards. Then she thought he was a guard who, for some reason, had a limp. Then she thought he was suffering a petit mal seizure. Finally, she realized he was just walking strangely. The men who were chosen to be the official guards were usually the very model of physical grace, but there was a jerky, forced uneasiness to this one's gait.

The guard walked up to her. His smile was slightly goofy, and his eyes almost glowed with manic energy.

The guard said, "Hi!"

Gwen said, "Hello."

There was a pause while the guard thought, then he said, "My name is Ampyx."

Gwen squinted at the guard. "Have we met before?"

Again, the guard calculated his response carefully before saying, "Yes, you chose me to escort the visitors from your homeland. Thank you for that."

"Oh," Gwen said. "How did you like my friends?"

"I did not like them," Ampyx said enthusiastically. "I found them distasteful."

"Oh," Gwen said.

"But I also realized that you made me endure them so that I, and only I, would see what it is you've been looking for in a servant all this time. No wonder you've rejected us. None of the men here were nearly weird, annoying, and uncoordinated enough to suit your particular tastes."

"And you are?" Gwen asked, equal parts amused and horrified.

"No," Ampyx said, his facade dropping for a moment to express his outrage at the very idea. Then, his forced goofy smile returned, and he said, "But if I concentrate, I can feign being *this way*, for you."

"That's . . . impressive." Gwen said.

Again, a moment's thought, then Ampyx said, "Thanks! Yeah, uh, of course, it would be a great shame to myself and my family if I acted like this in public. I'm only doing it now as a demonstration. Were you to choose me as your servant, I would put on this act for you only in our bed chamber."

"I see. And in public?"

"I would act like a proper man."

⊹═══⊹

At some point while nobody was looking, tables and chairs had appeared around the periphery of the room. They were probably brought in by servants, but nobody had noticed it happening, so it seemed like magic.

Brit the Younger sat alone at one of the tables, trying to be invisible. Phillip approached with two large, overtly decorative beverages.

Phillip said, "I asked for whiskey, but all they had were piña coladas and mimosas, so I got one of each. Take whichever you like, and I'll have the other," as he set the two drinks down.

She said, "Thank you. That's very sweet, but if you don't particularly want one over the other, and they didn't have what you asked for, why did you get them at all?"

Phillip thought about that as he settled into his seat. "Well, I didn't want to come back empty-handed. I considered just conjuring up two glasses of Scotch, but it felt like to do that when there was an open bar would be, I don't know, disrespectful to my host somehow."

Brit the Younger said, "You have a point. I suppose it would be." She lifted her hand in front of her face and swiped her finger through the air. The tip of her finger glowed and left a vapor trail as she moved it from her right to her left, then from the bottom of her field of vision to the top. To the uninitiated it probably seemed like she was casting some sort of spell, but to Phillip, or anyone else who had ever used a modern computer interface, she was clearly making selections from a computer menu that only she could see. Finally she jabbed her finger straight ahead twice, then traced a circle on the table top with her other hand. Two glasses of Scotch appeared. She handed one to Phillip, who took it happily. "Excellent," he said. "Next round's on me."

Phillip held the glass to his nose, and lightly breathed in through his mouth, letting the fumes from the drink gently ascend into his nostrils. "Ooh, that's nice," he said, before taking a sip.

Brit swallowed her first sip, savored it for a moment, then said, "I can make anything I want. I don't see any point in making crap."

Phillip leaned back, looking first at the glass in his hand, then at the woman who had given it to him. He thought for a long moment, then said, "I've been thinking I should give . . ." Phillip paused. Calling Brit the Elder *Brit* while talking to Brit the Younger seemed wrong, somehow, "my host a thank-you gift. Do you think a bottle of good Scotch would be nice?"

"Yeah," Brit said, "that'd be great. I'd love it if you gave her a bottle of Scotch. She hates the stuff."

Phillip looked at her for a long moment, then said, "I'm sorry. I have to admit, I'm having a lot of trouble getting my head around this."

Brit said, "Yeah, join the club." She took another sip.

Phillip looked into his drink again, but nothing he saw there made the situation easier to understand. He looked at the woman across from him again, enjoying her drink and seemingly not much else. Finally, he thought, *If we're going to talk, let's really talk.*

"There are those who say that because nothing we do seems to change the future, it means that whatever we do now has to be what we did in the past. Essentially, they say that all of our decisions were made for us, and that all we can do is play our parts. They tell us that any effort we make to change the course of history, or our own destiny, is futile, and ultimately results in us becoming the very thing we struggled to keep from becoming."

Brit peered at him over the rim of her glass, pulled the drink down from her mouth without actually taking a drink, then asked Phillip, "That's what they say. What do you say?"

Phillip smiled. "Usually, something loud and insulting. I am my own man. I make my own decisions. If the universe expects me to do anything different, it should prepare for a fight. I reject the idea that just because we can see the future that we're doomed to create it. I say free will and imagination are deeply linked, and if you don't believe you have one it just means that you lack the other." Phillip realized he was raising his voice. He took a deep breath.

"I get a little crazy when this topic comes up," Phillip said. "I'm sorry. I'll stop now."

"No," Brit said, "please, go on."

⊹⊱══⊰⊹

The evening was wearing on, and Martin felt overwhelmed. He'd met too many people, made too much small talk, and found too little of it interesting. He was under-stimulated. He decided to retreat to the nearest balcony and get some air.

When he got outside he was surprised to find Gwen there, leaning forward on the railing with her back to the door. Martin walked up, quietly enough to not demand her attention, but loudly enough to avoid startling her. He leaned back onto the railing so that he and Gwen were next to one another, but facing opposite directions. She looked up at the city, a thousand flickering light boxes, heaped all around them. He looked through the door into the party they were both avoiding.

Martin asked, "Who's that jerk who's been hanging around with you and Phillip this afternoon?"

Gwen chuckled. "Oh, he's just this guy I kind of almost had a thing with."

"He seems kinda needy."

Gwen turned to face Martin, but remained leaning casually on the rail. "He's not so bad. He's smart, and he's cute, and he makes me smile, which counts for a lot. He just needs to learn to cool it sometimes."

Martin turned to look at her. "Is that why you didn't want me to come here?"

Gwen said, "For example, this would be a good time to cool it," and turned her face back to the city, and away from Martin.

"Gwen, seriously, if you don't want me around, I'll keep my distance. I'm not interested in forcing my company on someone who doesn't want it. I can avoid you for the next two weeks, if that's what you want."

Gwen asked, "Do you want to avoid me, Martin?"

"I want us both to be happy. Being around you makes me happy, so that's one of us, but if it makes you unhappy, well, that's a problem."

"Having you around doesn't make me unhappy."

"Good." Martin said. "Not the highest praise I've ever heard. Wouldn't look good on a greeting card, but it's a start."

Gwen smiled. "Having you around makes me happy, Martin. Really. It's just, we only knew each other for a couple of weeks, then I had to move here. I thought I might invite you out to visit and see how things went, but then I got here, and . . . you've seen this place. Would you invite a guy here?"

"No, I would not," Martin admitted. "I have to admit, I was happy to hear that you haven't claimed a servant yet. I had some ideas about what a female-led society would be like. None of them featured 'scantily clad beefcake and sexual service provider' as a viable career path."

Gwen said, "Well, the sex-with-servants thing doesn't happen as often as the men would have you believe."

"That's good to hear."

"I mean, it does happen," Gwen said, "often, just not quite as often as they say. It's pretty bad, I agree, but don't judge the girls too harshly. If you think about it, it's the same arrangement as a wealthy old man and his trophy wife, only our way is more emotionally honest. Besides, a lot of the girls aren't romantically involved with their servants. They just picked a man they enjoy hanging around with.

"By the way," Gwen said, "One of the guards is acting weird. I think he's trying to imitate you."

"Oh, yeah, that would be Ampyx. How's his impression?"

"Pretty insulting."

Martin laughed. "Good. If we play this right, we could have him wearing silver sequins by the end of the week."

⊹═•═⊹

Inside the hall, the party was beginning to wind down. The conversation was getting quiet, and the crowd was getting sparse. Phillip had spent the better part of an hour telling Brit the Younger all of his theories that explained their apparent lack of impact on the future, while still allowing for free will. He had many possible explanations, but in the end, she shook her head and said that none of them really applied to her.

"See," she explained, "I decided to come back here and see if there was an Atlantis, and about a second before I left I thought, *if there isn't one, I could just go back in time a little further and build Atlantis myself.*"

"And what happened?" Phillip asked.

"Exactly that, I guess. I got here and found the city pretty much as you see it, only there was this huge welcoming ceremony all set up waiting for me. There was music and cheering, and some woman who looks exactly like me walks up and hugs me, and says that she's me, and that there was no Atlantis before

I came along, so I went back in time to build the city so it'd be here when I got here."

Phillip's face twisted in concentration. "That just makes no sense."

"Yeah," Brit said. "I noticed."

"But, if she's you, and she got here and found no Atlantis, then you'd have found no Atlantis when you got here."

Brit said, "Yes, but she didn't get here and find no Atlantis. She found Atlantis as you see it now, and another woman who looked just like her and claimed to be her, and to have built Atlantis. Then, fifty years later, she went back in time, built Atlantis, and waited for me to show up."

Phillip said, "So her memories do match your memories."

"No," Brit said. "Her memories match my present. Everything I do, she's done. Everything I think, she's thought. If I do something right, she gets the credit. If I do something wrong, she's the first to admit it, usually before or while I'm doing it. That's why none of your theories work in my case. You're explaining why we have no effect on the future. The future isn't my problem. She isn't in the future. She's here now, and as long as she's here, nothing I do affects the present."

Phillip looked at her, sitting there, staring miserably at the empty glasses in front of her. She made it sound so futile. *I'm sure that's just the booze talking*, he thought, then he thought, *No, it's her talking, but it's the booze thinking.*

He wasn't far wrong. The alcohol in her system was affecting her thinking. Brit looked at Phillip and thought, *He's cute, in a rumpled, worn in kind of way. Older me wanted me to get to know him. I don't know why, but I tend to think I wouldn't like it if I did.*

They made eye contact. They smiled. Then, there was a hollow, popping noise, like someone opening a bottle of champagne. Phillip looked alarmed, then in one movement stood up and swung his staff very fast overhand toward Brit's head. Brit instinctively cringed, shielding her head with both arms. Phillip shouted something she didn't quite catch, then her world was nothing but noise and confusion.

+≻═══≺+

Gwen and Martin heard the crash from the balcony. They ran into the hall and found chaos. The lights came up. Martin could see that one of the large goddess statues that stood around the circumference of the room had fallen. There was a base, a pair of sculpted feet, and a nasty, ragged break at the thinnest part of the goddess' ankles. In front of that there was a field of dust, shards of broken statue, crushed tables and chairs, and in the middle of it all stood Phillip, his staff held far out in front of himself like an axe stopped mid-swing. The debris on the floor was piled thick everywhere except for a perfect circle radiating outward from the tip of Phillip's staff. Inside the circle, free from any damage, were Phillip, the table he'd been sitting at, the chair that had been opposite him, and in the chair, directly under the tip of the staff, and as such, at the center of the protected circle, Brit the Younger, looking confused.

Phillip said, "*Forigi šildo*," and for an instant the outline of a dome of energy could be seen covering Phillip and Brit, before it disappeared. Phillip practically ran around the table and took Brit by the hand, helping her up.

"Are you all right?" He asked.

"Yes," she said. "I think so."

Martin and Gwen slid to a stop after running across the hall. "Are you two okay?" Martin asked.

"Yes. We're both fine," Phillip said. "Was anybody hurt?"

By this time, everyone who was still in attendance was standing around looking at the damage. Nobody seemed injured. It seemed that Phillip and Brit the Younger were the only people who had been in the statue's landing zone.

Gwen looked at the damaged statue's base and asked, "What happened?"

From across the room, a woman's voice called out, "I'll tell you exactly what happened." Everyone turned to see Brit the Elder walking serenely through the crowd. She reached the debris field, and said, "Just as I remembered it, Phillip was listening to me, complaining about the trivial things that seemed like problems to me at that age."

Brit the Elder walked to the table and looked at the three empty whiskey glasses in front of Brit the Younger's chair and shook her head. Brit the Younger's face turned bright red.

Brit the Elder said, "The hard stuff always did make me mopey. Anyway, dear Phillip saw the statue break and start to fall, and did some very quick thinking in his attempt to save me from being hurt." She bent at the knees, reached down, and picked up a broken piece of statue about a foot long. She stood up again and examined the chunk of debris.

Phillip said, "It really wasn't much. It's just a simple shield spell."

"It was very sweet of you," Brit the Elder said, "and also unnecessary. Much like you, we've manipulated the file to make ourselves impervious to damage." To emphasize the point, Brit the Elder smashed the piece of debris she was holding over Brit the Younger's head. Brit the Younger flinched and yelped, but it was out of surprise, not pain.

Brit the Younger said, "You didn't know that, though, and it's the thought that counts."

Brit the Elder said, "I agree." She turned to Brit the Younger and said, "And I think it's about time for you to go get some sleep."

12.

Jimmy stood in the corner of the room with one leg and both arms drawn up in front of him defensively. "Get that thing away from me!" he shouted.

Agents Miller and Murphy were both up on their feet, gesticulating wildly.

"What's wrong with you?" Agent Murphy cried.

Agent Miller yelled, "You idiot, get out of here before I smack you!"

They were in the conference room that Agent Miller and Agent Murphy had claimed as their command center at Seattle Police Headquarters, and they were all addressing an officer who was standing in the door, holding a laptop computer.

"What?" Officer Kyle asked. "You said you needed a computer."

"I said *we'd* need a computer. I didn't say I wanted you to bring it to me," Jimmy said, still forcing himself into the corner.

"Get that thing outta here!" Miller bellowed.

"What?" Officer Kyle said, still not understanding. "This is a good computer."

"Exactly," Jimmy said. "And if you get it too close to me I'll destroy the hard drive."

Officer Kyle asked Jimmy, "Are you threatening to damage Seattle PD property, old man?"

"He's not," Miller said, "but I promise to damage a Seattle police officer if you don't get outta here!"

Jimmy took on the most soothing tone he could muster while still actively cringing. "I'm not threatening to do anything, son. I just have a strong magnetic field, and I break any computer that gets too close to me for too long."

Kyle said, "Oh, that's nonsense. This computer works fine. I turned it on to make sure. Look, I'll show you." He opened the computer and looked at the screen. Nothing happened. After a second, he hit the space bar a couple of times. Still, nothing happened. He pressed the power button. When nothing continued to happen he said, "I'll be damned. It was just working a minute ago."

Officer Kyle timidly left the room. Agent Miller angrily watched him go. Agent Murphy and Jimmy reclaimed the seats they had hastily vacated when the officer had entered.

"Let me get this straight," Agent Murphy said. "You can't prove that what you're telling us is true without access to a computer, but if we get a computer anywhere near you, it stops working. You didn't think this out very well, did you, Jimmy?"

"I have a plan, Agent Murphy. I promise you I do, and the first step of the plan is to keep whatever computer we end up using far away from me."

"Great," Miller said. "Step one: You don't use a computer. Done. What's next?"

Jimmy said, "I have designed a system that will let me direct one of you while you use a computer. There's a list of items we'll need in one of the notebooks you confiscated. I assume they are locked in the evidence vault. Sadly, it's a rather bulky apparatus, so we'll need a lot more room than we have, even in this conference room. Once we have that, I will direct the two of you to the file that will prove that I've been telling you the truth."

Miller shook his head, "So, after we move you to a larger space and buy you a bunch of stuff, then and only then, you'll prove that the cock-and-bull story you've been feeding us is true. I don't like it. Not one bit."

"I assure you that none of the items on the list are expensive or dangerous," Jimmy explained.

Agent Miller walked to Jimmy's end of the table. He towered imposingly over the older, seated man. "Look," he said, "you know a bunch of things that nobody outside of our investigation is supposed to know, but that doesn't mean that Murph and I have to buy everything you say. You're asking us to believe that everything in the world, including us, is fake. Well, I wanna see some proof before I even bother to look at your list, let alone buy you any of the stuff on it."

Jimmy said, "First of all, I'm not saying that anything is fake. I assure you, Agent Miller, you and your partner are real. You're just real parts of a computer program, that's all."

Agent Murphy said, "There, Miller. Doesn't that make you feel better?"

Agent Miller didn't look like he felt any better. Jimmy continued. "As for proof, how much proof do you need? You've seen what my presence does to any electronics. I've noticed neither of you brings your cell phone anywhere near me anymore. You saw Martin Banks disappear right before your eyes when you had him in custody. How do you explain that? Come to think of it, how did you explain that? You can't have written 'the kid vanished' on your official report. If you could, I doubt you'd be desperate enough to still be dealing with me, would you?"

The door to the conference room swung open. Officer Kyle bounded in, triumphantly. "Good news, I found you another laptop!" He held the computer up like a prize as he started across the room to give it to Jimmy.

In an instant, Jimmy was back on his feet, pressing himself into the corner, trying to put as much space between himself and the computer as he could. "Don't bring it to me!" Jimmy cried. "I don't want it! Just keep it out there and let Agent Murphy look at it."

Officer Kyle stopped, confused. "You told me to get you a computer. I got you one. I'm sorry the last one didn't work, but this one does, I promise. Look." Officer Kyle opened the laptop, and instantly looked stricken. "I promise, it was just working. I'll reboot it."

Agent Murphy stood and guided the young officer to the door by the shoulder, saying, "You do that, and if this computer doesn't work, you find us another, and when you do, just leave it outside the door and come get us." Officer Kyle mumbled noncommittally as he left the room. Agent Murphy closed the door behind him, and the room returned to some sort of normalcy.

Agent Murphy said, "To answer your question about how we explained the Banks kid's disappearance, we just wrote that he escaped custody via unknown means. We don't really have to come up with an explanation until we catch and prosecute him."

Jimmy said, "Yeah, I'm sure your supervisors will find that real satisfying. You can't explain what Martin did, how it was illegal, or how he got away from you. "

"And you can?" Agent Murphy asked.

"And I will," Jimmy answered, "but for what it's worth, I don't believe you're going to end up prosecuting Martin, or anybody else. I don't think any of us have broken any laws."

"He deposited tens of thousands of dollars into his personal bank account without doing anything to earn it, and without being given it by anyone. How can he possibly do that in any way that's legal?"

"The way he did it is legal, as I've told you before, because nobody's made it illegal yet. He didn't steal it from anybody. Nobody was deprived by his actions. He didn't take the money from anyone. He created it himself."

Agent Miller smirked. "Sounds like counterfeiting to me."

The door blasted open again, and Officer Kyle bolted in, holding the laptop. It was open, and the screen was showing a desktop cluttered with icons. He held it facing away from himself, so as to show the men in the room. "Look, see, I told you it worked."

Jimmy didn't bother to get up this time. He just looked at Officer Kyle, pointed at the computer, and made a twirling motion with his index finger. The officer turned the computer around, looked at the screen, and yelled, "Damn!"

13.

The first full day of the summit got off to a good start. The same hall that hosted the reception had been converted overnight to house the summit. This struck Martin as odd, but Gwen would later point out that Brit had worked at a large resort hotel and had designed this room as a sort of convention center.

Tables large enough for two adults to sit comfortably were arranged in neat rows. Each table had a place card naming two representatives and the time-traveler communities from which they came. Also, the statue of a toga-clad Harriet Tubman that had caused all of the commotion the night before had already been replaced. Phillip asked one of the guards why the statue had fallen, and was told, "Brit the Elder seems to know what's going on," which Phillip agreed was true, but pointed out, was not an answer.

All of the delegates found their way to their assigned seats. The tables were arranged alphabetically/chronologically, so if there were two teams from a given place, whichever team was from an earlier point in history came first. This meant that the table next to Martin and Phillip's was assigned to Gilbert and Sid, the two dandies from nineteenth-century London who had been so hostile the night before.

The Atlantis delegation was last to arrive. Both of the Brits; Ida, the president; and several other women, Gwen among them, all arrived together. Brit the Younger and Ida took their places as delegates. At the head of the room, a dais held a podium where Brit the Elder took her assigned place as the speaker. The rest of the team from Atlantis took seats in the observers' areas set along both sides of the hall.

The proceedings began with a brief overview of the schedule and a list of the topics to be discussed during the summit. It was all perfectly straightforward. The first item of business was the adoption of a formal name for the time-traveling, magic-using peoples being governed by the summit. Brit the Elder mentioned offhand that she favored the term *Time Travelers*, and that until the formal vote, that was the term she would use—not that it mattered, since she also mentioned that she remembered that this was the term the group would vote to use anyway. Other than that, most of the agenda dealt with prevention of abuse by time travelers of the indigenous peoples and other time travelers.

The only part that confused those listening was when Brit the Elder announced, "Sessions will begin promptly at nine o'clock each morning, and will run until five each evening, except for next Sunday, which we will have off, and today's session, which will end abruptly this afternoon after something unexpected happens."

The morning session proceeded past Martin like a slow-motion blur. It was a room full of earnest people having serious conversations about topics of great importance and very little interest.

At one point Phillip caught Martin on the verge of nodding off. Phillip prodded Martin with his elbow. Martin sat up and tried to look interested, but he grumbled while he did it.

"What's wrong with you?" Phillip asked.

"Ugh, sorry. Watching parliamentary procedure always makes me bored and angry. I think it has to do with the *Star Wars* prequels."

Phillip furrowed his brow. "Wait a minute. They made prequels to *Star Wars*?"

Martin winced. He remembered that he, Tyler, Gary, and Jeff had all sworn never to tell Phillip about the *Star Wars* prequels. "There are some things about the future that he's better off not knowing," Jeff had argued.

Like all events designed to help people meet and better understand each other, most of the real progress took place during breaks. The highlight of the day was during the lunch break, when someone pointed out that Phillip, a pure-bred Englishman, was eating a burrito while one of the Aztec delegates had magicked up an order of authentic London fish and chips.

After lunch there was another monotonous barrage of absolutely vital discussions. Martin managed to stay awake, but just barely. During the afternoon break he made his way out to the corridor. He produced a large cup of coffee from his hat and was just about to take a sip when he saw Gwen. He made a bee-line for her, mostly because he loved spending time with her, but also because he knew that she was from a time near his and would understand his *Star Wars* prequel reference, which had sailed right over Phillip's head.

"Hey, Gwen. How's it going?" he asked.

"Good, Martin," she replied. "How are you today?"

"Fine. I'm fine. I gotta say though, this meeting, with all of these motions being raised and seconded, I feel like I'm in one of the *Star Wars* prequels."

"I know!" Gwen enthused. She proceeded to go on at length about how much she loved the *Star Wars* prequels, and how particularly the parts set in the Galactic Senate gave all of the events much more of a sense of gravitas.

Martin drank his coffee as quickly as he could and tried to pretend the conversation wasn't happening.

Finally, mercifully, a bell rang, announcing that the break would end in one minute. As Martin returned to his seat, he noticed that Phillip had apparently spent the break sitting in the president's empty seat, talking to Brit the Younger. Phillip walked back to his own seat, smiling. Brit remained at hers, smiling as well. Phillip was nearly to the table when the hall resounded with a dull pop. Phillip looked stricken. Martin saw Phillip make an involuntary grasping motion with his right hand, his usual staff hand. Martin also saw that Phillip's staff was still on the table next to where Martin sat.

Phillip spun around just in time to see Brit the Younger, still in her seat, looking upward at another of the toga-draped goddess statues, which, like the one the night before, was falling directly on top of her.

Martin yelled, "Phillip!" He threw Phillip's staff at him, but it was far too late. The statue hit the floor with astonishing force. A deafening crash reverberated throughout the hall. People dove for cover as chunks of statue flew through the air.

Once the noise subsided, the delegates turned to look at the damage. They saw the ruined base of the statue and a great deal of rubble. Phillip was still standing exactly where he had been when the statue first started to fall, and in the center of all the rubble, there was Brit the Younger, sitting on the floor amongst the splintered kindling that used to be her chair and table. She looked at the ruins around her, and at the empty space where the statue used to stand, and she said, "Seriously?"

The head of the statue rolled noisily to a stop. Martin looked at it, grimaced, and said, "Ugh, is that Ayn Rand?"

The sound of a gavel echoed through the hall. All eyes turned to the podium and Brit the Elder, who was rapping her gavel for order.

"As I stated this morning, something unexpected has occurred. I move that we adjourn for the day. Seconded?"

Brit the Younger seconded the motion.

14.

After the delegates had mostly cleared out, Gwen came back to the main hall. She wanted a look at the statue's base. Truth be told, she had wanted a good look at the base of the first statue that had fallen the night before and had gotten up early to sneak in to the hall to snoop around a bit, but the statue had been repaired during the night.

In the convention center she saw servants cleaning up rubble and Martin, leaning on his staff, looking at the podium, deep in thought.

Martin turned as Gwen approached. He nodded, smiled, then turned his attention back to the podium. It was pristine and undamaged from the floor up to the point where the ankles and gown tapered to their narrowest points. There, the material was sheared smoothly at an angle, as if cut with a saw then sanded to remove any imperfections.

"How often do those stupid statues break at the ankles and fall over?" Martin asked.

"Never," Gwen answered. "The entire time I've been here it's never happened, and none of the other sorceresses can remember it ever happening either."

"Well," Martin said, "I'd say that's suspicious, but I think you're way ahead of me on that."

"Yeah," Gwen said. "It's not very subtle, is it? I mean, at least last night the statue was posed with its legs together, so the statue only had to break at one point. This one had its legs apart, so the statue had to break cleanly in two places at the same time."

"I know," Martin said, "and even if the statues did fall over twice in two days, the fact that they both fell on the same person is just a dead giveaway. How is Brit, by the way?"

Gwen said, "Shaken up. It didn't hurt her at all physically, but that kind of thing still takes its toll on your nerves."

"Yeah, I know. Gwen, how well do you know Brit?"

"She's my best friend."

Martin thought a second, then asked, "Which one?"

Gwen answered, "Both of them. They're the same person. You get that, don't you, Martin? I mean, I thought I'd explained that."

Martin held up a hand in surrender. "Yeah, yeah, I know. It's just weird. I know they're the same person, and they look exactly alike, but they act so differently. And besides, they don't seem to get along that well."

"Yeah," Gwen sighed, "there's some tension there. They're just very different people."

Martin let this pass. He got up close to the pedestal, examining one of the broken ankles in more detail. "What is this made of? Not more diamond, is it?"

"No. Diamond is good for some things, but not as good for others. Besides, it'd be pretty boring if everything were made of diamond."

I suppose this is what passes for boredom when you're a time-traveling wizard, Martin thought.

Gwen continued, "Diamond is used for the large-scale structural pieces, but most smaller-scale construction and decorative work is actually a toughened glass."

"Really?" Martin asked. "Like Pyrex?"

Gwen nodded.

"Well, what do you know? Phillip was right."

Gwen looked around the room. "Hey, where is Phillip?"

"Dunno," Martin said, still looking at the shorn ankles of the statue. "He hung around for a few minutes after the crash, then said he had something he needed to do and took off."

Brit the Younger was curled up in her favorite chair looking miserable when the doorbell rang.

The second time it rang, she wondered why her servant hadn't answered it.

The third time it rang, she remembered that her servant had gone out to get her dinner.

The fourth time it rang, she realized that it wasn't reasonable to expect whoever was ringing to wait for her servant to return and answer the door.

The fifth time it rang, she realized that whoever it was doing the ringing was probably tenacious enough to wait for her servant, but she'd have to listen to this ringing the whole time. She hoisted herself up from her chair and walked to the door, slowly enough that ring number six occurred while she was in transit. She looked through the peephole and was delighted by who she saw.

Phillip said, "Brit, we need to talk. I think someone's trying to kill you."

"Of course they are. Come in."

Phillip entered Brit's home and immediately had to stop to take it in. He had been in Atlantis less than a day, and while he was accustomed to everything being beautiful, Brit's living room still came as a shock. Like his and Martin's quarters, one entire wall was the curved, transparent outer wall of the city providing a panoramic view of the ocean. Brit's home was much lower in the dish than Phillip's, so the wall was raked at a much steeper angle, and the ocean outside was a much darker blue. Brit's floor was a single slab of pristine white perfection with a subtle etched grid pattern to help give a sense of scale. Her furniture was sleek and modern, yet comfortable looking. It was the kind of room Phillip had seen pictures of in magazines and thought, *Nice, but no real human being could possibly live like that.* It was the kind of room he had tried to create in his attic back home, but hadn't had the taste to pull off.

Phillip said, "Nice place."

Brit said, "Eh," then curled back up in her favorite chair, which looked to Phillip like a matched set of comfy cushions supported by just enough milky glass to maintain structural integrity.

Phillip sat in the identical chair opposite her, leaned in for emphasis, and said, "Brit, I'm serious. I think someone's trying to kill you."

Brit replied, "Yeah. I know."

Phillip still wasn't sure his words were getting through to her. "I don't believe the statue was an accident."

"I know it wasn't, Phillip. Obviously. It wasn't even the first attempt."

Phillip nodded. "Yes, the statue last night." Phillip leaned back in his chair and took a moment to try to figure out what was going on. After a moment, he came to the conclusion that what was going on was that he didn't know what was going on, and that anything beyond that was uncertain.

"You don't seem very worried," he said.

"I'm not."

"Someone's trying to kill you, Brit."

"Yes, but they're failing at it, and they're going to keep failing."

"How can you be sure?" Phillip asked.

"Because Brit the Elder is here. She makes me miserable, but one bright side to her existence is that as long as she's around, I know I'll live long enough to be her someday."

Phillip considered this. "I guess that is a pretty good bright side."

"Yeah," Brit agreed. "It'd be even brighter if I liked her, or wanted to be her, but there it is. Even when your future is good, it's not necessarily the one you want. Anyway, as long as I know that whoever is trying to kill me will never succeed, then their constant attempts are just an inconvenience."

"That's one heck of an inconvenience," Phillip said.

"Eh, I dunno," Brit said. "It's always over fast, and they come to wherever I am. Really, as attempted murderers go, I think I'm getting pretty good service."

Phillip was about to comment on this when the door opened. Brit's servant walked in, carrying a steaming crock of some fantastic-smelling liquid. Unlike all of the other servants Phillip had seen, Brit's servant was average height, and while thin and in good condition, he was not so muscular as to be bulky. He was dressed in the same ridiculous mesh top and kilt as all servants, but he somehow wore it with more dignity than the others. As he entered, the servant said, "I'm back, and I got that soup you like. The shop was about to close, so I had to beg a bit, but I told them it was for you and there was no problem." The servant saw Phillip. "Oh, I didn't know you were going to have company for dinner. I'm glad I got extra soup."

Brit stood and said, "Ah, I should introduce you. This is my servant, Nikolas."

The servant bowed slightly, still smiling, and said, "Please call me Nik. You must be Phillip."

Phillip stood up and returned the bow. "It's good to meet you, Nik."

Nik looked Phillip in the eye, kept his smile turned up to maximum, and said "It's good to meet you, Phillip. I've heard a lot about you."

Phillip said, "I hope you heard good things."

Nik held the smile and the eye contact just long enough to make Phillip uncomfortable, then said, "I know you do." Nik and Brit shared a small laugh, which Phillip joined in an attempt to be pleasant.

Nik winked at Phillip so quickly that he wasn't really sure he'd seen it, then Nik started walking toward the door at the side of the room. "You two get comfortable," he said, "I'll pour this soup into a couple of bowls for you and be right back."

"Actually," Brit said, stopping Nik in his tracks, "I've changed my mind. If you could please keep the soup warm for a little while, I think I need to get out of the house and clear my head a bit."

Nik bowed again, said that this would not be a problem, and gave Phillip another smile. Phillip wasn't sure if Nik was smiling at him, or smiling with him.

Phillip said, "I suppose I should be getting back."

Brit said, "You could do that, or you could come with me. I wouldn't mind the company."

Phillip remembered the look Nik had given him and thought, *Okay, I guess he was smiling with me.*

Phillip had expected "getting out of the house" to entail walking out the door, but instead, Brit reached down to the floor next to her chair and brought up what appeared to be a small rectangular sheet of glass. She held it with both hands and the flat surface of the glass came alive with printed shapes and symbols. Phillip leaned in closer to get a better look. Brit tilted the sheet of glass so that Phillip could see it better. The buttons were all clearly marked. Phillip only had time to glance, but he could see that there were controls for the heat and lighting in the various rooms in Brit's home. Various other buttons did other things that Phillip was sure he could figure out if he had the time.

He had seen some gadgets from after his time, but nothing like this. There was literally no place for any electronics that he could see. It looked for all the world like a simple sheet of glass, except that animated symbols and text were flowing smoothly over its surface. "What year are you from?" Phillip asked, amazed.

"I'm from 1996," Brit answered, more than a little puzzled by tone of the question. She looked at Phillip, followed his gaze to the tablet in her hands, then laughed. "This isn't from the future. It's just a sheet of glass with the edges sanded. Our version of what you call the shell can project touch controls onto any surface, or into thin air. Usually the person using the controls is the only one who can see them, but I made this up so there'd be visible controls for Nik to use."

Brit pressed a button in the corner of the tablet, then pointed out the curved, wall-sized window into the ocean beyond. As if called into being by the act of her pointing, a glowing sphere appeared, dimly at first, then quite brightly before dimming again to be barely visible.

Brit lowered the sheet of glass, and extended a hand for Phillip to take. "Our ride is here," she said. Phillip reached for his staff, which he'd placed on the ground next to his chair. "You won't need that," Brit said. "Besides, it won't fit."

Phillip left his staff on the floor and took Brit's hand. She tapped the corner of her control panel with her thumb, and the next instant she and Phillip were looking in at the living room from outside the window.

Phillip looked around the interior of the sphere. At first it seemed to Phillip that he was simply floating at a fixed point under the sea, but he immediately realized that he was standing upright, perfectly dry, and breathing normally. They were inside the sphere that he had seen Brit conjure up just a moment before. It was perfectly transparent with a flat, clear floor and two clear chairs. She sat in one. He took the other. She pulled her legs up underneath her with her control panel on her lap. Phillip couldn't easily read it from where he was, but he could tell that she was scrolling through various options.

Phillip asked, "Do you just conjure one of these things up whenever you want?"

"I could do it that way. Really it'd be just as easy, but I keep this one around all the time. It just hovers outside my window until I need it. I like knowing that I have a vehicle, and that it's there when I need it."

Phillip considered telling her about his Fiero, but decided against it. *Not yet, at least.*

Brit turned to Phillip and said, "We have all of the oceans to choose from. That's two thirds of the Earth's surface. Anything you want to see?"

"Surprise me."

Brit looked at him thoughtfully for a moment, then scrolled through her list of options and selected one. Instantly, the world got much brighter. The deep blue that had surrounded them was replaced with a lighter shade that gave way to an undulating plain of silver above them, and an explosion of colors beneath.

Phillip had watched enough nature programs to know that he was looking at a reef. Bizarre organic shapes in colors Phillip had never imagined spread out beneath them, fading into the murky blue distance. As Brit piloted their craft between the silver boundary above and the neon obstacles below, a school of fish, swimming in tight formation, played chicken with their craft. The fish swam straight ahead, directly into Brit and Phillip's path, then parted silently, enveloping them for a moment before reforming behind them, as if nothing had been in their way to begin with. A strange shadow fell over Phillip. He looked up and saw that a manta ray was swimming overhead, briefly eclipsing the sun.

Phillip said, "I just can't get over it, Brit."

Brit said, "Yeah?"

"Yeah, this submarine, it's amazing. There are no seams, no moving parts. It's so elegant. And, the fact that I know exactly how it works just makes it more impressive. I mean, it's all the same basic things we've all been doing all along, replicating, materializing, levitating, and moving through time and space, but it just never occurred to us to put it all together like this."

"I'm glad you approve."

"I, uh," Phillip stammered, "I once made a car indestructible, and gave it unlimited fuel. I thought that was pretty clever. I see now that was so needlessly complex. I could have just made it move forward without the engine. It would have been silent, which would be a bit weird, but I'd have thought of some way around that."

"That's an easy fix," Brit said. "It's not hard to alter something's sound and light signatures. This bubble is completely silent and invisible."

"Seriously?"

"Oh yeah. We could hover over Disneyland watching kids ride the teacups for an hour and nobody would see us."

"That would be great for hopping around time checking out historic events," Phillip said.

"Yeah," Brit agreed, "I considered that, but then I realized that most of history is made up of things I'm actually pretty happy that I wasn't there to see."

"Good point. I once went to the Kennedy assassination. I wanted to see who that shadowy figure on the grassy knoll was."

Brit's eyes widened. "You actually went to the grassy knoll?"

Phillip nodded.

"Who was there?" Brit asked.

Phillip gritted his teeth. "Nobody, until I got there. Luckily, not many people saw me. I managed to stay in the shadows."

They continued their tour of the reef in silence for a moment, then Phillip continued. "Anyway, like I was saying, it just never occurred to me to assemble these kinds of complex constructions, like this sub, or the elevator platforms, or frankly, Atlantis itself. I'm just blown away by it all, and Gwen tells me it was all your idea."

"Yup," Brit said. "My idea."

Phillip said, "Well done."

Without turning to face him, Brit said, "I'll pass your compliment along to Brit the Elder."

Phillip cursed himself. Here he was trying to pay her a compliment, and he had said the exact wrong thing. He started to apologize, but Brit cut him off.

"No, Phillip. I'm sorry. You were just being nice, and I handled that gracelessly. I did come up with the ideas. Laying down materials an atom at a time, using the objects made that way to build complex structures and devices, building Atlantis if it didn't already exist, heck, going to Atlantis in the first place, they were all my ideas. The whole reason I wanted to go to Atlantis was that I had all these things I wanted to try, and it's hard to do that when you're living with your parents in Racine, Wisconsin."

"What did you do for a living in Racine?" Phillip asked.

"I was a tour guide at the Johnson Wax building. That Frank Lloyd Wright really knew how to design a building, except for the roofs. They always leak. Seems like a funny thing for the world's greatest architect to be bad at, roofs. It's kinda the primary reason to make a building in the first place, wouldn't you say? To keep the rain out?"

Phillip agreed.

"Anyway," Brit continued, "I had all these crazy ideas I couldn't wait to try, and no place to try them, so I go back in time to Atlantis, and when I get there, Brit the Elder is waiting for me with the good news that she already tried my ideas, and they all worked. She'd used them to build the city, just like I wanted to, and all of the people who live there are very grateful, to her."

"I can see why you'd resent that. Just trying to be positive, though, the whole reason she's here is that you go back in time at some point in the future and become her, so you will get to build the city, and you do get to try all of your ideas, and eventually, you will get the credit."

Brit turned, looked at Phillip, and said, "Please, Phillip, don't be so positive. It's not becoming for people like us," which got a small laugh out of Phillip. She continued, "And, when I do go back and build, I won't really be designing and building, I'll be copying what was here when I got here. I'll be copying from her."

"But if she's you . . ."

"Then who am I copying? Who designed Atlantis in the first place? I don't know, but I do know that it wasn't me, and really, that's all I care about right now."

Phillip started to say something, but Brit put a finger across his lips to silence him. She smiled, but with firmness in her tone, she said, "And, frankly, I'm talking about someone I can't stand. If the best thing you can think of to cheer me up is to tell me that I'll be just like her someday, I'd suggest that you probably shouldn't bother."

Phillip smiled and nodded. Brit took her finger away.

They rode in silence as strange, colorful sea creatures swam past. Brit piloted the bubble over a tall stand of coral, and before them, a vista of brightly colored shapes stretched on as far as they could see.

Brit said, "So, Phillip. You haven't had much to say about the reef. What do you think?"

"It's very nice," Phillip said. He looked around a bit then added, "Pretty."

Brit looked at him, a smile slowly growing on her face. She bit her lip, then turned her attention to the control panel in front of her. She scrolled through more menu options before looking back up to Phillip.

"Okay, Phil. I've shown you something pretty. Now, how would you like to see something really cool?"

"Yes, please!"

Brit tapped the controls and everything went black. Phillip's eyes strained to adjust to the light, but there was no light to adjust to. After a second or two he saw the control panel emit a subtle glow.

"Where are we?" Phillip whispered.

""Very, very deep," Brit answered in an equally hushed tone.

"Why are we whispering?" Phillip asked.

"I don't know. You started it," she whispered, then added in a more conversational tone, "Nothing can hear us while we're inside this sphere."

Phillip surveyed the vista around them. "I can see why you brought me here. This is definitely the darkest dark I've ever seen."

Brit said, "Just wait. It gets better," as she hit a few buttons, and the darkness around them flashed and took on a greenish glow. What had looked like nothing but a solid field of black was now a vast three-dimensional galaxy of faint, light-green stars, drifting slowly around them.

"What happened?" Phillip asked.

"I set the sphere to filter the infra-red spectrum so that it's visible to us. Also, the sphere is emitting infra-red, or else there still wouldn't be anything to see down here."

"Why is it all green?" Phillip asked.

"Because it looks cool that way. Kinda night-visiony. I can change it if you like."

"No," Phillip said, "please leave it. What are all of these things floating around us?"

"Debris. Dead krill. Fish poop. I don't know, to be honest. They're not what we came to see."

"What did we come to see?"

Brit smiled. "We'll get to that in a minute. First, Gwen tells me you're from the eighties, right?"

"Yes."

"Tell me, what do you know about giant squid?"

"Huh," Phillip said, thinking. "Giant squid. Let's see. Sailors used to tell stories about them, most likely to impress other sailors. They used to draw them on maps. They made a really cool mechanical one for the movie *20,000 Leagues Under the Sea*."

Brit hit a button, and the dots of light that surrounded them started to move in unison, and all in the same direction, telling Phillip that the craft was moving. The effect was much like driving in a snowstorm, or how Phillip imagined flying in an extremely fast spaceship would look. "Are they real?" Brit asked, then added, "Giant squids?"

"No," Phillip said. "I mean, I've read stuff about big tentacles washing up on beaches, but that's mostly tabloid stuff. I'd guess they're no more real than the Loch Ness Monster, or Bigfoot."

"Yeah," Brit said, "probably. Say, what's that?" She pointed straight ahead. At first Phillip didn't see what she meant. He squinted, and in the distance he saw a ghostly image of something, something graceful and fluid. It almost looked like an immense snake, reaching out for them. *Maybe an eel*, Phillip thought. It was getting closer, or, to be more accurate, they were gaining on it. As whatever it was came clearer, Phillip could see that it wasn't an eel. At the very least, it was several eels swimming together. As they drew even closer, Phillip saw some dark mass ahead of the things, whatever they were. Were they chasing it? *No,* Phillip could see now, *they're part of it!*

"It can't be," Phillip said.

"It is," Brit replied. "It's Bigfoot."

Brit maneuvered the craft out from behind the giant squid, accelerating to come up alongside of it. "Cool, isn't it?" she asked.

"Yes, very, in a ghastly sort of way. The way the tentacles move, it's almost hypnotic." Phillip watched for a moment, then asked, "Did you make it?"

"No," Brit said. "It's real. One of the girls is into marine biology. When she found out about this craft and what it can do, she went off in search of all the coolest things she'd ever read about. We've got them all cataloged so we can come check them out any time. It's better than any aquarium."

"Its eye is bigger than my head," Phillip said. "It can't see us, can it?"

"No, it can't see or hear us. It has no idea we're here."

"Good."

They kept pace with the squid, watching in silence as it barreled through the dark. After a long silence, Phillip said, "Brit, I haven't known you long, but I've been thinking about your situation."

Brit laughed. "Phillip, we're deep below the surface of the sea, looking at a creature that until five minutes ago you thought was a myth, and you want to talk about me?"

"What can I say," Phillip said, "I just find some things particularly interesting."

In the low light, Phillip couldn't be sure that she had blushed, but he chose to believe that she had. "Look," he said. "We know that we're in a computer program, and knowing that allows us to play around with it to do things. Make things, fly, travel through time, that sort of thing. But Brit, none of us knows how the program really works. We tell ourselves that we do, but really we just understand bits of it. We think we know what happened when you came to Atlantis for the first time, but really, we have no idea how the program handled it. We just know what your experience of it was."

Phillip paused a moment to give Brit a chance to tell him to shut up. She didn't, so he continued. "You're thinking of it as if your life has been an unbroken thread that just happens to loop back around on itself, but what if it's not? What if you are the end of the thread, like the rest of us?"

"But Phillip, Brit the Elder is here. You can't ignore her. Believe me, I've tried. She's here, she's me, and she remembers everything I do."

"Or, so it would seem," Phillip said, "but what if, the instant you got the idea to go further back in time and create Atlantis yourself if you had to, the program, whatever it is, took that to be the plan. Then, when you transported, it triggered the plan you had created, like a subroutine. So the program paused our reality—"

"Can it do that?" Brit asked.

"I don't know. I don't see why it couldn't, and if it did, we'd never know. So, anyway, it pauses reality, and creates a second copy of you, which then runs through a projected version of events, seeing that there's nothing here, treading water for a few minutes presumably, then going back in time and creating the city. Then the program blasts through a thumbnail version of the past, what, hundred years? Then, when it has the past laid out, it restarts the program and you turn up, for the first time, from your point of view."

Brit shook her head. "Maybe, but I don't see how that makes any difference, and besides, that doesn't explain how she remembers everything I've done."

"Yes, it does. And it makes all of the difference. It means that you're the real you, and she's an imitation, created as a placeholder until the real thing is ready to take over, and her memories are being created on the fly by the program to reflect her past, which you're creating now. You've been thinking the things she's done affect you, but in truth, the things you do affect her. She's just a puppet you, being changed constantly to reflect the actions you've taken, or are likely to take. Her past actions didn't create you. Your current actions create her."

Brit thought about it, then asked, "That explains how she remembers the things I've thought and done, but what about when she predicts the things that are going to happen to me?"

Phillip shrugged. "Maybe it's the power of suggestion. You believe she knows your future, so when she says something's going to happen, you make it happen. I don't know. The good news is, you're not doomed to be just like her if you don't want to be. Brit, you can become anything you like and she will change to reflect your choices. If I'm right, you have more control over her than she does over you."

"That is good news," Brit said quietly, as if not wanting to be over heard. "What's the bad news? There is bad news, I assume."

Phillip took a deep breath "There's always bad news. If I'm right, you can die."

"Which is why you're so worried that someone is trying to kill me."

"Yes."

They were both so absorbed in the implications of their discussion that they nearly didn't notice the hollow popping noise, like a champagne bottle being uncorked.

A shrill, brittle tearing sound surrounded them as the diamond sphere that kept Phillip and Brit safe and dry was clouded by thousands of tiny, spider-web cracks. They had just enough time to realize what was happening, then see the looks of panic on each other's faces before the sphere catastrophically imploded.

For any ordinary person, the implosion of a deep-sea submersible is an instant death. The violence of the event and the pressures involved will completely destroy the human body faster than its nervous system can register a single pain signal. Death is immediate and certain, like someone turning off a switch marked *you*. Phillip was not an ordinary person. He was a subroutine in a computer-generated reality, and he knew it. As such, he had made modifications to his parameters.

Phillip was badly stunned. He drifted in the water, his whole body screaming. He was impervious to physical damage, but the implosion had felt like being hit by a speeding car from every possible direction simultaneously. Normally, on the surface, he would take a few moments to recover from this. Phillip was not on the surface. He was deep under the ocean, and while the pressure was not killing him, it certainly wasn't making him comfortable.

Phillip regained some small portion of his senses. He tried to look around, but there was no light this far down, and he no longer had the sphere to create and convert infra-red light into something his eyes could use. All he saw was, literally, a sea of blackness in every direction.

The cold was not an issue. Phillip's modifications to his own statistics left him with a constant comfortable temperature regardless of the ambient conditions, so that was a victory. The oxygen situation was less positive. They had found ways to make people not need oxygen, but they hadn't found a way to make them not feel like they need oxygen, so the unlucky few who had tried this modification (or had it tried on them) spent the entire time feeling like they were suffocating, even though they were not. This was deemed so horrific that no wizard he knew of had ever chosen to keep that modification installed, so Phillip needed air, and there was no way he could swim to the surface in time.

Because of the darkness and the pressure, he didn't feel like he was drowning. He felt like he was buried alive, under a mountain of water, which was not an improvement.

Phillip flailed about helplessly. He was down far too deep to have any hope of swimming to the surface. He had no light, he had no air. He wasn't thinking in rational sentences, or even words. Just fast, panicked images, one of which was of his staff waiting for him back at Brit's home. It was too long to fit in the sphere, so he'd left it. Without it, the shell program he'd mostly invented would not recognize him as a wizard, and would not let him teleport to safety. It was meant to be a failsafe to keep the wrong people from using magic. Luckily, after the scare they'd all had two months ago, he had developed an emergency backup: a collapsible metal pointer that he'd modified to extend to the proper length for the shell to recognize it as a wand. All he had to do was pull it out, extend it, not make the obvious joke, and use his last breath to say the right spell, and he'd be back at home, safe. He knew that it wasn't possible to talk in any meaningful way underwater, but as long as his lungs expelled some air, and his mouth and vocal cords formed the words, he was hopeful that the shell would recognize the incantation.

Hopeful was the word.

He jammed his right hand into his pocket, searching for the pointer. He swept his left hand in wide arcs with his fingers extended. If he could get a good grip on Brit, he could teleport them both to safety, but he needed to find her first.

He hadn't had the chance to take a good deep breath before the implosion, and even if he had, the violence of it would have knocked most of the wind out of him anyway. His lungs were already aching. The pointer was easy enough to find in his pocket, but drifting underwater, it was surprisingly difficult to pull it out of his loose robe's large pocket. Every time he tried to pull his hand out of the pocket, the pocket moved with his hand. Finally, after several tries, he suspended his left arm's search for Brit, and sent it to assist his right arm. He grabbed the outside of the pocket with one hand, yanking the pointer out with the other.

He quickly extended the pointer, then started whipping his arms around wildly in a desperate attempt to find Brit. His lungs were on fire, but he did not want to leave without her. His movements got more and more frantic. Finally, he realized that if he didn't get out of there soon, he wouldn't get out of there at all.

His arms had yet to make contact with anything that might be another person. He was very quickly reaching decision time, when he felt something grab his left foot. For the first time since the implosion, actual words popped into his mind.

Oh God, he thought, *it's the squid!*

Phillip pictured himself materializing back at home with a fifty-foot, angry, dying squid. He didn't like what he saw. He jerked his leg upward, but it was held tight. He couldn't shake the squid off. He knew that squid or no squid, he needed air, now. He drew up his other leg to make one desperate attempt to kick himself free. He looked down, towards his captured leg, and at first he thought he was hallucinating from the lack of oxygen. His eye struggled to focus and adjust, but submerged in murky water without goggles, his vision was only going to be so clear. Still, blurry though it was, Phillip definitely saw light beneath him. He stopped struggling and saw that it was not the squid that had his left foot, it was Brit. She had his foot jammed into the crook of her right arm, and the index finger of her left hand was glowing. They briefly made eye contact. Brit stabbed her glowing finger at a floating button that only she could see, and the two of them disappeared.

15.

Martin and Gwen were waiting.

They had realized that something was up. They wanted to tell Phillip and needed to tell Brit. They decided that finding Brit first was their priority, and decided to start with Brit the Younger, since she was the one in direct danger. They went to her home. Nik knew Gwen well and let them in, but was adamant that when Brit went out on her little head-clearing trips, she was not to be disturbed. Martin saw Phillip's staff lying on the floor next to one of the chairs, and asked Nik if Brit had company.

Nik said, "Yes. A gentleman named Phillip."

Nik assured Gwen and Martin that Brit would be back soon and told them to have a seat, while he went and got them some refreshments.

Gwen and Martin had just settled into their seats when Brit and Phillip returned.

Brit had her legs pulled in toward her body, one hand pointing into space, the other trapping Phillip's ankle under her arm. Phillip had one leg (the one Brit was clinging to) stretched out and the other pulled up, with his knee to his chest as if he intended to kick Brit in the face. His back was hunched, his arms were akimbo, and in his right hand, he was holding a metal pointer like he had just been giving a science lecture. They both appeared out of thin air, soaking wet and several feet off the ground.

They fell to the floor with a wet thud, then lay there gasping for air. Gwen rushed to their sides to offer aid. Martin leaned forward in his chair.

Once she had caught her breath, Brit leaned up on one elbow, looked at Phillip, and said, "Were you going to kick me in the head?"

Phillip shrugged and said, "Sorry. I thought you were the squid."

Martin said, "Well, there's got to be a story behind that."

Gwen helped Brit to her feet. Martin watched, smirking as Phillip clambered to a standing position, then wrung some of the brine out of his hat. Brit said, "Thanks, Gwen. By the way, what are you two doing here?"

Gwen put a reassuring hand on Brit's shoulder and said, "We need to talk. Martin and I think someone may be trying to kill you."

Phillip turned to Martin and said, "You think so, huh?"

Martin replied, "It's a theory."

Just then, Nik rounded the corner from the kitchen, calling out, "Okay, who's thirsty?" When he saw Brit and Phillip's condition, he nearly dropped his tray of drinks.

Phillip and Martin teleported back to their room so Phillip could clean himself up. Brit used the time to make herself look and feel more human. Twenty minutes later they reconvened in Brit's living room to compare notes.

Brit and Phillip described how they had heard the same hollow popping noise when the submersible imploded that they'd heard before the two statues fell. Gwen and Martin talked about their inspection of the statue base and their belief that both statues had been brought down deliberately.

"What I don't get," Martin mused, "is why anyone would want to kill you in the first place, Brit."

Brit smiled. "Thanks, Martin. I appreciate that."

"I mean," Martin continued, "Brit the Elder being here proves that you survive to be her, so any attempt to kill you is doomed to failure. Am I right?"

Brit looked long and hard at Martin, then said, "Is that the only reason you can think of not to kill me?"

Phillip quickly added, "Besides, it's not really true." He went on to give Gwen and Martin a quick synopsis of his idea regarding Brit the Elder's existence, and Brit the Younger's killability.

Martin thought for a moment, then asked, "Is *killability* even a word?"

Phillip said, "If I use it, and you know what it means, it a word. Also, it's fun to say. Killability. Killability. It rolls nicely."

"I don't know," Martin continued. "It's not very elegant."

"The word is killability. Who cares?"

"No, not the word. Well, not just the word. Your idea, too. It's inelegant."

"Reality is inelegant," Phillip huffed.

"No," Martin said definitively. "Reality is stunningly elegant. Our understanding of it is not."

"Martin, we're not going to have this argument again."

"We never have this argument. Every time we start to, you get mad and start shouting."

Phillip's face began to turn red. "You're right. I shouldn't have said, 'we're not going to have this argument again.' I should have said, 'again, we are not going to have this argument.' Maybe you'd think that was more elegant."

Brit turned to Gwen and said, "I can see why you enjoyed hanging around with these guys. It's entertaining in its way."

"Yes," Gwen agreed, "but as usual, it isn't really getting us anywhere. Guys, arguments about Brit's killability . . . oh, that is fun."

Phillip smiled, and said, "I know, right?" Brit did not smile.

Gwen continued. "Maybe Brit can be killed, maybe she can't. Either way, Phillip can be killed, and he nearly was. Whoever it is who's trying to take Brit out could easily kill someone else in the process. We have to stop them, and that means figuring out who it is."

Brit said, "We know it's someone with powers. Gunpowder won't be invented until hundreds of years from now, and even if it were, it would take a heap of the stuff to bring down one of those statues, let alone to put a hole in my diamond sphere."

"Agreed," Gwen said. "Of course, this would happen during the one time that we have magic users from all over the world visiting. That won't make it easier to narrow things down."

"Who has the most to gain?" Martin asked. "Brit, if you were out of the picture, who'd benefit most?"

"Nobody," Brit said. "I'm completely unimportant."

Gwen said, "Brit, that's not true."

Brit waved her off. "Yes it is. Brit the Elder has all of the power. I get it. She's the one who's done everything. I'm just the one who's going to do everything, and in the end, what's that worth? Really, I'm only in the council of three to break ties."

"But you are on the council," Martin said. "Maybe someone wants you off. Maybe, maybe . . . maybe they want you and Brit the Elder both off of the council, and they think that if they kill you, it'll take her out too. Two birds with one stone."

Phillip said, "Martin, there are only two options. Either their fates are tied together, or they aren't. If they are, and someone kills Brit here, then she never goes on to build Atlantis, none of this ever happens, and whoever it is who thinks they're going to gain something most likely loses everything. If, on the other hand, their fates aren't joined, then whoever kills Brit will find that the only change they've created is that the most powerful woman in Atlantis is furious at them for killing her younger self and giving her an identity crisis. Either way, it's a stupid plan."

Martin shrugged. "Then maybe the murderer is stupid."

"Attempted murderer," Brit corrected. "They haven't succeeded at anything yet."

"Which proves my point," Martin said.

Gwen said, "Martin, you said we should look at the person who has most to gain. Well, that's Ida, the president. With both Brits gone, she'd be the only council member left. But, she's not stupid."

"Are you sure?" Martin asked.

Both Gwen and Brit nodded. "We both voted for Ida. We wouldn't vote for someone we thought might be stupid."

Martin accepted this, and the room fell into a sullen silence.

Eventually Gwen said, "Whoever it is, either they'll give up, which is good, or they'll try again, and that'll be a chance to catch them. Either way, I think the logical next step is to go tell Brit the Elder what's going on."

"Why?" Brit asked. "Shouldn't she already know? Having someone try to kill you is pretty memorable. You'd think she'd recall who did it, how many more times they'll try, and how they're stopped."

Phillip said, "Gwen's right, and so are you. Either she doesn't know, and we need to tell her, or she does know, and we need to ask her what happens next."

"No," Brit said flatly. "I don't want her to have the satisfaction of knowing that I came to her for help."

Martin asked, "And if you don't, you're okay with having her remembering that you risked your life rather than ask her for help?"

"Yes," Brit said. "I'm fine with that, because that gives me satisfaction."

Gwen said, "Brit, if your life might be in danger, and we knew about it, wouldn't you want us to tell you?"

"You know it," Brit said.

Gwen said, "And that's why we have to tell her. Because she is you." Gwen tried not to look triumphant as she said it.

Brit replied, "Then you have warned her, just now, when you told me." Brit made a deliberate effort to look triumphant as she said it. She looked at the faces of the other three people. She could tell she had lost the argument, but that didn't mean she had to act defeated. "Fine," she said, "we'll warn her, but it's not going to be me who does it. One of you three is going to have to go deal with her. Who's it gonna be?"

While Gwen, Phillip, and Martin all agreed that Brit the Elder needed to be warned, none of them was particularly eager to volunteer to do it in front of Brit the Younger. She clearly had issues with Brit the Elder and might take them out on anyone who seemed to be *Elder-friendly*. Gwen was her friend and didn't want to seem disloyal. Phillip was beginning to harbor hopes of becoming something more than her friend, and especially didn't want to seem disloyal. Martin had a life-long aversion to offending angry women. The three of them stared at each other, mute with indecision, until, mercifully, the doorbell rang.

Nik speedwalked across the room, saying, "Don't get up. I'll get that. You keep having your very serious discussion that I was definitely not listening to."

Nik opened the door. Outside there were two guards. One, Martin had not met, was wearing the normal guard kilt and net shirt. The other, Ampyx, was also wearing an apparently homemade pointy wizard hat. When Ampyx noticed that Gwen was there, he winked and flicked his eyes upward to call her attention to the hat. The other guard said, "We have been sent to collect the guest of Atlantis called Phillip."

Brit the Younger rose to her feet and asked, "Why? What for?"

The guard stated, "He is to meet with Brit the Elder."

Brit the Younger glared at Phillip, who looked uneasily back at her. Martin smiled broadly and said, "Say, that's convenient." Ampyx studied Martin, filing this away for later.

16.

The heat was unbearable.

Agent Miller tried to get his mind off of the heat by focusing on the noise, which was deafening.

After a few minutes of this, he tried to distract himself from the noise by focusing on his motion sickness, which threatened to make him throw up at any moment. In an effort to alleviate this he crawled closer to the open door of the unrefrigerated boxcar in which he was riding. *Maybe if I look at the horizon, I won't be sick. That's supposed to help. Besides, it's cooler there because of the wind.*

He crawled as close to the door as he dared. Close enough to feel that the wind was still unnervingly strong and gusty, and to see that the train was still cutting along the side of a mountain, so that the door of the boxcar opened to a life-ending drop. Not a straight drop. There was a painful-looking gravel berm just wide enough for him to bounce off before he fell over the side to his certain death. His innate fear of heights, and his lack of any decent footing, drove Agent Miller clambering back into the dark corner of the boxcar where it was safe, hot, and loud.

"I hate this," he shouted.

"What?" Jimmy shouted back. It would have been hard enough to hear each other if they had only had the train noise to contend with, but because of Jimmy's weird effect on electronic devices, they'd had to find a train going from Seattle to Los Angeles that had three non-refrigerated boxcars in a row that weren't transporting any sort of electronic devices, and in which the middle car had room for three adults to live for the three days the trip was going to take. That left them with a field of one car to choose from, this car, which was transporting tens of thousands of squeaky, bone-shaped rubber dog toys, manufactured in China, shipped by freighter to Seattle, now headed to a big box pet supply chain's distribution center in southern California.

For now the squeaky bones were held in large cardboard boxes that completely filled the interior of the box car to a depth of six feet, leaving them four feet of living space on the top. Not that they could stand on the loosely packed boxes anyway.

The agents and their charge had taped several of the boxes to each other and to the walls so that they could have the door of the boxcar open a bit and not be worried about the cargo falling out unexpectedly and taking one or all of them with it. Still, the three men had to live in a moving, rattling, cacophonous metal box, while lying, sitting, crawling, and involuntarily bouncing on a bed of cardboard and thousands of squeaky toys. The din was constant, but not consistent enough to become white noise. Any bump or shimmy on the part of the train, or shift in weight on the part of the men inside the car, caused a spike in the volume of the squeaking.

Miller envied his partner, Agent Murphy. At least he had a means of taking an occasional break. Twice a day they had to check in with their supervisor, but cell phones didn't work if they were too close to Jimmy and his magnetic field. Being trapped inside a steel box with him didn't make the cell phone work any better, so in order to check in, all Agent Murphy (who had no fear of heights, unlike Agent Miller) had to do was swing himself out of the open door of the shaking boxcar, grab the ladder that was just within reach, climb up to the roof of the moving train, and make his way far enough away from Jimmy that his phone would work. This meant walking toward the back of the train and jumping to the next boxcar back. Two cars in front of them was an open bin of some foul-smelling material Miller suspected was used in the manufacture of fertilizer.

Miller carefully crawled toward Jimmy, who was lying back on several partially mashed, squeaking boxes as if they were a deluxe bed in the most expensive suite at the finest hotel. Jimmy was wearing his suit pants and a Seattle PD T-shirt. He had his suit jacket folded and tucked under his head like a pillow.

It took great care to move around, not only because the unreliability of the surface made it hard to find footing, but also because it was very easy to carelessly put your weight on one of the seams between the boxes of squeaky toys, meaning that you could be crawling along without a care in the world, then trust your weight to the wrong spot and instantly find yourself falling head first between the boxes all the way down to the splintery plywood floor. If that happened, you'd have to crawl your way up, like a man buried alive, to the surface of your squeaking, cardboard-scented grave.

Miller finally reached Jimmy. He put his head right up to Jimmy's ear and shouted, "I hate this!"

Jimmy smiled and shouted back, "I know!"

"How can you look so happy?" Miller asked.

"Try being a middle-aged white man, riding a bicycle through Nicaragua. This is luxury."

Agent Miller put his mouth right up to Jimmy's ear and yelled, "I feel like I'm going to be sick!"

Jimmy replied, "Please don't do it while shouting in my ear."

Miller said, "I should be so lucky," and carefully slunk back to his corner of the boxcar. He could have stayed where he was, next to Jimmy, but the fact was he wanted as much distance between them as possible. Miller had begun to regret having ever laid eyes on the old coot.

Miller thought back to his life before meeting Jimmy. He was half of a two-man task force, assigned to investigate and possibly solve a series of possibly connected impossible occurrences that were possibly crimes. They had spent years chasing promising leads and had always come up empty-handed. At the time it was frustrating, but in retrospect seemed like some kind of golden age. They never enjoyed returning to their office empty handed, but now they were returning home with their hands full of Jimmy, and it was just as unsavory as it sounded.

Their original plan was to stay in Seattle. They would question Jimmy and decide if he was a crackpot or if he was on the level. Either way they'd get the information they needed and get back to Los Angeles, tout suite. Unfortunately, Jimmy proved to be both a crackpot and on the level, and instead of just answering their questions, he needed to demonstrate his point, and he had a whole list of weird household items he needed before he could stage his demonstration.

It was like trying to interrogate Bill Nye the Science Guy.

Most of the items on the list had been easy. Things like kite string, binoculars, a large scented candle—things you could get at any department store. The problem had been the last item: a room at least forty feet in length with a clear line of sight. The Seattle

Police Department had no such room in their headquarters, or at least had none that they were willing to hand over to Miller and Murphy. The SPD had started to tire of the two Treasury agents, their weird informant, and the rash of unexplained electronic malfunctions that followed him wherever he went.

Murphy had tried to find another facility in Seattle that met Jimmy's specifications, but they all suffered from the same flaw: they cost money to rent, and there was no way the Treasury Department was going to spend money when it had several storage facilities and garages in Los Angeles. Murphy pointed out that transporting Jimmy to California would cost money, but their supervisor pointed out that it would actually be pretty cheap, since, as Murphy himself said, taking an airline flight home was impossible anyway.

They quickly researched several possible ways to get Jimmy to L.A. without his magnetic field killing anyone. They considered renting the biggest truck they could and having him ride in the back, but his field would affect any car that tried to pass. They tried to talk their supervisor into renting an antique airplane, but any modern avionics would be useless, risking their safety, and worse, it would cost money. In the end, the boxcar was the only option. Since it is not actually legal to transport humans in a boxcar for any price, the agents had to sneak onto the train with Jimmy, and were now officially hobos, which cost nothing but their dignity, the one resource the Treasury Department was happy to squander with wild abandon.

Murphy and Miller found a train that suited their purpose, then happily checked out of their room at the cheapest hotel in the SeaTac Airport district. Their boss had gotten a substantial discount by renting their room on a nightly basis, instead of the usual hourly rate plan. They then had to transport Jimmy from the police headquarters to the rail yard, and they couldn't use any car that employed an integrated circuit, because Jimmy would render it inoperable. In the end, an officer was able to loan them his early-seventies Cadillac, which was barely operable to begin with. They transported Jimmy in the dead of night to minimize any effect he might have on traffic. The stealthy, cloak-and-dagger feel of the operation was spoiled by the Cadillac's faulty wiring, which caused the horn to honk in time with the left turn signal.

Agent Miller leaned back into the boxes and a miasma of self-pity. *Maybe if I lie on my back,* he thought, *I'll fall asleep, then throw up, and aspirate on my own sick. Then my body will slide between these cursed boxes and slowly sink down into squeaky oblivion.*

He fantasized about this for a while, then his backbone reasserted itself. *No,* he thought, *without me here, Murphy will just be kind to Jimmy, and I can't allow that to happen, not after all of this.*

Miller forced himself to look out the door of the train. He watched the world pass, fast enough to keep him motion sick, but slow enough to give him no hope of arriving at his destination any time soon. After a few moments, he saw a single hand swing in from beyond the door and clutch at its frame, knuckles white with exertion. Miller and Jimmy both scrambled as quickly as they dared toward the door. They had been traveling for nearly two days. This was the fourth time Murphy had made the transition from clinging to the side of the car to sitting inside, and it had already become routine. It was still utterly terrifying for everyone involved, but the terror was part of the routine, just one more item on the checklist.

Jimmy braced his legs on one side of the doorframe. Miller braced against the door itself. Murphy's second hand joined his first on the edge of the opening, then the very top of his head appeared. He was now standing on the floor of the boxcar, but would not be able to climb up on the stack of boxes without help. Jimmy took one hand, Miller took the other, and with much pulling, kicking, and cursing, he was pulled up onto the surface like a landed fish.

"What's the news?" Miller shouted.

Murphy lay there, panting from the exertion and the stress. Between gulps of air he yelled, "They have a facility set aside for us, and suitable transportation will be waiting at the rail yard's employee parking lot. All we have to do is wait for the cover of darkness, then sneak out past the railroad dicks."

"Excellent," Jimmy said. "This is great news. Smile, gentlemen. Things are going well!"

That was the last straw. Miller shrieked, "Going well?! I'm sick, I haven't slept more than a couple of hours in two days, and Murph is having to risk his life twice a day to talk to someone that we both avoid when we're in the same building as him. Then, to top it all off, we just found out that we're going to have to slink into the city where we both live like criminals!"

"Yes," Jimmy said. "Isn't it exciting?"

Miller looked at Jimmy, who beamed at him. He looked at Murphy, who shrugged, as if to say *Well, he's got a point.* Miller considered yelling at them both some more, but instead he simply relaxed and allowed himself to fall between the boxes, down to the bottom of the squeaking cardboard crevasse. There, he hoped to find some peace.

17.

Phillip's trip to meet with Brit the Elder was actually rather pleasant. Once he realized that neither of the guards escorting him had any idea why she wanted to see him, their conversation turned to a more pleasant subject: Martin. Ampyx spent the entire trip asking Phillip pointed questions about Martin, questions Phillip was happy to answer.

"He's impulsive," Phillip said. "He acts without thinking. He makes the same mistakes over and over and when he finally does learn his lesson, he often forgets it within a few hours."

"He sounds irritating," Ampyx said.

"Oh yes! He'll irritate you."

"You don't seem to like him much."

"On the contrary, he's quickly become my best friend," Phillip said.

"If he's irritating and stupid, why be friends with him?"

"Oh, he's not stupid, just a slow learner. Stupid people are useless. Slow learners are tremendous fun to jerk around."

Finally, they arrived at Brit the Elder's patio, where he had first arrived in Atlantis just the day before. There was a table, two chairs, two empty glasses, and a pitcher of some refreshing-looking reddish drink. The two guards took their leave of Phillip, telling him that Brit the Elder would be with him shortly.

Phillip walked to the railing and looked up at the city. It was getting close to evening. Due to the unique bowl-like shape of Atlantis, most of the city was in shadow. Only one part of the city still had direct sunlight, a small crescent along the far upper rim. The darkness of the rest of town made it stand out even more. The sky was a brilliant blue disk overhead, and the city was dark and cool. Lights were slowly beginning to come on, just a few for now, but with each passing moment there were more, and as they did, the buildings themselves glowed. You could see light and shadow moving within the buildings, not so well that you could tell what was happening, but enough to let you know that something was going on, and that it seemed pleasant.

Phillip wondered about the lights. He knew that his quarters had artificial lights. Brit's did as well. He knew that the vast majority of the people who lived in Atlantis didn't have the powers that he and his magical/time-traveling kind did. He wondered if they used candles, oil lamps, or some other lighting method he didn't know about.

Phillip was startled when a voice behind him said, "Magical." He jumped then spun around to see Brit the Elder standing behind him. He still couldn't get used to it. She had the same face. The same glasses. The hairstyle was different, but the hair color was the same.

"The lights," Brit clarified. "They're magical. Computer generated, if you prefer to call it that." She walked to the railing, standing closer to Phillip than he was comfortable with. He was happy to have her stand that close, which is what made him uncomfortable. "Of course," Brit continued, "all of their methods of creating light before I got here were variations on the theme of 'burning something.' It's really dangerous and wasteful when you think about it. Instead, I set up light sources. You make a light. Make a switch. Tell the system that one controls the other. You know how it works. You used the same basic technique to make the lights in your rumpus room."

Phillip looked down at her. "You know about my rumpus room?"

Brit replied, "Phillip, I've ridden in your Fiero."

Phillip noticed that she had the same smile as Brit the Younger as well.

"Anyway, when people move to Atlantis, part of the bargain is that they get free light, heat, and garbage and waste removal. It's funny. I became a time traveler and a sorceress just to end up going into the utilities business."

"So, all of the city's necessary functions are handled by magic," Phillip said. "That answers a lot of my questions, but don't the locals want to know how things work?"

"Did the modern people we left behind?"

Phillip said, "Yes, they did. The libraries were full of books about how every single thing in the world worked."

Brit took Phillip by the arm and led him across the patio to the table. She did it so smoothly that he didn't even notice it was happening until they were almost there.

"Yes, that's true," Brit said, "but how many people actually read those books? How many know how to rewire a lamp, or fix their own toilet?"

They reached the table. Brit poured two glasses of whatever the reddish drink was and they both had a seat. Brit continued, "People say that they want to know how things work, but really, most of them just want to know why things work."

"Why they work?" Phillip asked.

"Yes," Brit said. "You know, 'I flip the switch and the lamp turns on because of electricity.' Or, 'I put gas in the car, it burns, and the car moves.' Or, 'I press this thingy, that thingy lights up because Brit made it work with magic.' It's all the same to them. Please, have a drink."

Brit took a long drink from her glass. Phillip followed suit. "What is this?" he asked.

"Hi-C. I've loved the stuff ever since I was a kid." Brit took another appreciative drink, then spent a moment silently studying Phillip. Finally she asked, "How'd you like the giant squid?"

Phillip was surprised. Then he was surprised at himself for being surprised. "The squid was amazing," he said. "I could have done without the swim afterwards though."

"Yes," Brit agreed, "not a pleasant way to end the trip, but still, memorable."

"Clearly, since you seem to remember it," Phillip said.

Every time Phillip thought Brit's smile was as bright as it could be, it found a way to get a bit brighter. "Yes, I remember it well. I only took you to see the coral reef because it seemed like a nice, touristy kind of thing to show you. I was happy when it bored you. Your reaction to the squid made me even happier. It was good of you to listen to my whining. Sorry about that."

Phillip bristled a bit. "I wouldn't call it whining. Brit the Younger has some legitimate complaints."

Brit the Elder shook her head. "Phillip, there's no need to defend me to me. I know exactly what my complaints were. I made some good points. It certainly wasn't easy being Brit the Younger, but it's not really easy being anybody, is it? She thinks it's hard being her, but she hasn't tried being me yet."

"You think you have it harder than she does?" Phillip asked.

"Not harder, just differently hard. You're what, forty years old physically, fifty or so chronologically?"

"Yes.

"Well, Brit the Younger and I are both twenty-eight physically. She's thirty-nine chronologically. I am 167. She's a little over a quarter my age. Think back to what you were like when you were thirteen."

Phillip thought about it. It was not pleasant.

"No need to tell me what you were like," Brit said. "The grimace on your face says it all. Now, imagine spending the next fifty years of your life living with you at age thirteen, or, to be fair, let's make it twenty. Imagine watching twenty-year-old *Phil the Younger* live the life you led, express the opinions that now make you wince, make the mistakes you remember painfully. Now imagine that you cannot, under any circumstances interfere, because you know those experiences will make him the person he needs to become."

"You."

"Well, *you* in this example, but you're right, I am talking about me."

Phillip thought for a moment, then said, "You make a good point, but that doesn't excuse all of your behavior. You're taking credit for her ideas."

"I'm her. They're my ideas, too, and when I get credit for them, she gets it as well."

"It doesn't feel that way to her."

Brit stood up. "Not yet, but it will." She offered her hand. "Please come with me, Phillip. There's something I'd like to show you."

Phillip stood up, and again, Brit the Elder deftly took him by the arm and led him, this time down the steps of the patio and into the park that made up the center of the city. The sliver of the bowl that was still receiving direct sunlight was bathed in the orange glow that told Phillip it was sunset. The reflected light gave the rest of the city a golden aura. Even more of the city's lights had come on, making the entire panorama surrounding them look like a patchwork quilt made out of light. The path through the park was lined with lights, but rather than being hung from poles, they were simply balls of pure white light suspended in space, casting a glow on the path beneath.

As they walked, Phillip said, "If you remember our trip to see the squid—"

Brit looked up at him and interrupted, "Like it was yesterday."

"It was today," Phillip said. "Anyway, then you'll remember my theory."

Phillip expected that to sour her mood, but it did not. She said, "You mean that I am not actually me?" She let that hang in the air for a moment before correcting herself, "Her, I mean."

"Yes," Phillip said. "And I suppose you're going to tell me that I'm totally wrong."

"No, Phillip. You're not totally wrong. I think you're about fifty percent wrong."

Phillip said, "Well, that's not so bad, I guess."

Brit said, "I know that I . . . *she* told you how things happened from *her* point of view. Let me tell you how they happened from mine. I'll make it quick, because most of it will sound familiar. I decided to come to Atlantis. I did some research, picked a time and place, and thought, 'If it isn't there already, I can always jump further back and build it myself.' Then I made the jump, and the city, much as you see it now, was here waiting for me, along with a woman who claimed to be me but older."

Phillip said, "But logically, if you built Atlantis, it can't have been here when you got here."

Brit reached up and poked Phillip's nose. "Exactly. I think you're right, Phillip. I think the program did pause reality and did create an avatar of me that found no Atlantis here, then went back in time and built it according to how it knew I would. Then, when it got back to the point where I turned up, it restarted reality so I could experience it firsthand."

Phillip said, "But then, after fifty years you go back in time to do what, make Atlantis again?"

"No, I make Atlantis for the first time, exactly as the projection of me did before. The program knew exactly what I would do when it built it the first time. It's no surprise that when it was my turn I did exactly the same thing."

"Interesting," Phillip said, "but still, how can you prove that you're really you and not a simulated you?"

"I can't. All I can tell you is that I am absolutely certain that I am me, that I used to be her, and that I know everything that has happened to us in the intervening time while she becomes me."

"Of course, that's exactly what a projection of you would say as well."

Brit looked up at Phillip. "Do I look like a computer projection to you?"

"Yes, but everybody does, because we both know that that's what we are."

Brit squeezed his arm and said, "Touché."

They walked on in silence for a few moments. Phillip saw that they were walking toward the monument that stood in the middle of the park. It was a polished white spire that rose from the center of the park, which was itself the center of the city. It gave the impression of being the spindle around which the city revolved. Phillip asked Brit the Elder where they were going.

"Exactly where it looks like we're going," she said. "Philip, I owe you an apology. I've misled you. A long time ago, earlier today to you, I told you that I . . . *me*, was taking credit for my . . . *her*, ideas. There's some truth to that, but what I didn't say at the time was that I only really had two ideas."

"What?" Phillip said, stopping in his tracks. "You built this entire city. I mean, Brit the Younger's point is that she had all of the ideas that you built the city with, and that you got the credit for it. Are you telling me that you built this place with only two ideas?"

Brit laughed pleasantly and started leading Phillip forward again. "No, not at all. It took hundreds of ideas to make this place work. All I'm saying is at the time that I transported back to this time in the first place, I had only had two of them: fabricating objects one atom at a time using automated algorithms, and using those objects to create complex mechanisms with few or no actual moving parts. I liked the simplicity of it. It felt very Charles Eames to me. Anyway, I got here and the city was already built, so I just took notice of how everything worked. Later, when I went back in time and started building, I realized how many details there were, and how many problems needed to be solved, so I had to fall back on the things I remembered from when I was Brit the Younger."

"Are you saying that the ideas just sort of spontaneously happened, and thanks to the loop in your time line it's impossible to know which of you came up with them?" Phillip asked.

"No," Brit said, and stopped walking. "I know exactly who came up with the ideas." They were directly in front of the obelisk now. At its base there was a squared section, covered with engraved writing. Brit let go of Phillip's arm, gestured toward the monument, and said, "Go read what it says."

Phillip walked toward the monument, eventually getting close enough to make it out. It read, "The city of Atlantis would neither exist nor function without the contributions of the following people." Beneath that were a great many names, listed in alphabetical order. Phillip scanned the list. He, Martin, and Gwen were all listed, as were Jeff and, strangely, Jeff's trainee Roy. As he read, Brit walked up beside him.

"When I first got here and saw this list, I figured it was just people who had been supportive, or offered the occasional bit of advice. It wasn't until I actually started building the place that I realized these are all people from whom I copied some idea, some bit of code, some functioning idea, and incorporated it into the city."

Phillip turned on Brit. "You mean you stole ideas from all of these people?"

Brit just smiled. "I don't think *stole* is the right word, Phillip. You've made all of your work available to the wizards in your community to use. You haven't attempted to patent anything. You're not exploiting any of your ideas for profit, except for creating money from thin air of course, but you're hardly the only one of us to come up with that. I am giving you credit. Part of this summit's purpose is so I can talk to the leader of each group and show them the monument. If I wanted to steal the ideas, I could just claim to have thought of them first. After all, I did *use* them first."

Phillip put up a hand to stop her. "Okay, you're right. I'm sorry. I'm a little sensitive about people taking credit for my ideas."

Brit took his arm again, and squeezed it reassuringly. "I know. It's one of the things you and younger me had in common. You'll notice that your old friend Jimmy's name isn't on there."

"Good," Phillip said. "So, what ideas of mine did you end up using?"

"Two things. One, you know the interface you created to help you manipulate the file? You call it 'the shell.' We call ours 'the interface,' but if you look at it, you'll see that it functions in much the same way. That's an idea that has caught on much more widely than I think you know. All of the communities have some version of it. Some even use chunks of your original source code."

"Really?"

"A good idea spreads fast."

Phillip liked the idea that he had made life better for many people. He couldn't resist asking, "What's the other idea you used?"

Brit smirked, and said, "You mean you haven't noticed the lavatories? All of the restrooms in the city work on the same principle as the one in your home."

Phillip's facilities consisted of a simple latrine with a thirty-foot pit, but at the bottom of the pit there was a portal that instantly transported anything that fell through it *away*. Where *away* was had changed recently, because a statue he particularly disliked had been removed. Currently, *away* was a local farmer's fertilizer supply, which the farmer appreciated, although he was not pleased with the velocity with which the fresh fertilizer would arrive. It led to his fertilizer pile being messier than he liked, a concept which fascinated Phillip.

"Where do your lavatories lead?" Phillip asked.

Brit asked, "You haven't had a chance to look at the stars at night since you got here, have you?"

"No."

"I suggest you and younger me do so. Not tonight, as I'm still a little shaken, what with someone repeatedly trying to kill me and all, but soon. I think you'll notice that we have quite a few more shooting stars than you're used to. Now that you know why, I doubt you'll find it as romantic as you would have before."

They walked in silence for a moment, giving Phillip the opportunity to notice that she had started leading him away from the monument and back to her patio. They were most of the way back and he hadn't even noticed it. He remembered that he had business with Brit the Elder, and he needed to tend to it soon.

"You mentioned the attempts on Brit's life," Phillip said.

"Yes."

"So," Phillip said, "clearly, you're aware of them."

"Oh, Phillip, I remember them like they were yesterday."

Phillip said, "Two of them were."

"Not for me. For me they were a long time ago, but like I said, I remember them all too well. It's terribly disturbing to know that someone wants you dead, and every attempt is a clear reminder. The statues. The submersible. The thing tomorrow. Ghastly."

"What thing tomorrow?" Phillip said.

"You'll see. Don't worry. Obviously, I survive."

Phillip sputtered, "But . . . why? If you remember exactly what happens, why not tell us who's doing it?"

"Because I don't."

"Don't, or won't?"

"Both. I won't now, because I remember that I didn't then."

Phillip stopped walking and gently but firmly removed his arm from Brit the Elder's grasp. "So you're not going to lift a finger to help," he said.

"No, I'm going to help, as Brit the Younger. I remember going to quite a bit of trouble to figure out who's doing this, but I also remember that Brit the Elder stood by and did nothing, and now it's my turn to play that part, unsatisfying as it is."

Phillip shook his head, "I . . . I don't have a lot of respect for that."

Brit nodded in agreement. "Neither did I. The whole thing caused a lot of resentment on my part. It took a long time for me to get over it, but eventually, I understood, and forgave myself."

Phillip said, "Whatever," and started walking again. Brit walked beside him.

"I know this isn't the way you hoped this conversation would go," Brit said, in a soft, pleasant tone, "but you'll see in time that you couldn't realistically expect it to end any other way. After all, Phillip, you still don't believe that I'm really Brit. You still think that I'm a false projection. I've noticed that you still refer to me as two separate people."

"And I suppose you resent it."

Brit said, "Not at all," and stopped walking while softly grasping Phillip's elbow in a way that made him involuntarily stop and face her. She softly cradled his cheek with her hand. "I don't resent it at all. You don't want me to be Brit the Younger's future because when I was Brit the Younger, I didn't want me to be my future. You only doubt me out of a sense of loyalty to me. How could I find that anything but endearing?"

Phillip looked into Brit's eyes and said, "You confuse me terribly."

She kept her hand on his cheek, looked back into his eyes, and said, "I find that endearing too."

18.

The next morning, when it was time to go to the summit's second day of meetings, Brit the Younger was feeling edgy. Three attempts on your life will do that to you. Having Brit the Elder predict a fourth attempt didn't help.

Martin, Phillip, and Gwen were nervous as well. They gathered at Brit the Younger's apartment and escorted her to the summit. They considered just teleporting to the convention center, but Brit didn't want to look like she was living in fear, so they walked. Gwen walked in front, looking for anything out of the ordinary. Martin and Phillip walked on either side of Brit, ready to leap into action the instant anything went wrong. Three guards, one of whom was Ampyx (still wearing his new hat), brought up the rear. As long as Brit the Elder seemed unconcerned, this was all the official response the situation was likely to get, and like all obvious precautions, none of this did anything to help Brit relax or make her look less fearful.

Martin tried to reassure her. "If Phillip's right and she's not really you, maybe Brit the Elder's memory of today is wrong."

"You mean her memory that someone would try to kill me and fail?" Brit asked.

"Yeah," Martin said.

"Well," Brit said, "if her memory is wrong, then it may be that nobody tries to kill me today."

Martin said, "Exactly."

Brit said, "Or, she could be right about the attempt to kill me, but wrong about it being unsuccessful."

"Oh, I hadn't thought of that," Martin said.

Phillip said, "Maybe she was predicting your failed attempt to cheer Brit up."

Martin looked back over his shoulder, and found Ampyx was staring at him. He asked the guard, "What are you looking at?"

"You."

Martin said, "Yeah, I thought so," and turned back around.

They reached the lift station just before the lift departed on its trip down the wall of the city toward the center. There were few people on the lift platform already, but to Martin's chagrin, Gilbert and Sid, the angry fops, were two of them. They were wearing stifling three-piece suits with stiff, starched collars, top hats, and white gloves, and carried walking sticks. They regarded Martin and Phillip with equal parts amusement and loathing, much as one would look at a cockroach dressed as a clown.

Martin ignored them. Phillip hadn't dealt with them yet, and as was his way, met their scorn with attempted friendliness. Phillip said, "Good morning," and bowed slightly.

The shorter of the two men, the one with the waxed moustache, lifted his top hat and bowed in an extravagant manner. "Good morning, Phillip. It is so good to see you. Martin, Gwen, Brit, lovely to see you today as well. I take it the purpose of traveling in this tight formation is to protect fair Brit in case another statue falls on her?"

Phillip said, "Yes. You disapprove?" His veneer of friendliness was already wearing thin.

Sid, the taller, chin-bearded one who had been silent until this point, said, "No, not at all. If you choose to spend your time making sure nobody kills someone who is unkillable, who are we to judge? Besides, this way, if another statue comes down, maybe it'll take you two out instead. Then we can step in and give the ladies some real protection."

"Yes, ladies," Gilbert agreed, raising his walking stick, which was piano-black with ivory caps on both ends. He used the stick to tap Phillip's wizard staff as he said, "Theirs might be larger, but I promise we're better at using ours."

Martin grimaced in utter disgust. "Really? Making the obvious joke?" Any question in his mind as to why he and these two men didn't get along was now answered. "The first rule of using magic staffs and wands is that you never make the obvious joke."

"That's your rule, not ours," Gilbert said.

Gwen decided it was time to speak up. "Tell me, has any woman ever laughed when you made the obvious joke?"

"No," Sid said, "but that's just because women don't really have a sense of humor."

Gwen asked, "What makes you say that?"

Sid said, "I tell a lot of jokes, jokes my male friends think are hilarious, but women almost never laugh."

Brit nodded, and said, "Well, we can't argue with that. Your logic is as strong as your wit."

Sid bowed more deeply, and said, "Thank you."

Mercifully, the lift reached the lowest station and it was time to disembark. Soon Gilbert and Sid were lost in the crowd. The walkway was crowded with Atlanteans going about their business and delegates all milling around before the summit commenced for the day. Gwen had expected to have to lead the rest of the group through the crowd, but word had gotten out about the two statues that had fallen on Brit, and everybody seemed to be giving their group plenty of room.

They were nearly to the convention center's entrance when a voice rang out through the crowd.

"Brit! Brit!" The crowd parted and Ida, the duly elected president of Atlantis, ran through, followed closely by her towering servant. The president ran to Brit the Younger and hugged her tightly. "Oh, Brit. Are you okay? I heard about the statues. I know you weren't hurt, but are you all right?"

"Yes," Brit said. "I'm fine, Ida. Thanks for asking."

Ida released the hug, but held Brit at arm's length, studying her face. "Are you sure you're okay? I know how badly an accident like that can shake someone up. Having a statue fall on you once would be bad enough, but twice. What are the chances?"

Brit said, "It's impossible, Ida. It wasn't an accident."

Ida smiled and shook her head. "Brit, I admit, it's weird, but you can't think that it was anything but an accident. I mean, why on Earth would anybody try to hurt you?"

Brit opened her mouth to answer, but was interrupted by a whizzing noise, and a razor-sharp arrow streaked into view at high speed, striking her harmlessly on the forehead. Brit grimaced and said, "I don't know, but I'm already getting pretty tired of it."

Phillip, Gwen, and Martin all looked frantically around, trying to see who had shot the arrow. Luckily, a random bystander in the crowd shrieked, "It came from up there!" The bystander pointed to the roof of a building near the rim of the city. All eyes turned and saw a single person looking down from the roof.

From that distance, it was impossible to tell who the person was, but they could clearly tell that the entire crowd was looking at them, because the head quickly disappeared.

Phillip turned to Martin and saw empty space, a pair of feet, and a silver sequined hem, streaking out of his vision. Martin had muttered "*flugi*" under his breath, and was speeding toward the would-be assassin's position at top speed.

Phillip said, "There he goes."

"Yup," Gwen agreed.

Ampyx looked at them, then shielded his eyes to watch Martin's progress.

Martin kept his eyes on the distant rooftop where he'd last seen the assailant. The rushing wind blowing directly in his face made it uncomfortable. For about the hundredth time Martin made a mental note to try to program some sort of auto-deploying goggles into the shell.

Martin reached the top of the building and performed a perfect three-point *Iron Man* landing with his staff held behind and above him, designed to instill fear in the person he was pursuing, and it certainly would have if anyone had been there to see it. Martin surveyed the roof. Like all of the other roofs in Atlantis, this one was made of a thick, milky, crystalline material. In the far corner there was a shed-like rectangular protrusion with a door. Martin ran to it, opening it cautiously, in case his prey was waiting to ambush him. The area inside the door was clear, so Martin entered.

As his eyes adjusted to the lower indoor light, Martin saw that the door led to a long stairwell, much as you'd find in any high-rise building, except that it was a graceful curving spiral, and made of milky glass. Martin heard the sound of someone running down the stairs very fast. He peered down the shaft of the stairwell and yelled, "Hey!" The running stopped, and a person's head emerged into the shaft almost a third of the way down. He thought it was the same head as he had seen on the roof, but now he was much closer, and Martin could see the look of absolute terror on the man's face. The head disappeared as quickly as it had appeared, and the running noises resumed at a faster pace than before.

Martin knew that if the other man reached the bottom floor before him, he'd be lost. Martin also knew that he wouldn't catch up on foot: the other man had too much of a head start. The open shaft in the center of the spiral was just a little too tight to fly down at any speed without crashing. He briefly considered trying to fly down the spiral. He would catch up to the guy that way, but by time he did, he'd likely be too dizzy to do anything but throw up on him.

Martin smiled, and reached into his pocket. He pulled his bean bag out and simply dropped it down the center of the shaft. Martin watched it plummet silently then hit the floor at the bottom of the shaft with an echoing thud. Martin said, "Bamf," and instantly he was standing at the bottom of the shaft. He looked up through the spiral. The now more distant running noises stopped again, and again, the man making them stopped running and peeked into the shaft. He looked up first, then turned and looked down.

Martin smiled and waved up at the man. *That's right,* Martin thought, *I've got you and we both know it.*

The man looked stricken. His head disappeared again. Then, Martin heard the unmistakable sound of rushed footsteps and a door opening and closing. Then, the stairwell was silent, except for the sound of Martin cursing.

Martin burst through the first door he saw, which led to an irregularly shaped hallway with three more doors. Martin tried one and found a dirty old mop. He tried the second and found a supply of clean new mops. The third door led to another hallway, this one tastefully decorated and ending in a bend rather than a door. Martin ran down the hall, rounded the corner and stopped, momentarily flummoxed by what he saw.

Despite being placed in a time before the beginning of recorded history, Martin was not particularly surprised to find seemingly modern scenes here in Atlantis. Also, even though he had never gone to a spa in his life, Martin was savvy enough to recognize one when he saw it. The air was a heady mix of soothing music and the smell of lavender, as you would expect. Employees were busy giving massages, pruning finger and toe nails, and tweezing unwanted hairs. What surprised Martin was that all of the customers were big, beefy dudes.

The man nearest to Martin was sitting back with a hot towel on his face while another man gave him a foot massage. The man receiving the foot rub was talking listlessly while the man giving the foot rub pretended to listen. "Yeah, I've always been a natural athlete. I'm good with the javelin, but my real forté is the discus. Ladies love a man who can throw a good discus, and the ones who aren't ladies love it even more. It's that pose at the beginning. There's nothing manlier than that."

At the end of the room, Martin could see an open door. A man was walking in to get some part of his body tended to, and Martin saw broad daylight behind him.

Martin shouted, "Hold the door!" Then he took off flying at top speed, but at an altitude of about four feet. Martin smiled when he heard men shouting, things falling, and water splashing as he shot through the spa.

Martin emerged back into the outside world. He angled up at a forty-five degree angle to get some distance from the chaos he had just created. He circled around back to face the wall of the city, and saw that the building he had just left stood out a good distance from the upper curve of the wall. It had several entrances at its base at the front of the building, and other entrances on to the street behind the building about half way up. He estimated that the man who'd fired the arrow was about halfway down the tower when he exited, so Martin gained altitude and searched for anything that might tell him which direction the guy he was chasing had gone.

He did not have to search for long.

Martin had suspected that Phillip would not be far behind him, and he could see Phillip flying above the street a few hundred feet down the road, directly behind some sort of commotion. Martin headed in that direction, and found that he was following a path of mild destruction. Nobody seemed to be hurt, but many of the people he flew over were picking up dropped items or helping fellow pedestrians to their feet. As he gained on the traveling disaster, he saw that it was being caused not by one man running, but by two.

The man he was pursuing was still running, and looked more panicked than ever. Not far behind, the president's servant was chasing him, gaining ground fast. The man in front was shoving people, grabbing things and throwing them behind him, toppling vendors' carts, anything that might slow the man behind him. The president's servant looked as if he was just out for a casual jog, and was dodging various obstacles in order to give his workout some variety. Nothing stopped him, or even seemed to slow him down.

Martin could see that the president's servant was going to catch the other man. It was just a matter of time. The problem was that in the meantime a lot of innocent bystanders were going to be inconvenienced, or maybe worse. This guy had tried to kill Brit. Who knew what he might do if he got the upper hand?

Either the president's servant would catch the man, or the man would effectively catch himself if they were just patient.

Martin, having never been known for his patience, gained altitude and accelerated. He was momentarily distracted by the niggling thought that he hadn't seen a bow, not on the roof, nor now in the fleeing man's hands. He put the thought out of his mind until later, when there would be time to think.

+⟫━━⟪+

Back on street level, the hunted man was frantic. His legs were aching, his throat was closing up, and his breaths were shallow, stabbing barks that were barely bringing in enough oxygen to keep him from blacking out. He wanted to stop running. Each step was more agonizing than the last, but he knew that whatever was going to happen to him if he stopped would be worse. He'd thought he was in trouble when that foreign sorcerer in the shiny silver robe came after him, but he'd been easy enough to evade. Now, though, he was being chased by this hulking slab of beef with a murderer's eyes and a marathon runner's gait.

He fled through the market as quickly as he could. The people milling were doing a pretty good job of parting around him, not because they wanted to assist him in fleeing, but rather because they didn't want to be anywhere near him when he was caught. The man scanned the path in front of him looking for anything that might slow his pursuer down. He saw a merchant selling heavy woven rugs. As he passed, he grabbed one of the large rolled rugs, a hefty specimen that was taller than himself standing on its side, and he heaved it down in his wake. The gambit cost him most of his momentum, and he struggled to get back up to speed. As he stumbled forward, he turned for a moment, hoping to see the monster chasing him trip and fall, or maybe get knocked off of his feet by the mass of the rug. Instead, what he saw was the man catching the rug, and smoothly tossing it aside without ever breaking the rhythm of his stride. Even through his mounting panic, the man had the wherewithal to think, *At least he didn't throw it at me.*

The man turned his attention to the path ahead just in time to see a silver bolt of light shoot down out of the sky and land directly in his path. It was Martin, who had landed in a crouch, and was holding his staff out, parallel with the ground. The man tried to leap over him, like a hurdle, but the force field Martin had just created prevented that. He bounced like a rag doll, and would have landed in a miserable heap on the ground if the president's servant hadn't caught him. Instead, he stood, locked in place by the servant's muscular arms.

Martin said, "Good work. I'd have lost—"

But Martin was stunned into silence when the servant held the man upright with his left hand and brought his right fist down with all of his power onto the man's head. The servant stood a full head taller than the man he'd been chasing, so the blow effectively hit him on the top of the head, and caused his knees to buckle beneath him. The servant now held the man's full weight with his left arm, not that it mattered. The servant held him up more solidly than the man's own legs had. The servant drew his right arm back again, and hit the man again, this time in the face. He lifted his elbow so that it also hit the man's face as he followed the punch through. Then, he backhanded the man as he drew the arm back to punch him again.

Martin said, "That's enough." The servant took no notice. The man's head lolled back sickeningly as the servant struck him in the face again and again.

Phillip landed next to the servant, and yelled, "He's had enough!" It did nothing to stop the servant from hitting the man several more times. He adjusted his grip to hold the man's head upright, in a convenient punching position, as clearly the man's neck could no longer do the job on its own.

Martin ran forward and stuck his staff between the two men and said, "*Muro*," placing a force field between them. The servant still held the man up with one arm, but the other arm couldn't penetrate the barrier to strike him again, instead stopping as if he had punched a wall.

Martin said, "Let him go."

The servant kept his grip on the man, and felt the force field with his other hand, looking for a hole or a weak spot. Martin noted that for a moment the servant's hand actually left a smear of the other man's blood suspended on the surface of the force field as if it were a sheet of glass.

Martin growled, "I said, let him go. He's unconscious, he's not going anywhere. Let him go."

The servant finished his examination of the force field. He looked at Martin for a moment, smiled, then jerked his left hand in toward his body, smashing the man's face against the other side of the force field. He looked Martin in the eye as he rubbed the man's face into the force field, then, with a smile aimed at Phillip, he released his grip, leaving the man completely without support. With some effort Martin and Phillip caught the man and lowered him gently to the ground. The man had a pulse, but he was out cold, and looking at him, Martin wasn't sure when or even if he would wake up.

Martin was dimly aware of the crowd murmuring and receding away from him. He looked up and saw a clear disk slowly descending from the sky, carrying Brit the Younger and Ida. Gwen flew alongside under her own power. The disk hadn't reached the ground before Ida leapt off, shouting, "Nilo! Thank God you're not hurt!" She ran to her servant and threw her arms around him. Nilo smiled at Martin as he and the president turned and walked away.

Gwen looked down at the man lying unconscious and bloody on the ground. "Is this him?" she asked.

Martin said, "Yes."

Brit asked, "What happened to him?"

Martin glanced toward Nilo's retreating form and said, "He got carried away." Brit and Gwen exchanged a look that conveyed several emotions. Surprise was not one of them.

Brit said, "We have to get him to a doctor," and nobody disagreed. Phillip and Martin placed the man onto the disk. They all piled onto the disk as well, and at Brit's direction, it rose smoothly into the air. As they flew through the central empty volume of Atlantis, traveling as the crow flies to the nearest doctor, Martin shook his head.

"I don't get it," he said. "This is the guy I chased from the roof, and he was the only one up there, but I thought whoever was trying to kill you was using magic to do it. He's not one of the delegates, and there are no male wizards from Atlantis. Maybe we were wrong about the magic."

Brit said, "No, we weren't wrong."

Martin asked, "How do you know?"

Brit frowned and turned to Gwen, saying, "Go ahead. Show them."

Gwen held up the arrow that had been fired at Brit. Gwen held it motionless for a moment, then lightly threw it straight up into the air. It tumbled as it flew upward, then it straightened and flew, as if pulled by a powerful magnet directly at Brit. It struck her in the top of her head and stuck there. Brit winced a bit, and then pulled the arrow away.

Phillip said, "I guess it's a good thing nobody got between you and the arrow."

"Yeah," Martin agreed. "That could have happened really easily, too." Martin turned to Brit. "If we don't figure out who keeps trying to kill you soon, someone could get hurt."

Martin grabbed the arrow from Brit's hand and pulled it a foot away, holding it lightly enough that the razor-sharp tip remained pointed directly at Brit no matter how he moved it. Then, he let it go, and it immediately stuck back to Brit. Martin chuckled and said, "That's really cool."

"Is it?" Brit asked. "Is it really?"

Gwen put a reassuring hand on Brit's shoulder and in a sympathetic voice, said, "It is. Sorry."

19.

The Treasury Department's business generates paperwork, and that paperwork can't just be thrown away; it must be stored. Of course, all businesses generate some paperwork. Many generate enough for it to be worthwhile to hire an outside company to store it all in a secure manner. This approach doesn't work for the Treasury because outside contractors cost more than simply buying the cheapest warehouse in the worst part of town, stuffing it full of boxes of paper, and hiring a guy to guard it. Outside contractors wasted money on things like air conditioning.

The Treasury kept several such warehouses in Los Angeles. Miller and Murphy had visited them on more than one occasion, so they knew what to expect. They pulled up to the massive roll-away door in the beat-up old Ford Fairlane the department had left waiting for them at the rail yard. As instructed, they had waited until dark, and after a brief delay, they sprinted to the car, drove to the warehouse and flashed the headlights, or in the case of this car, the one working headlight, three times. The security guard pushed the door open and let them in. Murphy pulled the car into the warehouse, turned the key, and waited roughly ten seconds for the engine to finally die.

The warehouse was only about one-third full of musty old papers, so there was plenty of room inside to park. Miller,

Murphy, and Jimmy got out of the car. Here in the warehouse was the first chance any of them had gotten to look at the car in the light, and it was a good thing. If they had seen it clearly before, they might not have ridden in it voluntarily. The car gave one the impression that the faded paint was the only thing keeping the patches of rust together.

The security guard looked young and very tired. He shook Agent Murphy's hand enthusiastically. "It's good to finally see you gentlemen."

"Yes," Murphy said, "sorry we're late. Security at the rail yard was heavier than expected. We got cornered and had to hide inside a shipment of sewer pipe until the coast was clear."

The guard released the handshake and walked over toward the corner of the warehouse floor. It was obviously his workstation, as it had a chair, a table, an old boom box, and a walkie-talkie. The rest of the room was nothing but tall shelves covered with boxes full of paper. The guard said, "What's done is done. You're here now. If there's any trouble, just radio the supervisor. He'll send backup." The guard hoisted a backpack up from the floor next to the chair and started toward the door.

Agent Miller said, "Wait a minute, where are you going?"

The guard said, "Home."

Miller said, "Just hold your horses. You're being paid to guard this warehouse."

"Yes," the guard explained. "From five P.M. until one A.M. It is now 1:45. I waited around an extra forty-five minutes for you guys to turn up. You're welcome, by the way, and now I'm going home."

Agent Murphy stepped in to play the peacemaker. "Okay, fair enough, kid. Go get some sleep. Where's your relief?" Murphy pointed toward Jimmy. "We should talk to him about where our associate here is going to sleep."

The guard said, "You're my relief, and unless the table or the floor look comfortable, I'd suggest that he sleep in that car of yours."

"What do you mean?" Miller asked. "We're not your relief. We're federal agents."

The guard said, "Yeah, and the powers that be decided that if two armed federal agents were going to be here guarding a prisoner anyway, then paying for an armed guard just to watch the boxes of paper surrounding the prisoner was a waste of tax-payer money."

Miller said, "We can't stay here. We were supposed to just drop our prisoner off and go home!"

The guard said, "Well, I'm sorry, but there's nobody here to drop your prisoner off with, so you're either going to have to leave him in charge here, or you'll have to stay here with him."

Murphy buried his face in his hands. "Okay, look, Miller, none of this is the kid's fault. He's already put in a full day. It's the middle of the night. I say we let him get out of here."

The guard said a quick thank you and made tracks for the door. Before he'd made his escape, Murphy yelled, "Hey, kid, one last question. Where's the bathroom?"

The guard said, "There's a Porta-John out back."

Agent Miller turned bright red. He yelled, "A Porta-John?! We've spent the last five days living in a boxcar! Our only bathroom was an open door, a four-pack of TP, and a pint of Purell! Now we're back in civilization, and you tell us all we've got to use as a bathroom is a Porta-John?"

The guard shrugged. "Yeah. Sorry." The guard paused, and looked at the hand he'd used to shake with Agent Murphy. "I don't suppose you've got any more of that Purell left, do you?"

┼───═──═┼

In the end, it was decided that one of the agents would stay and keep an eye on Jimmy and the papers while the other went home and got a shower and some sleep. Murphy volunteered to stay for the first watch, because nobody was convinced that Jimmy would survive the night if he was left alone with Agent Miller. Miller called a friend to come get him and take him home so that Murph and Jimmy could use the Fairlane as an emergency means of transportation and as a dormitory. Nine hours later Miller returned in his own car. Murphy and Jimmy left in the Fairlane and went to Murphy's place. Murphy turned off all electronics and they took turns showering and shaving.

Once everyone was clean, rested, and ready, they reconvened at the warehouse. While they were gone, Miller had called in a favor from his brother, so there was now a camper parked in the warehouse. They would still have to leave to shower and buy groceries, but at least Jimmy and whichever agent was taking a turn guarding the place at night could live like civilized people, or, at the very least, like civilized people who were camping.

Now that they had set up housekeeping, they all agreed it was time to get to work. Miller went out and gathered everything on Jimmy's shopping list. He also stopped by the office to pick up a spare computer and to yell at anyone who dared ask him where he'd been.

When he returned, Jimmy and Murphy helped him unload the car. As he hefted the case of canned chili over the lip of the trunk, Jimmy said, "Gentlemen, if all goes according to plan, this should all be over very soon."

"All this crap is going to help you prove how all these people have been embezzling money and then disappearing for all these years?" Agent Miller asked, carefully placing the telescope and tripod on the floor next to the chili.

"Yes," Jimmy said, returning to the car's trunk for the last bit of equipment. As he rummaged in the ancient car's enormous trunk, he said, "You two set up the computer. It'll need to be connected to the Internet. Will we need to have someone come and install that?"

Murphy said, "No, I can tether it to my phone. It won't be a fast connection, but it'll work."

Jimmy came up from his expedition to the bottom of the trunk with a roll of kite string and a large red scented candle. Jimmy read the bottom of the candle. "Cinnamon and holly berry. A little Christmassy, don't you think?"

Miller replied, "It was on clearance," daring Jimmy to push the issue further.

Jimmy, wisely said, "Fair enough." He tucked the candle and the string under his arm and ripped open the plastic around the case of chili, picking up two cans. He started toward the camper, saying, "You two tell me when you have the Internet up and running."

"Yeah, will do, boss," Agent Miller said, "and just what are you going to be doing while we're out here working?"

Jimmy said, "I'll be heating up the chili," as he disappeared into the camper.

An hour later everything was set up. Agent Murphy was disappointed in himself that he hadn't figured out Jimmy's plan
earlier, but Agent Miller was disappointed in Jimmy that he'd
thought of the whole cockamamie thing in the first place, so it
all balanced out.

Miller and Murphy sat at the table with the computer
between them. Miller held an empty chili can. The can had a
hole punched in the bottom, and the string, which was coated in
holiday-scented wax, stretched one hundred feet to the far end
of the warehouse, where Jimmy sat in a lawn chair with the other
empty can, the telescope perched on its tripod in front of him,
and a steaming hot bowl of chili resting in his lap.

Jimmy heard some noise emanate from the can, but he
couldn't make it out. He shouted into the can, "You have to hold
the string tight and enunciate clearly!" He said it loud enough
that the agents could probably hear him without the can.

Agent Miller pulled the string so tight that it nearly came out
of Jimmy's hand. Jimmy put his ear to the can, and heard Agent
Miller shout, "I said, this can smells like chili!"

Jimmy put his mouth to the can and said, "Yes, that's why I
specified a scented candle. Most of it is still in the camper if you
want to light it up."

Jimmy took a spoonful of chili and watched the two men in
the distance talk, then felt the line stretch tight again. He put his
ear to the can.

"All right," the distant, tinny voice of Agent Miller said,
"Murph says he's tapped into Xerox's system. You know, you told
us that what that Banks kid and all the rest of you did wasn't
illegal. Well, I got news for you—Murph has already broken
about a dozen laws just to get to this point."

Jimmy said, "I didn't say it was legal, I said it wasn't illegal, and I was referring to the way he got his money, not the things he did to find out how to get the money. Besides, the way I'm showing you isn't the exact way he learned about this. It's the way I did."

Jimmy watched the screen through his telescope and sent directions through the cans-and-string telephone to help Agent Murphy navigate through the long-disused vestiges of Xerox's computer system. They went down many a blind alley as Jimmy tried to guide their way from memory. Jimmy surprised himself on more than one occasion by remembering seemingly nonsensical commands and near-random strings of characters needed to make the ancient UNIX system do what he wanted. Finally, after hours of searching, they found their way to the directory that Jimmy needed. He had dreamed of this moment, plotted, schemed, and worked toward this moment for thirty years, and now, through his cheap telescope, he could see the directory there on the screen, exactly as he remembered it.

The directory held one file, which was named *repository1-c.txt*.

Jimmy took his eye away from the telescope and said into the can, "Open the file."

Jimmy heard Agent Miller say, "He's opening it."

After a second, Miller said, "Okay."

Jimmy closed his eyes. A single tear rolled down his cheek. It was the happiest moment of his life.

Agent Miller asked, "Okay, Jimmy, what's the password?"

Jimmy's eyes snapped open. "What do you mean, password? The file isn't password protected!"

"I don't know what to tell you," Miller said. "It's asking for a password."

Jimmy looked through the telescope.

At the table, Agent Miller had his ear to the can. Agent Murphy asked, "So does he know the password, or not?"

Miller shushed his partner and listened intently to the can. Finally, Miller said, "He says you must have opened the wrong file."

"There's only one file in the directory."

"I know. He says he's watching this time, and you should close it and try again."

Murphy closed the password window and left the screen displaying the directory for a moment, so Jimmy could get a good look through his telescope. Then Murphy typed in the command to open the file, and the password dialog box opened, just as it had before.

Agent Miller put his ear to the can. Even without the can, Murphy could hear that Jimmy was speaking, and that he did not sound happy. A smile slowly spread across Agent Miller's lips.

"What's he saying?" Agent Murphy asked.

Miller shushed Murphy again. He continued listening, his smile growing wider.

When he couldn't stand it anymore, Murphy asked again, "What's he saying?"

Miller smiled and said, "Nothing useful." He kept his ear rooted firmly to the can.

"Then why are you listening to him?" Murphy asked.

Agent Miller said, "It's not often I get to listen to somebody else get this angry."

20.

Phillip paced around their quarters in Atlantis. Martin watched Phillip pace.

The day had started with an attempt on Brit's life and had managed to go downhill from there.

They had apprehended a suspect, but he was unconscious, so they took him to the doctor, a sorceress named Louiza from 2011 who had found the file hiding in her hospital's database.

Louiza woke the man up with some smelling salts, but he was no help. He claimed that he had simply been spending some time on the roof, taking an unsanctioned break from his duties as a masseur, when he saw the arrow materialize out of nowhere and zip away at high speed. He went to the edge of the roof to see where it went, and that's when everyone saw him.

It wasn't really a surprise. The arrow had been enchanted (a.k.a., programmed) to home in on Brit the Younger, and the man who had fled in a panic from Martin then been beaten senseless by Nilo clearly couldn't have done that. Also, the fact that he'd had no bow had puzzled Martin, though he chose not to dwell on it at the time.

It was frustrating. They had captured the suspect and he not only couldn't give them any answers, he had provided them with more questions.

The day's summit meetings were largely a discussion of the treatment of non-time travelers, the centerpiece of which was a lengthy presentation by Gwen, detailing the abuses Jimmy had perpetrated on the people of Medieval England in an effort to turn it into some sort of enchanted wonderland. That should have interested Phillip, since Jimmy had then moved on to trying to abuse Phillip and everyone Phillip cared about, but he'd been far too preoccupied to pay attention. He was worried about Brit the Younger's safety. It wouldn't have been so bad if everyone else had been as concerned as he was, but he knew they weren't; they didn't totally believe that whoever was trying to kill her could possibly succeed. Gwen was concerned mostly because the attempts were upsetting her friend. Martin was not convinced that there was any danger, but was helping just in case, and because he was Martin and liked some action. Even Brit the Younger hadn't totally bought into his reasoning that she was truly in danger. That left Phillip sitting in a huge room full of bored people, slowly going out of his mind.

At one of the recesses, Martin and Phillip had attempted to confront the president's servant, Nilo. They chose to wait until President Ida was not around. They approached him in the hallway.

They decided to start gently. Martin said, "Hey, Nilo. I just wanted to say that it was really impressive how you ran that guy down today."

Nilo nodded. Martin wasn't sure if he was acknowledging the compliment, or simply agreeing with it.

Martin continued. "When you caught him, did you have to be so violent about it?"

"Yes."

Phillip said, "You nearly beat the guy to death."

"You're welcome."

Martin and Phillip gaped at him, but before they could formulate a response, Ida joined the conversation. "Hello, gentlemen. What are we talking about?"

Nilo smiled and said, "Nothing. These two sorcerers were thanking me for helping them catch the man who tried to kill Brit the Younger."

"That's very nice," Ida said, "but really, *you* helped *them*? It seems to me it was more the other way around."

Nilo said, "True. They were helpful. If . . ." he looked at Martin. "I'm sorry, what was your name again?"

"Martin."

"If Martin hadn't stepped in, I probably would have had to chase the man quite a bit farther before I caught him."

For Phillip, the afternoon passed in a paranoid blur, followed by dinner with Martin and Gwen. They discussed their ideas about who was behind it all, which would have been great if the discussion had consisted of something more than all three of them repeatedly announcing that they had no idea.

Now Phillip was in his quarters pacing, running out the clock on a profoundly unsatisfying day, and Martin was watching him do it. Whether or not Martin found that at all satisfying, Phillip couldn't say.

Phillip walked to one end of the room and examined the arrow that had been fired at Brit. She hadn't wanted it, so Martin had grabbed it, explaining that it was cool. As soon as they got it back to their quarters, Martin tried to put it on the table, and predictably it slid off the table, across the floor, to the wall, and into the corner, where it sat now, presumably pointing toward Brit's the Younger's apartment.

Phillip tried to put the arrow out of his mind. He turned around and walked to the far side of the room. He looked out into the ocean, which was hard to avoid, as one entire wall of the room was a window directly into the sea. He looked out into what would have been a mass of solid black at this time of night if not for a school of fish that swam by, visible in the light from their room.

Phillip thought back to the day before, when he and Brit had gone out in that submersible and nearly been killed. He remembered how he had put off leaving until the last second in hopes of saving her life, just to have her save his instead. He grimaced and turned around, walking back to the far end of the room. The arrow was still there, pointing to wherever Brit was. He pictured her in danger, then quickly tried to put the image out of his mind. He replaced it with the image of Brit safe in her bed. He quickly tried to put that image out of his mind. Finally he announced that he was going to go check on Brit.

Martin offered to come along, but Phillip didn't hear him, since the door was already swinging shut behind him.

Phillip rang Brit's doorbell. After a moment, Nik opened the door, smiling.

"Hello, Phillip," Nik said. "I expected we'd see you this evening. Please come in."

Phillip entered and found Brit's living room empty. Nik explained, "Brit's had a rough few days. She decided to go to bed early."

"Oh," Phillip said, "look, I don't want to disturb her. If you'd told me I'd have just left a message. You said she was expecting me."

Nik said, "I said I was expecting you. Don't worry. She's still reading. I'll go get her. Please make yourself comfortable."

Phillip sat uncomfortably on the front edge of a chair. He heard Nik walk down the hall and knock on a door. Brit said, "What do you need, Nik?"

"Phillip's here." Phillip could hear the smile in Nik's voice.

Brit said, "Oh! Oh, um . . . tell him I'll be right there."

Nik leaned around the corner from the hall, smiled at Phillip for a long moment, then said, "She'll be right out." Almost that instant, Phillip heard a door open, and Brit the Younger emerged around the corner.

"Here she is now," Nik said. "Before I go, can I get either of you a drink?"

Brit and Phillip both said no. Phillip feared that if Nik smiled any harder his face would fold in half. Nik excused himself. The door to his room closed with a purposeful click.

Brit stepped from the entryway out into the room. She was dressed for comfort, not for having people see her. She wore a sweatshirt that had a drawing of an attractive woman in a skintight red and black court jester costume and clown makeup. Lettering beneath the drawing identified the clown as *Harley Quinn*, which meant nothing to Phillip. The fact that the sweatshirt was oversized and hung off of her left shoulder meant quite a bit to him. Beneath the sweatshirt she wore a pair of cotton shorts and heavy wool socks, pushed down around the ankles. She took a couple of steps forward into the room and stopped when Phillip met her halfway.

Phillip said, "I just wanted to check up on you. You know, see how you're doing."

Brit chuckled lightly and looked away. "That's sweet. Thank you, Phillip. Please, sit." She motioned toward the couch. Phillip sat as directed, and she sat next to him.

"I'm glad you came by," she said. "You never really told me what happened in your meeting with the Elder."

"There was nothing to tell. I didn't have anything to say that she didn't already know, and she didn't have anything to tell me at all, or at least that she was willing to tell me." Phillip chose not to share Brit the Elder's comments about the Younger's attitude and future.

Brit said, "So she knows that someone's trying to kill me."

"Yes."

"And she knows who it is and how they're going to try in the future."

"So she says."

"And, of course, she's not going to tell us any of it."

Phillip shook his head. "She won't. She says she can't now, because she didn't before."

"Yeah, I've heard that song and dance. It doesn't seem to occur to her that maybe she didn't before because she won't now."

Phillip said, "I can see why you find her so aggravating."

Brit put a hand on Phillip's shoulder. "Thanks. I'm glad someone does. Everyone else loves her."

"You too," Phillip blurted.

Brit looked at him sideways. "You think I love her too?"

Phillip did think that, just a bit, but he was not nearly dumb enough to say so. "No, I'm saying that they love you too. They all believe that you're the same person, so, yes, they do love her, but they love you too."

"What do you think of her?" Brit asked, looking intently at Phillip, waiting for his answer.

Phillip said, "Free will is a really big deal to me, Brit. When I was a child, my parents tried to raise me in the church like they'd been raised, but it didn't work out. I could never accept the idea that God was all-knowing, all-powerful, had created us, and yet sent us tests. I couldn't see a logical way for him not to already know how we'd react, and when I asked the priests and my parents to explain it, all I ever got was, 'The Lord works in mysterious ways.' So I couldn't embrace their faith, and instead I embraced free will. I fell in love with the idea that nobody knows what anybody's going to do next, not even God. I'm the captain of my own destiny, and while I can't control what happens to me, I'm in total control of how I react to what happens to me."

Brit said, "And then you found the file."

"Then I found the file," Phillip said, "and it said that I was just a subroutine in a larger program. It bothered me at first, but then I realized that it changed nothing. As long as a certain amount of randomness and self-determination are built into the Phillip subroutine, I still have free will. Then I went back in time, and found that nothing I did had any effect on the future. Some took that to mean that everything we did had already been done before we were born, but I took it as proof that we had been forked off into a new branch of the program."

"A whole new future, there for you to create," Brit said. She instantly saw the appeal.

"Exactly. The ultimate expression of free will. A future that is ours to mess up. Of course, I won't be able to prove this until I live to see the year 1985 again. If it's different from the 1985 I came from and can now visit, it'll prove what Martin calls my

'Big Fork Theory.' Until then, it's a matter of faith. And that's how things stood for many years. I'd gotten pretty secure in my beliefs. Then I came here."

"And you met me."

Phillip smiled. "Yes, I met you." His voice lowered, his eyes narrowed, and he said, "And I met her. To everyone else she's just you, many years later. To you, she's a constant thorn in your side. To me, she is a living, breathing refutation of my most cherished beliefs. It would be one thing to take a committed atheist and tell him that there is a God, but imagine if you could introduce him to God, and they drank Hi-C together. Would the atheist find religion, or would he find reasons to disbelieve the evidence of his own eyes? And which of those reactions would be correct?"

"You must hate her."

Quickly and emphatically, Phillip said, "No. I don't hate her. I can't. She didn't do anything to me. She just exists. I'm the one torturing myself, not her. Other people can just accept that they don't know things and get on with their lives, and I can too, about a lot of things, but not this."

Brit squeezed Phillip's hand.

Phillip said, "Besides, I couldn't hate her. When I look at her, I see you." There was a long pause, then Phillip added, "There's a bit of a resemblance."

They both laughed, harder than the joke really deserved. They went on to discuss many things—their childhoods, their families, their taste in music. All the things people discuss when they're saying anything but what's actually on their minds. The hour got late. Phillip did not go back to his and Martin's quarters that night.

Despite physical appearances, Brit and Phillip were both middle-aged mentally, and this was not the first time either of them had slept over with someone. It was the first time they had slept over with each other, and later they'd both remember it the way most people remember a first of this type: as having been absolutely wonderful, and technically, not that great.

21.

For practical reasons, prisons are often built in areas that will naturally discourage escape. Some prisons are too far from civilization for inmates to realistically ever return from, like Devil's Island. Some are close to civilization, but located in a place that makes attempts at escape a form of suicide, like Alcatraz. Some of the most feared prisons are located both far from civilization and in a life-threatening environment.

After a long conversation followed by a long flight followed by a long drive, Agent Murphy parked his rental car in the parking lot of the most secret prison on U.S. soil, near the southern tip of Florida.

To many it would seem counterintuitive to place an ultra-high-security secret prison in Florida. After all, the two impressions most people share of Florida is that it is a palm tree-infested family vacation destination and that it is the criminal's natural habitat. Murphy himself had expressed surprise when he was told where he was going and why.

After Jimmy's attempts to direct Agents Miller and Murphy into the mysterious file that was now mysteriously password protected, Jimmy had scoured his notes trying to recall everything he knew about how every other person who had accessed the file had done it. It seems that a popular pastime amongst those who found the file was sharing stories about how they found the file. Jimmy said that during his time in exile he had written down what he remembered, and using his notes and his increasingly hazy memories, they had managed to find twelve more copies of the file, all of which were password protected.

After they had followed every lead in his notes, Jimmy lapsed into a deep funk, sullenly pacing around the warehouse for two days, muttering to himself. Miller and Murphy had decided that Jimmy had been a costly and embarrassing dead end, and were about to pull the plug when Jimmy ran into the camper shouting like a crazy person. He said that someone they'd never heard of, named Phillip, had clearly put up the passwords on every copy of the file he knew about to keep him out. At first, Murphy thought this was just more reason to give up, but then Jimmy said that there was one person who had never told anyone where he found the file, another person they'd never heard of named Todd Douglas. Jimmy said Todd should be easy to find, as he was fairly certain that Todd would be in prison.

They searched for a prisoner named Todd Douglas and hit a brick wall. They learned that Douglas existed, and was "in the system," so to speak, but they didn't have high enough security clearance for any information beyond that. Murphy had to kiss a lot of backsides and Miller had to yell a lot of threats. On a few occasions, they had to do both at the same time, to the same person, but after three days of sustained phone action they finally got clearance for one of them to come to this secret federal facility and meet with the infamous Todd Douglas.

The phone call came in the middle of the night. It was Murphy's turn to sleep at home in his own bed while Miller guarded Jimmy, so it was Murphy whose phone worked. The voice on the other end of the line said that he was a high-ranking official in the federal corrections system, and would give Murphy the clearance to meet with Todd at a top-secret federal prison in Florida.

Murphy expressed surprise that there was a secret prison in such a popular and populous state, but the mysterious voice explained that Florida was the perfect location for a secret prison. "You might think that out in the desert in Nevada or New Mexico would be better, but the problem with putting a prison in the middle of nowhere is that you then have to ship the prisoners, the guards, and their supplies out to the middle of nowhere. That costs money. The beauty of Florida is that it's a thoroughly hostile environment with well-established supply routes and a surplus of people for whom *prison guard* sounds like an attractive career opportunity."

"But Florida's not very wide," Murphy said. "You're never that far from an interstate. An escapee could be two states away by nightfall."

The voice on the phone said, "If a prisoner did manage to escape, they'd have a choice. Face the swamp, or travel through towns.

"If they choose the swamp," he continued, "they get to deal with alligators that are dangerous enough to kill and eat a man, and snakes dangerous enough to kill him without eating him, which if you think about it is kind of a bigger insult. It's bad enough to die, but it would be worse to also go to waste."

Murphy said that he agreed, although he wasn't sure that he did.

The voice on the phone continued. "If the escapee stuck to well-traveled roadways and towns, they'd face an even greater danger. Floridians. Law-abiding Floridians suspect that any stranger they meet might be a violent criminal. They trust nobody, and they call the police at the drop of a hat. To a Floridian, 911 is like an electronic lottery ticket. If they report you and you turn out to be a wanted felon, they might get a reward. If they report you and you're not wanted, they still get to watch you get questioned by the police. The only way to lose is to not be the first person to call the cops. It's a race to see who can dial 911 the fastest, and the prize for second place is a ride in a squad car."

Murphy wasn't buying it. "I'm not sure—"

"Don't interrupt," the disembodied voice on the phone said, interrupting him. Just because Murphy wasn't buying it didn't mean the voice had to stop selling it. "And furthermore, if that's how dangerous the law-abiding citizens are, you can imagine how treacherous the criminals would be. There's no honor among thieves, and even less among Floridians. If a criminal finds an escaped convict, they see the perfect victim. They can rob him of whatever he's managed to steal with impunity, because what's he going to do, call the police? And if he hasn't managed to steal any money, clothes, or a car yet, you can just befriend him, help him steal all of those things, then take them yourself later. Agent Murphy, if I escaped from a prison in south Florida, I'd try to swim to Cuba. At least sharks play fair and the communists are up front about taking everything you own."

This was a lot to absorb at 3:00 A.M., and Agent Murphy had almost forgotten what they were talking about in the first place. The voice reminded him, telling him that he was to report alone to the front gate of the prison at 3:00 P.M. eastern time in two days, and that he'd be allowed to meet with the prisoner, Todd Douglas, for exactly twenty minutes.

Murphy, Miller, and Jimmy scrambled to make a plan, then they scrambled to execute it. By the time they were done, Murphy barely had time to make it to his flight. The Treasury had approved the expenditure to pay for his travel, but, as always, they made the arrangements with an eye toward saving their money, not his time. There are direct flights from Los Angeles to Miami, but Agent Murphy's itinerary had three legs and layovers in Minneapolis and Seattle (because fate has a sense of humor), before landing in Jacksonville, at the far end of the state from where he needed to be. Agent Murphy told his supervisor that this was a massive waste of his time. His supervisor replied that Agent Murphy was paid a salary, so his time was the agency's to waste.

The flights were awful, and the drive had been worse. Several times he had driven through swarms of black insects that died in such large numbers, and in such a gruesome fashion, that it made it impossible to see through the windshield. Every rest area and gas station had lines of bug-splattered cars waiting to use a hose. The first time he stopped to clean the car had been seriously unpleasant. The nose of his silver rental car looked like it had been scorched during reentry, but the black streaks weren't burn marks, they were bug corpses. The car reeked of death. He used the dirtiest squeegee he'd ever seen to clean as much of the windshield as he could without throwing up. He got back in the car, got back on the freeway, and within fifteen minutes drove through another swarm that obscured his vision all over again.

By the time he reached his destination, Agent Murphy longed for his days in the boxcar full of squeaky toys, but he made it. Murphy thought he was going to see a prison, but when he arrived he found a perfectly mundane, if over-sized industrial park. The front of the closest building was a long row of office entrances. He saw an unbroken line of tinted windows, tinted glass doors, and uninspiring signs with names like *Fan-rific Industrial Venting Solutions*, and logos that were capital letters tilted to the side to look like they were moving quickly, or leaning over, partially melted in the Florida heat, which seemed more likely. The building had probably been beige at first, but prolonged exposure to the Florida sun had left it a dirty eggshell color. Behind the one-story office fronts there were larger two-story structures that looked like the standard industrial park storage/workshop/loading dock, multi-use business space. The whole property was surrounded by a cyclone fence topped with vicious-looking razor wire.

Murphy drove up to the security booth, where a dull-eyed old man in a faded uniform slouched on a stool, watching a small TV. Murphy sat in his idling car, trying to ignore the oppressive heat and the smell of baked bug guts rising off of his car in almost visible waves. The guard glanced at Agent Murphy without turning his head. He sighed, then slid the window open so he could talk to this man who had the audacity to interrupt his stories.

The security guard said, "Wadja want?"

Murphy held up his badge and said, "I'm Agent Duane Murphy from the U.S. Department of the Treasury. I have an appointment."

The guard nodded, then looked down at a clipboard on the shelf next to his TV. His finger trailed down the document, then stopped sharply. The guard sat straight up, turned crisply to Agent Murphy, and smiled. He instantly seemed ten years younger and twenty pounds lighter.

The guard said, "We're expecting you, Agent Murphy. Come right in. Warden Brookes is waiting at the visitors' entrance. It's the fourth door down, labeled *My Shirt-List Novelty Tees*." He slid the window closed and raised the orange and white striped arm so Murphy could enter.

Murphy found the door. The logo was a drawing of a T-shirt with a capital T in an overly decorative font. He parked, got out of the car, and pushed the car door closed with one finger, pressing on one of the few surfaces of the car that wasn't streaked with sticky dried bug juice.

Murphy walked into the nondescript office entrance and was shocked at what he found inside: exactly what you'd expect.

A dropped-tile ceiling and fluorescent lights hung above off-white stucco walls and low-pile, high-traffic carpet. A metal faux wood grain desk and a black plastic desk chair were the only furnishings. The desk was covered with paperwork, a red stapler, and a black multiline phone. The only other door was behind the desk. It looked to be hollow core, and probably weighed about eight ounces. It had a cheap, shiny brass doorknob. The room reeked of dust and failure, which was better than humidity and dead bugs, but only a little.

Murphy had been inside less than five seconds when the door swung open. A man in a beautifully tailored black pinstriped suit entered. He was average height with thinning black hair. He looked like the kind of man who would play the president in a 1950s movie about giant wasps. He stepped forward, thrust out his hand, and said, "Agent Murphy, I'm Warden Brooks. Welcome to The Facility."

Murphy shook his hand, and asked, "It certainly is quite a . . . facility. I just realized that nobody's ever told me what this place is called."

Warden Brooks said, "I just told you, Agent Murphy. It's called *The Facility*."

"Yes, I understand that that's what you call it, but what's its official name?"

Warden Brooks smiled, but clearly had been through this conversation many times before, and derived no pleasure from it. "This facility's name, Agent Murphy, is The Facility. Any time anybody refers to The Facility in any capacity, official or unofficial, they refer to it as The Facility."

"What kind of name is that?"

"The kind that confuses people and makes them sound either stupid or crazy. It is, in short, the perfect name for this kind of . . . facility. Please follow me." With that, Warden Brooks walked out through the flimsy door he had used to enter. Murphy followed.

The cheap door led from the shabby office to a crummy hall. One side of the hall held two more faux-veneer hollow-core doors and too-shiny doorknobs. One had a drab brown plastic sign that said *Men*; the other had a similar sign that said *Ladies*.

Warden Brooks walked to the unmarked door at the end of the hall, but paused before opening it. "You need to use the restroom?"

Murphy said, "No."

"Good. We deliberately keep those bathrooms dirty and short of toilet paper. We must keep up appearances." The warden led Murphy onward through the door. Every characteristic changed. The hard carpeting was replaced with slightly softer-looking concrete floors. The stucco was displaced with painted cinderblock. The suspended acoustic ceiling was now exposed metal trusses and ductwork. The design aesthetic had changed from the kind of cheap that falls apart immediately to the kind of cheap that lasts forever.

The warden walked quickly and talked at the same pace, forcing Murphy to struggle physically and mentally to keep up. They passed through an endless maze of identical concrete walls and steel doors, interspersed with the occasional staircase and wrought-iron gate controlled by people in uniforms protected behind thick impact-resistant glass. Murphy never got a good look at any of these people, because they never stopped walking. The gates swung open before the warden arrived. They did this with such reliability that a few times Murphy thought Brooks was going to walk face first into the bars, but the bars always got out of the way before that happened.

"The Facility was created at an undisclosed point in the past," the warden said, "for an agency that is classified, by a president who shall remain nameless." He barely turned his head to the side to speak to Murphy as he walked. "The purpose of The Facility is to house the nation's most problematic prisoners."

"By problematic, you mean violent and dangerous," Agent Murphy said, finally feeling like he was getting a handle on the situation.

Warden Brooks said, "No. I said 'problematic,' and that's what I meant. The prison system doesn't consider violence much of a problem. They deal with it all the time. If prisons had a problem dealing with violence, the prisoners would just fight their way out of prison and we'd all have a problem, and violence, before too long. No. We get the prisoners that nobody else knows what to do with. Take your man, Todd Douglas. Do you know what he did to get here?"

Murphy didn't know, as it happened. He took a wild guess, based on his knowledge of Jimmy's other associates. "Embezzling?"

The warden laughed. "You're a Treasury agent, that's right. It's all embezzlement and tax evasion to you guys. Well, he might have embezzled too, but what got him here was killing a man.

The victim was his boss at one of those strip mall video game stores. Do you know how he killed him?"

"No, I don't."

"Yeah, well, neither do we. Well, we do, but we don't. That's one of the things that makes your guy problematic. We know what he did, and we know why, but we can't explain *how* he actually did it."

Murphy was lost. "How's that work? If you know he killed the guy, you have to be able to explain how."

"He made all of the atoms in his boss's body lose their molecular bonds at the same time. Can you explain how he did that? Is that something the Treasury deals with routinely? No, I didn't think so."

"If you don't know how he did it, how can you know that he did it?"

"Because he had a beef with his boss, because he tried to evade capture, and because of all the people who worked at the video game store inside a mall in Phoenix, in August, he was the only one who came to work wearing galoshes."

Murphy said, "Ick."

The warden nodded. "Damn straight, ick. The entire carpet was destroyed, every square inch of it. Whole thing got confiscated by the government for study. It's probably rolled up and sitting next to the Ark of the Covenant by now."

Murphy said, "If he's that dangerous, I can see why they'd send him to a place like this."

The warden shook his head. "No, you're making too many assumptions. We don't know how he liquefied that guy, but we've seen no evidence that he can still do it. We've had him here for six years, and he hasn't hurt a fly. Mr. Douglas is here for two reasons. One is that we can't explain what he did, how he escaped capture at first, or how he was captured in the end. The police got called and they immediately started questioning him. He was pretty cocky until they started asking about the galoshes, then he got nervous. He excused himself, went into a restroom that had no exits beyond the one door the cops were guarding, and he never came out."

"That's something," Murphy said. He chose not to share the story about how Martin Banks had disappeared right before his eyes.

The warden continued. "Yeah, well the weird part was at that exact moment, he turns up in the lobby of Phoenix City Hall, stark naked and hog-tied, and get this, his hair was longer and he had a beard."

Jimmy hadn't told Murphy much about this Todd character. He now suspected he was going to have a long conversation with Jimmy about him. For now, Murphy just said, "That's pretty weird, all right."

"Yeah, well, you should be grateful," Warden Brooks said. "The only reason we're letting you see the little weasel is that we're hoping that it will lead to some answers."

Murphy chose not to comment. Instead he changed the subject. "You said there were two reasons he's here."

"Yeah, you'll see."

The two men walked in silence through a few more twists and turns of the corridor. Murphy hoped the warden would lead him back out, or else he'd never find his way to daylight again, and might end up just getting a job there. Finally they rounded the last corner and approached the last gate. Where Murphy would have expected to see another electronically actuated lock, the gate was instead held fast with a very large, very old-looking mechanical lock. Several feet before the gate a guard sat on a stool, guarding a single, oversized key that hung from a spike driven into the mortar between the cinderblocks in the wall.

Murphy got the pleasure of surprising the warden with his lack of surprise. "Oh, his magnetic field is the other thing, eh?"

The warden scowled. "You knew about that?"

Agent Murphy said, "Yes." They eyeballed each other for a moment. It was clear that there was a battle for dominance going on, and that up until a second ago, Warden Brooks was certain he was winning. Murphy, as was his way, had won the whole game by pretending not to play until the last few seconds.

Agent Murphy had walked into this meeting knowing exactly two things about Todd beyond his name. He withheld the information about the magnetic field until after Warden Brooks shared a great deal of new information, and in doing so, gave the impression that he already knew much of what Brooks had told him, and had been humoring him. The other thing Agent Murphy knew he had already decided he could never share, because he didn't really believe it. Jimmy had told him that Todd had traveled in time to the distant past and had been rejected and sent back by Jimmy and all of the other time travelers.

The warden grumbled under his breath as he removed his watch and cell phone, placing them on a small table next to the locked gate. Murphy did the same. When all electronic devices were safely removed, the guard opened the gate and let them through.

The cinderblock hallway that stretched on beyond the gate was structurally identical to the hallway before, but felt entirely different. The overhead fluorescent light fixtures were dark.

Instead, bare incandescent light bulbs hung from the ceiling at regular intervals. Their cords stretched up to the ceiling, where they looked to have been hastily stapled in place. The cords led to the wall, then down to the floor, then back, along the floorboards and through the gate they'd just passed, finally terminating in a cheap power strip plugged into the wall outlet. The hanging lights were dimmer than the fluorescents, and swung slightly in the breeze, making the shadows wobble unnervingly.

Their footsteps echoed as the warden walked down the hall and around the corner. Murphy followed, and finally laid eyes on Todd Douglas.

Murphy saw a prison cell. The only furniture was a toilet and a bed. The only light came from more poorly hung light bulbs dangling outside the cell, well beyond the prisoner's reach.

The back wall of the cell was stacked from the floor to about waist-height with books, most of them so thin as to barely qualify as anything more than a magazine. A man in an orange jumpsuit sat on the bed, reading a skinny book with a glossy cover. The back of the book had a drawing of a little girl and a man in a diving suit.

The warden barked, "Douglas, get up. You have a visitor."

The prisoner slammed the book shut and turned to face Agent Murphy. He had a weak chin, a strong nose, dark hair, and bright eyes. Todd rose to his feet. His movements were slow, but his eyes darted around, taking in every detail of his visitors so voraciously that Agent Murphy almost felt violated.

Todd grabbed the bars of his cell and leaned forward, almost placing his head between the bars, as if trying to get as close to the other two men as possible. "Hello, I'm Todd Douglas. Thank you for coming to visit me."

Murphy stood tall and said, "I'm not here for pleasure, Mr. Douglas."

"Oh, but having you here is a pleasure for me," the prisoner said. "I see some of the guards every day, and I see Warden Brooks here about once a month, but other than that I never get any visitors. What's your name?"

"I'm Agent Murphy. I'm with the Department of the Treasury." Murphy produced his badge. Todd read every word engraved on it.

When he was finished Todd asked, "Do you play video games?"

"Not since I was in college."

"Oh, that's a shame. They've gotten so good! They're doing amazing things these days. The standards for the graphics have gotten so high, even the worst games look great, so they've had to start getting more creative with the story."

Murphy looked down at the thin booklet Todd had been reading when he entered, which was lying on the bed. It was indeed the strategy guide for a game called Bioshock 2. Todd saw where he was looking and said, "The Bioshock games are a good example. At first glance you might think it's just a game where you run around shooting people, but there's a lot more to do than that."

Murphy was trying to make sense of the image on the cover, which was a city, a whale, and a man in a diving suit with a drill for an arm. While pondering this, he absentmindedly said, "Is there?"

"Oh yeah!" Todd enthused. "There's a ton of ways to kill people in that game other than just shooting them. You can beat them, you can electrocute them, you can set them on fire. You can blow them up, you can throw them across the room with your mind, you can have them stung to death by bees. There's all kinds of ways to kill people."

"In the video game," Murphy said.

"Yeah," Todd said. "Just like in real life."

Murphy asked, "Do you enjoy killing people . . . in video games, Todd?"

Todd's expression soured. "I used to. I haven't been able to play any for a long time." Todd motioned to the giant stack of magazines. "I read the strategy guides, but it's not the same."

The warden cleared his throat, which Murphy interpreted as a signal to get on to business. Murphy said, "Mr. Douglas."

Todd interrupted, saying, "You can call me Todd."

The warden said, "No, he can't."

Murphy started again. "Mr. Douglas, I've brought you a message." He reached into his inside pocket and produced a sealed envelope. Todd's eyes followed the envelope.

"Who's it from?" Todd asked.

Murphy silently turned the envelope around so that Todd could see where Jimmy had written "Merlin" in the fanciest script he could muster with a number-two pencil.

Todd's expression changed instantly from a smile to a snarl. "What does he want?"

Murphy handed him the letter. "Read it and find out." Murphy hadn't told the warden about the letter. It wouldn't have made sense to the warden if he had.

Todd snatched the letter away before the warden had a chance to object, retreating to the back of his cell. He scowled as he tore the envelope open. He unfolded the letter and started reading, his lips moving slightly as he did so. He laughed bitterly, then he cursed, then continued reading in silence. When he finished the letter, he closed his eyes and clenched his fists, crumpling the letter in the process. Then he smoothed out the letter and read it again. When he'd finished the second read through, he turned to Agent Murphy.

"You got a pen and paper?"

Agent Murphy reached into his pocket and produced a notepad and a pen, which he clicked open.

Todd said, "You write this down, 'cause I'm only going to say it once."

22.

Phillip opened his eyes and saw a sideways landscape of unfamiliar pillows in the foreground, an unfamiliar wall in the background, and Brit the Younger's sleeping face in between. He took a moment to collect his thoughts. As his brain booted up, he replayed the previous night in his memory. When he was done, he went back and replayed a couple of his favorite bits a couple of times.

Pleasant though the past was, Phillip knew it was time to deal with the present. He looked at Brit and reflected on the fact that the present seemed pretty nice too. The future, however, was a minefield.

If I get up and leave, he thought, *I'm the selfish guy who got what he wanted and ran. If I stick around, I'm the clingy guy who overstayed his welcome. I'd better decide what to do fast, or else she'll wake up and I'll be the creepy guy who was watching her sleep with a worried look on his face.*

What Phillip needed was a distraction, something that would wake her up, and hold her attention through the awkward, *Hey, why is Phillip here, oh that's right,* phase of the morning. Phillip knew that his staff was nearby, and he might be able to magic up a diversion, but in order for that to work, he'd have to put on his robe and hat, and he especially didn't want her to wake up and find him getting dressed. Besides, all of the spells that he could think of to use as a distraction were sort of a dead giveaway. He pictured himself saying, *Ha, look at that, Brit, a six-foot pillar of flame here in your bedroom, for no reason. That's something, isn't it? Oh, and now it's gone. So, how did you sleep?*

Phillip felt despair. Then he felt anger at himself for being the guy that wakes up in bed with a beautiful woman and has it cause him despair. He rolled onto his back and resigned himself to wait for the inevitable awkwardness when Brit awoke. He looked at the ceiling for a few moments, then the door swung open.

Nik swept into the room with a tray of food and a glass of some sort of juice. "Good morning," he said, as he walked around to Phillip's side of the bed. Phillip sat up and Nik placed the tray on his lap.

"Good morning, Nik," Phillip said, grateful, not just for the food, but also for a far better distraction than he could have imagined. The plate on his tray contained eggs and some sort of fried meat. Phillip hadn't realized he was hungry until he saw the food, and now he could think of little else. He turned to look at Brit, and found her bleary-eyed but awake, and pulling herself into a seated position.

Nik said, "Don't go anywhere. Now that our guest has been served, I'll be right back with yours."

Brit and Phillip smiled at each other and said good morning.

Phillip said, "Nik seems to be in a good mood today."

"Yeah," Brit said, "I'm sure he's happy. He always says I should have a man in my life."

Phillip said, "What about him?"

Nik returned with an identical tray of food, which he placed on Brit's lap, and said, "I already have enough men in my life, but thanks for asking."

They enjoyed their breakfast in a cheerful mutual silence. When they were finished eating, Brit turned to Phillip, smiled, and said, "So."

Phillip returned the smile, and the "So." *Okay,* he thought, *the ball's in her court. Let's see what she does with it.*

Brit said, "I think last night went very well."

Phillip laughed, largely out of relief, and said, "I wholeheartedly agree."

Phillip thought he sensed some relief in Brit's laugh as well.

After a long pause, Brit asked, "Do you think Martin suspects?"

Phillip said, "I don't think he suspects. I think he's absolutely certain."

"Really?"

"Yeah, he knew where I was going. He knows I didn't come back. He's not concerned for my safety, or else he'd have called."

Brit nodded. "Yup, Martin knows."

Phillip looked at Brit sideways, and said, "Look, if that's a problem, I can just go back in time to an hour after I left. I could tell him that you were fine, and nothing happened. Of course, my internal clock would be eight hours off then, and I'd probably fall asleep in our meetings today, but I'll do it if you want."

Brit put her hand on Phillip's to stop him. "No, it's fine, Phillip. I don't mind him knowing. Do you think he'll tell anyone?"

"Gwen," Phillip said. "He probably already has."

"Really?"

"Yeah," Phillip said. "It's an excuse to talk to Gwen, and Martin never passes up one of those."

"But it's so early."

Phillip held up a finger, as if to say *one moment*, then he held up his right hand and said, *"komuniki kun Martin."* The empty space in Phillip's palm was filled with a silvery, glowing image of the bust of Santo, the Mexican wrestler from Martin's staff. Normally an eerie organ sting would have played to signify Martin's phone ringing, but it had barely started before Martin answered. The bust of Santo was replaced with the head and shoulders of Martin, who had a sickeningly happy look on his face.

Martin said, "Yeah?"

Phillip said, "Hi, Martin."

Martin kept smiling. Neither man said anything until Martin finally asked, "Are you . . ." His voice trailed off and he shrugged, but he still had the same nauseating smile.

Phillip sighed, and said, "Yes, I'm with Brit."

Martin laughed diabolically, and gave exaggerated thumbs up. The laugh went on much longer than was dignified, which was, of course, exactly how Martin wanted it.

Phillip said, "Okay, okay. Look, have you told Gwen yet?"

"Of course," Martin said. "She's here right now."

Gwen's head appeared over Martin's shoulder. She had the same sickening smile on her face. "Good for you Phillip! Where are you now?"

Phillip winced, and admitted, "I'm at Brit's place."

Gwen said, "Ooh, put her on!"

Brit leaned in close, and Phillip twisted his arm so that her head would be in view.

Brit said, "Good morning."

Instead of saying good morning back, Gwen gave an enthusiastic thumbs-up and laughed like a crazy woman. She did this alone for a moment, then Martin joined her, both in the laughing and the thumbs.

Brit and Phillip laughed a bit in spite of themselves, then Phillip said, "Oh, shut up. We'll see you both at the summit." He clenched his hand, hanging up.

The night before, Martin had waited for Phillip to finally do what they both knew he wanted to do: go check on Brit. Then he'd waited for Phillip to return. Then, when it became clear that he wouldn't be back that night, he waited until morning when he could talk about it with Phillip if Phillip showed up, and Gwen if he didn't. When morning came, it was clear that Phillip had not returned, so Martin arranged to meet Gwen for breakfast. That's where they were when they got Phillip's call.

They had a table at a surprisingly modern outdoor café. Martin was not surprised to find that coffee was on the menu, despite the fact that South America wouldn't be discovered by Europe for hundreds of years. He was surprised at how good it was, though. When Gwen arrived, they ordered their breakfast, then Martin shared his news, which made both of them very happy, not just because their friends were presumably happy, but also because they could good-naturedly rake both of them over the coals about it for a few days. The phone call came just before their food arrived. They spent the meal idly discussing the situation while they ate.

"I'm surprised that Phillip worked so fast," Gwen said. "He's never seemed all that romantic to me."

"Well, he doesn't show that side to you, Gwen. You're like a sister to him."

Gwen smiled. "Are you saying he's shown that side of himself to you?"

"Not directly," Martin said, just defensively enough to make it clear he was in on the joke. "But I know it's there. Guys like Phillip are like, hmm . . . You know those cheap frozen chicken pot pies you get from the grocery store? Phillip's like one of those. He's all bland and beige on the surface, a little bit flaky too, but underneath, on the inside, he's a scalding hot, bubbling mass of passion and gravy. And peas."

"And chicken?" Gwen offered.

"Less than you'd think," Martin said.

╫══╍══╫

Back at Brit's apartment, she and Phillip were dressed and ready to face the day, but not together. They had decided that it would be for the best to keep things quiet for now, and both of them emerging from her front door didn't feel like the way to make that happen. Instead, they decided that she would leave via the door and walk to the summit as usual, and that Phillip would teleport back to his room and go to the summit from there. Nik came out to the living room to see them off, but was not having much success at it.

"Go on," Phillip said. "Get going. Once you're gone, I'll teleport out and meet you at the summit."

Brit said, "No, you go first. Then I'll go."

Phillip shook his head. "No, you go now. Then me."

Brit crossed her arms. "I don't see why I should go first."

"Maybe I enjoy watching you walk away."

Brit blushed slightly, then said, "Maybe I enjoy watching you walk away."

Phillip said, "See, I'm going to teleport, so all you'd see is me disappearing. There's not a lot of fun in that."

Nik said, "I disagree. Look, you two kids have to get going or you'll both be late, and that'll look just as suspicious as you two leaving here together anyway."

Brit said, "Nik's right."

"Yeah," Phillip said.

Brit said, "I should go."

Phillip said, "Yeah, me too."

Phillip and Brit said, in unison, "Right after you." Then they laughed like teenagers.

Nik walked over and opened the door. He grabbed Brit by the hand and said, "Come on. Time to go. The sooner you two get to your meeting, the more time you can spend making googly eyes at each other," as he pulled her out the door.

⊹╼╾⊹

Gwen lifted her napkin from her lap and put it on her plate before pushing the plate away.

"You have to hand it to Brit and Phillip," she said, settling back in her seat. "They figured out what they wanted, and they didn't waste a lot of time getting it."

Martin took his time parsing Gwen's statement. After mentally double checking it, he leaned forward and said, "You know, when I realized that Phillip wasn't coming back, I seriously considered coming to visit you."

"Really," Gwen said.

Martin said, "Yeah."

They stared at each other for a moment, then Martin asked, "Should I have?"

Gwen shrugged and said, "If you have to ask, then probably not." She smiled as she said it, but that didn't alter the meaning much for Martin.

He chuckled once, mirthlessly, and said, "Then I'm glad I didn't," as he stood up to leave.

Gwen smiled and said, "Oh, Martin."

Martin leaned in and said, "Gwen, save it. Look, I've made my position perfectly clear."

"Perfectly," Gwen said.

"Yes. Gwen, you say that like it's something I should be embarrassed about, but I'm not embarrassed. I'm interested. I have been since day one, and I am now. If something's holding us up, it's not me, so please don't act like my uncertainty is the problem."

Gwen's smile disappeared. "What are you saying?"

"I'm saying exactly what it sounds like I'm saying. That's the beauty of me, Gwen. I'm clear. You, on the other hand, hint that I'm not direct enough, but every time I've tried to take the bull by the horns, you've shot me down."

"And then you've mixed your metaphors." Gwen's smile came back, but it had changed, and not for the better.

Martin said, "A mixed metaphor is like a beautiful woman."

"How so?"

"They can both make a guy look stupid."

Martin turned to leave, but only got one step before his right hand started glowing and emitting a chime. Martin's shoulders sagged as he lifted his hand, answering the call.

"What?" Martin said.

Phillip's face appeared in Martin's hand. He looked panicked. "Martin, is Gwen still with you?"

"Yeah."

"Good. You two come meet me at the doctor's, now. There's been another attack on Brit!"

Gwen heard. Martin hung up and a second later they both disappeared.

Across the street, Ampyx put down the brand new kilt he hadn't really been considering buying, shook his head, and walked away.

23.

"Shut up, Jimmy! I've heard enough out of you! I wish I'd never met you! You've been nothing but trouble to my partner and me, and I curse the day you turned yourself in!"

Agent Miller shook his head, put his hand on Agent Murphy's shoulder, and said, "Take it easy, Murph."

Murphy's calm façade was usually impenetrable, but a man can only take so much, and Jimmy had given them more than enough. In the short time they'd known Jimmy they'd gone from being federal agents, treated with fear and respect by the civilians, to being hobos, treated with scorn and contempt by railroad security, which was a clear demotion.

Then they'd gone from being hobos to being security guards at a warehouse full of old files, which, while less clear, they still saw as a demotion. At least hobos choose to do nothing. Watchmen are ordered to do nothing.

They'd been deprived of sleep, of their homes, of human interaction, and of their dignity. Miller had spent most of the time yelling, but Murphy allowed himself no such outlet, and instead kept it all bottled up. He'd remained good-natured and cheerful through the entire ordeal, including his trip to Florida. He even came back laughing about the flight home, in which he had the middle seat between two rather large people who both had raised their arm rests.

He had returned with Todd's answer to Jimmy. Murphy didn't have to read it; he'd had it dictated to him, and he knew it to be a string of tech gibberish. Arcane abbreviations, directions to do things that made no sense to him. Stuff like, "Type dir. Select menu item three. Use trumpet wind-sock." He knew roughly what it all meant, but he was unsure that it would have any effect. He'd transcribed the instructions as best he could, and delivered them to Jimmy. Now, together, they were trying to follow them, and it was slow going, made worse by Jimmy. He was clearly getting frustrated, and it was making him bossy, which was the last straw for Agent Murphy.

After Murphy finally blew up, it fell to Miller to be the voice of reason.

"Now, now Murph," he said. "Losing your temper won't accomplish anything."

Murphy sputtered, "But, but, you . . . you're always losing your temper."

"Yes, but I'm good at it. You're not. Watch and learn."

Miller looked at Jimmy, sitting there at the far end of the warehouse, holding his tin can and peering at them through his telescope.

Miller held his can up to his mouth, which Jimmy took as a cue to lift his can to his ear. The string pulled tight, and Miller spoke.

"Jimmy, I speak for both my partner, Agent Murphy, and myself when I say that we both deeply regret his outburst."

"I'm certain you do," Jimmy said, magnanimously.

"Yes. It wasn't nearly harsh enough."

With that, Agent Miller threw open the valve on a fire hose of profanities delivered at top volume, and with the occasional hint of vibrato that is the mark of a true virtuoso. Jimmy took the can away from his ear, then put it back, because due to the volume of Miller's voice, and the acoustic qualities of the warehouse, the obscenities were actually quieter through the can.

When Agent Miller had finally run through the entire Urban Dictionary, and good portions of the thesaurus, and a rhyming dictionary, the torrent finally petered out.

Through the tin can Jimmy heard Agent Miller say, in a quiet voice heavy with menace, "Now you look, Jimmy. My partner Murph has shown the patience of a saint. He's doing the best he can to follow those ridiculous directions, so you need to cool your jets, or I'm going to come over there and the last thing you'll ever hear will be my tinny laughter as I strangle you with your own soup-can telephone."

"Actually," Jimmy said, "if the string was pulled tight around my neck, the sound vibrations wouldn't carry through the string." There was a long silence, then Jimmy added, "I apologize. Correcting you then was probably not the smart move. I know that working with me has not been pleasant for either of you, and that so far there's been nothing to show for it, but I tell you, we're very close to our goal."

Jimmy took the silence as encouragement and continued. "It's just these instructions of Todd's. It's been years since he's done the things he's telling us to do, and, well, as Agent Murphy told you, Todd's not the brightest man. He's shrewd enough to be dangerous to others, but dumb enough to be even more of a danger to himself."

Miller finally broke his silence to ask, "So, do you think this is going to work or not, Jimmy?"

Jimmy said, "We are going to find the file, and when we do, I will prove that everything I've told you is true, but it's going to be a frustrating process. I promise, I'll be more patient. Please give Agent Murphy my apologies."

The three men got back to work. Jimmy deciphered Todd's instructions, and watched through his telescope as Agent Murphy attempted to follow them. Finally, they wound their way around the Internet and onto some sort of massive corporate database. Jimmy could tell from the address that it belonged to a large gaming company. After several more nonsensical blind alleys, they were looking at a directory with one file in it, a file called *repository1-c.txt.*

Jimmy told Murphy to open the file remotely using the terminal, as they had tried several times before. Unlike all of the other times, this time the file opened.

Jimmy said, "Okay, gentlemen. Here comes your proof. Do a search for my full name, James Isadore Sadler."

Agent Miller's voice came back through the tin can. "It's searching. How long will this take?"

"Usually about twenty minutes, but it depends on the speed of the server we're accessing."

Nine minutes later, the search returned a single match. Jimmy silently thanked his parents for giving him a ridiculous middle name, then instructed Murphy to pull up the entry that Jimmy knew defined him as a person. Jimmy didn't need to work very hard to remember which number they were looking for. He had rehearsed this moment thousands of times in his mind. He led Agent Murphy to a specific set of digits, and instructed him to read them aloud.

Murphy took the can from Miller. His tinny voice said, "It says five, zero, zero."

Yeesh, Phillip, Jimmy thought. *That's overkill.*

Jimmy put the can to his mouth and said, "Change that to twelve."

"Twelve?"

"Yes. Twelve."

Murphy hesitated. "What'll this do?"

Jimmy tried to sound calm as he explained, "If I've been telling you the truth, it'll reset my magnetic field so I can use electronics again."

"And if you're not telling the truth?"

"Nothing," Jimmy said. "I mean, it's just some random file some game company is holding onto, right? If I'm lying, the worst that can happen is it'll break some game and they'll have to restore a backed-up copy of the file. Besides, the file has my name in it, right? So this is my entry, and I'm having you adjust the number down, not up, so I can't possibly be stealing anything, can I?"

That seemed to satisfy Murphy. Jimmy couldn't hear the clicking, but he watched through the telescope as Murphy made the change. Jimmy sat for a moment, concentrating on enjoying the moment. Eventually, Agent Miller yelled, "Hey, what next?" from the far end of the warehouse.

Jimmy stood up, straightened his rumpled, secondhand suit jacket, and walked toward the agents, never taking his eyes off of the computer monitor. He walked at a normal pace, but to him it felt agonizingly slow. With each step, the screen got closer, and with each step he became more certain that at any second it would flicker and go dead. He kept walking like that, each step expecting the screen to die, until he couldn't walk any further without kicking the table on which the computer sat. Miller and Murphy both looked shocked, but Jimmy didn't know it.

He couldn't take his eyes off of the screen. It was the first time he'd seen a video display of any kind from closer than fifteen feet in thirty years, and it was the most beautiful thing he'd ever seen.

Murphy muttered several obscenities. Miller said, "Okay, so he can stand next to a computer. What's that prove?"

Jimmy said, "It proves I was telling the truth."

"Not about everything," Agent Miller said. "We didn't arrest the Banks kid for standing next to computers, we arrested him for producing money out of nothing. Frankly, I'm still not convinced this whole *magnetic field* thing hasn't been a trick from day one."

Agent Murphy rolled his eyes. "Miller, how could he possibly fake that?"

"If I could tell you that, it wouldn't be much of a trick."

Jimmy expected this. Circumstances had forced him to prove that what he was saying was true, but proof, as is often the case, wasn't very convincing. Luckily for Jimmy, he was convincing, even when he had no proof.

Jimmy smiled and said, "Agent Miller has a valid point. None of the people you've been pursuing were wanted for damaging electronics. I can show you how all of the other things were done, but it will take a little time."

Agent Miller laughed contemptuously, and said, "Yeah, I knew it. How long will it take, Jimmy? How much longer are you going to string us along?"

Jimmy said, "About fifteen minutes." He walked lightly over to the camper and grabbed one of the folding lawn chairs they'd been using to augment the warehouse's furnishings. He brought it back to the table and plunked it down in front of the keyboard. "In the meantime," he said, "you gentlemen might want to turn on your cell phones and check your voicemail, since you can now."

Jimmy ran a search on the file for Agent Miller's full name. While it ran, he pulled up the text editor and started typing out strings of code, largely from memory. Agent Murphy asked what he was doing, and Jimmy explained that he was writing a quick script that would automate the process of accessing the file in the future, so they wouldn't have to repeat the whole process they'd just been through. There was a lot that Agent Murphy didn't understand about computers, but neither he nor Miller wanted to go through all of that rigmarole ever again, so they let him proceed.

Jimmy checked on the search, and found that it had returned four people with the same full name as Agent Miller. He got the agent's birthdate, and that allowed him to narrow it down to one.

"Okay, gentlemen, for my next trick: Agent Miller, I'll need you to tell me your current checking account balance, down to the penny."

Miller shook his head. "If you think I'm going to give you my checking account number, you're crazy."

"I didn't ask for your checking account number," Jimmy said, "just the balance, as I said, down to the penny."

Miller didn't know his balance, but he was able to call the phone number on the back of his debit card to find out. He carefully guarded his keypad as he entered the number on his debit card, but he needn't have bothered. Jimmy was occupied, putting the finishing touches on his script.

After navigating a phone tree, shouting at a phone tree that he didn't want to open a new line of credit, talking to a human, then shouting at the human that he didn't want to open a new line of credit, he got the number he'd wanted.

"Okay, my checking balance is $3,762.43"

Jimmy said, "Splendid. Now please hang up the phone."

Jimmy did a quick search, typed few characters, then told Agent Miller, "Now call again and ask for your balance."

"What? Aw, man, I had them on the phone. I could have just asked the guy to double-check it. Now I have to go through the whole phone tree again."

Jimmy said, "Please, just call again."

Miller had murder in his eyes, but he made the call, climbed the phone tree, and refused the credit line. Jimmy and Murphy watched with growing anticipation as he got closer and closer to his bank balance. Miller said, "Okay, for bank balance, it says to press one." He'd opted to stick with the computer tree for this run, since it aggravated him automatically and impersonally, while the human had done so deliberately for his own enjoyment. He looked at his phone, pressed one, put the phone back up to his ear, and immediately went white as a sheet. He looked at his phone, pressed one again, and held it back to his ear a second time.

"What is it?" Murphy asked. "What does it say?"

Jimmy looked at the computer screen, and said, "It says that his balance is $5,003,762.43, doesn't it, Agent Miller?"

"What did you do?!" Agent Miller shouted.

"Exactly what I said I would."

"Whose money is it?"

Jimmy shrugged. "It's in your account. I'd say it's yours."

Miller stood up, towering over Jimmy and bellowing down at him. "Don't you give me that! Who did you take it from?"

"Nobody," Jimmy said. "How could I have? All I did was type a number into the file. You've been sitting right here, and Murphy's been watching me like a hawk the whole time. I haven't pulled up any other systems, or accessed any other files. I haven't even contacted your bank. I've been typing away in a text editor the whole time."

"You better be able to take it back! Now!" Miller's face was beet red. Spittle rained down on Jimmy.

"I will. But, first, a little credit please. I've lived up to my end here. I told you I'd show you how Martin and all the others got their money, and I have."

"By making me a criminal?"

"I can change it back if that's what you really want, but gentlemen, tell me, is this embezzling? Have we broken the law? We didn't take the money from anywhere. We didn't deprive anyone of anything. Are there laws against altering reality at a fundamental level?"

Miller shouted, "You haven't altered reality! I'm not stupid. All you altered was a bank record."

"By changing a plain text file that has nothing to do with online banking, on a server that belongs to a gaming company?" Jimmy asked, calmly.

"Don't give me that," Miller said. "I don't care where this stupid file of yours is. It's computers. They're all tied in together these days. You and your buddies just found a back door or something. That's all."

Jimmy's smile remained in place, but it did become a bit less genuine looking. "Okay, Agent Miller, say that's true. What about my magnetic field, then?"

"It's a trick!" Miller whined. He turned to his partner. "Murph, you've gotta see that this is some kind of trick!"

Jimmy turned to Murphy and asked, "How? How could I have made any integrated circuit that got within fifteen feet of me stop working?"

Agent Murphy asked Agent Miller, "That's a good point. How did he do that?"

"I don't know," Agent Miller cried. "Maybe he keistered an electromagnet!"

Jimmy said, "Really now, how likely does that sound?"

"A lot more likely that you getting God-like powers out of a government-issue Dell."

They both turned to Murphy, who had somehow assumed the role of judge in their group dynamic. Murphy thought for a while, then said in an even tone, "I'm sorry. I just don't buy it. If he'd keistered an electromagnet, he'd have stuck to the side of the boxcar."

Jimmy put up his hands and said, "Look. This is a lot to take in, I understand. And you're right that all you've seen me do is change a number on this computer and have it change a number on another computer. I can show you the fancier stuff."

Miller bared his teeth and said, "I think you'd better do that then."

Jimmy said, "Okay." He turned to the computer and typed in a command.

At first, nothing happened. Then, more nothing happened. Agent Miller scowled. Jimmy held up a finger and said, "I'm sorry, one second." He turned back to the computer, looked at the script he'd been writing, muttering to himself. The two agents shared a look that would not have made Jimmy feel safe.

Jimmy said, "Ah, there it is. I tell you, you miss one slash . . ."

He stood up again, and said, "Sorry about that, guys. It should work this time." He typed the command, hit enter, and disappeared.

The two agents blinked in disbelief. They looked at the space where Jimmy had stood, then they looked at each other, then they looked around the warehouse to see where Jimmy had gone.

They didn't see him anywhere.

Murphy quickly turned to the computer. Miller saw his partner's head turn and followed suit, just in time to see the screen go black. He looked at Murphy, whose face had gone white.

"What happened?"

Murphy said, "The last thing I saw was 'reformat C drive.'"

"What's that mean?"

A distant voice shouted, "It means the memory has been erased."

The agents looked to the chair and telescope at the far end of the warehouse, and saw Jimmy, wearing a beautifully tailored suit. He had shaved, gotten a haircut, and was holding a tablet computer. "Of course," Jimmy continued, "a good data recovery specialist could get it all back, but by then I'll have password protected the file anyway, so there's really no point."

Jimmy reached down to the chair, picked up the notebook that contained Todd's instructions, and said, "Just came back for this. Thanks for your assistance, gentlemen."

The two agents started running as fast as they could toward Jimmy, who said, "Keep the five million. Consider it a tip. You can use it to pay for anger management classes."

Jimmy poked at the tablet screen and disappeared.

24.

Louiza had been a surgeon in Sao Paulo before getting sidetracked into the medical technology field, then eventually finding the file and emigrating to Atlantis. When people arrived in the past, they eventually realized that they still had to do something, and what the people who already lived in the past were doing, such as struggling to find food and shelter, was not in their case necessary, nor was it fun. Most time travelers ended up doing pretty much the same thing they did in their original time, and for Louiza, that meant setting up a medical clinic. It passed the time, she was helping the community, and it allowed her to explore the medical applications of the file.

Her facilities were beautiful, clean, and modern. Her waiting room was comfortable, spacious, and attractive, and her receptionist was a large, muscular man who knew how to look at her in just the perfect way to put butterflies in her stomach.

He was sitting at his desk filing his fingernails when Phillip and Brit materialized in the waiting room. Brit was clearly in great distress, and Phillip was holding Nik, who had an arrow sticking out of his side.

Brit shouted, "We need Louiza, now!"

The receptionist scarcely had time to stand before Martin and Gwen appeared. Martin immediately helped Phillip support Nik, who was moaning and clutching at the arrow. Martin could see that Nik also had deep cuts on his arms.

The receptionist hit a button which was not technically connected to anything, but which still alerted Louiza whenever it was pressed.

Martin asked, "What happened?!"

Brit answered, "We were being silly and Nik was dragging me out of the apartment. As soon as we got out the door, a bunch of arrows flew at me from both ends of the hall."

Gwen said, "And poor Nik got in the way."

"No," Brit said. "They bounced off me and hit him."

Louiza materialized. She took a second to survey the scene then leapt into action. Within moments she and her receptionist had Nik on a gurney that hovered in midair and whisked him away to the examination rooms. They instructed the others to remain in the waiting room. Five minutes later, Louiza came out to tell them what was happening.

"Luckily, the arrow didn't penetrate very far into his abdomen. I'm going to have to do surgery, but he should pull through just fine."

Brit asked, "Is he in pain?"

"No," Louiza said. "I froze him in time. He's not even aware that anything's happening."

"And you can perform surgery on him that way?" Phillip asked.

"Close. I can't do it with time stopped. With time frozen, he's essentially a statue, but I can slow time to a crawl for him while I do the surgery. I'll have the whole thing done before he has time to flinch."

Brit asked, "And he won't feel any pain?"

"Oh, he'll feel a tremendous amount of pain, but only for half a second, from his point of view."

Brit said, "I don't want him to feel any pain."

Louiza said, "He was in pain when you brought him in. He'll be in pain after the surgery, no matter what I do. We could put him under general anesthetic, I'd have to train someone to monitor his vitals and make sure he doesn't die. We'd have to intubate him. He'd take a long time to wake up, and he'd be groggy and disoriented when he did. Or, we can do it my way, and get the same result, only I can have it done safely all by myself, and we'll be done in a half hour."

Phillip said, "You make a convincing argument."

"Also," Louiza continued, "the slow-motion facial reaction to the surgery is usually hilarious."

+⊨━━⊨+

They left Nik in Louiza's capable hands. She promised to repair the damage, keep him comfortable after the procedure, and record his reactions for them to enjoy later, when they were in the mood.

They walked to the summit. They weren't concerned about a new attack because the killer or killers seemed to need time to regroup after each failed attempt on Brit's life. Besides, they wanted time to talk.

Gwen asked, "How many arrows was it this time?"

Brit said, "I didn't take the time to count, but at least ten."

Martin said, "If one arrow doesn't do it, maybe ten will. I mean, whoever's doing this, they're either stubborn or stupid, right? It's like 'one statue didn't do it. Let's try a different statue.

No? Maybe an arrow? No? How about a bunch of arrows?' What will it be next time, a hundred? Poor Nik getting hit is bad enough, but there could be serious collateral damage if this keeps up. We have to figure out who's doing this."

"Yes, thank you," Phillip said. "That hadn't occurred to the rest of us."

"Well then, let's hear some ideas," Martin said. "We need some suspects."

Phillip asked, "Well, what are your ideas, Martin? Or does realizing that we need an idea count as your idea?"

Martin knew Phillip was on edge, so he didn't return the snotty tone when he replied, "I don't know the possible suspects nearly as well as Brit and Gwen, but I'll say again that we need to look at who has the most to gain from Brit being out of the picture."

Gwen put her hand on Martin's shoulder. "Martin, we've been through this. Nobody has anything to gain. Anybody who has enough knowledge of magic to make the attempt will know that they can't possibly succeed."

Martin shifted to face Gwen, and in doing so, pulled his shoulder out from under her hand. "Then there has to be something we're missing," he said. "Brit, think about it. Let's forget motive for a minute. Has anybody been acting weird around you lately?"

Brit said, "No, but they wouldn't, would they? If they were trying to kill me, they'd make a point of not tipping their hand."

Martin said, "What about those two dandies, Fauntleroy and Fancy Pants? You know, the guys in the tuxedos. They were pretty rude to you yesterday."

Brit said, "No, as I remember it, they were rude to you."

"Okay, you're right. But they were rude *near* you; that's a start."

Gwen said, "Martin, your problem is that you're trying to figure this out with logic. You can't. It's illogical. They're trying to kill someone who can't be killed. You can't make sense of something that's senseless."

Martin glowered, and said, "Everything's senseless until someone makes sense of it. Life doesn't explain itself."

"Be that as it may," Phillip said, "we do have to stop these attacks. Not just because of collateral damage, but for Brit. I don't think her fate is tied to Brit the Elder's. I'm absolutely sure that she can be killed."

Brit the Younger took Phillip by the arm, and said, "Isn't he sweet?"

Gwen smiled, and glanced at Martin, but he wasn't looking at her.

━┿━━━┿━

They arrived late at the summit and attempted to enter quietly during the morning session. Their attempt was foiled by Brit the Elder, who was making some announcements as they entered. She smoothly, as if waiting for her cue, announced, "Both members of the Medieval England delegation and one member of the Atlantis delegation have arrived. As I informed you all this morning as the day's deliberations commenced, there was another attempt on my life, which, of course, failed, but did result in the injury of a servant, who will make a full recovery."

Instead of slinking unnoticed into their seats as they had planned, they slunk into their seats with everyone in the room watching them.

The morning's program involved discussion of various methods of testing whether a person who found the file was well versed enough in its use to be allowed to remain. A man of Indian descent who identified himself as Vikram explained his group's method, which involved making a new recruit publicly perform with a deadly cobra. If the recruit understood the uses of the file well enough to make himself impervious to the cobra's venom, then he had enough mastery to remain. Martin looked to his left and noticed that one member of the delegation of traveling faith healers from the 1940s was furiously taking notes.

After a couple of hours it was time for a break, and the four of them just naturally congregated together to continue discussing the problem.

Brit told the other three, "Look, I think we all agree that we have to put an end to this, and I think we all agree that we don't really have any good suspects. What if instead of hunting them down, we trap them instead? That way they identify themselves."

Gwen, Phillip, and Martin agreed that it sounded like a good idea, so she continued.

"We've been looking at the fact that all of these delegates are here doing magic as if it's complicating things, but I was looking at them and I realized that the only reason they can all do magic here is that we've got copies of their interfaces and shell programs running on a local machine in this time, and all of the users are registered with the various programs. I figure I can write another program that will monitor all of those, and the Atlantis Interface. Next time someone tries to kill me, we'll be able to see exactly who did it."

Martin said, "That sounds like a good idea."

A voice that sounded exactly like Brit's said, "I agree. It does sound like a good idea."

They all turned to see Brit the Elder standing behind them. Martin asked, "Will it work?" Phillip didn't ask because he wasn't convinced her answer was trustworthy. Brit the Younger and Gwen didn't ask because they knew not to bother.

Brit the Elder said, "I'm still alive, aren't I?"

Martin said, "That didn't really answer the question."

Brit the Elder replied, "It tells you all you need to know though, doesn't it?"

Martin scowled and said, "Now you're just being evasive."

Brit the Younger said, "Maddening, isn't it?"

Brit the Elder held up her hands in a gesture of surrender. "I don't want to upset anybody. I just wanted to come over and touch base with everyone. I know the last day or so has been . . . *eventful*." She looked straight at Phillip as she said this, and smiled a knowing smile.

Phillip said, "We're fine."

Brit the Elder said, "I'm sure you are." Her smile got wider, and more knowing. Phillip smirked, in spite of himself. Brit the Elder nodded, now beaming. Phillip blushed a bit, then chuckled. Brit the Elder laughed as well. They both looked at the ground, laughing softly, and peeking up at each other and blushing.

Phillip glanced to his side, and saw that Brit the Younger was also turning red, but she didn't look embarrassed. She gritted her teeth, turned silently, and walked away at high speed. Phillip exhaled sharply, shot Brit the Elder an irritated look, and followed the Younger.

Gwen said, "That wasn't very nice, Brit."

Brit the Elder said, "No, it wasn't, but eventually, I was able to forgive myself."

Gwen watched Phillip's back as he disappeared through the crowd and down the hall. She leaned toward Martin and said, "You'd think a love triangle would be less complicated if it only had two people in it."

Gwen heard no answer, so she turned, and only then saw that Martin had walked away. Judging by his distance, he clearly had left immediately after Phillip.

Brit the Elder said, "When it comes to romance, two people are more than complicated enough, wouldn't you agree?"

<hr />

Brit the Younger reached the door to the outside. Phillip was right behind her, calling for her to slow down. They emerged into the open air at the top of the gleaming white staircase that led to the meeting hall. Brit stopped walking and started swiping at the air with her finger.

Phillip ran up behind her panting and said, "Brit, please, we need to talk about this."

Brit scowled at Phillip, but placed a hand on his shoulder and with the other hand, poked at the interface only she could see. An instant later they were standing on a beach of one of the uninhabited islands near Atlantis.

Phillip spun around and asked, "Where are we?"

"I took us somewhere we could talk in private," Brit spat. "I certainly wasn't going to take you back to my place. You've been there enough."

Phillip saw Atlantis shimmering in the distance. They were miles away. He said, "Brit?" Even to himself he sounded miserable.

"You slept with her!" Brit shouted.

"No! I never!" Phillip shouted back. Brit stared at him for a moment, then he said, "I mean, well, uh, I don't, I don't think I did."

She continued to smolder and stare. He continued to stutter and stammer, "Uh, ugh, okay, I, I guess, depending on how you look at it, I guess I kinda did, but Brit, that was a long, long time ago!"

Through gritted teeth, Brit the Younger asked, "When?"

Phillip said, "Brit, you know . . ."

"When?" Brit interrupted. "When did you sleep with her? You say it was a long time ago. When was it, Phillip?"

"Last night."

Brit turned and stormed off down the beach. Phillip followed. "From our point of view! From hers it was decades ago! Over a century!"

Brit kept walking, but she did start talking. "Oh, so now we are the same person!"

"What?"

"Up until now, when you were trying to butter me up, you were sure that she wasn't really me, but now, when I'm angry, you decide she is!"

"Look," Phillip shouted, "you're the one insisting that when I slept with you I also slept with her! I very clearly stated that I didn't sleep with her!"

"So I suppose I should think better of you for having denied it at first!"

"I still deny it! I only entertained the idea that you're the same person to show you how silly . . ." Phillip trailed off, but he knew it was a word too late. He took a second to rephrase his thoughts. Brit passed the time by attempting to kill him by staring him to death. Phillip, his voice much quieter and much sadder, said, "Brit, I'm just hoping I can get you to look at this logically."

Brit spoke in a voice that was also much quieter, but also much angrier. "Phillip. Am I the first woman you've ever been in a fight with?"

"No."

"Am I the first woman you've ever told to be more logical?"

"No."

Brit asked, "Has that ever worked out well for you?" She said, "Don't answer that. I'll tell you what. I'll do as you say, and look at the situation logically. Martin keeps saying we should look at who has something to gain from trying to kill me. Well, it occurs to me that one person has gained. He's gained an excuse to be around me. He's gained from me being emotionally vulnerable and grateful to him for his support. And, it just so happens that the attacks started right after I first met him, and he's the only person who's been present every single time I've been attacked. What does that tell you, logically, Phillip?"

Phillip gaped at her, wounded and confused, then in a small voice he said, "Why am I always a suspect? I'm just about the most harmless person on earth, and yet everyone I get close to is suspicious of me."

Brit said, "Good question, Phillip." She started swiping her finger through the air. Phillip realized that she was setting up the teleport back to Atlantis, which meant that the argument was over. He sighed heavily, and held out his hand.

Brit looked down at his hand, laughed mirthlessly, and said, "No, I'll let you get your own ride back." She disappeared, and left him standing alone, on a beautiful island, in an ugly mood. He raised his staff into the air, took flight, and swung low over the waves, on a direct heading for Atlantis. In his state of mind, he made even flying look like a miserable ordeal.

25.

On a chilly fall day in Butte, Montana, Jimmy materialized next to a dumpster in the parking lot of a fast food restaurant. He closed his brand new laptop and tucked it into his brand new leather suitcase. He straightened the jacket of his brand-new, blue-pinstriped suit and walked around to the front of the restaurant.

He looked up at the restaurant's sign, which read "Pork Chop John's."

Good, he thought. *I'm where I want to be. Now let's see about when.*

The sign featured a cartoon drawing of a pig wearing a crown. According to the sign, the pig's name was "Pork Chop King." *Not much of a king,* Jimmy thought, *if all he promises is to let people eat his subjects.*

Jimmy entered the restaurant and casually perused the menu, which was made of plastic-tab letters and hung on the wall above the electronic cash register. It still thrilled Jimmy to see things like cash registers work in his vicinity.

Jimmy ordered a fried pork chop sandwich and a ten-piece order of pork nuggets. He paid with an extremely beat-up twenty-dollar bill he'd purloined from Agent Miller's wallet when nobody was looking. It was wrinkled and filthy and taped together, but it was also minted in 1998, and would not arouse suspicion.

As he waited for his meal, he nonchalantly picked up the top copy from the stack of *Penny Press* classified ads next to the door. The issue was dated September 21, 2003, just as he'd expected.

Jimmy ate his sandwich and pork nuggets. He had the dining room to himself for most of the meal, but toward the end two men drove up in a dirt-encrusted Geo Metro. One was a bit heavy with thinning hair and a beard. The other was thin with shoulder-length hair, black-rimmed glasses, and an inhaler. They loudly discussed which fried pork items to purchase, and whether they wanted to get a fried egg on top for an extra dollar. Jimmy discarded his last three pork nuggets and left, grateful to not have to listen to their inane chatter anymore.

Jimmy walked across the parking lot, across the street, across another parking lot, and up to the entrance of a small apartment building. It looked like it had originally been a motel, but had been converted to more permanent housing within the last few years.

Jimmy walked to the door of the unit farthest from the office and closest to the road. The room where plumbing noise would be least likely to bother the neighbors. Jimmy put his ear to the door, hearing nothing, as he'd expected.

Jimmy raised a fist to knock politely on the door, but then thought better of it. He turned his fist sideways, shifted his weight and pounded on the door loud enough to be sure he'd be heard even from the far corner of the apartment.

After a moment passed with no answer, Jimmy pounded again. In the far distance, Jimmy heard a faint voice say, "One minute! I'm in the bathroom!"

"Yes," Jimmy muttered, "I expect you are."

Jimmy waited patiently for a moment, then heard the deadbolt and saw the doorknob turn. The door swung open, and for the first time in thirty years, from Jimmy's point of view, he was standing face to face with Tyler.

Back when he was chairman of the wizards of Camelot, Jimmy had made a point of talking to every wizard in his area about their lives, their interests, and where and when they had come from. Knowing that Tyler was from Butte, Montana, had made finding his address simple.

Tyler had not aged a day. Literally, that was one of the chief perks of being a wizard. Jimmy had aged quite severely, which was one of the chief drawbacks of being an ex-wizard who had spent thirty years mostly outdoors. For a moment Jimmy was worried that Tyler wouldn't recognize him, but that fear evaporated when Tyler said, "Oh, it's you."

Jimmy said, "Tyler, it is so good to see you again!"

Tyler silently turned around and retreated back into his apartment. At first, Jimmy wasn't sure if he was being invited in, or being told to go away, but Tyler hadn't shut the door, and eventually he gave an irritated look back over his shoulder, as if to say, *Well, what are you waiting for?*

Jimmy was surprised by Tyler's robe. It was different than he remembered. It was still red and purple vertical stripes, but now it had gold decorative accents, and much fancier cuffs. Jimmy asked Tyler what time he was living in currently.

Tyler said, "The Renaissance," but offered no further information.

Jimmy did some fast mental math, and realized that Tyler had lived through at least three hundred years of European history since they'd last seen each other.

While Tyler's robe was a surprise, his apartment looked exactly as Jimmy had expected. It was packed half full of bulk-packaged rolls of toilet paper and paper towels. The other half was mostly filled with full garbage bags, stuffed with empty packaging, used paper towels, and hundreds of cardboard tubes.

Tyler's bathroom habits were legendary amongst the wizards. He was the only time traveler who had never gotten used to using the bathroom facilities of the distant past, simply because he had never tried. Instead, anytime he had to move his bowels, he simply teleported and time traveled back to this apartment, and used his modern bathroom, *like a civilized person*. He would appear, use the restroom, disappear, then, as far as the apartment was concerned, reappear immediately, and use the restroom again. After another round of lightning-speed mind math, Jimmy figured that if Tyler hadn't skipped any large chunks of history, his toilet must have been in constant use for well over a year by now. He considered asking to see the toilet, then decided that, should the opportunity arise, he would specifically ask not to see it.

Tyler sat on a bale of rolls of toilet paper, and looked sullen. Jimmy knew that of all the wizards, Tyler had the most reason to hold a grudge against him. He'd put Tyler through a torturous ordeal. He'd "ghosted" Tyler, making him invisible and insubstantial, and as a side effect, making him feel as if he had spent many days suffocating. After being caught, Jimmy had tried to kill Tyler and all of the other wizards and had never shown any real contrition after he failed. He chose to let Tyler set the tone for this conversation, and he did so by staying quiet until Tyler chose to speak.

"I knew you'd show up eventually," Tyler said.

"How'd you know that?" Jimmy asked.

"Because you showed up in my past and told me that you'd visited me in the future."

"Yeah," Jimmy said. "That's a pretty good hint."

"You said," Tyler continued, ignoring him, "that you'd come to me in the future and convince me to help you."

Jimmy said, "I was hoping you'd say that."

Tyler remained expressionless. "I always wondered what you, of all people, could have possibly said to me that convinced me to help you."

Jimmy was on shaky ground here. Clearly, Tyler remembered some interaction between them that had taken place in Tyler's past, but was still in the future, from Jimmy's point of view. "I never told past-you what I say right now to make you want to help me?" Jimmy asked. "Interesting."

Tyler winced. "Me telling you that just now is why you won't tell me, isn't it?"

Jimmy said, "Probably. Sorry."

Tyler sank slightly, and rolled his eyes. "Okay," he said, "you're here now. At least I'll find out. Go ahead, say what you're going to say. Say whatever it is that convinces me to help you, the man I hate most in this world."

Jimmy shrugged, took a breath, and said, "Well, Tyler, you've lived through my future. You know what I have planned. You already know that you will give me the information that I need, and clearly, it can't work out too badly for you, since you're still here, so, I guess the best reason you have to help me is that you know it's going to happen, and you might as well get it over with."

Tyler sagged even further and said, "I was afraid you were going to say that."

26.

For the second day in a row, Brit the Younger traveled to the summit meetings on foot, accompanied only by Gwen.

For the second day in a row, Phillip and Martin were waiting at the door when they arrived.

For the second day in a row, Brit pretended not to see Phillip as she passed.

For the second day in a row, Gwen made eye contact with Martin, who nodded a polite but curt greeting and went on his way.

All four of them were particularly edgy this morning, because for the second day in a row, there had been no further attempt on Brit the Younger's life. There were a few theories as to why this might be, and none of them was particularly pleasant.

It might be that the attempted murderer was taking his time, planning his next attempt, an attempt that might have some chance at success. Perhaps the perpetrator had given up and would make no further attempt, which would be a good thing except that they might never find out who it was and would never be sure that they wouldn't strike again. It could be that whoever it was was in fact planning another, possibly deadlier attack and was waiting to make them think he or she had given up so that they'd drop their guard.

The sad fact was that no matter which of those possibilities was true, their course of action was the same. They had to go on about their business, remain ever vigilant, and slowly go insane from the suspense.

What was worse was that the sharp decline in attempted Brit-killings had started at almost the same moment as when Brit's electronic surveillance system had started. If and when another attempt was made, Brit would be able to look back through the database her new program was creating and find out who was using magic at that precise moment. All of the sorceresses in Atlantis and every delegate in town for the summit were registered and easily identifiable. The next time someone tried to kill Brit, they'd know who did it, which put them in the strange position of hoping for a violent attack that never seemed to come.

Brit took her seat next to her fellow delegate, Ida, the president of Atlantis. Once seated, Brit fell into her new routine of making a point to look everywhere, *anywhere* but at Phillip. She wasn't angry at Phillip specifically. She was angry at the situation. Unfortunately for Phillip, he was the only part of the situation that cared that she was angry; therefore, when she chose to withdraw from the situation, it effectively meant that she was withdrawing from him. She missed him, but she knew that making up with Phillip would just give Brit the Elder a happy memory of making up with Phillip, and that felt like Phillip was cheating on her. She knew that made no sense, and that just made her angrier, both at herself for acting crazy and at Brit the Elder for making her crazy.

Most people can't have their cake and eat it too. Phillip couldn't have his cake without eating it too, and as such, he would get no cake at all.

Phillip and Martin sat at their table and waited for the day's meetings to begin. Beside them, Gilbert and Sid, the tuxedo-clad dandies representing London in the late 1800s, sat down with broad smiles on their faces, placing their top hats on the table in front of them, their white gloves folded and tucked neatly inside.

"Well," Gilbert said, "I think that went well for our friends from Camelot today. Brit the Younger is clearly warming up to Phillip."

"What do you mean?" Sid asked. "I thought she ignored him again."

"Oh yes! You are right Sidney. She ignored him. Quite so. A finer demonstration of the art of ignoration, I've never seen. But did you not notice how she ignored him?"

"Sorry Gil, it seems I'm ignorant of the art of ignorance. Please enlighten me, that I may take note of her future ignorances."

"See, Sid, that's your problem right there. You fell into the all too-common trap of watching the ignorer. In this case, as in all cases, it is worthwhile to pay close attention to the ignored. Regard our friend, Phillip, the object of the lovely Brit's inattention." Both magicians turned to study Phillip in mock studiousness.

Gilbert continued, "Note the ostentatious sky-blue wizard robe. Observe the ridiculous matching pointy hat. Take a mental picture of his clichéd wizard staff, festooned nonsensically with its bottle of what appears to be V-8 juice. Would you not think any rational person would find it difficult to ignore a man with such a buffoonish appearance, even if he weren't accompanied everywhere by an assistant who dresses like a disco traffic cone?"

"I see your point," Sid said. "It'd be easier to ignore a thumb in your eye."

"Indeed! That, Sidney my friend, is why the fact that the enchanting Miss Brit is going to the trouble to actively ignore Phillip must be interpreted as an act of love."

"Love?" Sid asked.

"Indeed!" Gilbert said, rapping his cane on the table for emphasis. "In fact, in Phillip's case, I suspect it's the only act of love he ever receives."

Sid shook his head. "I think you're right that to ignore a buffoon like Phillip would take so much effort that it could only be motivated by love, but I don't think it follows that Brit must logically love Phillip. She might love ignoring him."

Gilbert considered this. "I will admit, it would be a pleasure to ignore Phillip."

Gilbert and Sid looked at Phillip and Martin, who did not look back, or move in any way.

"Oh dear," Gilbert said. "Phillip and Martin appear to be ignoring us."

"Which, by your reasoning, means that they love us?"

"I fear so, Sidney."

"What do we do?"

"We'll just have to signal our lack of interest in the only way they seem to understand, by continuing to watch every move they make."

Brit the Elder called the meeting to order. As she started her daily opening remarks, Martin leaned over to Phillip and whispered, "What could we have done to those guys to make them hate us this much?"

Phillip muttered, "I don't know, but we have a few hundred years to come up with something good."

The day's meetings included a debate on how to best prevent the abuse of power.

A delegate from the United States in the 1890s, whose costume indicated some experience as a traveling patent medicine dealer, was arguing in favor of draconian punishments for any time traveler, sorcerer, or wizard, who was found abusing their power, up to and including, in extreme cases, death. He argued that one could never stop all abuse, but that fear of punishment would keep the vast majority of people in line, and that those who did still abuse their powers would do so more quietly, and to a lesser degree.

He, said, "I know that most of you have no stomach for violence." He paused to smooth his thinning hair. Martin was impressed at how comfortable he looked. This man was clearly used to speaking to large groups of people. "The beauty of capital punishment," he continued, "is that you only have to do it once to make your point."

Toward the back of the hall, someone let out a quiet cough that echoed through the hall. The man speaking shrugged, as if the cougher had made a valid point. "Okay, once in a while. Occasionally. We'll only have to kill people occasionally, but only people who deserve it. Evil people, who really have it coming. People who we can all agree need to be put down like rabid dogs, and we will do it humanely, and without taking any pleasure in it."

There was a long silence. Martin was still impressed with how relaxed the patent medicine salesman from the Old West seemed. Clearly, he was used to large groups of people not believing him. The silence was broken, not by crowd noise, or

Brit the Elder's gavel, but by a hollow popping noise followed by a groaning creak.

All eyes turned to the source of the noise, one of the large statues (Hedy Lamarr, in this case) that decorated the outer perimeter of the room. It had been damaged at its thinnest point, near the base, and to nobody's surprise, it was slowly toppling over, directly toward the table where Brit the Younger and President Ida sat.

The delegates from the surrounding tables instinctively scattered, as did Ida. Brit had been through this before, and did not look concerned. She just rolled her eyes and said, "Really?! We're back to this?"

The statue came down directly on top of her with a deafening crash, followed by the now-familiar cloud of dust and flying debris. One could just make out the form of Brit, sitting on the floor in the rubble. Her chair was destroyed but she was unharmed, as expected. What nobody expected was the hail of arrows that zipped over their heads from the back of the room, plunged into the heart of the dust cloud, and struck Brit the Younger.

Despite the familiarity of the attack, Martin was instantly in full panic mode. He knew the instant it started that this time was different somehow. In a frenzied half-second of observation, Martin saw that there were more arrows than ever before, easily a hundred of them, if not more. The arrows didn't seem to have conventional, sharp arrowheads, which in the past had bounced off of Brit's skin harmlessly. Instead these arrows were tipped with some formless black material. Martin suspected tar. Whatever it was, the arrows were clinging to Brit, rather than bouncing off. The arrows each seemed to trail a thin cable, no bigger around than Martin's pinky finger. On their own, the ropes were most likely not very strong, but the hundred of them together were likely quite strong indeed, an idea that was reinforced when the cables pulled tight and dragged Brit across the floor with great speed.

Brit tumbled sideways. Martin's eyes followed the ropes, and saw them terminate at the far end of the hall, disappearing into a seemingly unbroken section of the wall. Martin glanced back to Brit, and saw that Phillip had already sprinted the distance between them and was lunging to grab her. He got a grip on Brit's outstretched hand and planted his feet on the floor. Phillip's staff tumbled to the ground. He discarded it to grip Brit's free hand with both of his own.

The ropes pulled tight, lifting Brit off of the ground. She tried to extend her other arm, but couldn't. Her entire left side was covered with the tar arrows, and she wasn't strong enough to fight the pull from the ropes.

Phillip slid across the floor like a water-skier, barely slowing Brit's progress toward the wall. Without thinking, Martin reached into his pocket, and in one deft motion withdrew and threw his beanbag with all of his might. It shot forward like a line drive and hit Phillip square in the back. As the beanbag made contact, Martin said "Bamf," and was instantly standing behind Phillip.

Phillip was still moving forward quite quickly, so Martin dove, and seized Phillip by the ankles with his free arm, which caused Phillip to fall forward and, without being able to catch himself with his hands, land directly on his face. Brit also fell fast and landed hard, then the three of them slid across the floor with no discernible change in their speed.

Martin didn't have time to think. He just knew on an instinctive level that he needed to do anything he could to slow them down. His brain ran through everything it knew looking for an idea, and when it got one, he acted on it without hesitation.

Martin kept his left arm hooked around Phillip's ankles, and with his right, he pointed his staff in Phillip and Brit's general direction and said, "*Ekskuzi vin!*"

A foul-smelling jet of purple smoke erupted from Brit's ribcage. In the cavernous hall, the sound was more like a pulse jet than a whoopee cushion. The spell had landed, as Martin had hoped, in a place on Brit's body that aimed at least a bit toward the wall, so their progress did slow. Unfortunately, the jet also vectored toward the side, so most of its thrust sent Brit sliding across the hall.

Brit slid in an arc, pushing through a tangled mass of tables, chairs, and slow-moving delegates. Most of the objects Brit went through fell directly on Phillip and Martin as they were carried along helplessly behind her.

Phillip coughed in the thick, malodorous vapor trail, and shouted, "Ugh, wha . . . what is that?!"

"Something Gary invented!" Martin replied.

"Oof! Shoulda guessed."

The three of them came to a crashing, clattering halt in a massive heap of jumbled furniture against the wall, but while their sideways motion had stopped, they were still being pulled relentlessly toward the portal in the wall. They were dragged painfully through the thicket of table and chair legs. Martin tried to hook his legs into the furniture, but that just resulted in a portion of the pile being dragged along with them and did nothing to slow them down. He kicked his legs free and attempted to get traction against the wall and the floor, trying to wedge himself between them somehow, but it was no good. He became aware that someone had grasped his left leg. He peeked down and saw Gwen hugging his leg to her torso with both arms, but she could get no more traction than he could, and they were all sliding toward the portal.

The purple jet sputtered out and their speed increased. Martin caught a quick glimpse of the path ahead and saw that the ropes, rather than extending straight out of the wall, now bent at the edge of the otherwise invisible portal and stretched along the wall until they attached to Brit.

Martin felt the stretching force on his spine increase, and their progress slowed again. He glanced toward his feet and, to his surprise, saw that Gilbert had taken hold of Gwen's waist and Sid had hold of his. Sadly, their shiny black dress shoes provided almost no traction at all.

Sid extended his white-tipped ebony cane and shouted "Abracadabra, ala trahere!" An undulating blue energy field extended from Sid's cane to the nearest firmly anchored object, another of the massive goddess statues. Their motion stopped again. Sid's spell momentarily counterbalanced the pull from the ropes. They all were lifted off of the ground as the ropes stretched tight. It was a tug-of-war between the irresistible force and the immovable object, and they were the rope.

Straining from the exertion of keeping his grip, and the pain of Gwen keeping hers, Martin found the strength to say, "Really? Abracadabra?"

From the back of the group, Sid shouted, "Shuuuuuuut uuuuup!"

Brit was unable to move her head, due to the several tar-tipped arrows that were stuck to it, but she could swivel her eyes just enough to look at Phillip. He had a two-handed death grip on her free wrist and a look of desperate determination on his face.

"Just let go, Phillip," Brit said. "Thanks, but just let go."

"No!" Phillip barked.

"I won't die, Phillip."

"We don't know that!"

"We do. She's here. I can't die."

Gwen and Gilbert were both shouting about something, but neither Phillip nor Brit took any notice. Whatever it was couldn't be as important as this.

Phillip said, "We don't know that! We can't know that! You might be killed, and I'm not going to let it happen!"

"Phillip! I'm not going to die!"

"I'm not willing to take that chance!"

"If you get dragged in with me, maybe we both die!"

Phillip said, "I am willing to take that chance."

Brit said something else, but her words were drowned out by the horrendous sound of the destruction of the statue that was anchoring them.

Like her sisters before her, the statue of Mary Dyer gave way at its thinnest, weakest point. Unlike her sisters, she broke with a terrible cracking noise, not a pop, and she did not fall gracefully to the floor, but instead was slammed down by the force of Sid's spell directly onto Sid, Gilbert, Gwen, and the lower half of Martin. They all would have been hit if they hadn't shot forward the instant the statue gave way.

The shock from the impact caused Gwen to lose her grip, and Martin, Phillip, and Brit slid along the floor at breakneck speed. Brit finally reached the portal, and disappeared into the wall. Phillip went into the portal up to his shoulders, then pulled his head and one arm back out. He held his grip on Brit with one hand, flailing desperately for something to hold onto with the other, but there was nothing. Phillip's arms, head and torso were consumed; only his legs remained visible. Martin held his grip, but his motion stopped. He was aware that something was keeping him from moving forward, but Phillip's legs were still being drawn in. Martin strained for a moment, but then Phillip was gone, and Martin was holding a pair of empty boots.

Martin was pulled away from the portal. It was instantly clear that he'd been kept from going in himself by spells cast by one of the fakirs, two Atlantean sorceresses, and a gypsy. They all had finally realized what was happening and how they could stop it. He didn't blame them for the lateness of their actions. Though it had felt like an eternity to him, the whole ordeal may have only taken less than thirty seconds.

Martin gazed miserably at the blank patch of wall that had just swallowed his friends. He saw Gilbert approach the wall and knock on it with his cane. It was solid. Wherever the portal went, it was closed now. The meeting hall was a scene of utter devastation. The furniture was all wrecked and thrown about willy-nilly. Two of the statues were destroyed, and a malodorous purple haze still tainted the air and hung in a sinister cloud around the ceiling.

Martin felt a gentle kick at his ribs. He looked up, and saw that Sid was offering him a hand up, which he accepted. As he got to his feet, Martin said, "Thanks for pitching in. I know you don't much like Phillip and me. Why is that?"

Sid ignored the question, instead saying, "Doesn't matter. We have nothing against Brit. Any idea where they went?"

Martin shook his head.

"Well then, do you have any idea who's behind all this?"

"Until recently, my chief suspect was you two."

Sid let out a resigned sigh and said, "And you wonder why we don't like you."

Gwen ran up and hugged Martin. Martin smiled. Sid grimaced. Then she hugged Sid, which made Martin grimace and Sid smile.

Gwen said, "Thank you for your help."

Sid said, "We'd have jumped in sooner, but we didn't think there was any real danger until Brit disappeared."

Martin said, "But you both jumped in before Brit went into the wall."

Sid shook his head. "No, not that Brit. The other one."

Gwen said, "We tried to tell Brit the Younger that, but clearly none of you were listening. While you were sliding across the floor, Brit the Elder vanished."

Martin was aghast. "You mean she left?"

"No," Gwen said. "She looked surprised, then she disappeared."

Martin's blood ran cold. It would take some time to make sense of this, if it was even possible, which was never a sure thing when time travel was involved. Brit the Elder disappearing was bad news. Heck, Brit the Elder looking surprised was bad news.

Martin had the sudden, sinking feeling that maybe Phillip had been right all along, which, for several reasons, was the worst news of all.

A single voice rang out strong and clear above the confused chatter in the room. All eyes turned to the podium, Brit the Elder's podium, and saw Ida, the duly elected president of Atlantis.

"I think," she said, "given what just happened, that we should adjourn for the day."

27.

The woods were dark and deep, but nobody would ever describe them as "lovely." Jimmy had materialized a good distance away from his eventual goal, and was spending his walking time preparing for what would happen when he reached it. Despite the difficulty that had marked the last thirty years of his existence, Jimmy knew that in many ways the most difficult part was still ahead of him.

Directly ahead of him, in fact.

Bicycling back to North America had been a matter of patience, persistence, and risk avoidance. Getting what he'd needed out of Martin's parents and the treasury agents had just been straightforward social engineering, which had always been Jimmy's forte. The task Jimmy was starting now was more social engineering, but of a much higher difficulty level. If he pulled this off, it would be his proudest achievement.

It was mid-afternoon, but the light was flat and gray. Jimmy walked through the decaying, lifeless forest and let his mind wander. He could have materialized at his destination and saved himself some effort, but he found that before attempting something difficult, it was helpful to take some time and think about anything else.

Also, walking up on foot would be good showbiz. It would make him seem small and harmless, which was always a good approach when dealing with someone who wants to be seen as big and powerful. As he entered the clearing and saw the sacrificial pyre, the imposing cliff, and the cave that had been carved to look like a fearsome skull with its angry brow and its sharpened, elongated canines, he knew that he had chosen the right approach.

Jimmy walked to the dormant sacrificial pyre in the center of the clearing. He sat his briefcase to the side, extended his arms as if praying to the cave, and bellowed, "Oh mighty wizard of the cave, I come to you in this, my hour of great need, in hopes that you might offer aid!"

The cave remained dark and silent.

Jimmy continued, "In exchange for fair compensation, of course."

The skull's eyes burst to life, emitting gouts of fire that burned an unnatural blood-red. The mouth spewed forth a thick red fog that rolled down the cliff and pooled in the clearing, quickly obscuring the ground from view. The cold sacrificial pyre in front of Jimmy burst into flames. A thunderous voice echoed through the forest, so loud Jimmy felt it in his bones.

"Who dares to seek the assistance of the necromancer? What challenge do you face that could drive you to risk my wrath, and what did you mean by 'compensation'?"

Jimmy dredged up his friendliest, most harmless-sounding tone of voice, and said, "I invite you to come and find out for yourself."

For a moment the fire and fog continued to pour from the skull, but there was no sound and no other movement. Then,

Jimmy barely made out a dark shape moving in the fog-filled cave mouth.

That's it, Jimmy thought. *Take a little sneaky peek.* He didn't need Gary to recognize him at first; in fact it would be better if he didn't. The sight of a sixty-something-year-old man standing here in his medieval clearing, wearing a smart business suit and attempting to summon a necromancer should be more than enough to whet his curiosity.

Jimmy saw the dark shape moving in the cave get more distinct, then he clearly made out a head in a pointed hat, and an arm attempting to wave some of the red fog out if its way.

One of the keys to persuading people is to get them to like you. One of the keys to getting people to like you is to behave like the kind of person your mark likes. People try to be likeable, so they tend to act like the kind of person they like, which is a mistake, because they invariably get this act wrong. That's why acting exactly the way another person acts is a sure way to make that person dislike you.

Jimmy knew that the key to making someone like him was not to act how that person acts, but to act like that person thinks they act. In Gary's case, that meant good-natured teasing that, unlike Gary's "good-natured teasing," was demonstrably good-natured and actually amusing to someone other than the person doing the teasing.

Jimmy said, in a proud voice, "Your cave has fangs."

Gary looked up at the sculpted teeth hanging down just above his head and said, "It's a skull."

Jimmy asked, "Is it a vampire skull?"

The mouth glowed with an eerie green light that, when combined with the red fog, made Jimmy think of Christmas. The glow enveloped the circumference of the cave opening, and then dissipated. When Jimmy's eyes had readjusted, he saw that all of the teeth were now sharpened.

The voice from the fog said, "Is that better?"

"Yes," Jimmy said. "Very necromantic."

Gary said, "Who is that?" He walked forward so that he was clear of the fog. Clearly, the sight of a gray-haired man in a suit did not alleviate his confusion.

Jimmy stood still, hands at his sides, and said, "Hello, Gary. It's good to see you."

Gary tilted his head to one side, then flew down, landing across the pyre from Jimmy. He looked at Jimmy in the dim gray light, clearly trying to place his face. Recognition hit him like a jolt of electricity, and in an instant he was pointing his staff like a rifle, directly at Jimmy's face.

Okay, Jimmy thought, *what emotions am I trying to communicate here?*

Jimmy was happy to be back, so he smiled. He knew that Gary wasn't happy that he was back, so he raised his eyebrows apologetically. He was being threatened, so he raised his hands, but he knew that Gary wouldn't just attack without warning, so he only raised them to head height. He knew that Gary had good reason to distrust him, so he bowed his head submissively. He knew that Gary was probably more scared than he was, so he kept his voice low and his tone friendly.

"You!" Gary yelled.

"Yes," Jimmy said.

Gary yelled, "Shut up!"

Jimmy pursed his lips and nodded.

Gary circled slowly, keeping his staff aimed at Jimmy's head. He nudged Jimmy's leather briefcase with his foot, then asked, "What's in this?"

Jimmy spent half a second considering making a smart-aleck comment about how he was told not to talk, purely because that was what Gary would do in that situation, but he quickly decided that the non-threatening posture was more important than currying favor.

"My computer, and some socks and underwear," Jimmy said.

Gary considered this, then continued circling until he was behind Jimmy. He thought for a moment, then tucked his staff under his arm and frisked Jimmy quickly and inexpertly.

"Got a wand hidden on you somewhere?" he asked.

"No. I'm unarmed. Even if I had a wand, I'm short a hat and robe, so the shell wouldn't obey my commands, not that I'm in the shell anymore. We both know I had my privileges revoked."

Gary seemed satisfied. As he circled back around to Jimmy's front, Jimmy saw that instead of holding his staff like a rifle aimed at Jimmy's face, he pointed it from the hip, in Jimmy's general direction. This, in Jimmy's life, was what passed for progress.

Gary studied Jimmy for a long moment, then asked, "How did you do it?"

I mustn't sound angry, Jimmy thought. *I can sound happy to be here, sad for what I did, grateful that he's talking to me, but I can show no anger.*

"How'd I manage to return?" Jimmy said, clarifying and subtly reframing the question. "It took thirty years and a great deal of effort."

"Why'd you come back?"

"Wouldn't you, Gary? Think about it. If you got kicked out of the shell and sent back to your time without file access, wouldn't you spend the rest of your life trying to return?"

Gary thought about this, then smiled, and said, "So we should have killed you."

No anger, Jimmy reminded himself. He shrugged, and made his eyes about ten percent sadder, an amount he calculated to be noticeable without overselling it. "I'm glad that you didn't, but I guess yes, Gary. If the goal was to make sure I'd never turn up again, then you should have killed me. I have to admit, I had it coming."

Gary raised the end of his staff slightly, as if readying himself to use it. "And now you're here to kill us."

Jimmy fought a smile, which would have been just as damning as showing anger. He was delighted at how Gary had phrased that question. He hadn't said that Jimmy was here for *revenge* or *payback* or *to give us what's coming to us* or any other ambiguous clichés. He'd made the delightfully concrete statement, "You're here to kill us." Jimmy could reply to that both directly and honestly, which was good. As Jimmy always said, the easiest way to keep people from thinking that you're lying is to not lie.

"No," Jimmy said in a firm tone of voice. "I'm not here to kill anybody. I'm done with that. I know that for you, that all just happened, but for me it's been decades. I've had plenty of time to think about what I did and how you all reacted."

All true, Jimmy thought.

Gary said, "I don't believe you."

Jimmy took this as more good news. *If he didn't believe me at all, he'd just hit me with a spell, call all the other wizards, and they'd either kill me or send me back to my time, but he didn't. He took the trouble to tell me that he doesn't believe me, which tells me that he doesn't totally disbelieve me either. Even if he's only five percent unsure, I can use it. It's a seed of doubt that will grow into a tree of trust, which I can sit beneath for shade or cut down for lumber as I see fit.*

"You don't have to believe me," Jimmy said, his hands still raised to head height. "I wouldn't ask you to after what I did. Look, we both know that I'm not in the shell, so there's only so much I can do, right? I only got back file access yesterday. You're the second person I've visited. I've stopped my aging, set up time travel and teleportation, and expanded my bank account, but that's all. I have no weapons."

Jimmy risked lowering a hand to point at his briefcase. "My computer is right there. We can go into your cave. You can fire up my laptop and look for yourself."

Jimmy could see the wheels turning behind Gary's eyes. A question was coming. Jimmy thought about all of the possible things that might still be bugging Gary, and figured about a ninety percent chance that he would ask Jimmy why he'd come back here, and not to some other time and place.

Gary gave Jimmy a shrewd look, and asked, "Why'd you come back here? Why not just go to some other time and place?"

"Good question," Jimmy said. "I don't want to be a fugitive for the rest of my life, especially if I'm immortal. If I'd gone to some other time, I'd have to live in fear of one of you all finding me, and eventually you would. Naturally you'd attack me, and send me back to exile, if I was lucky. There's a good chance you'd just kill me and be done with it. No, the only way for me to have peace is to come back here, to the scene of the crime and . . ." Jimmy chose his next words very carefully, "try to make things right."

"Jimmy, you killed a town. A whole town! And when we told you that you shouldn't have, you tried to kill us."

Jimmy said, "Yes. I know. I'm not saying that I can ever truly make things right, but, Gary, I have to try."

Gary said nothing.

Jimmy slowly lowered his hands. "We can just go inside. You can look at my computer. You know you'll be able to see exactly what powers I have, and what powers I don't. Then, I'll tell you what I plan to do. If you disapprove, you can easily incapacitate me and call everyone else to come and decide what to do with me, and I don't mean that I'll let you incapacitate me; we both know that I wouldn't be able to stop you."

Gary thought, let out a long sigh, then rolled his eyes and gestured with his staff, indicating the cave mouth. Jimmy picked up his briefcase, and said. "Thank you, Gary. Thank you so much."

He meant it. He'd never been more grateful in his life.

He's willing to listen to reason, Jimmy thought. *That means that as long as I can keep coming up with reasons, he'll keep listening.*

28.

Gwen and Martin materialized outside Brit the Younger's front door. They rang the doorbell, though they had little hope of Brit being home. They knew Nik was there, convalescing after his relatively gentle arrow injury and horrifically sudden and violent surgery.

After a moment, Nik opened the door. He looked weak, but his manners and spirits were intact. He invited them in and offered them a cold drink. They refused, and told him to sit down. Martin asked if he needed anything. Martin leaned Phillip's mislaid staff against the wall, then went to the kitchen to get Nik a drink while Gwen told Nik what had happened at the summit meeting. Nik seemed unconcerned, until Gwen told him that Brit the Elder had disappeared as well, at which point he became deeply concerned.

"I always thought nothing could hurt Brit," Nik said. "You know, as long as the other Brit was around."

Gwen said, "That's what we all thought." She was sitting on the couch next to Nik, holding his hands. As Martin entered and handed Nik a glass of water, he reflected on the fact that he'd only known Brit less than a week, and Phillip only a few months. As upset as he was, he could only imagine how Gwen must feel. She'd known Brit for two years, and Phillip for over a decade. Martin felt young and foolish.

"Well," he said, "we don't know for sure that anything bad has happened to them. We just know that they got pulled violently into the wall. Okay, let me rephrase that. We don't know that anything else bad happened to them after they got pulled into the wall."

"Isn't there some way you can use your magic to find them?" Nik asked.

Gwen chose not to tell Nik that she and Martin had both tried to call Phillip and Brit with no success. Instead she said, "There may be. You live with Brit. Do you ever see her looking into an object? It may look like a book or a box. It would glow and change colors."

Nik showed them into Brit's bedroom and pointed to a rect-angular shape under a velvet cloth. Martin could tell instantly that it was a one-piece Macintosh computer.

Gwen said, "Thank you, Nik. You should go rest. We need to be alone for this."

Nik smirked, and looked at Martin.

Martin said, "Don't worry. We won't do anything naughty."

Nik smiled at Gwen and said, "Oh, I know you won't."

Once they were alone, Gwen whipped the sheet off of the computer and looked for the on switch. Martin said, "It's on the back, on your left there."

There was a clear, sharp click, followed by a muddy, muffled bong, and the screen came on. The computer was a plastic rectangle with one disc slot and a screen slightly larger than the screen on Martin's phone, but with a much lower resolution. It wasn't an original Mac, but was from the dark years when Apple had churned out endless repetitions of the same basic designs. Martin knew that the computer had started out a tasteful shade of light gray, but as with all early Apple products, time had caused it to fade to a urine-like shade of yellow, a major problem for a computer that was often purchased as much as a fashion accessory as a business device. *A problem,* Martin thought, *unless you're the one trying to get people to buy a new one every two years.*

Their plan was so straightforward that neither Martin nor Gwen had felt it necessary to even say it out loud. Plan A would be to try to find Phillip's or Brit's entry in the file with a name search, but that could take a while, and if another person had their exact name, which could happen, it would slow them down. It would be much faster to simply use either Phillip's or Brit's computer, and hope they had some sort of bookmark or shortcut to help them find their own entry. Phillip's computer was a text-based relic, and was on a different continent, and hundreds of years away, so Brit's was the obvious choice.

When the Mac had finally booted up, there were several shortcuts on the desktop, one of which was named "Repository." Gwen clicked on it, and a program called Hypercard slowly loaded up. After an interminable wait, a new window opened up, asking Gwen to input a password.

Gwen said, "Huh. That's odd."

"Yeah," Martin agreed. "I wonder why she'd password protect the file. Oh well. I'll go check Phillip's computer. You wanna come with?"

"No, I'll keep nosing around on Brit's computer."

Martin said, "Cool," and teleported away. Five minutes later Martin was back, and he didn't look happy.

"How did people ever get anything done on those things?" Martin asked.

"Phillip has a Commodore 64, right? I'm not sure anyone did get things done on them. I think they were mainly designed for playing Omega Race. Didn't you get him an upgraded model?"

"Yeah, it has all modern guts, but he still works in an emulator. I think just to annoy me."

"The important thing is that he's getting enjoyment out of your gift. Did you find him in the file?"

Martin shook his head. "Yeah, but it was password protected."

"Weird!"

"I'll tell you what's even weirder. The password screen looked exactly like the one on Brit's Mac. Same font and everything."

Gwen shrugged. "Hmm. Maybe it's something they decided to do together."

Martin said, "Yeah, who knows. We'll ask them when we find them. Just means we have to do this the hard way." Martin reached into his pocket and pulled out the ornately carved box that he used to disguise his smartphone. He removed the phone, tapped a few times, swiped a few times, tapped a couple more, then stopped dead. He gave Gwen a look that she did not find comforting.

"What?"

Martin silently turned his phone around to show Gwen the exact same password box they'd seen on Brit and Phillip's computers.

Gwen said, "I'll try mine." By the time she had finished the sentence she had produced her iPhone, and was already looking at the screen.

Martin said, "You do that. I'll go try my laptop," and teleported away.

Gwen sat alone in Brit the Younger's bedroom, hastily swiping and jabbing at her phone. Finally, she cursed and put the phone away. She looked out the glass wall to the ocean beyond and muttered, "What's going on?"

Martin reappeared. "It's no good. I'm locked out on my laptop too."

Gwen said, "Same goes for my phone."

Martin said, "Yeah, I figured, and that's not the worst of it." Martin held up the first arrow that had been fired at Brit. It was enchanted to be relentlessly drawn to her. Even if there was some barrier that kept it from moving forward, it would get as close to her as it could. He held the arrow in the air, then let go. It fell straight to the ground. Gwen kicked at it with her foot. It moved a bit, aiming a different direction.

Gwen said, "I'll go try my computer."

Martin said, "Knock yourself out."

Gwen was only gone thirty seconds before she returned, looking stricken. "This is bad, Martin. This is *really* bad."

Martin said, "Yeah. It is. The good news is that our powers still work. Even though we're locked out of the file, clearly the shell and the Atlantis Interface still have access."

Gwen sat in front of Brit's computer. "We don't know what's happened. We can still figure out who's responsible." She peered at the flickering screen and said, "Brit had a program running that was monitoring the shell, the interface, and all of the other various programs the delegates use to make manipulating the file easier. It was constantly cross-checking any activity with the list of registered delegates and resident sorceresses. Since magic was used to take Brit and Phillip, it'll tell us who did it."

She moved the mouse, clicked a few times, and got even closer to the screen, really studying the line she was reading.

Martin stood up, moved behind her, and asked, "What's it say?"

"That whoever took Phillip and Brit is not a summit delegate or a resident sorcerer."

"Great," Martin said. "That narrows it down to just people we don't know about." Martin walked to the glass wall and stared out into the murky, blue-green ocean. Gwen got up from the useless computer and joined him.

"Nobody took it seriously," Martin said. "Not even us, really. Brit didn't even entirely believe that she could be hurt. Phillip believed, and Brit wanted to believe Phillip, and we helped them because they were our friends, and, frankly, it was kinda fun."

"I don't like the way you're using the past tense, Martin."

"I don't either."

Gwen said, "Look, everybody's taking it seriously now. We don't know that Brit and Phillip are dead. We don't even know for sure if they've been hurt. All we know is that we can't contact them."

"Very reassuring."

"It is. As long as we don't know, there's a chance. And now it's not just you and me trying to figure this out. Everybody loves Brit, both of her. All of the sorceresses, all of the delegates, everyone knows how serious this is. Someone's going to think of something, and even if they don't there's still you and me. Come on, Martin. You're down right now, but we both know you don't give up easily."

Martin turned to face Gwen. Their eyes locked. Martin muttered, "You're right, I don't give up easily." Their attention remained focused on each other's eyes until Martin said, "I'll see you later. I need to go think."

Martin walked out of Brit's bedroom, said goodbye to Nik, who was laying on Brit's couch, and left. Gwen followed him silently, and watched him walk out the door.

Nik sat up, wincing a bit at the pain in his side, and asked, "What happened?"

Gwen shook her head and said, "I'm not sure."

Nik patted the empty space on the couch next to him. Gwen sat down and pulled her legs up to her chest.

Nik said, "None of this is any of my business, but let me say what I think is going on and you can tell me if I have it right."

Gwen nodded.

"Martin likes you, and has for a long time, yes?"

Gwen said, "I thought you meant the situation with Brit and Phillip being gone."

"What? No, that's magic stuff. I can't be any help there. I don't know anything about that, so I'll stay out of it. You and your young man, I know all about that kind of thing. There I can help, if you want. Shall I continue?"

Gwen nodded.

"So, as I was saying, he likes you and has for a long time. You, on the other hand, took a little longer to decide that you liked him. Am I right?"

Gwen nodded again. She asked, "How do you know all this? Are we that easy to figure out?"

Nik said, "You are, but I had help. You're Brit's friend. He's Phillip's friend. Brit and Phillip have to talk about something, and I'm in earshot a lot more of the time than they think."

Gwen enjoyed hearing Nik refer to Brit and Phillip in the present tense.

Nik continued. "I don't know Martin well, but I'd bet that he's been pretty obvious about his feelings."

Gwen nodded emphatically.

"But now," Nik said, "he doesn't seem to like you so much anymore, and he's being pretty obvious about that as well."

Gwen didn't nod. She didn't have to.

Nik put his arm around her shoulders, squeezed gently, then asked, "Have you told him how you feel?"

"Yes. Many times."

Nik smiled, then asked, "The positive feelings, or the negative ones?"

Gwen said, "I tried to, you know, get the message across. I was just subtle about it, you know?"

Nik squeezed her again. "Gwen, have his messages to you been subtle?"

Gwen laughed. So did Nik.

"So, if he doesn't act with subtlety, what on earth made you think he would react to subtlety?"

Nik let that sink in, then continued, "It's fun to be pursued. It's fun to be desired. It's also fun to pursue and to desire, but the thing is, it's not as much fun, and it gets old a lot faster. Eventually, if you don't show an interest, he'll lose his."

Gwen said. "I just, you know, I just thought maybe he was showing enough interest for both of us."

Nik shrugged and said, "Clearly not."

29.

It was a clear day in Camelot. Happy citizens went about their business beneath a blue sky, populated with just enough clouds to remind one that there were such things as clouds, and that they could be rather pleasant. The sun shone down, illuminating the streets and alleys of the city, and reflecting off of the gold-plated castle at the heart of Camelot, blinding anybody foolish enough to look directly at it.

The castle had been covered in genuine gold for the same reason that the castle had been built in the first place, and for that matter that the name of the city had been changed from London to Camelot, because Jimmy could.

Of course, one of the great advantages to having a gigantic castle covered with genuine gold is that anything that happens in front of that castle will seem mundane by comparison, even a wizard and a man in a modern business suit, both wearing sunglasses, appearing out of thin air.

Gary turned to Jimmy and said, "Okay, we're here. I don't think this is going to work, but we might as well get it over with."

Jimmy held up a hand. "Please, Gary, may I have a moment? I haven't seen this place for a very long time."

Gary had been there the last time Jimmy had seen the castle, but had to remind himself that while it had only been a couple of months to him, to Jimmy it had been over thirty years. He chose not to dwell on the fact that on that occasion Jimmy had attempted to kill all of the other wizards.

Jimmy put his hands on his hips and took a deep, satisfied breath. For the most part, the castle was exactly as he'd remembered it. The spires, the buttresses, the grand entryway with its golden steps, they were all still there. The golden outer wall still shone just as brightly. The gilt castle gate was just as immense as ever. There were fewer guards at the entrance, but that was a minor detail. The only noticeable change was the statue that stood in the middle of the courtyard.

When Jimmy left, there had been a massive statue of the former king and the current king, both being guided protectively by Merlin, which was what the locals had called Jimmy, because he told them to.

It did not surprise him that the statue had been replaced. He had feared it would be a depiction of Phillip standing triumphant over Jimmy's own defeated form, but that was not the case. Instead, the statue represented four figures: the king, a nobleman, a wizard, and a peasant, all the same size, and clearly equal in importance, standing together, hands joined in the spirit of unity with their arms raised in triumph, over Jimmy's defeated form.

Jimmy had long ago realized that he was not a popular figure in Camelot, but it was unpleasant to have the idea demonstrated for him so vividly.

"All right," Jimmy said. "Let's do this."

Jimmy had managed to convince Gary to cooperate, but it had not been easy, and his hold on Gary's loyalty was shaky.

"Like I told you back at the cave," Gary said, "I'll do what you want, but on my terms, and I do all the talking, got that?"

Jimmy thought, *Doing what I tell you to on your terms is still doing what I tell you to.*

Jimmy said, "Got it."

"Good." Gary strode impatiently up the stairs to the main entrance to the castle. Jimmy followed behind.

As they approached the top of the stairs, Jimmy got a good look at the two guards who were stationed at the castle's open doors and did not like what he saw. The guards were taller than average with a slight bluish cast to their skin, and teeth that didn't quite seem to fit in their mouths. Clearly, these were some of the men that Jimmy had attempted to turn into orcs. Jimmy feared that they would recognize him, and remembering that the transformation process had not been painless, might not be too happy to see him. Or, even worse, they might be entirely too happy to see him.

As they reached the top of the stairs, Jimmy braced himself for a confrontation, but none came. He and Gary passed by the guards without exchanging a single word. As they passed into the cavernous, gold-trimmed antechamber, Jimmy whispered, "They didn't remember me."

"Oh, they remember you," Gary said. "They just didn't recognize you. Remember, the last time they saw you was only a month ago to them. You were thirty years younger and dressed like a wizard. Trust me, if they'd seen Merlin, they'd put those teeth you gave them to good use. Lucky for you, all they saw was a weird old guy dressed like a weirdo."

"Lucky me," Jimmy said.

Instead of passing into the grand hall of the castle Camelot where much of Jimmy's final battle with Martin had taken place, they turned and went up a large, sweeping staircase that led to what had once been Jimmy's office. Along the way, they passed another former orc. Once they were beyond his hearing, Jimmy said, "I'm glad to see that the process of changing them back to humans is going well."

Gary said, "If by *well*, you mean *slowly and painfully*, yes it is."

Jimmy decided to drop the subject. Instead, he turned his thoughts to the task ahead. It would call for a slightly different approach than the one he'd used on Gary. Of course, Gary was doing the talking, at least at first. Jimmy would jump in if need be, of course, but he was curious to see what Gary would say. Most people had hidden talents, and someone with Gary's sense of humor didn't keep friends long unless he was pretty good at smoothing ruffled feathers.

They finally reached their goal, the door to Jimmy's former office. Gary opened the door without knocking, but entered carefully, asking, "Is anybody here?" in a loud voice. Gary was through the door and had entered what used to be Jimmy's lobby when Eddie emerged from his and Jimmy's former office. Eddie smiled when he saw Gary.

Eddie was wearing his red silk robes, just as Jimmy remembered them. They helped sell his cover as Wing Po, the mysterious wizard from the east. Of course, his cover would have been utterly destroyed by Eddie's thick New Jersey accent if any of the locals could recognize it.

Eddie said, "Hey Gary, how're you . . ." Eddie's words trailed off as he saw Jimmy enter. Given the changes in Jimmy's appearance, it took a moment for Eddie to make sense of what he was seeing. By the time Eddie started shouting inarticulately and wielding his staff threateningly at Jimmy, it was clear that Eddie recognized him.

Gary threw himself between Eddie and Jimmy and spread his arms wide. *Okay,* Jimmy thought, *let's see what the kid has to say.*

Gary shouted, "Dude! Dude! Dude."

Eddie stopped yelling, but kept his staff pointed menacingly, murder in his eyes.

Gary said, "Dude?"

"What is this?" Eddie asked, through gritted teeth.

Gary said, "It's Jimmy."

"I know it's Jimmy! What's he doing here?"

"He showed up at my cave a half-hour ago. He was able to get access to the file again, but it took him a long time. He can't hurt us. He's still locked out of the shell, okay? You know that. You're the one who controls the shell, so you know he can't hurt us."

Eddie calmed down, but only enough to look like he wanted to kill Jimmy slowly and methodically, instead of in a blood frenzy. He turned to Jimmy and asked, "What do you have to say for yourself?"

Jimmy knew this would be a tough one. Eddie had been his right-hand man for years, obeying Jimmy's every order and hanging on his every word in the belief that they were a team and had no secrets from each other. When Jimmy's secrets were discovered, Eddie was as surprised as anyone, and when Jimmy then attempted to kill all of the other wizards, Eddie included, he had been more surprised than anyone.

What emotions am I trying to convey? Jimmy asked himself. *Regret. Happiness to see my old friend, mixed with sadness that he doesn't want to see me. Resignation and acceptance, certainly. Contrition and affection in equal measures.* It was a tall order, but Jimmy had an idea.

Jimmy projected sadness with his eyes, spread his hands to signal surrender, and in a quiet voice, said, "Dude."

"Don't you dude me! Don't you ever dude me!" Eddie shrieked. "Do you understand?! Do you?!"

Jimmy nodded, and raised his hands above his head.

"What do you want?" Eddie bellowed, then looked back to Gary. "What does he want?"

Gary looked back to Jimmy. Jimmy shrugged. Gary looked Eddie in the eye and said, "He wants you to give him shell access."

Eddie belted out a wail of pure anger, and hauled his staff back as if he had given up on using magic on Jimmy and instead intended to bludgeon him.

Gary again threw himself between Eddie and Jimmy, shouting, "Dude!"

30.

Martin walked sullenly through the streets of Atlantis.

He had decided to call them streets even though there were no cars or wheeled vehicles. There were some pushcarts and the occasional wheelbarrow, but unless someone was riding in them, he couldn't call them vehicles. By the same token, he didn't think he could justify calling them streets without wheeled vehicles, but he decided to let that one go. *Walking sullenly through the pedestrian footpaths of Atlantis* just didn't set the right tone.

Of course, he could have just teleported back to his hotel room and avoided the whole problem, but teleporting, like driving a car, is best suited to situations where you're either traveling a long distance in a hurry or trying to impress people. For short distances, walking is still preferred by most wizards because it gives you time to talk if you're with someone and time to think if you're not. Walking can be very pleasant. Moving slowly through an environment gives you the opportunity to really see it. Besides, teleporting around everywhere gives one's life a frantic, disjointed feeling, and doesn't help one's cardiovascular health either.

Also, it's impossible to teleport sullenly. It's over too quickly, and nobody witnesses it. If you want to travel sullenly, you pretty much have to walk, and given Martin's mood, if he was going to do anything he was going to do it sullenly.

Martin heard someone shout his name. Martin turned, and said, "Hi, Vikram," sullenly.

Vikram was a fakir from one of the Indian delegations. When they'd first been introduced at the big meet-and-greet on day one, Vikram had worn ostentatious robes and a cartoonish large, bejeweled turban, but since then he had worn his usual daily uniform, a simple loose-fitting orange robe.

Vikram ran to catch up to Martin, then said, "Look, Martin, I just want to apologize. I feel terrible that I didn't do anything to help today."

Martin started walking again. Vikram kept pace.

"Don't worry about it, Vikram. There were a lot of people there who didn't help. Heck, if you look at the results, I didn't really help, did I?"

"At least you did something, and please, call me Vic. Most of us just stood there and watched."

"It's understandable. You were all in shock."

"It's no excuse," Vikram spat.

They both walked sullenly for a moment, then Vikram asked, "Any idea who's behind it?"

"Well, we've ruled some people out."

"Who?"

Martin chuckled mirthlessly, and said, "Pretty much any suspect we had."

After another long silence, Vikram said, "We all should have been helping you. There are so many of us. Whoever did this, they were smart to make today's attack so chaotic. It kept us from acting until it was too late."

Martin shook his head. "Really, Vic? I don't think so. I mean, really, Phillip and I created most of the chaos ourselves. All the attacker did was drop another statue and throw some more arrows. Sure, he added some ropes and tar, but really, it's just a slight variation on all the stuff they'd done before that didn't work. It was an act of stubbornness, not intelligence."

Vic nodded. "Sadly, I find that stubbornness often beats intelligence eventually. Stubbornness will beat anything eventually. That's the whole point of stubbornness."

Martin didn't like that idea. He agreed with it, but he did not like it.

"Look," Vikram said, "none of us really took any of this seriously before today. Logic seemed to dictate that Brit the Younger couldn't be killed, so we didn't think the Brits were in any real danger."

Neither did I, Martin thought.

"But now we are taking this seriously," Vikram continued, "and we feel like jerks."

So do I, Martin thought.

"If there's anything I can do to help, please let me know. I'm sure that goes for all of the other delegates. We want to help. We just don't know how."

Neither do I, Martin thought.

With that, Vikram said goodbye and Martin continued his sullen trek back to the room he had been sharing with Phillip.

When he reached the door, Ampyx was waiting.

"What do you want?" Martin asked, then immediately waved his hand to stop any forthcoming answer. "Never mind. Don't say it. I know what you want. Go for it. I hope you have better luck than I did."

Martin opened his door and went into his room. He didn't close the door behind himself, so Ampyx followed him in. Martin slumped down in a chair and looked at Ampyx, clearly irritated and confused. "What? I told you, she's all yours. Just take my advice, don't try to get anywhere with Gwen by acting like me, because I can tell you, it doesn't work."

Ampyx shook his head and stepped to the center of the room as if he were about to recite the Gettysburg address. "Martin," he said, in stilted tones, "I have come here to say something to you."

Martin's irritation faded, clearly being pushed out of his brain by his increased confusion.

Ampyx said, "I have watched you closely since you've arrived. I have discussed you with your friend, Phillip. I have observed you interacting with the sorceress, Gwen. I have witnessed your attempts to prevent harm from coming to Brit the Younger."

Oh great, Martin thought. *Just what I need, criticism from a walking pituitary gland.*

Martin opened his mouth to interrupt, but before he could, Ampyx said, "And I've come here today to tell you that you have earned my respect."

Martin squinted and said, "I'm sorry. Could you repeat that?"

"Do not gloat about it, Martin. This is hard enough for me as it is."

"I'm not gloating. I just . . . I can't believe what I'm hearing."

"It is true. Martin, you are a man of action. You intervene, while others stand and watch. Then, by the time they take action, you are already several steps ahead. You are often out of step with those around you, but that doesn't mean that they're on the correct foot."

"Thank you, Ampyx," Martin said. "That's one of the nicest things anyone's ever said to me."

"That does not surprise me. My biggest criticism of you is in your choice of friends. Phillip doesn't respect you as much as he should."

"Well, in Phillip's defense, he was my teacher. In a lot of ways he still sees me as a student."

Ampyx sat on the chair opposite Martin. "No. You still look at yourself as a student, and it keeps you from seeing yourself or him clearly."

"Look," Martin said, "Phillip might be dead, at any rate he's missing and in trouble. I appreciate what you're saying, but now's not the time."

"No, now is not the time for honesty? When is? I was at the summit today, guarding one of the balconies. I saw what happened. You acted, while the other wizards and sorceresses stood there like sheep."

"Ampyx, that's not fair."

"True. Sheep are useful."

Martin said, "Phillip helped. Heck, he got to Brit first."

"Yes, and what did he do? He held on to her, and he yelled. You used your magic. You attempted to anchor your legs to pillars, tables, even the wall. And nobody else thought to come to your aid until failure was practically a forgone conclusion."

"Thanks, but I think you're giving me too much credit. None of that did any good."

"I give you credit for trying and failing. It's not much credit, but it's still more credit than most of your peers deserve."

Martin asked, "Well, why didn't you and the other guards help?"

"We don't get involved in issues regarding magic. What if I had tried to push Brit the Younger out of the path of a falling statue? I'd have been crushed and she wouldn't have gotten hurt either way. What if I'd thrown myself between her and the arrows? I get impaled, she is unhurt either way. We guards are there to keep angry citizens from troubling the sorceresses, but in truth, we are largely ornamental. Most of us do the job in hopes of catching a sorceress's eye. Otherwise, we'd probably wear something more substantial."

Martin tried to imagine fighting while wearing a mesh t-shirt and a kilt, and decided that Ampyx had a point.

"You do things, Martin. Not smart things, but still, things. While Phillip criticizes and Gwen hides, you do things."

"What do you mean, Gwen hides?" Martin asked.

"I've only been watching you for a short time and it's obvious to me that Gwen is yours. You are the only man she is interested in, and everyone else can see it. Yet she refuses to show you. She hides from you, and from her feelings. You know it is true, Martin. That is why she frustrates you so."

Martin shook his head. "I don't know."

Ampyx asked, "Martin, how many women have you wanted in your life?"

Martin answered, "Many."

Ampyx asked, "How many of those women have wanted you in return?"

Martin answered, "Not many."

"And how did you respond to their lack of interest?"

"I dunno. I guess I got the hint and left them alone."

"Yes. But you haven't given up, even after she left and moved far away. Even after all the times she's rebuffed your advances. Even now, when you claim to have let her go, you still hold out hope. It's because some part of you, some part that sees things clearly, some part that isn't your brain, knows that she is hiding. She hides. It is her nature."

Martin frowned. He didn't like being psychoanalyzed. He especially didn't like being psychoanalyzed accurately. *Is it true?* Martin asked himself. *No. She's very outgoing. Everybody in Leadchurch liked her. She ran that shop, where she spent ten years pretending to be a tailor, hiding the fact that she was a wizard.*

"Okay, Ampyx, say you're right."

"I am right."

"I didn't mean that literally."

"I do."

"Whatever. So what? How does any of this help me now? Phillip and Brit are gone and Gwen is still hiding."

"And you are sitting here in your room, doing nothing."

Martin asked, "What should I do?"

"Something."

"I can't just go out and start doing crap at random. I need a plan."

"Who has been coming up with the plans so far?"

Martin thought back to the time right after what he'd started referring to as "The Big Squid Implosion." Martin felt a stab of embarrassment when he recalled having suggested that Ida, the president, was behind it, and having to have it explained that nobody as smart as her would do something so stupid. Martin had instantly seen that they were right, and handed over the strategy to them. Martin said, "Brit and Phillip and Gwen made the plans."

"Why them?" Ampyx asked.

"Because, if I'm being honest, they're smarter than I am."

"Are they smarter, or do they just know more?"

Martin asked, "Is there a difference?"

"Yes, a big one. Even I know that. Martin, you say they made the plan. Was that plan to simply let the murderer keep trying over and over again, until they either gave up or got it right?"

"Well, that's not how they put it," Martin mumbled. "Besides, this last time the idea was to use our powers to identify who did it."

"Did that work?"

"No."

"And you're certain that they are smart?"

"Yes, look, you're right. You have a point. I am usually the one who acts first, and Gwen and Phillip tend to do a lot more standing around talking than I like, but I make a lot of mistakes. More mistakes than they do."

"Because you try more things than they do."

"I'm not sure that's a good thing. There's something to be said for planning and strategizing, and they are smart people. It's just their plan this time that turned out to be stupid. Smart people do dumb things some times."

Ampyx stood silently, thinking about this.

"Smart people do dumb things," Martin repeated.

They sat in silence. Martin's eyes got wide. He looked at Ampyx, then stood up urgently. Ampyx stood as well, alarmed that Martin seemed alarmed. Martin looked around the room, opening and closing his mouth as if silently arguing with himself. Ampyx asked, "What's wrong?"

Martin looked up at Ampyx and said, "Smart people do dumb things!"

"Dumb things like repeating themselves?" Ampyx asked.

31.

It isn't possible to teleport sullenly, but it is possible to teleport urgently. Martin and Ampyx materialized outside Brit the Younger's door. Martin was perched on the balls of his feet, ready for anything. Instead of anything, he found nothing, nothing out of the ordinary anyway, and it seemed to confuse him for a moment. He swiveled his head around, making sure the coast was clear, then removed his hand from Ampyx's shoulder and rang the doorbell.

As they waited for Nik to answer, Martin kept looking from one end of the hall to the other.

"Is something wrong?" Ampyx asked.

"Yes. We're onto something."

"And that's wrong?"

"Of course it is," Martin said. "It's always when you feel like you're onto something that life knocks the wind out of you."

Nik opened the door. "Oh, hello again, Martin. Who's your friend?"

Martin said, "Nik, this is Ampyx. Ampyx, Nik. Is Gwen still here?"

Nik smiled, but shook his head. "No, the poor thing left a little after you did."

"Where'd she go?"

"Home, I guess." Nik turned his attention back to Ampyx. "You don't talk much, do you?"

Ampyx said, "No."

Martin said, "Thanks, Nik. You rest. We'll go to Gwen's."

Nik said, "You should."

The three of them stood in silence, then Nik asked, "You don't know where Gwen lives, do you?"

"No," Martin admitted. "No, I don't."

+══╼ ╾══+

Martin and Ampyx materialized urgently outside Gwen's door. Unlike Brit's apartment and Martin's hotel room, Gwen lived in the Atlantean equivalent of a townhouse. Her front door faced the pedestrian thoroughfare. Atlanteans went on about their business, but the city's mood was decidedly less upbeat since the events of the morning. The worse the news, the faster it travels.

Martin took a quick look at the façade of Gwen's home. Its Atlantis-standard white-crystalline walls were interrupted by pleasant, rather conventional-looking windows. Martin could see the backsides of curtains and plants just inside. The place gave off an air of cheerfulness. He'd have wanted to go inside even if he hadn't known that Gwen was in there.

Martin knocked on the door. He heard nothing. He knocked again, then yelled, "Gwen, it's me! We need to talk."

A few seconds later, the door swung open violently. Gwen looked at Martin. She seemed to be both angry and relieved. Martin didn't know if she was angry to feel relieved at seeing him, or relieved to feel angry at seeing him.

"Gwen, we need to talk. Can we come in?"

Gwen seemed to notice Ampyx for the first time, and his presence clearly confused her. "Uh, sure," she said, stepping aside.

Martin went in the door, but Ampyx hesitated. Martin turned around and said, "Come on in. You might as well watch us from up close for a change." Ampyx followed Martin into Gwen's home.

From the outside, peeking in through the windows, Gwen's home had exuded happiness, and Martin could see why. What with the curtains, the flowers, and the decorative furnishings, the areas right next to the windows almost reeked of cheerful good taste. The rest of the house seemed to be storage space for rolls of fabric, dress dummies, work tables, and sewing machines. The whole back wall of the room was covered with racks of garments in various stages of completion.

Martin spun around, taking it all in. "You still make clothes?" he asked.

"Yes," Gwen answered.

"Why?"

Gwen said, "Because I enjoy making clothes."

Martin walked to one of the work tables and felt a piece of dark fabric that was pinned to a pattern. "Do you make things for the other sorceresses?"

"A few things, mostly for the Brits. To be honest, I mainly just make things for fun. What I really enjoy making is outerwear, and we don't get much call for it here." She walked to a female dress form that was wearing a sleek moto-inspired jacket that was made from the dark wool material of a longshoreman's coat.

Martin looked at the coat, and the other projects strewn around the space, and said, "This is really cool, Gwen!"

Gwen smiled, then glanced at Ampyx. She turned back to Martin and said, "Why is he—" She stopped herself, realizing that she was being rude. She turned to Ampyx and asked him, "Why . . ." She stopped again, then realized that she didn't know how to ask what she wanted to ask without it sounding a little rude, so she just went for it.

"Why are you here?" she asked.

Ampyx said, "I don't know. He brought me."

Martin said, "I think better with Ampyx around. He helped me figure out what to do next. Besides, the non-magic folk live in Atlantis too, so they should have a hand in preventing this."

Gwen asked, "Preventing what?" She looked at Ampyx, who shrugged. Clearly, he was as lost as she was.

"First things first, Gwen. When we were at Brit's place, and she and Phillip came back from the giant squid implosion, what did I say?"

Ampyx repeated, "Giant squid implosion?" He looked even more lost.

Gwen said, "It's not what it sounds like. The squid didn't implode."

"Never mind that," Martin continued. "What did I say?"

"About what?" Gwen asked.

"I said that we should look at who had the most to gain from Brit and the other Brit being out of the way."

Gwen nodded, "Yes, I remember, and we told you that wasn't helpful."

"Because?" Martin asked.

"Because you said that the person with the most to gain was Ida."

"Because?"

"Because she's the president, and with the Brits gone, she'd be in charge."

"She is in charge," Martin pointed out, "but let's not get ahead of ourselves. You all told me that was a stupid idea."

"And it is," Gwen said. "Ida's not behind this."

"How do you know?"

"Because Ida knows just as well as anyone that it's logically impossible for Brit the Younger to die, because Brit the Elder is here."

Martin and Ampyx exchanged a look, then Martin continued. "Your logic has two flaws. One is that it would appear that harm *did* come to Brit the Younger, and that it seems to have removed Brit the Elder, but that's not the main flaw. You couldn't have known that would happen back then. No, your reasoning has an even more fundamental error."

Gwen asked, "And what is that?" She did not like the way this was going.

"Gwen," Martin said, "it's not your fault. You and Brit, heck, even Phillip agreed, and he didn't buy into the idea that Brit the Elder's existence made Brit the Younger invulnerable. You all fell prey to the same fallacy. Ida is smart, isn't she?"

"Yes. Very."

"And to even attempt to kill Brit the Younger would not just be immoral, but it would also be stupid, wouldn't it?"

"Yes, very."

Martin walked to Gwen, and gently placed his hands on both of her shoulders. "Gwen," he said, "smart people do stupid things."

Gwen looked at Martin, her expression a mixture of confusion and disgust.

Martin smiled as if sharing a bit of good news. "Smart people do stupid things!"

Gwen replied, "Smart people do stupid things?"

Martin nodded slowly, and said, "Smart people do stupid things."

Ampyx muttered, "Like repeating themselves."

Martin said, "You said that already," then turned his attention back to Gwen. "Just because someone's smart, that doesn't mean that everything they do is going to be smart. Look at you!"

"What?" Gwen asked.

"You're one of the smartest people I've ever known."

"Go on."

"But you refuse to admit that you're crazy about me. That's stupid! You want something, yet you're pushing it away. You're smart, but you're doing something stupid."

Gwen shook her head. "I never said I was crazy about you."

"I know! That's my point!"

Gwen looked like she might explode. Martin held up his hands, and in a calming tone said, "Look, never mind that. Forget I said anything. I'm sorry. Now's not the time for that conversation anyway. But think about my point for a second. Really think about it. You have to admit, I'm right. Smart people do stupid things."

After a long, angry silence, Gwen said, "Yes. You're right."

Martin thrust a triumphant finger in the air, and yelled, "Ah ha! HA! Ah ha HA!" He turned to Ampyx, smiling broadly, and said, "Huh? Eh?"

Ampyx crossed his arms, nodded in deep satisfaction, looked at Gwen and said, "Mmm-hmm."

"Oh, what?!" Gwen shouted. "What are you so happy about?"

"I've convinced you," Martin said. "That means that my argument was convincing, and the only example I gave to try to make my point was that you're into me. If that example convinced you, that means—"

"That you should shut up," Gwen interrupted.

Martin looked to Ampyx, who nodded silently.

"Okay," Martin said. "We'll table that for now." His words were contrite, but he sounded like he was on the verge of giggling. "We have to go and question Ida."

Gwen rolled her eyes. "Martin, we've been through this. She wouldn't have thought that killing Brit was possible."

"Yes, yes, and as such her even trying would be stupid, which I've demonstrated, is not the same thing as impossible."

"But that's not evidence."

"I'm not claiming it is. I'm just saying that we can't rule her out, and you have to admit, she is the person with the most to gain from the Brits being gone. You saw her after they vanished today. She's practically the whole government now. Even if you don't think she did it, talking to her is the logical starting point."

Gwen looked unconvinced.

"Unless you have any better ideas," Martin added, trying not to sound smug.

After a long, smoldering silence, Gwen said, "It can't have been Ida anyway. She would have been caught by Brit's surveillance app."

"Yeah, I've been thinking about that. The app was looking for any known magic users, right?"

"Yes."

"And since magic was used, but the app didn't catch anyone, that means it was an unknown magic user, right?"

"Yes, and Ida is well known. If it'd been her—"

Now Martin interrupted, "Yes, I know. Clearly she didn't actually do the magic, but someone had to, and every legitimate magic user in the city would have shown up in the app, right?"

"Yeah," Gwen said, wearily.

"Then, logically, it had to have been an illegitimate magic user. Someone who snuck into the city unannounced."

Gwen said, "Yes, in which case we can't—"

Martin raised a finger and said, "Or, OR! Or, some magic user gave powers to a local."

They had both nearly forgotten that Ampyx was still there, but now he reminded them. "Wait, you can do that?"

Gwen said, "No! No we can't!"

Martin said, "That's not true. We can, and you know it." He turned to Ampyx, and said, "I mean, obviously, we can't. We're not supposed to. We'd be in big trouble if we did and the other wizards found out, and even if they didn't it would be tremendously dangerous. It'd probably end in horrible bloodshed, so no, we can't give powers to non-magical folk."

Martin turned and looked Gwen in the eye. "But, it is technically possible. You know better than anyone, the Camelot shell program gives powers to people who are wearing a certain kind of robe, a particular kind of hat, holding a staff or a wand," Martin shook his staff to emphasize the point. "Give someone all that, have them recite the Konami code in Esperanto, then memorize a few key phrases, and they're in business."

Gwen shook her head. "Martin, Ida would never do that."

"Why? Because it's stupid?"

"Martin, I grant you that smart people do dumb things sometimes, but this is Ida. She doesn't go around doing dumb things all the time. She's not an idiot. We wouldn't have made her president if she were."

Martin slowly took a step toward Gwen. He put his hand on her shoulder, looked deeply into her eyes, and said, "Gwen, I don't deny that you're much smarter than I am, and have been around longer, and that you know Ida far better than I do. That said, you just used the fact that she's an elected official as evidence that she wouldn't have done something stupid. Are you even listening to yourself?"

32.

Everybody saw them flying down to the ring of grand buildings that surrounded the central park of Atlantis and served as
the sorceresses' seat of power. The sorceresses seldom flew anywhere, deeming it far too ostentatious, so the sight of Martin and
Gwen streaking purposefully across the vast empty bowl of the
city's skyline would have gotten a great deal of attention even if
Martin hadn't been carrying Ampyx, who was shouting with glee
at the top of his lungs.

They slowed, gliding through the entrance doors and finally
landing in the grand space where the summit meetings were
held. The tables and chairs had all been replaced, but without
Brit the Elder there to assist with the cleanup, the two statues
that had fallen were still represented by the shattered stumps and
empty plinths where they had stood. If you knew where to look,
and Martin did, you could still see the streaks where Phillip's
shoes had slid across the smooth white floor.

"Hard to believe it only happened a couple of hours ago,"
Gwen said.

Martin looked at the blank patch of wall that had swallowed
Brit and Phillip. "Yeah. Wherever they are, I hope they're all
right." He turned to Gwen. "So, you say Ida has an office in this
building?"

"Yes, there are offices for all three members of the council. Brit the Younger never uses hers."

"Why not?"

"It has an adjoining door with Brit the Elder's office, and the Elder doesn't see a reason to knock, since they're the same person."

"Wow," Martin said. "I'm surprised the Younger didn't try to kill the Elder before now."

"We used to joke about that. Even if the Younger did try to kill the Elder, the Elder would remember making the attempt and avoid it."

Martin said, "You could go crazy thinking about this."

Gwen glanced ruefully at the empty base of a broken statue and said, "Maybe someone did." She shuddered. "Come on. The offices are this way." She and Martin took several steps before they realized that Ampyx was not following them.

Martin asked, "You coming?"

"Should I?" Ampyx asked.

"Sure. Why wouldn't you? I mean, you locals like the Brits, right? If I'm right you don't want to be ruled over by someone who seized power this way, and besides, as president, she's your elected leader. I figure there should be a representative of her non-magical voters."

Ampyx looked confused. Gwen cleared her throat, and mumbled something that Martin couldn't make out.

"I'm sorry. What was that?" he asked.

Gwen repeated, only slightly louder, "Um, non-sorceresses don't get a vote."

"What? That's most of the city! A huge majority, and you're telling me that they don't get a say in who's president?"

"Well, the council of three only really rules the sorceresses."

"Then who runs the city?"

"The sorceresses."

Martin gestured toward Ampyx, using him as a stand-in for all non-magical Atlanteans. "So they don't get to pick their leaders, or the leader of their leaders?!"

Gwen said, "I told you, there are things about this city I'm not proud of. I've only been here two years. Brit says that they'll get the right to vote eventually, she just hasn't told us when."

"Well I'm sure Ampyx and his friends find that very reassuring, don't you, Ampyx?" Martin turned to Ampyx, looking for support.

Ampyx said, "Sure. I mean, I guess. It depends. What's a vote?"

With that argument ended in a three-way tie for loser, they made their way to a side exit, through a labyrinth of beautifully decorated hallways, and eventually to a door marked *Ida Cooke: President.*

Martin said, "Let me do the talking."

Gwen replied, "She knows me, Martin. She'll be much more comfortable if I ask the questions."

Martin said, "Which is exactly why I'll do the talking. Trust me, I know how to handle this. I've been interrogated by the best."

Gwen knew that Martin had once been captured by federal agents. She didn't know that when he referred to being interrogated by the best, he was talking about his mother.

Martin looked at the closed door and asked, "Does she have a secretary or anything?"

"No. We like to keep things informal."

Martin knocked on the door, three forceful blows, then waited. After a moment, the door opened. Martin was grateful that Ida herself answered the door, not her violence-prone bodyguard Nilo. She looked tired and concerned, but not overtly so, as if something awful and upsetting had happened, but not to her, which was the case.

Ida smiled and said, "Oh, Gwen and . . . Martin, isn't it? Hello. I don't believe I've met your servant."

Martin stared at her silently, radiating anger.

Ida narrowed her eyes and asked Martin, "How can I help you?"

Martin continued staring directly into her eyes. Gwen and Ampyx fidgeted uncomfortably.

All friendliness drained from Ida's demeanor. She glared at Martin, and spat her words. "Do you have something you want to say, Martin?"

Gwen started to speak in a conciliatory tone, but Martin raised one finger and glared over his shoulder at her. He turned his attention back to Ida with one raised eyebrow and a grim smile on his lips.

Ida's shoulders slumped inward slightly and she seemed to age ten years in a single second. She sighed and said, "Come in. I'll try to explain."

As he entered, Martin looked at Ida with cold contempt. Gwen and Ampyx tried not to look amazed.

Ida closed the door behind them. Her office was, like almost every other room Martin had seen in Atlantis, beautiful and serene, made up of clean lines and uncluttered white, polished surfaces. The room was dominated by a large desk that looked exactly like the desk of the President of the United States, only smaller, and made of milky-white glass. Ida walked around the perimeter of the room and sat behind her desk. There were chairs and a couch, but Martin chose to remain standing. Gwen and Ampyx followed his lead.

Martin sneered at Ida, and asked, "Why?"

Ida slumped in defeat. "He wanted it so badly."

Gwen asked, "Who? Who wanted what?"

Ida, furrowed her brow, looking at Gwen. Then she looked back to Martin and asked, "You didn't tell her?"

Martin smiled.

Shock registered on Ida's face as she said, "You didn't know?" Her eyes darted across the faces of her three visitors, then she said, "Nothing! I'll say nothing further. Get out of my office."

Martin turned to Gwen and Ampyx, and said, "Nilo. Nilo wanted powers."

Her brief hopes dashed, Ida looked even more defeated.

Gwen was stunned. "Ida, why did you do it?"

"It started innocently, Gwen. I love him, and I couldn't bear the idea of him getting old and dying, not if I could prevent it."

Ampyx said, "You can prevent that?"

Gwen turned to him and said, "We've been through that."

Ida smiled at Gwen, pointed to Ampyx, and said, "Oh, you and him?"

Martin said, "We've been through that too."

Ida shrugged, and continued. "So, I fixed that for him, then I told him what I'd done, you know, as a gift for him."

"That's some gift," Martin said.

"I know, right?" She turned back to Gwen, "But you know how men are. They always want more. Anything he saw one of us do, he wanted to do it too. I set him up with kind of a simplified, baby set of powers. I made him impervious to physical damage. He can teleport within Atlantis city limits."

"Of course," Martin said. "That's how he got up to where I was so fast. You know, when we were chasing the arrow guy."

Gwen shook her head. "No, he sprinted up the stairs. I saw him do it."

Ida got a dreamy look in her eye. "Yes. He just doesn't get tired. He can go like that for hours."

"Thanks to you, I suppose." Gwen said.

Ida smiled. "No. That's all him. He's always been able to do . . . that."

Gwen and Martin rolled their eyes. Ampyx smirked, and nodded approvingly.

Gwen was at a loss. "Ida, I can understand wanting to keep him alive, and giving him a few small powers was wrong, but understandable, I guess. Why would you ever give him the power to blow things up and enchant arrows?"

Ida shook her head. "I didn't!"

Gwen looked relieved. Martin looked concerned.

Ida continued. "Not really. Not at first."

Gwen looked concerned. Martin looked relieved.

Ida waved her hand dismissively. "I made him the arrows, and some little lumps of clear putty that explode with the force of a pound of C-4, but the damage is contained and shaped into a wedge so he could direct where the statues would fall, like a lumberjack chopping down a tree. I set it up so he could trigger them, though. Makes him feel powerful."

"So you helped him?" Gwen asked.

"Well, yeah. Gwen, he was just so cute. He was making all these plans, and figuring out how to best use the arrows and the explosives." Ida smiled at the memory of it. "He thought of the thing with the submersible himself. Of course, he thought they'd just drown. He didn't know about the water pressure, but still. It was sweet. He just wanted me to be in charge. And it was nice to see him getting so excited about a project of his own."

Gwen shouted, "His project was murdering Brit!"

"Which isn't possible, Gwen. I mean, obviously, if Brit the Younger dies, then Brit the Elder never existed, and the whole city would disappear, which it hasn't, so clearly she's still alive, somewhere."

"Then where is she, Ida? Either of her, or Phillip, for that matter?"

Ida, smile faded slightly. She said, "Oh, I'm sure they're all right."

"Where are they?"

Ida laughed at how silly Gwen was being.

Gwen did not laugh. "Where, Ida?"

Ida's laugh died, horribly. She shrugged and said, "I don't know."

Martin asked, "What do you mean, you don't know?"

"I gave Nilo the ability to make his own portals. Setting up the arrows was such a pain. He was very particular about getting the angles just right so that the arrows would hit Brit exactly where he wanted them to. It turned into such a hassle. I just gave him portals and told him to go nuts." Ida paused for a moment, then said, "That sounded really terrible, didn't it?"

Gwen, Martin, and Ampyx all agreed that it did.

Ida held up her hands and whined, "She's fine! Lighten up, okay? She's clearly fine! We wouldn't still be here talking if she weren't!"

Martin asked, "What about Phillip?"

Ida replied, "What?"

"What about Phillip?" Martin shouted. "Wherever your boyfriend sent Brit the Younger, Phillip went there with her, and while the city still being here might, *might* prove that she didn't die, which is a very different thing than being fine, by the way, it doesn't prove anything as far as Phillip's safety is concerned."

Ida said, "Huh. I hadn't thought of that. Well, that's a shame, but, really, it is Phillip's own fault. I mean, if he hadn't gotten involved in the first place . . ."

"By trying to save Brit's life?" Martin interrupted.

Ida said, "Yeah. That sounded really terrible again, didn't it?"

Again, Gwen, Martin, and Ampyx agreed.

"So, you don't know where Nilo sent them?" Gwen asked, clearly out of patience.

"No"

"Then we'll have to ask Nilo. I don't suppose you know where he is."

"Yeah," Ida said. "He's in there." She pointed to a small door behind her desk.

Martin and Gwen looked at the door, then at each other, then at Ida. Gwen asked, "Has he been listening this whole time?"

Ida laughed. "No, he's asleep. After the meeting he dragged me straight back here to celebrate. After that, he fell asleep, and he's been out ever since. Anyway, even if he was awake he wouldn't have heard us. When I moved a bed in there I also made the room soundproof." Ida arched her eyebrows and stuck her tongue out mischievously.

Martin feared that Ampyx would have a sore neck later from all these approving nods.

Ida quickly saw that neither Martin nor Gwen was sharing her delight at how naughty she was being. Her expression darkened. "I suppose you want me to go get him."

Gwen said, "Yes."

Ida got up from her seat and opened the small door behind her desk. In a kittenish voice that, under these circumstances, sickened Martin, Ida said, "Honey? You awake?" In the distance, they heard a faint but very deep groan. Ida turned, gave Gwen a look that clearly meant *I'll be back in a minute*, then went into the room, leaving the door slightly ajar behind her.

They couldn't make out words, but they heard Ida mutter something in her softest, sweetest tone. They heard another deep groan, followed by a mumble and a laugh.

Gwen said, "I can't believe this. How could she be so stupid?"

Martin shrugged and said, "Love does that to people."

Gwen said, "Shut up."

Martin said, "No, Gwen, I'm sorry. I wasn't talking about you."

Gwen said, "Good."

After thinking for a moment, Martin said, "Of course, the fact that you thought I was clearly—"

Gwen said, "Shut up."

The tone of the nothings being whispered in the other room had become noticeably less sweet. Ida sounded insistent. Nilo sounded defiant. Finally, Ida appeared at the door and said, "He'll be right out."

Nilo shuffled into the office, looking surly. His demeanor clearly showed that he had simply dragged himself out of bed, pulled on his uniform, and come straight out to face his accusers.

Gwen took the lead. "Okay, Nilo. What have you done?"

Nilo laughed. "You don't understand? No, of course you don't. You sorceresses, you all think you're smarter than everyone, but I've shown you. I've shown you all." He looked at Gwen and Martin with a mixture of amusement and disgust. He shook his head and said, "Isn't it obvious? Can't you see what I've done? Do you really need me to explain it to you?"

Uh-oh, Martin thought. *I don't like this. Have we underestimated him? Has he been playing Ida all along?*

Nilo said, "I have killed Brit the Younger."

That answers that question, Martin thought.

Ida said, "Dear, you haven't killed Brit."

"Yes, I have," Nilo said. "I killed her!"

Ida said, "Okay, okay, you're right. You killed her." Nilo turned back to Gwen, feeling vindicated. Ida smiled at Gwen and winked.

"Why?" Gwen asked. "Why did you do it, Nilo?"

Nilo shook his head. He looked amazed at Gwen's stupidity. He turned to Ida, who play-acted his amazement back to him. He turned back to Gwen and replied, "Because I wanted her dead, obviously."

Ida looked as if she might laugh, but she peered up at Nilo with adoration in her eyes, like a pet owner watching her clumsy puppy trip and fall.

"Well, I knew that," Gwen said.

"Sure you did," Nilo said. "That's why you had to ask. Because you knew."

"Clearly if you were trying to kill her, you wanted her dead. That much is obvious."

"Obvious now that I've told you. I suppose you also realized that killing Brit the Younger would also kill Brit the Elder, and with both of them gone, Ida is in charge."

"Well, of course," Gwen sputtered, "but that can't work!"

"It has worked, and anyway, if you already knew everything, why didn't you stop me?"

"Well," Gwen said, "we didn't know it was you doing it."

Nilo laughed contemptuously. "You're making yourself look dumb. If you didn't know I was the one doing it, then you can't have known what my plan was, because you didn't know it was my plan. Think!" He pointed at his head to drive his point home.

Martin felt for Gwen. She was arguing with a dumb person, which never works. For a smart person to argue with a dumb person, they have to dumb down their logic on the fly, while the dumb person thinks in dumb logic naturally, giving them an advantage. Martin decided to end Gwen's suffering.

Martin stepped forward and asked, "Where'd you send them?"

Nilo asked, "What does it matter? You're all so much smarter than I am, and you say my plan can't have worked, so it can't matter where I sent them, can it?"

Martin tightened his grip on his staff, gritted his teeth, and grunted, "Where?"

Nilo laughed, clearly unconcerned. "Okay, big man. Don't get upset. I'll tell you. I had two ideas. I thought I might just throw them high up in the sky over the city and then watch them fall to their deaths."

Gwen said, "That wouldn't have worked."

"Could have," Nilo replied.

"They can fly," Gwen persisted.

Nilo shrugged. "So you say."

"You've seen Phillip fly with your own eyes!" Gwen yelled.

"Eh," Nilo said. "I don't know. Maybe he needs to run real fast to take off. Maybe he was being held up by very thin ropes. Point is, it was worth a shot."

"No it wasn't!"

Nilo smiled, "Well, luckily, that's not what I did."

Gwen shouted, "Obviously!"

Martin put a calming hand on her shoulder, and repeated his last question. "Where did you send them, Nilo?"

Nilo said, "The middle of the ocean."

"The middle of the ocean," Martin repeated.

"Yes. I picked a spot far away from any land, and placed the exit portal just above the surface of the sea. As soon as your friends disappeared into the wall, they reappeared out among the waves, and immediately sank into the sea and drowned."

Ampyx muttered, "A terrible way to go."

Martin, Gwen, and Ida all knew that while wizards, sorcerers, and all other magic users were impervious to physical damage, disease, and aging, they could still die of thirst, starve, suffocate, or drown. Martin looked at Ida. She didn't look angry or horrified. She had a slightly disgusted look on her face, like a cat owner who has found her beloved kitten playing with a freshly killed mouse.

Quietly Gwen said, "That wouldn't work."

Nilo asked, "What?"

Gwen said, "That would never work! You know that can't work! You blew up Brit's sphere when they were hundreds of feet beneath the surface and it didn't kill them! Why should dropping Brit in from the surface be any different?"

Nilo puffed up his chest, raised his nose in the air, and revealed his master stroke, "Because those arrows that were stuck to her were tied to a very heavy rock."

"But she has magic," Gwen was yelling again. "Both she and Phillip can do magic!"

Martin leaned toward Gwen, and in a quiet voice, said, "Phillip couldn't. He dropped his staff before he went through, remember? Without that, the shell wouldn't recognize him." Martin didn't add that Phillip very well could have drowned. He didn't have to.

Gwen said, "Well, that's always been the shell's main design flaw. Brit doesn't use the shell anyway. She uses the Atlantis Interface."

"Yeah," Martin said. "You use that flicking through options with your hand, right? Her arm was gummed up by the arrows."

Gwen said, "You can use either hand, Martin."

Martin said, "Phillip was holding on to the other hand."

It was too terrible to think about, but also too terrible to put out of their minds. Whether out of love, or panic, or just plain stubbornness, it was possible that in trying to save Brit's life, Phillip had killed them both.

Martin noted that for the first time, Ida looked genuinely concerned. "Well, there you have it," he said. "Through a combination of dumb luck, and just dumb . . . ," Martin trailed off, looking at Nilo, trying to find the perfect word. Finally, he continued, "Dumb, dumbness! Your boy toy may have killed two people, and you helped. What are you going to do about it?"

Ida thought for a moment, then said, "That is the question, isn't it? I guess I do have to decide how we proceed from here, since I am the only surviving member of the council of three."

Gwen said, "Ida, you don't honestly think that means anything, do you? The council only existed because Brit the Elder wanted it to and even if it did mean anything at all—"

"True," Ida said. "But Brit the Elder is gone, and so is Brit the Younger, and I was popular enough to get unanimously voted president. I think there's a good chance the sorceresses will follow me now that there's nobody else to follow."

Gwen asked, "But what's the point? We already have all the food, money, and security we could ever want. Why do you have to be in charge?"

Ida laughed. "So that everybody will do what I say, hang on my every word, and look up to me, like they do to Brit the Elder. Being president has given me a taste. Turns out I like it. I didn't plan any of this, but I think we might be able to make the best of it."

Gwen said, "There's no way the sorceresses are going to let you stay president once they know what you two have done."

Ida said, "I suppose that's true."

Nilo stretched himself to his full height. He glared down at Martin and said, "I'll just have to stop you from telling anyone."

Martin glared back, and said, "Try and stop us."

Nilo cracked his knuckles, then quickly swiped his finger through the air and poked it forward, making a selection. The floor beneath Martin, Gwen, and Ampyx shattered with the sound of several champagne corks popping. The three of them fell several inches into the portal that Nilo had set up just beneath the floor in case of a situation like this.

33.

When Gwen, Martin, and Ampyx fell through the portal, emerging in a shower of shattered floor fragments thousands of feet in the air over the city of Atlantis, they were all surprised and angry. Ampyx was surprised and angry at Nilo for trying to kill him. Gwen and Martin were surprised and angry at themselves for allowing someone to get the drop on them again.

Of course, the last time they had been amongst twenty other wizards, and they had all been stripped of their powers. This time was not nearly as bad. Gwen was tied into the Atlantis Interface and the Camelot shell. She was already flying toward Ampyx with great speed.

Unfortunately, Martin's staff had gotten hung up on the side of the portal as he fell through, and in his shock, he had let it slip from his fingers.

Martin's eyes darted about, stinging in the wind as he reached terminal velocity. *I'm okay,* Martin thought. *Even if I don't get my staff, the fall won't kill me. It'll hurt like hell, especially if I hit one of those glass and diamond buildings in the city. Those don't look very soft. I could hit the water, but they say that's as bad as landing on concrete.*

Martin quickly decided that plan A was to get his staff and fly gently to the ground, and plan B was to aim for a grassy area in the park at the center of town. He preferred plan A.

After a moment of panicked searching, he saw his staff tumbling end over end as it fell, a black speck suspended between the blue expanse of the sky and the darker blue expanse of the ocean. He straightened out and pointed his body toward his staff. Progress was slow at first, but he soon started gaining on it.

Martin thought, *Why haven't I ever made a macro that makes my staff fly into my hand on command? That'd be sweet! Like Thor's hammer! I'm about to be attacked, I hold out my hand and yell "Santo, aqui," and it sails through the air right into my hand, and whoever's about to attack me then wets themselves. Of course, the shell won't execute the macro unless I have the staff already. That's a problem. Maybe I could sew a wand into my robe somewhere. The shell might recognize that. But then I wouldn't need my staff in the first place. Hmm. Oh! Hey! I need my staff!*

Martin snapped out of it just in time to overshoot his staff. He cursed, then arched his back and spread his arms like he'd seen skydivers do on TV. He swung around and made another attempt to reach his staff, which was now falling straight down like a spear due to the wind resistance caused by the bust at the staff's top.

Time slowed. The wind was deafening. The light was unbearably bright. Colors seemed more vivid. The ground was getting unnervingly close. Martin's fingers were inches from the staff, and closing.

This is pretty James Bond right here! he thought.

He pictured himself grasping his staff, saying the flight spell (rather than the obvious joke), and soaring back into the sky just before he hit the ground. He wished there was a way to get a video of it to show the guys later.

His hand was getting closer. Closer. He was almost there. It was within his grasp. He stretched and closed his hand.

Martin's fall stopped abruptly. His hand closed on thin air as the staff continued its fall. He would have cried out in anger and shock, but the wind had been knocked out of him. He could tell from the glow that surrounded him that he was being held in a force field. He groaned, and rolled onto his back. The force field was coming from Gwen, who was far above him. She had her wand in one hand, generating the field that held Martin. The other hand held Ampyx by the shoulder as he floated weightless beside her.

The force field had stopped him more gently than the ground would have, so it hurt less, but that pain was spread out over a longer deceleration, so Martin figured it was a wash. Anyway, he had plenty of time to recover, since Gwen and Ampyx were hundreds of feet above him, and took their time coming down to his altitude. Martin looked below. He figured he was about five hundred feet above the rim of the city; the city center was substantially farther away. From this height, the city looked like a bowl full of sugar cubes with a bad ant infestation. Martin scanned the roofs that lined the inner bowl of the city. Luckily, since the roofs were white and the staff was dark, it stood out. It had come to rest on one of the smaller buildings, just below the rim. If the wind had pushed it just a little further, it would have landed in the ocean beyond the city wall. It might have sunk and been lost forever.

Martin turned over onto his back again, and saw that Gwen and Ampyx were almost to him. He yelled up at them, "That hurt!"

Gwen yelled back, "Would you rather I let you hit the ground?"

Ampyx yelled, "My ears hurt!"

Martin said, "I wouldn't have hit the ground. I almost had my staff."

"No you didn't," Gwen said.

Ampyx asked, "It's like they're stuffed with something."

"Gwen, I nearly had it. It was in my hand."

"Well, I'm sorry. I didn't know that, did I? I was all the way up there tending to him."

Ampyx yelled, "What's in my ears? I can't hear so well!"

Martin said, "Okay, thanks for trying."

"Look," Gwen shouted, "if your heart was set on falling all the way to the ground, I can still make that happen."

"No, no. You're right. Thanks for catching me. Out of gratitude I won't point out that I was right all along."

"Yeah, thanks for not pointing that out."

"But, I was," Martin said. "Right, I mean. All along."

"Yes, yes, Martin. You have a gift for understanding stupidity. Can we focus, please?"

Ampyx stuck a finger in his ear and shook it. "It's like I've been swimming!"

Martin said, "My staff is down there." He pointed to the staff.

Gwen looked down at a totally different part of the city, and said, "Uh oh."

Martin said, "No. It's not over there, it's right here, below me."

Gwen said, "Martin, look." She pointed toward the government buildings at the center of town. Two of the tiny black dots were clearly flying toward the general location of Martin's staff.

"Ida and Nilo?" Martin asked.

"Yes," Gwen said. "I saw them leave from her balcony. They probably watched us fall."

"Then they're looking for my staff. They know I'm powerless without it. Then they'll only have you to deal with. Gwen, I gotta get to my staff, now!"

Gwen smiled and withdrew the spell that was holding Martin in the air.

Martin shouted, "Thaaaaank youuuu!" as he streaked away toward the ground.

It won't hurt me. It won't hurt me. It won't hurt me, Martin thought, as the rooftop and his staff got larger and larger in his vision. His memories of being tossed around the courtyard of the castle Camelot by Jimmy flooded back, and he corrected himself. *It will hurt me, but it won't kill me. It won't kill me. It won't . . .*

Martin and Phillip had wondered about the exact makeup of the buildings in Atlantis. They knew that the outer bowl was made up of molecularly pure diamond that Brit the Elder had laid down one atom at a time, but the white buildings inside the bowl had seemed more like glass. Later, Martin would find out that all of the structural, non-decorative elements of the city were indeed made of diamond, but that walls, floors, and ceilings had a thin coating of white silicon, because it was quite strong, and could be made opaque (or at least mostly opaque) without weakening its structure. Also, it was easy to clean. The incredible strength and rigidity of structures made of diamond meant that when Martin hit the roof of this smallish building, the roof did not buckle or give in any noticeable way. Martin's body, however, did both of those things. For the second time in a five-minute span, he lay groaning, trying to get his wind back. He was in the center of a radiating pattern of spider web cracks in the thin glass veneer. As he lay there, he saw Ida swoop down and deposit Nilo on the roof before rising back into the sky, turning sharply and zooming in the direction from which she had come.

Nilo sprinted across the roof, snatched up the staff, kicked Martin in the head, and jumped down to the street. Martin scurried to the edge of the roof, not bothering to get to his feet, and leapt down after Nilo. By the time Martin had his bearings, Nilo was already running away, down the narrow, crowded footpath between the rows of shiny white buildings. Martin gave chase.

It did not take long for Martin to realize that he was not gaining on Nilo. Even with the traffic slowing him down, Nilo moved fast enough that Martin was struggling to keep up. Actually catching him did not seem realistic. Martin shouted, "Gwen! Little help here?!" He didn't know that she was within hearing range, but he suspected she was, and was relieved when he heard her reply from overhead.

"I've gotta go after Ida," Gwen said. "Here's some help though."

In his peripheral vision, he saw Gwen gently lower Ampyx to the ground at running speed. As soon as the guard's feet were on the ground, she was gone, off to deal with the president of Atlantis.

Far from being disappointed, Martin was delighted to have Ampyx on his side. *He might not be the smartest guy,* Martin thought, *but I trust him, and he's just as big and strong as Nilo.*

His spirits buoyed by not being in this alone, Martin found some extra speed. He might have gained slightly on Nilo; it was hard to tell at this distance. What he could tell instantly was that he was outrunning Ampyx. Martin slowed slightly, looked over, and could plainly see that the big guard was already winded.

"What's wrong?" Martin asked.

"I . . . don't . . . run . . . very . . . often," Ampyx answered.

"What?" Martin couldn't believe it. "Look at you! You're a walking wall of muscle and tan! How can you be in such terrible shape?!"

Ampyx said, "I . . . don't . . . know . . . I'm just . . . lucky . . . I guess . . . I don't . . . even . . . exercise."

"Clearly," Martin said.

Martin looked toward Nilo, still in the distance, gracefully weaving through the pedestrians with his staff. *I'm not going to catch him on foot,* Martin thought, *and neither is Ampyx. Come on, Martin. You've seen plenty of movies. What does the chaser usually do in these situations?*

He cursed quietly, then shouted, "Stop! Thief! Somebody stop that man!"

Martin thought, *These battles are never quite as epic as you hope they're gonna be.*

Ida flew at a fairly relaxed pace, clearly not concerned that anyone might be following her. As such, Gwen did not have to follow her for long, and was soon flying next to her.

"Gwen," Ida said. "I'm surprised to see you. I figured you'd want to help Martin get his ugly stick back."

Gwen said, "Nah. I figured I'd let him and Ampyx take care of it."

Ida smiled. "Nilo's gonna beat Martin like a drum. You know that, right?"

"Oh, I dunno, Martin can take . . ." Gwen's mind quickly flashed back to Martin's famous battle with Jimmy. She reformulated the end of her sentence. " . . . a beating pretty well."

The two stared at each other for a moment and slowly came to a halt, high above the park that marked the center of Atlantis. Gwen broke the silence.

"What are you going to do, Ida?"

"What are you going to do, Gwen?"

"That depends."

"On what?"

Gwen said, "On what you do, because if you do anything other than go to a public place, admit what you've done, and beg for forgiveness, I'll have to try to stop you."

Ida seemed galled by the unfairness of the situation. "I haven't done anything, Gwen."

"You gave your servant powers!"

"Limited powers."

Now Gwen was galled. "Limited to only things that could do people harm, and why? Because he wanted to kill Brit."

"No," Ida said. "I didn't give him powers because he wanted to kill Brit. I gave him powers because I loved him, and wanted him to be happy, and he wanted to kill Brit because he loves me and wants to see me happy."

"Has killing Brit and Phillip made either of you happy?"

Ida rolled her eyes. "Gwen, I never would have given him the powers if I thought he had any chance of succeeding! Logic says that he couldn't, and hasn't. He hasn't killed anybody."

Gwen shouted, "We don't know that!"

Quietly, Ida replied, "We don't know that he has. Do we?"

Another icy silence passed, then Gwen said, "You're not going to apologize and you're not going to give up, are you?"

Ida answered, "I don't see why I should."

They continued to hover in mid-air, staring each other down. Ida pondered her next logical move. Gwen also pondered Ida's next logical move. Gwen considered her best response. Ida also considered Gwen's best response. They were both as still as statues, trying desperately not to let slip any hint of what they intended to do next. An eternity seemed to pass, then, almost in unison, they each made identical swiping motions in the air and disappeared.

Martin was still keeping pace with Nilo, albeit from many yards behind.

"Stop him! Thief," Martin yelled. "Somebody, call the police!"

Ampyx had given up on keeping up with Martin, and was somewhere behind, presumably gasping for air. In the distance, beyond Nilo, Martin could see that the narrow footpath between buildings widened out into some sort of large public space, like a plaza or a market. *Oh no,* Martin thought. *I'm going to lose him.*

Nilo emerged from the tight confines of the footpath into the open space beyond, and as predicted, the crowd filled in behind him, completely blocking him from view. Martin continued to run, but his heart was no longer in it. He was certain that he would reach the opening, spend several seconds frantically searching the square, and not find Nilo or his staff.

Martin emerged from the narrow path into a public square with shops and market stalls around the edges and a fountain in the center. Three sides of the square were lined with buildings; the fourth was open to the great bowl that formed the city of Atlantis. It wasn't so much a public plaza as it was a public balcony. He could tell all of this at a glance because the people who had been filling the stall were crowding out toward the edges like a flock of birds instinctively avoiding a hawk. In the center of the square, directly in front of the fountain where he had plenty of room to maneuver, Nilo stood facing Martin, wielding Martin's own staff menacingly.

Martin stopped running. He took a second to catch his breath, then walked casually out into the now empty space in the center of the square until he stood close enough to count the teeth in the smug smile on Nilo's face.

Martin said, "I've got you now."

Nilo said, "You have nothing. Look at you. You think you're so smart. You and your girlfriend, and all the sorceresses and those other ridiculous men in their stupid-looking clothes."

Martin said, "You're wearing a shirt made out of a net."

Nilo ignored him. "You all think you're so smart. You don't even know what smart is! I've shown you who's smart."

Martin continued, "I mean, a shirt has three jobs. Cover you up, protect you from the sun, and keep you warm. Your shirt fails on all three counts."

"No, a shirt's main function is to make the wearer look good. I'm sure covering your torso makes you more attractive, but showing mine off works for me."

"You've got me there," Martin admitted.

"Listen to you," Nilo said, still smirking. "You still think you're smarter than me! Well, I've been one step ahead of you from the beginning."

"Well, of course you were one step ahead. You started first."

"Yes," Nilo said. "That was my first great move."

"What?" Martin asked. "Trying to kill Brit before we decided to try to stop you?"

"Yes. You never saw it coming."

Martin said, "Well, I suppose you've got me there, too."

Nilo laughed. "For someone who thinks he's so smart, you seem to lose a lot of arguments. You ever wonder why? It's because you think all there is to being smart is being clever and knowing things. There's more to it than that."

"No," Martin said. "I'm pretty sure being clever and knowing things is pretty much all there is to being smart."

"You're missing the most important part. Winning!"

"What?" Martin shook his head. "That's the dumbest thing I've ever heard!"

"Or you're the dumbest man who's ever heard it."

"Winning makes you smart?" Martin asked.

"Yes," Nilo replied. "Of course it does. It's smarter to win than to lose, so whoever wins must be the smartest. Isn't that just logic?"

Martin said, "An interesting idea. We'll discuss it again after you've lost."

Nilo said, "I'm not going to lose. I've got the staff."

Now it was Martin's turn to laugh. "Nilo, you know you can't use my staff, right?"

Nilo arched one eyebrow. "Can't I?"

Nilo swung the staff with all of his strength, hitting Martin in the ribs. Martin cried out in pain and surprise. Physical blows could not injure him, but they did hurt, and all animals, wizards included, instinctively dislike and avoid pain. Martin used his arms to protect his head, neck, and face, so Nilo continued to pound on his ribs and midsection like a crazed toddler who doesn't understand the rules of T-ball. After several savage blows to the breadbasket, Martin lowered his hands and attempted to catch the head of the staff mid-swing. Nilo expected this, and altered his swing to catch Martin in the ear. The crowd of

Atlanteans who were still gathered around the square groaned in unison as the dull, hollow *thunk* of the blow reverberated off of the buildings, like someone had dropped a coconut from a great height.

Martin slewed sideways sickeningly, pushed off balance by the force of the blow. Nilo wound up for another swing, but Martin took off running. Nilo pursued him, still striking him with the staff whenever an opportunity presented itself. Unfortunately, by that time, all exits from the square were blocked by gawkers, and Martin had nowhere to go, so he ran in a large circle, completing a full lap of the square with Nilo close on his heels, striking him in the hips, thighs, and buttocks with his own staff.

On his third lap of the square, Martin saw Ampyx finally make his way to the front of the crowd. He had caught his breath, and was eating an apricot he'd clearly bought from one of the fruit stands.

As he ran past, Martin cried, "Ampyx! Help me out!"

Martin and Nilo completed another lap. As they came close again, Ampyx said, "I'm not really much of a fighter!"

Again, Martin ran out of conversation range, taking several more painful blows as he orbited away from and then back toward Ampyx.

"But you're a guard!" Martin shouted as he ran past again.

Ampyx waited for Martin to come close again and yelled, "We never get into any real fights."

As they ran around to the far side of the square again, Nilo bellowed, "Maybe *you* don't," and cracked Martin in the right hip.

Ampyx knew he had to act. He waited for Martin and Nilo to come around again, and when they did, Ampyx lost his nerve.

He watched them for another orbit, psyched himself up, then, when they came close he gave chase.

"Hey!" Ampyx yelled. "Hey, stop that!"

They ran two more laps that way, Martin fleeing, Nilo striking him, Ampyx yelling at him to stop. Ampyx realized that yelling wasn't doing the trick, so he threw his half-eaten apricot, hitting Nilo on the back of the head. Nilo stopped, felt the sticky mess dribbling down his neck, and started chasing Ampyx. Martin barely had time for a few deep breaths before he had to chase Nilo. The three men were back to running laps of the square, but in the opposite direction.

Ampyx was setting a faster pace than Martin had. *Great,* Martin thought, now *you can run!* He knew that Ampyx's newfound speed was probably inspired by the fact that Ampyx could get injured, and that Nilo would probably be happy to do it. Martin had been running to avoid pain. Ampyx was running to avoid death. Ampyx had risked his life to help Martin, and Martin felt a duty to make sure that he came out of this in one piece. That said, he was not going to be able to outrun Nilo any time soon.

For some crazy reason, Martin's brain flashed on the film *Star Trek: The Wrath of Khan.* Specifically, Martin clearly heard Spock saying, "His pattern indicates two-dimensional thinking."

Martin cut across the square, sprinted hard, and dove head first, intercepting Nilo, and catching his neck in the crook of his elbow.

Nilo staggered, but remained on his feet. Martin clung to his back, hanging on with his right arm and repeatedly but ineffectually punching him in the side of the head with his left. Nilo retaliated by swinging the staff backward, as if he were an overweight Russian man in a sauna, whacking himself on the back with eucalyptus branches. While Nilo was thus distracted, Ampyx attacked by darting in, kicking him in the shins repeatedly, then darting out of staff-range to wait for his next opportunity to strike.

Vikram the fakir pushed his way to the front of the crowd. He didn't know what was going on, but he figured that if that many people were watching it, it was most likely something he wanted to see. His reasoning, it turned out, was sound.

He watched the three men floundering in their pathetic stalemate for a moment, then scanned the crowd for familiar faces. The first ones he found were Gilbert and Sid, who were also at the front of the crowd, and seemed in the verge of bursting with delight.

Vikram shouted to them, "The wizard from Camelot is in trouble!"

Gilbert shouted back, "Yes!"

They watched the struggle for a moment. The sounds of grunts, curses, and smacking noises echoed around them.

"Shouldn't we help him?" Vikram asked.

Sid said, "No!"

Vikram stared at him. Sid looked shamed, then said, "Oh, of course we're going to help him, just not yet. Let us have just a little more of this, will you?"

Nilo staggered toward the middle of the square. Martin's arm was clamped over the larger man's eyes, and Martin was pulling on his ear, causing him to spin involuntarily to the left. Nilo swung the staff blindly in a wide arc, trying to find Ampyx, who was well out of range, throwing small rocks at him from a safe distance.

Nilo stopped spinning, despite Martin's continued ear-pulling. He also stopped swinging the staff in his futile effort to hit Ampyx. He knew that he needed to get his vision back if he was going to end the fight. He stood still for a moment, then leapt into the air and flopped to the ground directly on his back. All of his considerable weight came down on Martin's diaphragm, a move that loosened Martin's grip on Nilo's head.

Nilo jerked his head forward, free of Martin's grasp, then spun at the waist, driving his left elbow into Martin's ribs. Nilo quickly located Ampyx, and hurled the heavy staff as hard as he could. It pinwheeled through the air until the heavy plaster bust of Santo connected with the side of Ampyx's knee. The guard's leg bent at an unnatural angle. He cried out in pain, dropping his handful of throwing pebbles to clutch at his injured knee.

Nilo rose, grabbed Martin by the throat, lifted him to his feet, then slammed him back to the ground. Nilo repeated this process several times, laughing as he did so.

Vikram gave Sid a look that said, *I'm going to do something, even if you're not.* Sid rolled his eyes, but bellowed, "All right, bub, that's quite enough!"

Nilo had Martin back on his feet, but stopped short of slamming him to the ground again when he heard the magician. Martin took advantage of this lull in the action to savagely swipe at Nilo's face, but since Nilo had him by the throat, and Martin's arms were substantially shorter than Nilo's, he connected with nothing but empty air.

Nilo turned to face the voice that had dared interrupt his fun. He saw Sid and Gilbert, resplendent in their Victorian formal attire, wielding their white-tipped canes at him, and Vikram in his orange robe, holding what appeared to be a flute.

Nilo faced the three of them smiling. "Do what you will," he shouted. He shook Martin by the throat, and said, "But choose your next move carefully. I doubt you want to hurt your friend."

A blindingly fast bolt of sparkling-green energy sizzled from the end of Gilbert's cane and struck Martin directly in the chest, violently tearing him free of Nilo's grip and sending him skidding to a stop several yards back.

Nilo stared at his stinging hand in disbelief, then looked at his three attackers in anger. He swiped at the air with the index fingers of both hands. Arrows materialized in midair. Nilo looked surprised when they fell straight to the ground, but immediately realized that since he'd eliminated Brit, the arrows had nobody to be attracted to. He quickly adjusted, summoning two more arrows, catching them in midair, and throwing them overhand at Sid.

He quickly found a rhythm, and was soon producing and flinging arrows at an impressive rate of speed. Vikram had just as quickly played a few notes in his flute, which had thrown up a force field. Once it was in place, he didn't need to keep playing, so he and the magicians were free to talk while the arrows bounced impotently off of the shield.

Gilbert said, "Good work with that . . . what is that, part of an old bagpipe?"

"It's called a pungi," Vikram answered. "It's played with circular breathing, like a didgeridoo."

Sid said, "Thank you, Wikipedia. Anyway, when do you think he'll stop throwing arrows at us?"

Vikram said, "Dunno. When he gets tired, I guess. He certainly doesn't seem to be letting their lack of effectiveness stop him."

"Yeah, about that," Sid said, "Those arrows look familiar. I think this little display answers the question of who was trying to kill young Brit."

Gilbert watched several more arrows bounce lamely off of the force field and add to the pile that was forming on the ground.

"Indeed. I think it also explains why you've never heard anyone described as the world's deadliest arrow-thrower."

━━━

The two guards who were assigned to watch Brit the Elder's patio were at ease. They didn't know that Brit's powers, like all of the sorceress' powers, were derived from a computer program called "the Atlantis Interface," or that the computer running the Atlantis Interface was located in Brit's home (because she wrote it), or that the rules built into the Atlantis Interface made it impossible for a sorceress to teleport directly into another sorceress's home, even if that sorceress was missing, like Brit the Elder was. They might have been dimly aware that the best way to gain entry to Brit the Elder's home would be from the very patio they were guarding, but they weren't worried about it, precisely because they did not know that Ida and Gwen were coming their way, both intent on denying the other the use of their powers.

The two sorceresses appeared at the same time, materializing out of thin air and falling about three feet to the ground. Ida hit the ground running, but facing the wrong direction, so she had to make a sharp turn to aim herself at the door into Brit the Elder's home. This gave Gwen time to react, and she did, by creating a force field that blocked Ida's path. Ida bounced off of the invisible field, a chaotic cloud of flying hair and flailing arms. She fell to the ground, looked up, and saw Gwen sprinting for the door herself.

Gwen only made it a few steps before she struck the force field Ida threw in her way.

Ida rose to her feet. She and Gwen stared each other down a bit, then Ida lunged hard to her right in an effort to catch Gwen by surprise. Gwen had expected this, and quickly threw another field, which Ida struck before she had gained any real momentum. Gwen capitalized on Ida's surprise by sprinting to the side to get around Ida's force field, but she wasn't fast enough and ran face first into Ida's second field.

Again the two women stared, each trying to guess what the other was thinking without letting any sign slip of their own thoughts.

Gwen got an idea, carefully thought through the motions required to make it work, then took a deep, calming breath. In one swift action, she sprung backward, while at the same moment placing a force field behind Ida, in case she followed suit.

Ida did not follow suit. Rather, she did the exact same thing at the exact same time. Both women bounced off the fields behind them, and fell to the ground cursing. Gwen took some comfort from the fact that they chose different curse words.

Both women knew that they each only had two unrestricted directions left in which to escape: up and to one side. They were now engaged in a high-stakes guessing game. Which direction would the opposition move next, and which would they block?

Ida quickly tilted her shoulders to her left, an obvious feint. Gwen placed a force field directly above her just in time to watch Ida fly directly into it. Gwen quickly cast one last force field, blocking Ida in completely, then she darted to her own right, and made it several steps before Ida managed to get a field in place to stop her.

Gwen picked herself up off of the ground, sneered at Ida, and raised her hand above her head. It hit a force field. Gwen was boxed in as well.

"Well," Ida said, "here we are."

"Yup," Gwen agreed, spreading her arms out. "At least the box I'm stuck in is bigger." It wasn't much of a victory, but Gwen was happy to take it.

Ida, it turned out, was also willing to take it away from her. "Oh, it is, is it? Let me fix that." Ida moved her left hand inward, causing the force field next to Gwen to move inward, pushing her along with it, her feet sliding on the patio floor until she was standing where she had started.

"Ooh," Ida said, "that's interesting!" Ida constricted her hands as if she were squeezing a large sponge. Gwen felt the walls and ceiling of her invisible prison start to constrict, forcing her to hunch over and curve her shoulders inward. She quickly followed suit, forcing Ida to bend at the knees in sort of an extended curtsey. The two of them stayed like that for several seconds, hunching and grunting and straining to remain upright while exerting as much pressure as possible on the other.

The two guards looked at each other, unsure how to proceed. One of them cleared his throat, and asked in a timid voice, "I'm sorry. May we be of some assistance?"

Neither Ida nor Gwen said anything, but they both gave him a look that answered his question more eloquently than words ever could. He reacted the way any intelligent man does when he receives that look: he stopped talking, looked straight ahead, and concentrated his energy on wishing he was somewhere else.

The guard did not know it, but he did help. He distracted Gwen and Ida just long enough for them to see the futility of what they were doing. When they turned their attention from glaring at the guard to glaring at each other, they did so with anger, but not blind fury. Wordlessly, they eased the pressure on each other. Soon, they were both standing upright. Gwen chuckled at her own stupidity and teleported five feet forward. She was free of the invisible cage in which she had been trapped. Ida followed suit.

The two women stood facing each other for a moment, then Ida cautiously turned toward the door into Brit the Elder's abode. Gwen started to cast another force field, but stopped just shy of committing, instead saying, "Ida, you don't really want to start that again, do you?"

"I suppose not. Okay, Gwen, what's your next move?"

Gwen said, "You won't like it, I know I don't. I really hoped it wouldn't come to this."

Ida's face fell as she realized what Gwen intended to do, but by then it was too late. Gwen's hand had selected the menu item that opened a direct voice link with every sorceress in Atlantis. It was meant for emergencies and Gwen had decided this was one.

Gwen shouted, "Come quick to Brit's patio. Ida and her servant are the ones who've been trying to kill Brit, and she just tried to cut me out of the interface! Without the Brits here, she figures she's in charge! I need help to stop her!"

It wasn't a bad speech for someone who was under stress. It was concise, informative, and fraught with genuine emotional content. Unfortunately, once Ida realized what Gwen was doing, she put out a distress call of her own, basically blurting out, "No! That's not true! I can explain! Don't listen to her! She was going to cut me out too!"

Gwen's entire message after "Brit's patio" was unintelligible because of the cross-talk. None of her accusations got out and she knew it. She gave Ida a look that would have utterly destroyed a person who was capable of feeling shame. Ida smiled and shrugged.

Gwen took a second to ponder her next move, then realized she didn't have to, because sorceresses started materializing en masse. The bulk of her message had been garbled, but the most important part, "Gwen and Ida are fighting at Brit's patio" got through loud and clear, and it was obviously enough to draw a crowd.

⊹⊱══⊰⊹

After many dozens of arrows had been thrown, even Nilo realized that they were not going to hurt anybody as long as the wizards had a shield up. The act of throwing them had distracted him long enough for Ampyx to hobble out of harm's way, into the crowd, which was getting larger by the second. Ampyx was greeted by the two wizards from China, who used magic to dull his pain and listened as Ampyx told them the story up to this point.

Martin had gotten his wits back, and that's why he kept quiet. He was in a crouch behind Nilo, whose attention was focused on the shield Vikram had raised. Martin knew that if he engaged Nilo without his staff, the result would just be another ignominious beating until Gilbert or Sid chose to shoot him out of Nilo's hands again. He could see his staff lying on the ground only ten yards away, but it was in front of Nilo. If Nilo saw him dive for it, he'd likely grab Martin before he could get to it. Martin waited. Soon Nilo would get distracted, and that was when he'd strike.

Nilo was not one to keep doing something futile when he had another equally futile idea to try. True to form, he stopped throwing arrows and started producing and throwing what appeared to be small lumps of clear putty. Vikram, Gilbert, and Sid, standing safely on the other side of Vikram's shield, looked at each other, confused, as several lumps of the stuff clung to the shield, apparently hanging in midair. Nilo traced another crude shape in the air, and they all exploded with a sound like a twenty-one-gun salute, delivered with bottles of champagne instead of rifles.

Of course the explosions, though powerful, did not penetrate the shield. Their main effect was that they caused Sid to say, "And that explains how he brought the statues down."

"Yes," Gilbert agreed. "Of course, it's an open question as to how he got his powers, and what all powers he may have."

"I don't know," Vikram said, "I suspect the arrows and the explosions may be his whole bag of tricks."

"Either his repertoire is limited, or his imagination is," Gilbert said. "Either way, I dare say the advantage is ours."

Sid saw that other delegates had started arriving. He didn't know if they'd been drawn by the noise or the excitement, or if word had simply gotten out that there was a magic battle underway. He recognized John and his cohort from the Chinese delegation, the Romany Gypsies, the Egyptians, and at least one Incan. He also saw Richard, the wizard who wore only a loincloth and a hat made of a wolf's skull. Sid said, "We have plenty of backup if things go pear-shaped. Let's give him a scare and see how he reacts."

Gilbert smiled. "Splendid idea. On three?"

The two men counted to three, then doffed their top hats in unison, swirling their canes with a decorative flourish. They were enveloped in a shimmering blue light. When that light dissipated, they were both transformed.

Gilbert's head was smooth and bulbous. His eyes glowed red. His lower face was obscured by a tangled mass of twitching, coiling tentacles. A pair of leathery bat wings sprouted from his back and flapped, making a noise like someone opening an umbrella made of suede.

Sid's hair had grown long and matted into jet-black curls. His forehead had swelled and distorted with countless ridges. His eyes were glistening, evil jewels that peered out from deep, cruel eye sockets. His nose was a pair of nasty holes in the middle of his now equally nasty face, and his mouth was a slathering mass of viscous saliva and fangs.

Both men had grown by several feet, and had become much more physically massive, but their suits had expanded with them. Sid nodded to his counterpart and placed his now much larger top hat atop his mass of oily black curls. He tilted his head toward Nilo, who had been momentarily stunned into inaction, and said, "Shall we?" His mouth emitted as much saliva as it did sound.

Sid put on his hat, got a firm grip on his walking stick, and with a hand that now featured five squirming tentacles where fingers had once been, gestured toward Nilo. In a tentacle-muffled voice, he said, "After you."

The monstrous magicians advanced on Nilo, their walking sticks held before them menacingly. Nilo screamed as if all of his nightmares were coming true, but he stood his ground and defended himself the best way he knew how, by throwing arrows with one hand, and exploding goo bombs with the other. Wearily, the magicians raised their own protective force fields.

Sid snarled, "We'd better think of something quick. If he ever thinks to start sticking the exploding goo to the hand-thrown arrows, we're all done for." Gilbert wouldn't have thought it was possible to sound sarcastic and dismissive while snorting and drooling, but Sid managed it.

Martin saw that Nilo was in a blind panic. Clearly, none of the sorceresses had ever brought a copy of *Fangoria* back for their coffee table. Martin knew this was his chance. He made his way to the outer edge of Nilo's peripheral vision and prepared to make a dive for his staff. He planned what spell to use as soon as his fingers made contact. All he needed was the right moment.

Gilbert parted his face tentacles to be heard clearly. "This is no good," he said. "Scaring him is not enough. We need to subdue him."

Sid slobbered, "We could just pin him to the ground with a force field."

Gilbert shook his head, causing his tentacles to swing like the tassels on a ballroom dancer's dress. "Let me rephrase. We need to subdue him, in the most entertaining manner possible. We don't get to use our powers this way often. It would be a shame not to capitalize."

Sid said, "Fun is fun, but the longer we draw this out, the better the chances are of one of these spectators getting hurt."

Vikram shouted, "I have just the thing! Gentlemen, shield the crowd! Just leave a hole in front of me!"

Every delegate in the crowd did as they were asked, instantly surrounding the open space in a protective field, sealing in Nilo and Martin as well. As Vikram again raised his pungi to his mouth, Martin made his move, diving for his staff. Sadly, it was too late. He saw some sort of dark mass shoot at high speed from the end of the pungi, and was driven to the ground under the weight of what people outside the force field could see was an undulating mountain made up of millions of live cobras.

The crowd that had gathered to watch the battle dispersed instantly, screaming and fleeing from the horrific scene. They ran far enough away to not be afraid of the cobras, but not so far away that they couldn't see what would happen next.

The delegates from different cultures and times worked together to keep the snakes contained, and Nilo and Martin contained, buried beneath the squirming serpents like children hiding in the ball pit at a Chuck E. Cheese. Vikram looked proud. Gilbert and Sid looked delighted, or as delighted as they could in their current condition.

One of the Egyptians turned to the other and said, "Asps. Very dangerous. You go first," which got a nice laugh out of all of the delegates.

⊷══•══⊷

Brit the Elder's patio was large, more than large enough to host every sorceress in Atlantis, and that was a good thing, because they had all teleported in, drawn by the promise of some genuine drama. At first there was quite a bit of chaos. They were all accustomed to deferring to Brit the Elder, but she wasn't there, leaving a power vacuum. The next obvious authority figure was Brit the Younger, who was also gone. That left Ida, but to Gwen's relief everybody seemed to recognize that neither Ida nor Gwen should be running the show, since they both clearly had an agenda.

After a brief conversation, Louiza, the doctor, took charge of the situation and nobody argued, which in this case was all the vote they needed to take.

Of course, Gwen already had the crowd on her side. She wasn't sure this would be the case. After all, Ida was popular enough with the other sorceresses to get herself elected to the only elected office they had. Happily, as the other sorceresses started to arrive, they all noticed that Gwen seemed genuinely happy to have other people involved in the argument, while Ida seemed frantic and skittish and tried to hide it under an increasingly unconvincing front.

Once all of the sorceresses had arrived, Louiza told the guards to leave, which they did gratefully. Then, the sorceresses set about trying to figure out what was going on. They formed a rough circle with Gwen and Ida in the center and told them both to explain themselves. This might sound like a less aggressive approach than the male delegates were pursuing further out toward the rim of the city, but from Ida and Gwen's point of view it didn't feel less aggressive.

"All right, you two," Louiza said. "You called us all here. What's going on?"

Ida said, "I didn't call you here! She called you all here, not me! I told you not to listen to her!"

Louiza held up her hands to make Ida both quieter and calmer. "Okay, okay," Louiza said. "Fine, Ida. You didn't call us here. This meeting is Gwen's doing."

Ida smiled, feeling as if she'd scored a point.

Louiza said, "Okay, Gwen. You called everyone here. What's going on?"

"Wait! What?" Ida shouted. "Why does she get to explain things? How's that fair?"

Louiza squinted at Ida, then, in a slow, even tone said, "She's the one who called us here. I think we'd all like to know why. It seems logical to ask her for an explanation."

"Actually, Ida," Gwen said, "I think it would be better for everyone if you did explain what's going on." She softened her expression as much as she could, and looked Ida directly in the eye. "Go ahead, Ida, tell them what's happened, from your point of view. They'll listen." She hoped her message was piercing through all the layers of ego and embarrassment and panic, actually reaching Ida's brain. Gwen thought this might be Ida's only chance at redeeming herself.

Ida muttered, "I don't know." Then she broke her eye contact with Gwen, shrugged, and in a loud, clear voice said, "I don't know why Gwen called you all here. I can't think of anything she'd have to say, unless she intends to lie."

Gwen grimaced. Ida misinterpreted this as a sign that she'd scored another point.

Louiza squinted again, then said, "Well, I can see why you fought to get the chance to say that you don't know what she's going to say."

"Except that I know it'll be a lie," Ida corrected her. Gwen realized that on a certain level, she missed Jimmy. At least he'd been a good liar. Ida was panicking, and there's a reason you never hear anyone say, "Luckily I panicked and did something really smart."

"Noted," Louiza said, in an effort to placate Ida. She turned to Gwen. "Okay, your turn."

Gwen said, "Ida is in a romantic relationship with her servant, Nilo."

Most of the sorceresses laughed at this. Louiza smiled and shook her head. She started to say something, but Gwen cut her off. "Because of her feelings for Nilo, she used the file to stop his aging."

Louiza's expression changed. She no longer looked amused. She looked concerned. The other sorceresses stopped laughing as well, but Gwen noted that instead of looking concerned, many of them looked embarrassed.

"And," Gwen continued, fearing she might lose what little momentum she had, "when she told him about it, he talked her into giving him other powers!"

Gwen saw a lot less quiet embarrassment among the sorceresses and a lot more quiet shock. Louiza looked at Ida and asked, "What powers?"

Ida said nothing, so Gwen answered, "The power to make small explosives, powerful enough to bring down a statue. The power to create enchanted arrows that home in on a specific target. The power to create portals in space. He told her he wanted these powers to eliminate Brit the Younger. He believed that if he did, Brit the Elder would be out of the way as well, leaving Ida, as president, in charge."

Now, Gwen could detect no embarrassment in the crowd, just anger. All eyes turned to Ida, who also looked angry. Louiza asked, "What do you say to that, Ida?"

Ida said, "See? Lies!" Several of the women listening groaned. "Yeah," Ida said. "I know. Why would she make up a lie like that?" Ida nodded vigorously and wagged her index finger. "You know what I think?" She continued nodding and wagging slightly longer than one would expect before continuing. "I think she, Gwen, and that guy, that Martin, I think *they* are the ones who were trying to get rid of Brit. Yeah! *Yeah!* It all makes sense!"

Ida spread her arms wide and spun around, making sure that she had everyone's attention. She did.

"Yeah, Gwen wanted Brit out of the way because she wanted that other wizard guy, the old one—"

"Phillip," Gwen interrupted.

"Yeeeees, Phillip! You liked Phillip, didn't you? Yeah, and you knew that he and Brit the Younger were an item, so she had to go!"

Gwen asked, more out of curiosity than any concern, "Why would Martin help?"

Ida said, "Because, because . . . because he, he wanted you! Right? I mean, it's obvious that he's into you! Obviously he wanted Phillip out of the way so he could have you to himself!"

Gwen shook her head. "So, you're saying that we killed Brit so I could have Phillip, and we killed Phillip so Martin could have me. That's stupid."

Ida said, "No stupider than the plan you say Nilo and I had."

"Well," Gwen said through gritted teeth, "I can't argue with that."

"No, you can't," Ida smirked.

"But tell me this," Gwen asked, "what about Ampyx?"

Ida asked, "What's an Ampyx?"

Gwen, speaking more to the gathered sorceresses than to Ida, said, "He's a guard who was in the room when Ida admitted her plan to Martin and me."

"Well, clearly, he'll back you two up, because he's in on it, too. He probably wants you as well."

Gwen was amazed. "You're saying that I killed Brit because I wanted Phillip to myself, and that Martin and Ampyx both helped me, killing Phillip in the process, because they both wanted me instead."

Ida shrugged, smugly.

Gwen rolled her eyes. "Look, if we were just going to get rid of Phillip along with Brit, then there's no point in getting rid of Brit in the first place. Also, even if that made sense, the plan you just laid out still leaves me, Martin, and Ampyx here in Atlantis, so neither of them has me. The math doesn't work out."

Ida said, "Oh, I dunno. Maybe you're into that kind of thing."

Gwen said, "If I were, then they'd have no reason to get rid of Phillip."

Ida said, "Look, it's your stupid plan. I can't explain it."

Louiza decided it was time to take back control of the meeting. "A lot of accusations have been made here. Some plausible, some less so. I propose that we don't do anything rash until we've had time to talk to Martin, Nilo, and . . . what's his name?"

Gwen said, "Ampyx."

Louiza looked at Ida and said, "We'll talk to them, then we'll do something rash. I further propose that I continue to refer to the guard in question as what's-his-name." The wave of head nods and muttered affirmations made a vote unnecessary.

Louiza opened her mouth to say something else, but was interrupted by a blinding flash of light coming from a gap in the buildings up near the rim of the city. All of the sorceresses looked up and saw fire, chaos, and panic. An instant later, loud, horrific sounds of screaming and explosions reached their ears.

"What in God's name is that?!" Louiza gasped.

Gwen said, "The boys."

⊹══✠

Every window, door, and alleyway that fed into the square was packed full of people craning their necks to see what would happen next, but the square itself appeared to be populated entirely by wizards and cobras. Nilo was there too, but nobody could see him, because he and Martin were buried under the cobras.

The wizards wore many different disguises. There were sha-men, medicine men, philosophers, con men, holy men, magi, and magicians, but they were all, when you got down to it, wiz-ards, and now they were acting like it. Once Vikram had finished producing the cobras he joined the rest of the wizards in creating and maintaining the invisible walls that were holding the squirm-ing mass of horror in place. The cobras were piled at least ten feet deep, and where the force fields held them in, they formed a solid wall of slick, coiling blackness.

Gilbert, still disguised as a tuxedoed mass of tentacles, asked Vikram, "What if the cobras bite him? We're not trying to kill anybody."

Vikram said, "Oh, they're not actually poisonous. They're not even really snakes. They look and feel real, but all they do is slither around. They don't bite."

A small light spot appeared in the undulating wall of snake flesh. It grew, and became recognizable as a hand. A second hand joined it, pushing against the invisible force field, then Nilo's face became clear, contorted both by the pressure of being pressed against the force field, and by the horror of what was doing the pressing.

Nilo struggled and scrambled and clambered his way to the top of the pile, which looked a bit like tall marsh grass swaying in the wind, only instead of grass, it was hooded cobras, all poised as if ready to strike. Gilbert was so amazed by the sight of Nilo fighting his way to freedom that he didn't even think to extend the force field until Nilo was already vaulting over the top of it.

Nilo landed clumsily on the ground between Gilbert and Sid, neither of whom made any move to stop him, as they were busy holding back a wall of snakes. They knew the snakes weren't real, but they didn't have time to think. They were acting on instinct, and the "avoid being buried under an avalanche of cobras" instinct is pretty strong.

Nilo rose awkwardly to his feet, looked at the wall of snakes behind him, looked at the monsters on either side of him, and ran away from all three of them as fast as he could.

Sid shouted, "Someone stop him!"

Nilo was running toward the open end of the square that led out to empty space and a spectacular view of the city. If he reached the edge, he could jump. As steep as the bowl was at this level, the tops of the buildings on the next level down could probably be only thirty feet or so down. He would have to vault over the railing, but he could survive that jump, and then would have an excellent chance of escaping.

John, the Chinese wizard, heard Gilbert's call, and in one smooth motion redirected his energies from maintaining the wall to shooting some sort of glowing energy ball toward Nilo. The ball of red light passed through him as if he weren't there, continued straight out into the empty expanse of the city's airspace, then flashed a blinding red light. When the light died, in its place, suspended in midair, was a massive Chinese dragon. Its body, at least fifty feet long, undulated through the air like a gymnast's ribbon, but at the front end, instead of a fourteen-year-old Ukrainian girl with a stick, there was a head like that of a lion, but much larger and much less sleepy. Its claws looked like daggers. Its eyes looked like hatred itself, and it made a beeline for Nilo, who scrabbled to an undignified stop, shrieked, and darted away to his right.

John would have found it quite gratifying if he'd seen it. Unfortunately, he had lowered his force field to create the dragon, and as such had been buried under an avalanche of snakes.

The dragon changed direction to follow Nilo, who ran a full, panicked lap of the cobra pile until he emerged on the other side of the square with an unobstructed run to the open air and freedom again. Luckily, John had shown the way, and the Incan shaman at the other side of the pile had paid attention.

The Incan dropped his force field and reached toward the open air. In the space between Nilo and the railing, a mounted conquistador appeared, glowing like a fake ghost in an episode of Scooby Doo. Steam burst from the ghostly horse's nostrils as it reared up on its hind legs and flailed menacingly with its hooves. The rider leveled a flare-fronted musket at Nilo, but Nilo had already altered his course to run another lap of the pile. As he ran around the back side of the square, each wizard he passed abandoned the wall and did something to add to his problems. By the time he emerged again on the other side of the square he was pursued by the dragon, the conquistador, a three-headed wolf, a stone golem, and a small pack of vicious Chihuahuas. The cobra wall had also unraveled behind him, giving the impression that he was fleeing from a nonstop wave of deadly snakes.

As he again sprinted toward the railing and, Nilo hoped, freedom, he was passed by another bolt of energy that struck the railing and exploded into a wall of solid flames that filled his entire field of vision. He stopped dead in his tracks, shielding his eyes from the light and his face from the searing heat. His shoulders sagged, and he turned to face his tormenters. He saw the people of his city, his people, watching from every available vantage point, waiting to see how he would be tortured next. He saw the wizards, the monsters, and the tiny yapping dogs all waiting for him to make his next move, and all standing ankle deep in the pile of snakes (except for the Chihuahuas, who were standing on the surface of the snakes).

It was almost impossible, but Nilo managed to keep his fear in check.

For an instant, the central mass of cobras emitted a glow, as if they were piled on top of a theatrical spotlight that had been quickly turned on and then off again. Then the pile began to swell, bulging and pulsing outward. A circular wave of wriggling snakes rolled outward like a ripple in a pond as a swirling mass of what appeared to be small silver boxes broke the surface of the pile. The boxes coalesced into a larger version of the recognizable form of a crouching wizard, Martin, who had finally managed to find his staff.

Giant Martin rose to his full height, cobras rolling off of his shoulders and back like rain. He planted his gigantic staff on the ground with a sound like two wrecking balls colliding. He looked down, surveying the scene. He saw the fearsome creatures, the wall of flame, the large audience, and the international task force of wizards, all clearly ready for action, standing in what he had to admit were mostly bad imitations of kung-fu poses. Martin took this all in, then opened his giant mouth and in a voice so deep and so loud that you could feel it in your viscera, he said, "See! This is more like it!"

With that, the last of Nilo's self-control disappeared. His mind was wiped clean of all rational thought. All he knew was that he wanted to get away. He turned, screaming, and leapt through the wall of fire. He emerged on the other side, hair and clothes smoldering, and fell thirty feet to the roof of a building below. He landed badly, rolling on his side. He speed-crawled to the edge and then slid over. He fell another twenty feet to street level. He landed on his back, groaning, just in time to see giant-Martin burst through the wall of fire with his legs tucked up under him, one hand in a fist and his staff held out before him like a sword. All of the hideous creatures, and all of the wizards who had created them, followed Martin through the wall of fire. Most flew under their own power, but the distinguished gentleman from China rode his dragon.

Martin made a three-point landing, taking up most of the street. Nilo ran like he'd never run before, literally. In his terror he'd forgotten all grace and technique, and was shambling like a toddler, arms flapping uselessly. His hair and the heavy fabric of his kilt had stopped smoldering, but his netting shirt burst into actual flame. Luckily for him, there was very little of it to burn, and the fire was mostly light and flash with very little heat. Still, Martin caught up to him in one massive stride, more a short flight than a single step, and kindly put out the fire by mashing Nilo to the ground with the flat of his hand.

Nilo yelped piteously as Martin grasped him around the waist in his giant fist, and lifted him up two and a half stories to Martin's eye level. (In truth, Martin was located in the giant's torso, but lifting him up to the head was better showbiz.)

Nilo pushed and struggled and beat at the immense fingers with his fists, but Martin did not feel it, so it had no effect. Nilo screamed insults and curses, ranted and raved, and made specific threats about what he'd do when he got loose. Martin wanted to squash him like a bug. He'd tried to kill Gwen and Martin and Ampyx. He'd beaten Martin mercilessly and had tried to kill Gwen. He may have killed Phillip and Brit, both of her, and what made it all worse, he'd tried to kill Gwen. Martin wanted to squeeze him until he popped, but he didn't. He showed some restraint. Instead, he raised the hand that was holding his immense staff and gently flicked Nilo's head with his index finger. Nilo's head flew to the side as if he'd been slapped.

Martin looked to the assembled wizards, who, along with their various creations, were hovering around him like planets orbiting a star. He said, "Thanks for the help, everyone. That was great!" Martin's eye was caught by Gilbert and Sid, who had not yet taken the trouble to revert from their monster forms. He looked at Gilbert's wings and tentacles and said, "Cthulhu, obviously."

Gilbert's face tentacles parted, and he replied, "Obviously."

Martin turned to Sid, and asked, "Are you Fek'lhr, guardian of the Klingon afterlife?"

Gilbert slobbered, "As envisioned by Ardra in the *Star Trek: The Next Generation* episode 'Devil's Due.'"

Martin laughed and asked, "How is it that we're not friends?"

Gilbert said, "Maybe in our time you're just a jerk."

Sid added, "Or maybe we are friends, and Gil and I have just been messing with you."

A distant voice shouted, "Hey! Hey Martin!"

Martin turned, and back at the railing that marked the edge of the public square where all the action had occurred, amongst the throng of Atlanteans, he saw Ampyx waving his arms. Martin covered the space between them in one long, gliding step, standing on one of the rooftops beneath the railing.

"Ampyx! Are you okay?"

Ampyx said, "Yeah, my knee hurts, but it could have been much worse. I see you caught him."

Martin said, "Yeah. Always knew we would in the end." He lifted Nilo up for the crowd to see, like a child showing off his favorite toy. "Look everyone, it's Nilo! Say hello to Nilo."

A surprising number of people actually did yell, "Hi, Nilo."

"So, what do we do now?" Ampyx asked.

"Go find Gwen, I guess."

"Can I come?"

Martin said, "Sure," then looked at his hands. One was holding his staff, the other was holding Nilo. He couldn't really let go of either. He looked perplexed for a moment, then jammed Nilo into one of his armpits and stretched out his now free hand to carry Ampyx.

34.

The sorceresses watched the distant lights and listened to the horrific noises coming from the upper ring as if it were some bizarre fireworks show. Most of it had been just a little too distant to make out from their vantage point, near the lowest part of the city. It was mainly distant shrieking noises and weird, faint glows, but the Chinese dragon was large enough to get everyone's attention, then the wall of fire held their attention. The tiny-looking, normal-sized man bursting through the wall, pursued by a giant silver wizard, made for a pretty satisfying finale for everyone except Ida.

Gwen knew who the giant silver wizard was, and when he started standing around casually, with what appeared to be a human being clamped helplessly in his hand, she knew what that meant.

Gwen asked Louiza, "Mind if I send them a signal to come down here?"

Louiza said, "Knock yourself out. It should be interesting to hear what they have to say."

Gwen poked and swiped at the air in front of her, then traced an arrow shape, and in the sky directly above her position, a huge blinking-blue arrow appeared directly overhead. The sorceresses had a chuckle when they saw the silver giant notice, then point at the arrow.

Martin placed Ampyx on the back of the Chinese dragon along with John, the dragon's rider. Martin retrieved Nilo from his underarm, and slowly flew down to the center of the city. All of the wizards who had assisted him followed. As they flew, Martin heard Vikram shout, "I put out a call to all the delegates I know to meet us at the arrow and pass the message along. Whatever happens, I think it would be good to have plenty of witnesses."

Soon, Giant Martin touched down in the park, just beyond the railing of Brit the Elder's patio. He looked down to the sorceresses, said, "Ladies," and touched the squirming and protesting Nilo to the brim of his hat as a sign of greeting.

It took only a moment for Martin to lose the undivided attention of his audience. He looked over his shoulder and was a bit disgusted by what he saw. He knew the Chinese wizard was riding his dragon down, giving Ampyx a lift in the process, but he hadn't expected the Incan to bring the ghost-conquistador along, and he'd assumed that Gilbert and Sid would go ahead and ditch their Cthulhu and Fek'lhr disguises. He certainly hadn't expected to see winged Chihuahuas flying in behind him. They had Nilo in custody. There was no need for all of this shock and awe, but then Martin remembered that they'd been able to see that many of the sorceresses had gathered at their destination, and Martin realized that these guys would not choose to turn off their most impressive spells *before* the ladies got a chance to see them.

I guess I'm lucky that Vikram didn't bring the snakes, Martin thought bitterly. There's nothing a showoff hates more than a competing showoff.

Vikram's call had been more successful than expected. Most of the city had become aware of the chaos Martin and Nilo had started, and when the call to the delegates went out saying that the danger was probably over, but the interesting bit was not, they all came running—or rather, flying. Less than a minute after Gwen had sent up her arrow, every magic user in Atlantis was gathered together—the sorceresses on Brit's raised patio, and the delegates in the park below.

Rather than try to get everyone up to speed herself, Gwen simply asked Ampyx to tell everyone what had happened when they confronted Ida. He stood, surrounded by his audience, and explained the whole thing. Gwen was betting that he, as a naïve non-magical type, would be believed more readily than she or Martin, and by the time he finished, she could see that she'd been right.

Louiza thanked Ampyx, then turned to Ida and asked, "Would you like to say anything in your defense?"

Ida started to say something, but she saw the looks on the faces of the sorceresses, her former friends, and realized that more talking was not the solution to her problems. The jig was up, all the way up. Any attempt at a defense would just be perceived as a new crime, like a child who steals a cookie, then lies to his parents about it. She simply shook her head no.

"And how about you—Nilo, is it? Anything to say for yourself?" Louiza shouted.

Nilo shouted, "How dare you question her? How dare you question either of us? She is your president! She is your rightful ruler! You should defer to her as she defers to me, her man."

Louiza said, "Interesting."

"Silence, woman! You've forgotten your place. You've all forgotten your place! This whole city you've built is a perversion, and I've tolerated it for about as long as I can. You have forgotten your place. You are women. *Women!* You are here to serve the needs of men."

With commendable calm, Louiza said, "Women built this city and invited you to live here. We rule the city and make sure everything works. We bend the laws of time and space. We do that. We women."

"Yes," Nilo said triumphantly, as if she had made his point for him. "That is how you serve us. That is your place, to make a peaceful and pleasant place for your men while we do the important work."

Louiza said, "You do what we want you to."

Nilo sneered derisively, "And that's what is wrong. We should do what we want."

"While we do everything else?" Louiza asked.

Nilo said, "If that's what your man wants. Always remember, you are here to serve men. It is not natural for men to do women's bidding!"

Louiza said, "Then you're not gonna like this. Martin, please shut him up."

Martin said, "Yes, ma'am," then flicked Nilo's head again, and sent him back to the giant armpit for a time out. Nilo's legs kicked furiously, but he was effectively silenced.

Louiza stepped forward, and in a loud, confident voice said, "I am not in charge here. Nobody has elected me. I have no official rank. I only stepped forward to organize things because I saw that someone had to. While we are on Atlantean ground, the crimes committed here have affected one of our guests as well, so for this matter, I personally think the delegates should have an equal say in how we proceed. Does anyone object?"

The silence was long and pronounced enough to be a clear answer.

"Okay," Louiza continued. "Good. Delegates, rest assured that Ida and Nilo will be punished, and we can certainly discuss who will determine what that punishment will be. But before that, I think we need to find out definitively what happened to the wizard Phillip, and the sorceresses Brit the Elder and Brit the Younger. Does anyone object to that?"

Brit the Elder raised her hand and said, "I object to you referring to me as if I were two separate people, but I'm willing to let that go for now."

Louiza said, "Fair enough. Thanks, Brit." Then she, along with almost everybody else, spent the next few moments silently freaking out, and listening to Ida curse.

Brit the Elder smiled and said, "Ida, if I didn't know any better, I'd think you weren't happy to see me."

Ida's unbecoming anger faded, and was quickly replaced with an equally unbecoming expression of hope. "No! Brit, on the contrary, I'm very happy to see you. All these people thought Nilo had killed you and that I'd helped, but the fact that you're here proves that he didn't do it."

"Ida, dear, the fact that I still live only really proves that Nilo didn't succeed in killing me. I am living proof that he failed. Usually I say a miss is as good as a mile, but in this case I'm willing to give him full credit for having tried his hardest. As for you, you tried to help him, and you succeeded."

Ida cried, "But I didn't—"

"Yes, you did," Brit the Elder said, interrupting.

"I didn't think—"

"No, you didn't," Brit agreed.

"I was sure he couldn't—"

"But you were happy to let him try."

"But, then where are—"

"Younger me and Phillip are fine. We'll get to that. Don't jump ahead."

Ida whined, "But I didn't do—"

Finally, Brit the Elder had had enough. She snapped, "I know what you did. I know exactly what you both did. I saw the whole thing, twice, from two different angles. I lived through what your houseboy did to me, then I had over a century to think about it, then I got to spend the last week watching you do it all over again, so don't talk to me about what you did and didn't do, because at this point I know it all better than you do. I know what you did, I know what all these good people have done, and I know how we will all decide to punish you."

Ida gave a sickly smile, and said, "Really, do you know about this?" She hastily traced a shape in the air with broad, slashing gestures, shouted, "Evac, evac, evac!" and she and Nilo both disappeared.

Brit said, "As a matter of fact, I did."

She turned around to address the throng of magic users who surrounded her, both on her patio and on the turf below. "Don't worry, everyone. I know exactly where they went. I'm going to let them have one more happy night together, thinking they got away with it, just to make it that much more painful for them when they're caught. When they wake up tomorrow morning, they'll find me, younger me, and Phillip waiting at the foot of their bed, and believe me, the look on their faces will be priceless."

Louiza asked, "But what if they get away from you?"

"They won't."

"But, how can you be sure?" Louiza persisted.

"Like I said," Brit explained, "when I was younger, I came along. Besides, you know full well that thanks to the file there's nowhere they can possibly go where we wouldn't easily find them."

Gwen spoke up. "Um, there might be a problem there. The file's been locked down. Martin and I both tried to access it from several different places, and it's been password protected."

Brit smiled. "First of all, thank you, Gwen, for trying." She raised her voice so all could hear. "Thank you to everyone for having helped bring Nilo and Ida to justice, but particularly, I'd like to thank Ampyx, Gwen, and Martin, and to Gwen and Martin I also want to apologize. I'm the one who locked you out of the file. Think of it as a proof of concept for things we'll be discussing later in the week. Besides, I couldn't have you bringing Phillip and me back prematurely, could I? Speaking of which . . ."

Brit the Elder swiped her finger through the air, scrolling through options only she could see. Finally she jabbed at the air before her, and Brit the Younger and Phillip materialized. They were both wearing T-shirts, shorts, and sneakers. Brit had a pair of black mouse ears with "Brit" embroidered on the back in gold thread. Phillip had a similar set of ears that said "Phil."

To the other sorceresses, Brit the Elder had always seemed a little aloof, a bit above them. They all adored and respected her, but from a distance. Brit the Younger had always been more approachable, so they approached her from all sides, making it clear that they were happy she was back and was all right.

Phillip looked out over the assembled wizards, nodded, and said, "Hey, guys."

Some of the wizards waved. All of them muttered some variation on the phrase, "Hi, good to see you."

While the sorceresses were greeting Brit the Younger to within an inch of her life, Gwen caught a glimpse of Brit the Elder watching them, and she could have sworn that Brit the Elder looked jealous, but then Brit the Elder made a few quick swipes at the air, raised her hand, and projected a force field over the sorceresses just in time to stop the hail of arrows Nilo had created during his battle with the wizards, arrows that had fallen uselessly to the ground before, but were drawn to Brit the Younger as soon as she reappeared. With that, Brit the Elder no longer looked jealous.

Martin reverted to his normal size and appearance and went to join Phillip. They shook hands and mumbled some bland greetings, expressing their feelings by making an obvious effort to ignore them, as was their way.

"So, what happened?" Martin asked.

Phillip said, "We went through the portal and immediately found ourselves underwater. We sank for a few seconds. I couldn't do any magic without my staff. We should really do something about that, by the way."

Martin said, "I've come to the same conclusion. Go on."

"Well, I realized that Brit couldn't do any magic with me holding onto her hand. So I let go, and just as she started to work a spell, we teleported again. We found ourselves in a hotel room. We coughed and sputtered for a bit, then we realized that Brit the Elder was standing there watching us."

"What did she say?" Martin asked.

"She offered us towels. Then Brit yelled at her until she got tired. Then she explained that you and Gwen would sort things out, and that everything would work out for the best, but for that to happen, the three of us had to disappear for a little while. How long have we been gone?"

Martin said, "Hours. You disappeared into the wall this morning. Why? How long have you been gone?"

"A week. Brit the Elder did two great things for us. She got us a week at Walt Disney World during EPCOT's grand opening, and she left us alone to enjoy it. The only catch was that we couldn't contact anyone. We had to let events here unfold the way she remembered."

"Did you stay on-property?" Martin asked.

Phillip said, "The Polynesian Resort."

"Nice," Martin said.

"It was. It gave us something to do together that didn't require us to just focus on our relationship problems the whole time. Real problems stick around, of course, but the nice thing about the unimportant, made-up problems is that if you ignore them long enough, they really will just go away."

Martin smiled. "I'm glad you two had a good time. I've spent the afternoon arguing with Gwen, grieving my best friend, and being savagely beaten in front of a large audience."

Phillip said, "I'm sorry I missed it." Martin believed him.

Brit the Elder raised her hand to get everyone's attention. When that didn't work, she cleared her throat. When that didn't work, she said, "Pardon me." When that didn't work, she summoned a lightning bolt that struck her, temporarily blinding, deafening, and terrifying the whole group.

"I apologize," she said as the wizards and sorceresses tried to compose themselves. "All these dragons, monsters, and giants sort of got me in the mood. Anyway, I believe we've all had enough excitement for one night. I move that we adjourn for the evening, then reconvene the summit in the morning at the usual time. I suggest all sorceresses attend as well. I think all will agree that we have pressing business to deal with, and that we are now prepared to deal with it in a manner we were unable to before today. Together."

"That's not to say that there will not be difficulty," she said. "While we are all smiles today, I know that tomorrow, many of you will not be happy with me, because, to be honest, I have manipulated you all. I know this because I remember it." She gestured to Brit the Younger, who clearly still did not enjoy being used as a prop by her older self. "See?" Brit the Elder continued. "You can tell from the look on my face that even I am not happy with me. More so by the second, it would appear."

Everyone looked to Brit the Younger, to see how angry she looked. Brit the Younger looked around angrily. Everyone quickly looked away.

Brit the Elder said, "Anyway, as I said, tomorrow we start the real work of this summit. Deciding on a punishment for Ida and Nilo, setting up a mechanism for all of us time travelers to govern ourselves fairly, and making the hard decisions necessary to ensure that nothing this stupid and pointless ever happens again."

35.

The open-air café was busy, full of Atlanteans and more than a few delegates enjoying their last meal in town before going home, now that the summit had ended. Ampyx sat alone at a table for several minutes before Martin and Gwen arrived, both looking terrible. Ampyx stood as they approached. Martin smiled and winced simultaneously, a move that is almost impossible unless you are hung over, in which case it is difficult to avoid.

"Amp," Martin said, "I see the knee is better."

Ampyx shook Martin's hand, hugged Gwen, and said, "Yes, it's like nothing ever happened. That Louiza is a great doctor. It's a shame you had to make her president."

Gwen said, "Eh, don't worry. She'll still be spending most of her time as a doctor. Being president of Atlantis is a part-time job."

"And besides," Martin said, "she goes up for re-election in a year, just like the chancellor, and both jobs are limited to only two consecutive terms, so that should ensure lots of turnover in the council of three."

Ampyx said, "There's a lot I don't understand about how you all do things, and one of them is why you still call it the council of three when there are four people in it."

Gwen said, "Well, after a lot of arguing, mostly from Phillip, it was decided that the Brits counted as one person, so they only get one vote."

"Yup," Martin said, "between that, and the fact that the chancellor has to be a non-sorceress, voted into the job by the non-magical citizens of the city, I suspect things will be a little different around here."

"Yeah, though the sorceresses still outnumber us on the council by two to one," Ampyx said, "while we outnumber them out here by over a hundred to one."

"Yeah," Martin allowed. "I said *a little* different, not *very* different."

Ampyx leaned in and lowered his voice. "Look, they don't tell us a lot about what you've been doing in there. What ended up happening with Ida and Nilo?"

Gwen said, "Part of why you haven't heard is that we didn't really do anything until yesterday. Dealing with them was the last official act of the summit. Phillip and the Brits went and retrieved them, as Brit the Elder said, the morning after they escaped, and dragged them in front of the summit. We gave them one last opportunity to justify their actions, listened while they failed to do it, then we punished them."

Ampyx clearly wasn't satisfied with that answer, so Martin elaborated. "They were both stripped of all powers. Nilo was banished from Atlantis for life. He's back in the little fishing village he came from. I'm told he always hated it there, so that's nice. Ida was sent back where she originally came from too. You realize that none of us are really from here, right?"

Ampyx nodded.

"Okay," Martin continued, "anyway, like I said, she was stripped of all powers including her immortality, and was sent back to where she came from, never to return."

"That's it?" Ampyx asked. "Banishment? That's all the punishment they get?"

Gwen explained, "When you know what's possible, what you could do, where you could go, how long you could live, believe me, Ampyx, knowing that you had all of that and that you squandered it because you wanted just a little more . . . that's enough punishment for almost any crime."

"But enough about punishment," Martin said. "Ampyx, let's talk about rewards. You helped us, you helped me, and for that, we've all decided that you should be rewarded."

Ampyx said, "I really didn't do much."

Martin said, "That's true, but the point is, you did something, and you could have been killed doing it. You helped me figure things out. You went with us to confront Ida, not knowing what she might do, and you tried to stop Nilo from pounding me into a puddle even though it would have been easy for him to kill you."

"I wouldn't say easy."

"*Very easy*, Ampyx. Anyway, we all discussed it, and we can't give you powers or immortality, but if you're careful, and avoid doing anything too stupid, you will live a long life, and you will be healthy until the day you die. Also, if you like, you have been offered a position as Brit the Elder's personal servant."

"Really?" Ampyx said, clearly very grateful and impressed. "Brit the Elder!" He pictured it for a long moment, smiling broadly. Then he asked, "Doesn't she have a whole team of servants?"

"Yes, and she still will. They'll continue to do pretty much all of the work. Yours will mostly be a ceremonial position. Nice work, if you can get it."

"Will I be expected to—"

"No," Gwen and Martin said in unison. "You will not."

"Okay," Ampyx said. "I won't be expected to, but . . . will I—"

"No," they repeated. "You will not."

"Fine," Ampyx said. "I understand, that's not part of the deal. At least not for now, but who knows what the future holds?"

Gwen said, "Brit the Elder does, and she wanted us to make it clear to you that your services in the bedroom will not be required, not now, or ever."

Ampyx looked disappointed. Martin said, "I don't think you're quite understanding what we're telling you. Brit has very limited need of a personal servant. Your duties will consist entirely of light cleaning and attending the occasional dinner party."

"The sort of work women are ill-suited for," Ampyx said.

"Yeah, whatever," Martin said. "Anyway, that's all you have to do, and in return, you have income and a place of your own to live in for life, and you can pursue any woman you like, sorceress or not."

The more he thought about that, the more Ampyx liked it. There would be a major change in the way he approached women. Instead of trying to use his physical assets to attract someone of higher status who could take care of him, he would be using his ability to take care of others to attract someone of equal status. It would take a while to get used to, but Martin and Gwen thought he'd figure it out.

The three of them made pleasant conversation until breakfast was done, then exchanged thank-yous and goodbyes.

As he shook Martin's hand, Ampyx said, "I guess I won't see you again."

"Nonsense," Martin said. "There's another summit in ten years. And also . . ." He looked at Gwen, who nodded. "I plan to come back for visits from time to time."

Ampyx looked at Martin, then at Gwen, then he laughed the kind of laugh that said that he knew exactly what was going to happen while at the same time making it much less likely that what he thought would happen would.

Gwen and Martin took their leave of Ampyx and walked through the streets of Atlantis like two people who had someplace to go but were in no hurry to get there. After far too little walking and far too brief a lift ride for their liking, they arrived at their destination, Brit the Elder's patio, where—to Martin's surprise—they were immediately invited inside.

Brit the Elder's quarters looked very similar to Brit the Younger's, what with the Scandinavian-inspired crystalline furniture and the lack of clutter. The primary difference was that there was no giant window onto the ocean. Because her home was so low in the bowl of the city, having a transparent glass wall was not an option. Instead, she had windows built into the walls that were constructed of modified portals, which allowed light through but nothing else, and in only one direction. Because of this, while her apartment was at the very bottom of the city, it commanded views from the top of the tallest building on the rim.

Brit the Elder stood to welcome Gwen and Martin. Brit the Younger and Phillip remained on the couch, holding hands. Martin saw Phillip's hard-sided brown Samsonite suitcase sitting on the floor next to his own black-fabric flight attendant's special.

Brit the Elder said, "Martin, it's such a shame to see you go, but it's not forever, and besides, we did get a lot accomplished, didn't we?"

"A bit too much, if you ask me," Phillip grumbled.

Brit the Younger beamed at him and said, "We don't have to ask you, dear. Everybody knows how you feel about it."

"Well, I'll keep repeating it until someone listens," Phillip said.

"We have listened to you, Phillip. You gave a speech in front of the entire summit and everybody listened."

"If you were really listening, you wouldn't have voted against me."

"Or," Martin offered, "maybe we voted against you because we were listening."

Brit the Elder tried to calm things down, saying, "Phillip, I never said my proposal was without its problems."

"It's not without problems? It's all problems! It's a cluster of problems packed so tightly together that it appears to be one big problem! I mean the technical problems involved in password protecting all known instances of the file—"

"All of which I've already solved." Brit the Elder said.

"—pale in comparison," Phillip continued, "to the logistical problems of finding every instance of the file that every wizard and sorceress found and used to come back here, then password protecting them, but removing the protection just before that instance was found in the first place, and putting it back just after the time traveler in question was told about the plan. Even saying it out loud is a confusing nightmare, let alone trying to implement it!"

"But," Brit the Elder said, patiently, "we have many very smart people working on it, and we have literally all of the time in the world to work it out."

Martin said, "I don't know why you're complaining. Thanks to your forethought as chairman, our colony is one of the few that had a census of all of our people and where they found the file ready to go. You should be proud."

"Besides," Brit the Elder said, "we've gone to the future to check, and the plan is already working. All instances of the file are locked down. Now we just have to live up to our end and do the locking." Brit the Elder stopped, as if something important had just occurred to her.

"That's what's bothering you, isn't it?" she asked. "The fact that the plan seemed to go into effect before we did anything to make it happen except decide we would do it. It flies in the face of your free-will fetish."

"For the record," Phillip seethed, "it didn't go into effect the instant we decided to enact the plan. It went into effect the instant you told us about the plan. The fact that they all later decided to go along with it is incidental. And while I'm setting the record straight, my love of and belief in the simple truth of personal free will does not now, nor will it ever meet the clinical definition of a fetish."

"Well, in any case," Brit the Elder said, "I can see now why it upsets you so."

"No, you can't! Because that's not the biggest problem with your plan. The biggest problem is the moral problem."

"If the problems were Voltron, the moral problem would be his torso," Martin added, trying to be helpful.

"I don't know what that is," Phillip said, letting Martin know that he had failed. "It's like we've built a nice treehouse, climbed up into the treehouse, and now we're pulling the ladder up behind us because if we don't, someone we don't like might come in."

Brit the Younger squeezed Phillip's hand and said, "You're right, Phillip. You are. No one denies that. The problem is that she's right too. Actually, you're all three right. Martin's Voltron analogy was quite apt."

"Thank you," said Martin.

"The file has been a tremendous benefit to those of us who have found it," Brit the Younger told Phillip, "and it feels horribly selfish to deny that to the rest of humanity, but if we don't take steps to control it, the file will be used for evil again."

Phillip said, "But it's already been used for evil, several times, and besides, we're just as likely to use it for evil in the future as anyone else."

"Exactly," Gwen said. "That horse has already left the barn. We can't undo the damage that's already been done. We can only try to prevent more from happening."

"There might be ways to undo things. We are time travelers," Phillip protested.

Gwen asked Phillip, "Are you, of all people, about to suggest that we should go back in time and prevent ourselves from finding the very thing that allows us to go back in time? Phillip, you know better than that. That's the kind of thing Martin would suggest."

Martin started to argue, but then decided it was unwise. Why start an argument with Gwen when things were going so well? And she did have a point.

Phillip stopped arguing, but he was clearly unconvinced. "Okay, okay. We've been through this already, I know. The summit debated this for two days. It just feels wrong to me, that's all. The file, it's bigger than any of us. It belongs to the whole world. Arguably, it *is* the whole world. Who are we to try to tell others they can't have it?"

Brit the Elder said, "We're the ones who found it, who had the imagination to see how it could be used, and who have the responsibility to make sure that it's used wisely."

Phillip said, "I don't know that you'll ever convince me of that."

"You're right," Brit the Elder said. "At every summit after this you move that we lift the password protection and get voted down. Eventually we make it part of the opening ceremony."

Phillip smiled weakly. "Wonderful."

Martin laughed. "Cheer up, man. Look at it this way. With all of the known instances of the file password protected, we know Jimmy can never weasel his way back into the past to seek revenge."

"We knew that already," Phillip said, his mood lifted by the memory. "We fixed him but good. Yes sir, we can all rest easy knowing that we'll never see Jimmy again."

With that, Phillip and Martin started the familiar leaving ritual. They said their goodbyes, then talked for several minutes. Then they resaid their goodbyes, then talked for several more minutes. Everyone had a good laugh at how silly they were being, then they talked for several more minutes.

Finally, they all got serious. Gwen hugged both men, hugging Martin noticeably longer, then said, "I'll see you both soon."

"You will?" Phillip asked, confused.

"Yeah, I'm coming out to visit Martin. Please keep it quiet. I don't know how the locals would react if they knew the witch was returning."

Brit the Younger shook Martin's hand, then kissed Phillip goodbye. She said, "I'll miss you."

Brit the Elder said, "So will I."

Phillip sighed. "You know, I still don't buy into the idea that you two are the same person."

Brit the Elder touched Phillip's cheek. "I know, Phillip. I know."

Phillip asked, "Do I ever?"

Brit the Elder fought back a small laugh. "Phillip," she asked, "if I'm not the future version of Brit, how would I know the answer to your question?" Then she kissed him on the cheek.

While Phillip was working through his irritated silence, Martin took the initiative. He tipped his hat, said, "Ladies," and teleported himself and Phillip back home to Medieval England.

They materialized in Phillip's rumpus room.

"Here we are," Martin said. "Two weeks later. I can hardly wait to hear about all of the nothing that happened while we were gone."

Phillip said, "It's just less confusing to keep track of things this way. I never liked returning to places the instant after I time traveled out. It never felt quite right to go away and come back without really having left. Besides, if anything interesting happened while we weren't around, we can always go back and be there for it."

Martin shook his head. "And for us, that's what passes for 'less confusing.' Awesome."

Phillip put down his suitcase, sat in his easy chair and said, "So, Gwen's coming to visit you, eh?"

Martin smiled and said, "Yeah." He may even have blushed slightly. He sat on Phillip's couch and tried to avoid eye contact, instead staring at the GORF machine.

Phillip persisted. "And by *visit you*, we mean . . ."

"We mean visit me. She's coming for a visit and the last thing I need is anybody insinuating that I claimed anything else is going to happen."

"Okay," Phillip said, smiling.

"Seriously," Martin said.

"Sure," Phillip agreed.

"No, seriously, Phillip," Martin said, locking eyes with him. "I mean it. We need to be clear on this—she's just coming for a visit. That's all it is."

Phillip studied Martin's face for a moment then said, "Really? That's it, huh?"

"Yeah," Martin said, leaning back. "Things are good, but we're going to take things slow. It turns out, Gwen's a little old-fashioned."

"Oh," Phillip said. "I see. Well, that's good, isn't it?"

"Yeah," Martin said. "I guess."

Phillip said, "Well, since you've opened up to me, I might as well tell you that Brit and I have a date next Saturday."

"Whose Saturday, yours or hers?" Time travelers have to think about these things. "And which Brit?"

"The Younger, of course. And her Saturday, but at my place. I'm going to bring her to the rumpus room, show her my Fiero."

Martin said, "That all sounds filthy."

They laughed, then Phillip said, "Yeah, Brit's not old-fashioned."

Martin groaned, and said, "Okay."

"She's quite progressive, in fact."

Martin said, "Eww."

"Yes, eww," Phillip agreed.

They sat for a moment, Martin shaking his head in disgust, Phillip nodding his head in delight. Finally, Phillip stood up, clapped his hands together, and said, "I'm going to pop downstairs, make sure the place is still standing."

Martin stood as well, saying, "I should go to my place and do the same."

They grunted a cursory farewell, more a *see you later* than a *goodbye*, then Martin touched the handle of his suitcase, said the magic words, and the next second he was standing in his warehouse as if he'd never left.

Martin breathed deeply, savoring the sensation of being home and alone. Martin and Phillip enjoyed each other, but they had been in close proximity for the better part of two weeks. Martin wasn't quite sick of Phillip, but he was getting close, and he knew that there was a better than average chance that Phillip had had enough of Martin.

Martin dragged his suitcase over to the work table and had started to unpack his computer when he heard the chime that meant another wizard was trying to contact him.

That's weird, Martin thought. *Nobody knows I'm home but Phillip.*

Martin lifted his hand in front of his face. A small, semitransparent image of Phillip's head appeared in the palm of his hand.

"Really?" Martin said. "You miss me already?"

"Have you found your invitation?" Phillip's head asked.

"No, what are you talking about?"

"Go look under your front door," Phillip's head said. "I'll wait."

An envelope was waiting on the floor just inside Martin's warehouse, as if it had been slid under the door.

Martin reached down and picked up the envelope. He tried to open it, but found it awkward with Phillip's miniature floating head hovering in his hand. "Um, sorry," Martin said, "I'm going to have to hang up on you to see what it says."

Phillip said, "Don't bother. If it's like mine, it says that they're giving your former apprentice Roy his dinner and trials tonight at the castle."

"Huh, that's convenient."

"Yeah," Phillip said. "They probably held it for us. They knew we'd be back today."

Martin said, "True. Waiting for us gave them time to plan something special."

36.

The ability to teleport made distance irrelevant, so it was not a surprise that Phillip got to the castle before Martin, even though Phillip lived very far away, while Martin could see the castle from his front door.

As Martin walked across the cavernous grand hall of the castle Camelot, with its gold trim, gold statues, and marble floors with gold inlay, he was struck by how cheap it looked compared to even the simplest dwelling in Atlantis. The reason for this, of course, was that the castle was designed by Jimmy, specifically for the purpose of looking expensive, and just like a truly powerful person never needs to tell people that they are powerful, a truly rich person doesn't need to demonstrate that they are rich.

The wizards were already seated at the banquet table. Just as they had been at the last trials banquet, which, as it happened, had been Martin's. That evening Martin, as the guest of honor, had sat at the head of the table, next to the chairman, Jimmy at the time. Phillip had sat at the far end with Jeff, Gary, and the Magnuses, and the rest of the wizards had worked out a sort of self-created seating chart, sorting themselves in order of their own obsequiousness.

Now things were different. Roy, the guest of honor, sat at the head of the table. Phillip was the chairman, and was already sitting to Roy's right. Jeff, Roy's trainer, sat across from Phillip, and the rest of the wizards were seated around the table, almost randomly, except for the Magnuses, who still sat at the far end of the table, because that's what they were used to.

Everyone wanted to hear about Martin and Phillip's trip to Atlantis. Phillip said that he would write up an official report of all the business that got done, which he would distribute as soon as it was done.

Good, Martin thought, *we don't want to turn this into a debate about locking down the file. That's not what tonight's about. This is Roy's initiation.* It struck Martin that it would also be the last initiation. *All the more reason to let everyone enjoy it,* he thought.

Phillip and Martin took turns describing the city and its architecture, and ignoring questions about the sorceresses and their architecture. After a few minutes of this, Phillip said that all of the details would be in his report, and shifted the focus back to Roy, who entertained the wizards with tales of what it was like to work at the Lockheed Skunk Works, which might not sound interesting to many people, but to this crowd it was endlessly fascinating.

Eventually dinner was over and Phillip proclaimed that it was time to see Roy demonstrate his macro. It was how the trainee demonstrated his mastery over the shell program, and gave the other wizards an idea of what kind of behavior they could expect from the new guy. Fireballs, whirlwinds, and explosions were par for the course, but if the trainee did anything genuinely dangerous in an attempt to impress them, it would give the wizards something to think about.

Before Roy could respond, Gary raised his hand and cleared his throat. Something about it unnerved Martin. *I don't know why,*

Martin thought. *He's being perfectly polite.* Then Martin realized, *that's why it seems odd. Gary's being polite.*

Gary said, "Guys, before we get to Roy's macro, Eddie and I have a surprise for you."

Everybody looked to Phillip, and Phillip looked weary. Gary enjoyed surprising people, but he favored the kind of surprise that you announced afterwards by laughing, pointing, and yelling "Gotcha." The fact that he was announcing a surprise in advance was out of character, and that led Phillip to believe that Gary's surprise probably wouldn't be anything too bad. After all, he was already announcing the surprise in a manner that was out of character. The surprise would likely be out of character as well, meaning it might be something pleasant.

Eddie wasn't a natural leader, but he was a born organizer. Nobody would ever follow him into battle, but at his word, they'd happily form a single file line once they were there. When Eddie asked the wizards to step into the vast, empty portion of the room and form a circle, they did so with little hesitation. "Oh," Eddie added as an afterthought, "and leave your staffs at the table. You'll need your hands free."

There were only twenty-four of them, so the circle was not particularly large. Martin was reminded of P.E. class in elementary school, when they'd play with the parachute.

Once the circle was formed, Gary said, "Okay, now everybody join hands." Nobody moved. Phillip turned to Eddie and asked, "Do we have to?"

Eddie said, "Yes." With some grumbling, they all joined hands.

Martin's left hand held Tyler's. His right held Gary's hand who also held hands with Phillip, who also held hands with Eddie, who craned his neck around to look at everybody's hands.

"Okay," Eddie said. "Looks like we're ready to go." He and Gary made eye contact, nodded, then in unison said, "All is prepared."

There was a modest-sized flash of light, a small cloud of black smoke, and then Jimmy was standing in the middle of the circle with his hands clasped behind his back. With his green and gold wizard hat covering most of his gray hair, and his old wizard robe obscuring his gaunt, wiry frame, he was instantly recognizable.

Phillip spoke for everybody, or rather, he shouted random noises in inarticulate alarm and rage for everyone. He struggled to get his hands free so that he could attack his nemesis, but he could not, as Gary and Eddie had a firm grip on them. As the three men struggled against each other, Gary grunted, "This is why we needed to hold hands."

All of the wizards, save for Jeff and Eddie, were shocked. The air was full of questions, obscenities, and obscenities stated in the form of questions. "How?!" Martin shouted, as he tried desperately to pry his other hand out of Gary's grip. He tried letting go of Tyler so he could use his left hand to help free his right, but found that he couldn't release his grip. Martin repeated, "How?!" At the moment, that was the best his mind could come up with.

Gary, struggling with both hands, said, "Come on, guys, settle down. Let us explain!"

Martin yelled, "How?!" again.

Jimmy smiled. "*How* what, Martin? *How* am I back here? *How* can they possibly explain themselves? *How* are your hands stuck together? Which *how* do you want answered?"

"All of them," Tyler spat, "and make it fast, so we can get to killing you."

Jimmy turned to face Tyler. "Tyler, I know you're angry, and with good reason, but don't exaggerate. We all know you aren't murderers. You're better than that. And even if you were killers, you couldn't kill me with your hands all joined together like this. You can't attack me physically, and without your staffs you can't do magic. The worst you can do is give me a particularly aggressive group hug."

Martin asked, "How are you doing this? I don't see a staff in your hand!"

Jimmy said, "I have a wand in my pocket." He reached his robe's deep side pocket and produced a wand. He turned to Phillip and said, "And no, I'm not going to make the obvious joke."

"Go ahead," Phillip cried. "It can't make me like you any less."

"Wait," Jeff said. "I got my wand in my pocket too! *Transporto hejmo!*"

Nothing happened. Jeff wasn't transported home. Jimmy's plan wasn't foiled. Gary and Eddie didn't look surprised.

Gary said, "Okay, be cool! Be cool, everybody. We'll explain. Everything's going to be fine."

Eddie added, "Yeah, Gary and I have the situation under control. You all don't have your powers right now, but Gary and I do. Jimmy has some powers, but they're limited, and there's nothing he can do that Gary and I can't stop, okay? Jimmy just wants to say something, then you'll all be released."

"What can he possibly have to say that'll make any difference?" Phillip asked. "He played God with people's lives, ghosted Tyler, accidentally killed an entire town, then tried to kill all of us!"

"That's the thing, " Eddie said. "He wants to apologize."

Phillip couldn't believe what he was hearing. "He told you he wants to apologize?"

"Yes," Jimmy said, "I told them that I want to apologize. I also told them that if I came before you all without powers, you'd never believe that my apology was genuine. You would just think that I was trying to manipulate you into letting me be a wizard again. I told them that in order for you to see that I was genuinely sorry, I would have to have the upper hand when I apologized, and that meant that Gary and Eddie would have to give me some of my powers back so that I could trap all of you, so that I could demonstrate how sorry I am."

"That makes no sense," Martin said. "The logic doesn't hold up. It doesn't matter if you've got the rest of us in check, if Gary and Eddie are still more powerful than you and can stop you from harming us, then you don't have the upper hand and your whole argument falls apart."

Jimmy nodded appreciatively. "That's a very good point, Martin. I guess it's a good thing I stripped Gary and Eddie of their powers, too."

At the same moment, as if they had rehearsed it, Eddie and Gary looked stricken, attempted to teleport away, and failed to go anywhere.

Jimmy said, "Problem, guys? The wands in your pockets aren't working like they used to?" He turned to Phillip. "Sorry about that. Sometimes the obvious joke makes itself."

"This isn't possible," Gary shouted. "I would have seen it if he'd taken my powers too! I stood behind him and watched over his shoulder while he wrote every line of this macro."

"Not every line," Jimmy said. "You may remember there was a brief moment when you were distracted."

"No."

"I distracted you," Jimmy assured him.

"Not a chance."

"By breaking wind," Jimmy reminded him.

"Oh yeah," Gary groaned. "It was foul. Really, guys. You should've been there."

Jimmy shrugged. "Garlic. It has that effect on me."

Martin shook his head at Gary, "And what, you left to open a window?"

"No," Gary said. "I was doubled over laughing. I was standing right behind him. It was classic!"

Jimmy said, "I knew Gary's fatal weakness. Scat humor. While he was distracted, I wrote a small bit of code that called out to a much larger chunk of code I'd written before I came back in time. It's housed on a server I set up, and when triggered, it relieved Eddie and Gary of their powers, among other things."

"Other things?" Phillip snarled.

"Yes, it reinstated all of my powers, not just the limited range Eddie and Gary granted me, and it has surrounded me with a circular force field, in case any of you tries to kick me. Go ahead," Jimmy urged them, "give it a try."

After a long moment in which nobody moved, Jimmy said, "Pity. I always enjoyed the Rockettes."

Jimmy got face to face with Phillip. "So you see," he said, "you are completely helpless. I have all of my powers. You have none of yours." Jimmy tapped Phillip on the forehead with his wand, just to drive the point home.

"I can do anything I like with you." Jimmy flicked his wand upward, and the circle of wizards rose into the air as one unit. They stopped gaining altitude at about forty feet, well below the height of the great hall's ceiling, but more than high enough to get their attention. They hovered there, stationary. It would have been almost majestic if they hadn't all been yelling threats and profanities.

Jimmy called for silence, and was ignored. He tried again, with no more success. Jimmy sighed, then flicked his wand again, causing the ring of wizards to spin.

Jimmy shouted, "The spinning will stop when the yelling stops."

After a moment, the room went quiet. Jimmy jerked back on the wand and the rotation stopped abruptly. *Sadly, I've just traded yelling for moaning,* Jimmy thought. *As long as it doesn't escalate further, that'll be fine, and if it does escalate to throwing up, well, I have my force field.*

Jimmy drifted into the air until he was floating in the center of the circle.

"So," Jimmy said. "You are all helpless, I am in control, and you will listen to me. I had a lot of time to think about what you all did to me. You foiled my plans, passed judgment on me, then sent me away to live the rest of my life in poverty and squalor, if I was lucky. If I was unlucky, you knew there was a chance I'd be beaten to death by Argentinean soccer fans. Well, I was lucky. After they got tired of using me as a hacky sack, they turned me over to the police. It took me months to talk my way out of prison, years to get out of South America, and decades to finally get back here."

Jimmy started slowly lowering himself and the wizards to the floor, but he kept talking as they went.

Jimmy continued. "Every step I took, slogging through the middle of nowhere on foot, pedaling a broken bicycle someone else had thrown out as trash. Begging for coins on muddy foreign streets. Wherever I was, I always remembered where I had been, and how I'd gotten from the one place to the other." He faced Phillip. "I've pictured your face a million times. Imagined what I'd do if we ever met again."

The ring of wizards touched down on the solid marble floor, but it did little to make them feel more secure. Jimmy had demonstrated that he could do whatever he wanted with them. The idea that it might involve the floor was not reassuring.

"So here we are," Jimmy continued. He spoke to the entire group, but he seemed to face Phillip, Martin, and Tyler more than the others as he did so. "I've survived your punishment, and using my own resources, I have regained access to the file and the shell. I have undone all that you have done to me. Now that I am powerful and you are powerless, I can do what I came here to do."

"Just get it over with," Phillip spat.

"Okay," Jimmy said. "I will."

Jimmy centered himself within the circle of terrified wizards, spun around once, savoring the moment, then fell to his knees, raised his hands above his head, and in a voice drenched in emotion, he cried out, "I am sorry! I apologize! I was wrong, so terribly wrong! I was wrong to play God. I was wrong to cover it up, and I was certainly wrong to try to kill all of you."

"What the hell is this?" Tyler asked in disbelief.

"It's me apologizing," Jimmy said. "I don't blame you for being confused. You've never seen it before."

"You're not here for revenge?" Phillip asked.

"I don't deserve any. It's not like any of you wronged me. I deserved the punishment you gave me for what I did to Tyler alone. I deserved far worse if you throw in my attempt to have you all beaten to death by orcs, making the orcs in the first place, and what happened to Rickard's Bend, which was an accident, but that doesn't make those people less dead, does it?"

"No," Martin agreed. "As a matter of fact, it doesn't."

Jimmy turned to Martin. "I know, I can never truly make up for any of it, even that awful, humiliating beating I gave you in this very room. The shame and anger must be terrible. The embarrassment must still feel fresh for you. Can you ever forgive me, for humiliating you with your own macro like that?"

"It wasn't that humiliating," Martin said. "I mean, I held my own pretty good."

Jimmy smiled. "That's very gracious of you, Martin, but please, don't sugarcoat it. I attacked you brutally with a macro you yourself designed, making you look pathetic and inept in front of a large crowd of spectators. Can you ever forgive me?"

Martin said, "I doubt it."

"I don't blame you. I don't blame any of you. Not one bit. I am asking you to forgive me, though. I have returned to ask you all to please forgive me for what I've done, not because I deserve your forgiveness, but because you deserve the opportunity to forgive."

Gary said, "So you were telling me the truth."

"Yes," Jimmy said. "The easiest way to manipulate someone is to tell them the truth."

"After you've twisted the truth to fit your needs," Phillip spat.

"I prefer to think that I pruned the truth like a banzai tree. I removed some of the ugly bits, and made it more elegant. Gary, Eddie, you wanted to believe that I was here to apologize, and the truth is I was here to apologize, but for the apology to be believed

I needed everyone to be helpless. I told you that. I just glossed over the fact that you are part of everyone. Most people forget that they are part of everyone. You say everyone, and everyone hears *everyone else*."

Phillip said, "Does this really seem like the best way to apologize to us? Manipulating us like this?"

"I see your point," Jimmy said, "but what can I do? It's what I'm good at. It's part of my nature. I can't help manipulating people any more than you can help being sarcastic."

"Oh, that's brilliant," Phillip said.

"Well, here's some more truth," Tyler said. "Your apology is a load of crap. You say your apology wouldn't hold water unless we saw you as a threat. Well, if we accept it, that won't hold any water either, for the same reason. Saying 'forgive me, or else' doesn't show a lot of remorse."

"Quite right," Jimmy said. "That's why your powers were all reinstated, and mine were taken away, when I said, 'I am sorry. I apologize'. That's why I had to lower us back to the floor. If I didn't, we'd have fallen."

The wizards glanced around the circle at each other, then quickly let go of each other's hands as if they'd all received a mild electric shock. Jeff produced his wand and tested it by levitating Jimmy, holding him helpless in the air. He started to put Jimmy back down, but Phillip stopped him.

"No, leave him up there. I have some questions to ask."

Jimmy said, "That's fine. Perfectly understandable. You have my permission to keep me suspended here if it makes you all more comfortable."

"Shut up," Phillip barked. "So you're here to apologize, huh? And you expect us to just welcome you back with open arms?"

"That would be wonderful, but no, I don't expect that. You can't truly trust me now, but I hope you'll give me the opportunity to earn your trust."

"What if we don't? What if we take your powers away again and send you back where you came from?"

"Then I've lost nothing. In fact, I've already gained the knowledge that I at least offered an apology."

Tyler said, "Great! So either we send you back, and you win, or we welcome you back like nothing ever happened, and you win."

Jimmy shook his head. "I don't really win in either case. I either lose my powers again and get sent back to the future to die, or I stay here with thirty years' worth of wear on my body and bad memories in my head, struggling to regain your trust and respect, which I probably will never get. I can't really call either of those *winning*. They're just better than where I was before."

"There's a third option you haven't mentioned," Martin said. "We decide not to forgive you, and you disappear with your powers intact. You may be sorry for what you did, but you've admitted that you're willing to omit parts of the truth to get your way. Do you honestly expect us to believe that you don't have an escape plan in place?"

"That's a very good question, Martin, but I can't answer it. If, hypothetically, I said 'yes, I do have an escape plan,' it would undo all of my arguments. If I say no, you won't believe me anyway. What can I say?"

"Tell the truth," Martin said. "Do you have an escape plan?"

Without any hesitation, Jimmy said, "No. I don't. Now you tell the truth, Martin. Do you believe me?"

"No."

"I don't blame you."

"I don't care."

Jimmy was left floating in the middle of the hall while the wizards huddled in the far corner and argued for a good long time. Jimmy could identify which wizard was speaking, and their general tone of voice, but he couldn't make out what they were saying. There was almost always at least one wizard peering at Jimmy nervously. Occasionally, all debate would stop and all of the wizards would turn as a group to stare at him for a moment. The first time it happened, Jimmy smiled and waved. He could tell from the tone of the voices he heard immediately after that that it had been a bad move. He spent the rest of the time trying to convey a sense of nervous hopefulness with a slight note of desperation.

Finally he heard Phillip say something in that loud, stilted voice guys like Phillip use when they're trying to sound like a leader. Then he saw the majority of the wizards raise their hands. Phillip said something in the tone of voice guys like him use when they've dropped something heavy on their foot, and Jimmy knew things had gone his way.

The wizards came back to where Jimmy floated, but they stayed grouped together, rather than reforming a ring around him. Phillip snarled with obvious distaste, "Okay, we've come to a decision, but before we tell you what that is, we have some questions."

Jimmy said, "Ask me anything."

"Why did you come back now? From our point of view you just tried to kill us all less than two months ago. Some of the guys are still having nightmares about it. Why not give us a year or two to calm down?"

"It's almost always best to apologize as soon as possible after you've wronged someone. It shows more remorse, and while sometimes people do get less angry over time, just as often they actually get angrier. The more they remember what you did, the worse it can seem to them, until eventually they blame you for doing things that are much worse than what you actually did."

Tyler asked, "What would be worse than ghosting me, killing an entire town, trying to murder all of us, and trying to kill Martin with your bare hands?"

Jimmy said, "I don't know, and I didn't want to find out." The wizards grumbled, but nobody argued, so Jimmy continued. "I would have come back right after you banished me if I could, but I also needed a time when, well, I can't think of a better way to put this. I needed the coast to be clear. I knew that you, Phillip, or Martin might just attack me at first sight, so I had to find a time when all three of you were scarce, and my informant told me that this week they were in Atlantis, which I can't wait to hear about, by the way, and that you were away researching your next book, *Dragon Wagon*."

"*Dragon Wagon*?" Jeff asked.

"Yeah," Tyler said, "it's an idea I have about a guy who hitches a wagon to a dragon, and uses it to haul freight. It's sort of a sword and sorcery meets *Smokey and the Bandit* kinda thing." Tyler's curiosity overwhelmed his anger. He asked Jimmy, "How does it turn out?"

"My informant says it's some of your best work, but it doesn't sell very well."

"Who's your informant?"

"You are, Tyler. I visited you in the future and persuaded you to help me."

"What could you possibly say to make me want to help you?"

Jimmy said, "I can't tell you. The only reason you even talk to me in the future is to find out what I'm going to say to you to get you to help me. If I say it to you now, it won't work then."

"Tell me!" Tyler yelled.

"I will, just before you help me."

Phillip put a hand on Tyler's shoulder. "Okay, look, we're getting sidetracked. Tyler, you two can discuss it later."

Jimmy added, "And we do."

"Shut up," Phillip barked. "Next question; how'd you get access to the file? We fixed you so that no computer would work anywhere near you. How'd you get around that?"

"I found someone who would be motivated to help me."

"Who?" Phillip asked.

"The federal agents who tried to arrest Martin. I figured since Martin had vanished right in front of them twice, they'd probably want to know how he'd done it."

Martin asked, "How did you find them?"

Jimmy smiled. "Your parents gave me their number."

"What?! You . . . what did you do to my parents?"

"I told them that you hadn't hurt anybody, and that you hadn't broken any laws that I knew of, and if they'd give me the number of the agents who'd been there, I could prove it. I told them the truth. They're lovely people, by the way."

"You told the feds about the file?" Phillip asked.

"Yes, and I understand your concern, Phillip, but think it through. If the men I worked with ever figure out how to use the file on their own, what are they going to do, come back here and arrest us? No, they'd join us if they could. Anyway, don't worry. They'll never find their way back to the file without my help, and even if they do, we'll have password protected that instance of it just like you did all the others. How'd you do that, by the way?"

The wizards were confused by this. Phillip put up a hand to silence their muttering, and said, "All known copies of the file have been locked down, but we still have total access. It'll be in the report." He turned his attention back to Jimmy. "How'd you get into the file? I know the copy you found was locked down. It was the first one I told the Atlanteans about."

"I know. I checked," Jimmy said. "We hunted down every copy I knew of and they were all locked. Eventually I remembered that there was one wizard who'd never trusted any of us enough to tell us where he found the file."

"Todd," Phillip said. "You went to Todd."

"I went to Todd."

Todd was the one wizard nobody ever wanted to talk about. Martin didn't know why, because nobody wanted to talk about it.

"How is he?" Phillip asked.

"In prison for life," Jimmy answered.

"That's good. Nice of you to point him out to the feds. I'm sure they have a lot to talk about. They'll probably tell us all about it when he leads them here."

"That's not going to happen, Phillip. However your friends in Atlantis locked down all of our file instances, now they can do it to his as well. I can tell you exactly where it is."

Tyler asked, "What did you tell him to get him to help you? You banished him. He must hate you nearly as much as I do."

"He hates all of us," Jimmy said. "So I told him that giving me the means to come back here would make the rest of you very angry. In essence, I am his revenge. You should be grateful. It could have been much worse."

Phillip said, "I'll be the judge of that."

The wizards retreated back to their huddle. They had another hushed conversation. They took another vote. From the sound of it, Phillip suffered another disappointment.

When the wizards returned, Phillip spat his words at Jimmy. "You've got a choice. You can either go back to the time you came from, with your magnetic field restored and your access to the file cut off, for good this time. Or—"

Jimmy said, "I choose the second option."

"Wait," Phillip sputtered. "I haven't even told you what it is!"

"It'll be preferable to the first option. I'm sure of it."

"It could be something awful. It could be that we'll kill you."

Jimmy laughed. "Phillip. You'd never be a party to that. As much as you hate me, you'd never kill me unless it was self-defense. You're a good man, and we both know it."

Phillip was disgusted. "You say 'you're a good man' like it's an insult."

"No," Jimmy protested, "I mean it as a high compliment. You just hear it as an insult when it comes from me. Honestly, I wish I were more like you, Phillip. The last thirty years of my life would have been very different if I were."

"So you want to be good, for selfish reasons."

Jimmy shrugged. "It doesn't sound great when you put it that way, but you gotta admit, it's progress."

Phillip decided to just plow ahead as if he hadn't been interrupted. "The second option is that you stay here where we can keep an eye on you, and that is exactly what we will do. Rest assured, we will all be watching, just waiting for you to do anything we don't like. The file modifications that stop the aging process and make you impervious to physical damage and illness will be left in place for now, but at the first sign of anything we don't like, you're cut off and sent back to the future to die in squalor."

"Or find my way back again," Jimmy said, instantly regretting it.

"Oh, don't worry about that!" Phillip said. "I intend to spend every moment between now and the day you step out of line thinking up new, awful ways to prevent that from happening."

"What if I never step out of line?"

A bitter smile crossed Phillip's lips. "Then I get to spend an eternity imagining demeaning things to do to you. Not a bad consolation prize."

"I see," Jimmy said.

"If you stay," Phillip continued, "for a probationary period your access to the shell will be severely limited."

Jimmy asked, "How limited?"

"Oh," Phillip said, "look who has questions all of a sudden. Mister 'I'll take the second option' wants some details."

Jimmy said, "Make no mistake; I'll take the second option. I just asked out of curiosity."

"You can conjure up food and water. You can create money, but there will be limits on how much you can make per week. You can teleport, but only to certain defined geographic locations. If you want to go anywhere else, you need permission from at least two other wizards, or you can fly. By the way, your flight will be limited to an altitude of fifty feet above ground level and a speed of twenty-five miles per hour. We only gave you that so that the locals wouldn't be able to beat you to death as soon as they see you. I lost that vote. You will have no access to edit the shell, which means no macros, and for the duration of your probation, every time you use magic it will automatically be logged in a document that any of us can read at any time. That way we can keep tabs on you."

Jimmy nodded as if all of this were expected. After a moment, he asked, "How long is the probationary period?"

Phillip said, "Until we unanimously vote to lift it, so pretty much forever."

Jimmy said, "Fair enough."

Jimmy was allowed to touch the ground again, and was treated to a full round of mumbled greetings and suspicious looks. He graciously thanked everyone for this second chance, then had the good sense to keep his mouth shut and try to blend into the background. He figured he'd be doing a lot of that from now on.

Roy's macro was quite impressive. With the clenching of his fist he caused a volcano to emerge from the ground spontane-ously and erupt in a thick lava flow. It would certainly make an impression on any local who witnessed it, and it impressed the wizards even more so, since they could all instantly recognize that the volcano was papier-mâché and the lava flow was made up of baking soda and vinegar foam and food coloring.

The next morning, Martin called Phillip to discuss the Jimmy situation.

Martin said, "I don't like it."

"Then why'd you vote in favor of it?" Phillip asked.

"It's like I said last night: he's demonstrated that he's not going to just slink away and leave us alone. We're not going to kill him. At least this way we can keep an eye on him."

"Yeah," Phillip said. "If only there was a way to keep an eye on him without having to look at him all the time."

"Well, I guess the good news is that he'll probably avoid the two of us for the most part. And Tyler, I'd assume. Heck, especially Tyler."

Phillip said. "I wish that made me feel better. That's the worst thing about this. There's no way to win. I don't want him anywhere near me, but I'm uncomfortable having him out of my sight. There's nothing he can do that will make me comfortable. He has my complete distrust."

"But, to be fair, that's nothing new. You never trusted him."

"No," Phillip said, "that's not true. There are different kinds of trust, and up until yesterday, I knew in the bottom of my soul that I could count on Jimmy to do what was best for himself. Now, though, he's trying to prove that he's changed, and that means he'll try to do the right thing for everyone."

Martin said, "That sounds pretty good."

"Yeah, but it isn't, "Phillip said. "Because he's got such a twisted view of morality, there's no telling what he'll think the right thing is."

EPILOGUE

862 years later.

Agent Miller leaned against the wall. His hard-soled dress shoes were killing him, and the hard concrete floor wasn't helping, but the warden had been adamant that nothing that could be used as a weapon could be allowed anywhere near the prisoner. Given the prisoner's familiarity with professional wrestling, a folding chair definitely qualified as a potential weapon.

Miller asked, "What's our next move, kid?"

"Uh-uh-uh," Todd said, scolding Agent Miller. "That's not how we do things. We have an agreement. I give you information, you answer a question. Squid pro quo."

"I told you, kid, it's 'quid pro quo.'"

Todd rolled his eyes. "Yeah, and I told you, I've seen *Silence of the Lambs* like, three times, and it's 'squid pro quo.'"

"We've been through this, kid. 'Squid pro quo' makes no sense."

Todd snorted. "Oh, and 'quid pro quo' makes all the sense in the world." Todd crossed his eyes, made his teeth stick out of his mouth, and flapped his arms limply while repeating "Quid pro quo! Quid pro quo!" He laughed at how stupid Agent Miller was being, and said, "I told you, the hero, that Hanimal guy, was a fancy chef, and squid pro quo was like, the name of his favorite dish, or something."

Miller growled. "'Quid pro quo' is Latin."

"Oh yeah? Do you speak Latin?"

Agent Miller asked, "Is that your question?"

Todd stiffened. "No. I wouldn't waste a question on something that stupid. Here is my question, Agent Miller. Have you ever shot a man in the face?"

"No," Miller growled. "I have not."

Todd chuckled as if he was disappointed, but not surprised. "Fine," he said. "Your answer is satisfactory. The next step is to type in 'dir.'"

"Dir?"

"Yes. Obviously. It stands for 'directory.' Tell your partner. Now."

Miller said, "Don't tell me what to do, kid."

Todd snorted again. "Miller, the whole reason you're here is so I can tell you what to do."

Miller attempted to kill Todd with nothing more than prolonged furious eye-contact. When it became clear that it wasn't working, he shouted, "Murph! Type 'dir!'"

From around a corner, down a hall, through a locked gate, and well beyond the range of Todd's magnetic field, Murphy yelled, "Dir?"

"Yes," Miller shouted, without tearing his eyes away from Todd. "D-I-R! It means 'directory'!"

"Obviously," Murphy replied. Miller's attempt to stare Todd to death backfired, in that it only gave him a good view as Todd laughed at him.

After a few seconds, Murphy's distant voice called out. "It's giving me a big long list of stuff. Do I need to read it all out, or does he know what we're looking for?"

Miller asked, "Well, you heard him. Do you know what we're looking for?"

Todd smiled. "Squid pro quo. Agent Miller. Have you ever shot a man in the junk?"

Miller said, "Not yet."

SECOND EPILOGUE

2,492 years earlier.

Puffy white clouds coasted over a choppy blue-gray sea, which surrounded an island with swaying palm trees and white sandy beaches.

Brit materialized, closed her eyes, and exhaled. Five seconds ago, she had been Brit the Younger. A hundred years later, she knew she would become Brit the Elder, but for now, finally, she was just Brit.

Her farewell from Atlantis had been a pretty heavy emotional scene. Live anywhere for fifty years and you're going to feel some emotions when you leave, even if you've been looking forward to moving on. The fact that she knew she was just leaving to build Atlantis in the first place, and that she was doomed to return whether she wanted to or not, didn't seem to matter to her tear ducts.

She had wanted to keep things low key. She invited Gwen and Martin out to see her off, and asked Brit the Elder to come over, and to please bring Ampyx.

Ampyx was in his sixties now. He was still technically Brit the Elder's servant, but since he had aged and she hadn't, she spent more time taking care of him than the other way around. It had been interesting to watch Ampyx's role in Brit the Elder's life change over the years. He'd gone from grateful servant to trusted assistant, to loyal confidant, to wise advisor, and had finally settled into funny old crank. He had also married and had several children and been widowed in the meantime.

Brit didn't see the need for her transitioning to this new chapter of her life to be a major event. Thanks to teleportation and time travel, relocating to another time was no more of an inconvenience than moving to a new apartment. She could still go visit anybody she wanted any time she wanted. Really, she still lived in the same place, just a century or so earlier. There was no need to make it a big deal. She just wanted to be seen off by a few friends. In retrospect, she felt foolish forever thinking that she might get her way.

The first sign that her goodbye had been hijacked was when Brit the Elder showed up early, with Ampyx and Phillip.

"Why did you bring him?" Brit the Younger whispered just quietly enough to be certain that Phillip would hear it.

Phillip said, "Look, I can go. I don't want to—"

Brit the Elder turned and pleasantly shushed Phillip, then told Brit the Younger, "I invited Phillip because he's Phillip."

"Yeah, I know he's Phillip. Phillip and I aren't getting along right now."

Phillip said, "Seriously, I'll just go—"

Both Brits shushed him, one pleasantly, the other not so much.

Brit the Elder said, "I know you two aren't getting along right now. Maybe he and I are?"

"Well, your relationship with him has nothing to do with me."

"Well, I'm the future version of you, so my relationship has everything to do with you."

Brit the Younger furrowed her brow. "Okay, wait. Is that some future Phillip, or is he my Phillip?"

Brit the Elder smiled. "Your Phillip? I thought you weren't getting along."

"Yeah," Phillip added. Both Brits shushed him. Neither one was very pleasant about it.

"I am not going to miss you," Brit the Younger seethed at the Elder.

Brit the Elder said, "Yes, you are," and hugged Brit the Younger. When the unidirectional hug ended, Brit the Elder said, "And now it's time." She swiped her finger through the air a few times, made a selection, and all four of them—both Brits, Phillip, and Ampyx—were transported to the park at the center of the city. Every sorceress in Atlantis, along with every important merchant in town, all of the citizens, elected officials, representatives from most of the other time-traveler colonies, Nik and his husband, and Gwen and Martin. Looking up at the city, Brit the Younger could see that every window, every balcony, every public space with a view of the bowl was filled with people.

The next twenty minutes were a blur of heartfelt speeches and firm handshakes. In the end, she managed to say a few words without blubbering too horrendously. The last person she spoke to before officially leaving was Brit the Elder. They both understood that it was just good showmanship for their goodbye to be saved for last.

To Brit the Younger's surprise, she heard herself say, "Thanks for arranging this."

Brit the Elder said, "Are you kidding? It was my pleasure. You earned it by putting up with me all these years, and besides, how often do you get to plan your own goodbye party?"

Then Brit transported to the place and time she'd always known she'd go eventually, and the Brit the Younger part of her life was over.

Right now, in Atlantis, she thought, *well, not* right now. *Right now is right now, and I haven't built Atlantis yet. But in the future, just after the time that felt like right now a minute ago, Brit the Elder is just Brit, and so am I. We're both flying solo.*

The thought both scared Brit and made her laugh. *Of course, she's flying solo for life. In a couple of hundred years, I'm going to have Brit the Younger to deal with. As I remember, she could be kind of a handful.* Brit laughed again.

That was a problem for another day. For now, she could enjoy her solitude. Tonight, she would build a shelter. She was picturing a perfectly clear dome made of diamond, the world's most expensive igloo. It would keep wind and rain off, but allow her to look at the stars and the waves whenever she wanted, and because there was nobody around, she didn't need to worry about anyone looking in at her.

Brit cracked her knuckles, then limbered up her fingers, and started scrolling through menu options, preparing to start construction of her new home when she was severely startled by a voice behind her.

"You'd better get to work, girlie. Shelter's not going to build itself."

Brit spun around and found herself face to face with herself, only the other version of herself was wearing some kind of shawl.

"I know, dear," the other Brit said. "You didn't expect to see me here. You see, I've been the only Brit around for a few hundred years now, and it's been great, but I've always felt guilty that you got stuck building Atlantis on your own, so I figured

I'd come back here, keep you company, and kinda, you know, supervise."

Brit made several confused, guttural noises.

"I know. It's a surprise. If it makes it easier to keep things straight, you can call me 'Brit the Much Elder.' Or how about 'Grand-Brit'?"

Brit made more inarticulate noises. Grand-Brit looked concerned for as long as she could, before finally cracking up and laughing.

"Kidding!" Grand-Brit said. "I was kidding."

Grand-Brit disappeared, and Brit was left alone.

ACKNOWLEDGMENTS

I'd like to thank my wife Missy for continuing to put up with me.

I'd also like to thank Allison DeCaro, Jen Yates, John Yates, Debbie Wolf, Mason Wolf, Rodney Sherwood, Leonard Phillips, Ric Schrader, David Pomerico, everybody else at 47North, and the readers of my comic strip, Basic Instructions.

ABOUT THE AUTHOR

 Scott Meyer has worked as a radio personality and written for the video game industry. For a long period he made his living as a standup comedian, touring extensively throughout the United States and Canada. Scott eventually left the drudgery of professional entertainment for the glitz and glamour of the theme park industry. He and his wife currently live in Orlando, Florida, where he produces his acclaimed comic strip *Basic Instructions*.

Spell or High water is the follow up to Scott's debut novel, *Off to be the Wizard*.